The Farm

By Shannon Wallace

Acknowledgments

There are many people I would like to thank for their support during the chaotic process of writing my first novel. My father, whose long distance telephone conversations added many twists and turns to *The Farm* that expressed themselves, sometimes even subconsciously, in my writing. My son Mickey, for his help with research that added realism to the novel. My partner Chris, for showing me a male's view of the world. My friend and cousin Derek for his Bigfoot expertise and his divine editing. To Tony-el, for making the Farm was it is. To my mother, grandmother, and maternal side of the family, thank you for the discovery of the Farm and all the wild times, including you too, Johnsons. To Dr. Goldberg, for teaching me how to kill my demons without ending up in jail. My husband Mike, for his neurotic editing and patience while I worked on my book. To Joe, for his extensive work on my book cover, web design, and technical support. To David Blumenfeld, who inspired me in many ways, and reminded me that Bigfoot was closer than I realized. And to my biggest inspirations of all, my dogs: Okeano, Mako, and Neptune.

I will never forget all the people who read early versions of the story and who propelled me forward with the novel because of their encouraging words and insightful suggestions. I thank you all.

To
Derek

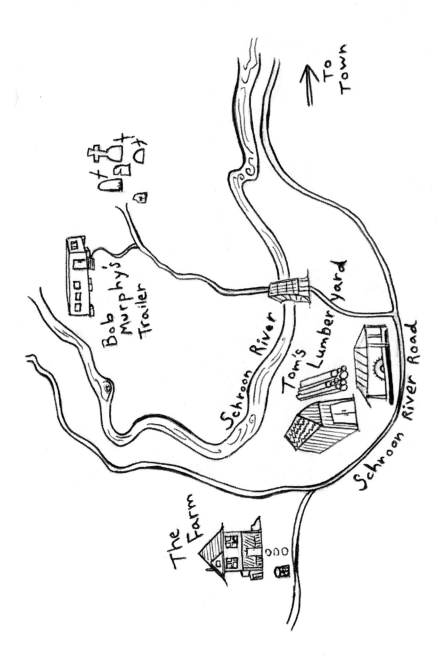

Bob Murphy's Trailer

Schroon River

Tom's Lumber Yard

Schroon River Road

The Farm

To Town

7

Chapter 1

"Have another drink, Tom?" said the bartender. "Or you going home to your ol' lady, in hopes to get lucky!"

"He'd be lucky if his ol' lady wasn't there when he got home!" laughed Bob.

"O.K., one more drink, but put it on Bob's tab."

"No can do," replied the bartender, "Bob still owes ninety four dollars from last week, and that's not counting what he drank tonight."

"Bob, man, you just don't get it, do you?"

Bob looked up from his empty shot glass. "You're Mr. Money 'round here, Tom. Why don't you spread some of that lumberyard cash around and buy all us dead-beats another drink?"

"You guys are pathetic. But you're still the best friends a man can have. Mike, another round for my friends!" The men lifted their beers in the air and chanted Tom's name as if he were Dionysus himself. Tom reveled in the chant while he nodded his head and splashed back another shot of rum. And that's how it always went when "one more round" turned into three or four. The usual crowd had shown up at the Brew N' Stew that night, a bar handed down to its owner Mike from his doting father. Mike's father wouldn't have remained so enthusiastic about having his son take over the business, however, had he been able to foresee where Mike and his friends were taking it. After all, the business had the potential to be lucrative, but Mike and his friends drank away half the profits, and Mike himself spoiled the rest of the profit during the college football season.

Warrensburg was a small town, with a population of just over four thousand living within a sixty- mile radius. Everyone knew everyone, so it was no big deal to see neighbors helping each other paint houses or tow a tractor or give one another a lift when their vehicle broke down and the warranty was out. And you were either liked or disliked by the local police. The cops in this town thought they were better than most everyone else. They used their powers to bleed some of the local business owners of their weekly profit, or to hit on any female they deemed attractive.

At around 3:30 A.M, Mike called, "Last round," and started closing up the bar. One by one, the drunkards staggered out of the bar, disorganized and disoriented. One man held his hand against the wall, breathing like he'd just finished a marathon, another fumbled unsuccessfully to insert his keys into a truck that didn't belong to him, and yet another dropped his keys on the ground and then kicked them under his truck. Pretty much everybody in this town drove a pick-up truck, and every one of them lived within twelve miles of the bar. The only thing they feared at this time of night were the local police officers. The police were known to wait outside the bar, and then tail the drunks almost all the way home before they pulled them over. The cops loved to make the men sweat it out—losing a license around here was as good as losing your job. But when they finally flashed their lights and pulled the men over, more than likely they weren't looking to spend the night filling out paperwork just to take away a guy's privilege to drive. The cops would demand some money, maybe throw a few cheap punches and then let them on their way. Not that assault and robbery by a police officer was a welcome nightcap, but most considered it better than a DWI. And most knew better than to hit back. There were a few self-proclaimed tough guys who tried their hand at it, but who rarely tried twice.

Anyone who had lived around Warrensburg for a few years had heard the tragic story of Jim Healy. The one man who always seemed to believe that the next time

10

would be *his* time to put the police in their places. One night Jim was driving home from his buddy's house, with a few beers under his belt. Jim was feeling good that night. He and his pals had recently negotiated a contract with a company named Jard Construction. Jard had offered each of them eight hundred dollars a week to build an extension on the Warrensburg Nursing Home. As he slowly drove the four miles back to his house, he dreamed about what he would do with all that money. Maybe he would put his daughter through college, maybe send his wife to that spa she had been saving up for. And he would put a swimming pool in his back yard. Not just a typical four-footer, but a built-in one like he'd seen on television. Jim was just pulling into his driveway when a dark sedan almost collided with his truck head on. The two vehicles screeched to a halt just inches away from each other. Jim breathed a sigh of relief, but it was short-lived. Stumbling out of the sedan came Officer Demitres, with Kankro not far behind. These two were the town's dirtiest cops of all.

Demitres had the full, corn-fed build of his pioneering family. Thick, sinewy arms that ended in bulging fists—knuckles calloused over from weekly wrapping on the local's skulls. His eyes were dead, his expression blank, until, all at once, he would erupt with all the caged anger of three generations of alcoholic rage. He'd been on probation twice for assaulting suspects, but things like that had a way of getting forgotten in Warrensburg. Demitres was the precinct's biggest liability, but that was part of his effectiveness. Not many people dared to cross him, few suspects even dared to talk back to him, whatever few words he might have mumbled. Demitres was everything he looked like and not much else. Unmerciful muscle hell bent on taking full advantage of every ounce of power foolishly entrusted to his care.

Kankro was half Demitres' size but twice as sinister. He had a way of intimidating people that was

11

second to none. And with Demitres as his partner, his violent promises weren't hard to bring into reality. He wore a thick mustache that was stained with smoke from his cheap Tipparillo cigars. His breath was acrid and sour, so much that not a few unfortunates had fallen victim to their own stomach's violence before they could experience his. His pockets were full of dirty money, which he used for all of his dirty habits—cheap whores, smokes, and meth. Once he'd been so spun on the drug that he shot a dog's eye out because he thought it was laughing at him.

Jim had just stepped out of his car. Now Jim wasn't exactly a big guy, he was of a descent height but rather skimpy where you'd normally picture muscles on a man. In his case, skin and bones. He rounded the hood when he felt a harsh blow to his right kneecap. He fell to the ground instantly, looking up at Demitres leaning over him with a baton in his hand.

"Well, well, well. Now what do we have here? It looks as if you've been drinking. That's a violation of the law. And do you know what we do to perps like you?" barked Demitres.

"I'm not driving. I'm walking to my house," said Jim while trying to conceal his pain.

"I asked you a question. I said, 'Do you know what we do to perps like you?'"

Jim answered as he stood up, "I guess you try to break their kneecaps."

"Wrong, dipshit! We make them pay. And I hear you've made yourself quite a little fortune, with that Jard contract."

"You heard wrong. They turned down our offer. Hired some city boys instead."

Demitres backhanded Healy with a force so hard that it echoed through the trees. "You lyin' to me, boy?"

"So what if I am? What are you going to do about it? Hit me again? Go ahead. Take your best shot!"

Demitres thought Healy must have drunk enough to fill a lake that night, if he thought he could take on this tag team. At that moment Healy heard a sound like a slinking skunk searching for garbage. It wasn't a skunk, although it could have been. Kanko came walking up behind Demitres.

Kankro took it upon himself to lay down his version of the law to Mr. Jim Healy. "Let me tell you how it's going to be from now on. Every Friday, starting today, you are going to give me and my partner one hundred dollars each. If you do not cooperate, you no longer have a deal with Jard. You see what I mean? 'Cause uh, I really don't like to repeat myself."

"Fuck you," replied Jim. He walked backwards towards his front door as he admonished them. "Everybody else 'round here is afraid of you, but not me. No sir, I know you two are nothing but greasy cow pies who slobber on each other's sausages in that pig mobile all night long."

Demitres' voice was surprisingly calm in the most unnerving manner. "Now that's some real poetry. However, tastefully unnecessary, and unfortunately, it's gonna cost you another hundred dollars per week. Do we have a deal?"

Jim ignored the threat and went inside. The following Monday when Jim showed up for work, Jard told them they found somebody else to do the job. With a second mortgage taken out to pay off his credit cards, a daughter on her way to college, and three young boys who still needed his wife to wipe their asses, the reality of this loss rained down on him like hot ash from an exploding volcano. Adrenaline soared as he sped towards the police station at over one hundred miles an hour. Jim's thoughts were a nightmarish frenzy of spattered blood and stifled screams. Images of Kankro's neck crushed between Jim's hands floated past his vision of the curving road.

Suddenly Jim felt weightless, and the truck stopped humming along the road. The road was above him somehow, and then all at once he realized what was happening. His truck rolled three times before it came to rest on the other side of the divided highway. Flipping the truck around the turn wasn't nearly as bad as what happened next. The vehicle had skid into oncoming traffic, and a second after it came to rest he was struck by a car speeding around the curve. When Jim came home from his six- week stint in the hospital he was paralyzed from the waist down. Jim's wife began working eighteen hours a day, and his daughter gave up her dream of going to college to attend to her younger siblings. And since Jim's complaints were officially considered "unfounded' by the local police chief, it would only be a matter of time before Demitres and Kankro would ruin yet another life.

In any case, Jim Healy's sad feud was *not* what happened to be in Tom's mind as he sailed home in his truck, barely visible as the thick fog made its way across the river and covered Schroon River Road. Tom, buzzed from the seven rum and cokes he guzzled beside his buddies, reminisced about a story Frank had been telling them in the bar. The tale concerned a Zambezi shark that swam up a river in New Jersey during the summer of 1916. During a record-breaking heat wave and a polio epidemic, people came to New Jersey for the refreshing beaches. Apparently one or more of these Zambezi sharks had developed a taste for humans. Within twelve days, the Zambezis had swum up a local river and killed four swimmers. A fifth was left legless and in critical condition. The horror of these shark attacks was unparalleled in 1916. Both the townspeople and members of congress put their lives on halt to seek and destroy these vile creatures. *How insane!* Tom thought to himself. He then tried to imagine a large shark traveling along the Schroon River, where his son used to kayak and fish daily in the warm weather. The shark could feed for months on the large supply of salmon, turtles, water snakes, frogs and of course, people. People from all over.

Warrensburg was located only four miles north of Lake George: a vacationing spot for travelers from as far north as Quebec or as far south as Miami. Lake George was well known for its hotels, restaurants, souvenir shops, ice cream, mini golf, and, of course, breathtaking sightseeing tours aboard the lake's most famous boats: the Minne-Ha-Ha and Saratoga steamships. These cruises toured the seven-mile lake and its many small islands. Along the way sightseers would be treated to gorgeous views of the lush mountainside, including a fascinating vision of the steep rise of Tongue Mountain, the feature responsible for creating the lake's famous northern forks. The tours also including talking points on the many mansions resting against the lake's shores, and if the sightseers were truly lucky, they might even catch someone outside who would wave at them. The men could enjoy parasailing and jet skiing on the lake while the women could kick off their sandals on the shore and sip on a bay breeze. From arcades to glass bottomed boats, Lake George had something for everyone.

Only a handful of people knew about Warrensburg. More than likely they stumbled into it by accident, usually by taking a scenic side road out of the shore town of Diamond Point. Warrensburg had all the necessary amenities of a slightly off the beaten path hick town: a Stewart's to fill up one's stomach and car, a crappy diner that refused to cook egg whites, and an antiques shop which was little more than an overpriced garage sale. Not that the town was without charm. If the tourists wandered into the bait and tackle shop next to the antiques store, friendly "Pat" would boost her sales by informing them of Schroon River's big adventures and even bigger fish. Many families took the bait and spent the rest of the

15

afternoon picnicking along the beaches of Schroon River. Warrensburg offered peaceful diversions from the crowded streets of Lake George.

Tom's mind went back to the shark. He thought about how a beast such as that could set this small community into an uproar. He chuckled to himself, imagining Bob in his backyard with a shotgun aimed at the river, mosquitoes swarming around his face. Tom continued his ride home along Schroon River Road. He was just passing by his lumberyard when he suddenly saw somebody crossing the dark road. "Holy Shit!" he yelled as he slammed on his brakes. The truck swerved violently from right to left and then right again before screeching to a halt. Tom screamed through his window, "You crazy son of a bitch! You damn nearly got yourself run over!" But before Tom could finish his sentence, he realized it was not a person, but a bear he was yelling to. The bear stopped dead in his tracks and looked at Tom. Tom stared back at the bear in disbelief. In all his fifty -two years living in the Northern Adirondacks, he had never seen a bear of this caliber. It was walking across the street on two feet. "Jesus fucking Christ!" he stated out loud. In a flash, the bear was gone. Tom sat there, as if frozen in time, and then tried to move but couldn't. As he tried to ponder his thoughts, there was only one word that ran through his mind: Bigfoot. Suddenly, as a bolt of adrenaline ran through his body, he shifted the car into drive and turned the wheel 180 degrees, then quickly put his brights on to view this creature. He looked straight through his windshield, out his driver side window, out his passenger window, through the rear window…nothing. He was alone on the dark road. Tom, recapping what had just happened, said, "That was no fucking bear." He wondered if it was the alcohol playing tricks on him. "This can't be. This can't be!"

Tom lived only one hundred yards from the lumberyard, and was home in under a minute. He ran to his front door faster than a greyhound chasing the big white bone at the Multnomah Greyhound Park. His hands were shaking so badly that he could hardly get the key in the front door. He was so scared, it seemed like ten minutes went by before he got into his house. He made it through the door and quickly reached for the lock. He ran into the bedroom and woke up his wife.

"Sherry! Sherry!" Tom huffed as he shook her body awake. Later she would complain to him that he had bruised her shoulders. He then leaped over her and turned on the light switch.

Sherry jumped up, falling off the edge of the bed. "What is it? Are you alright? What happened?" she shouted, still not fully awake but demanding one hell of an explanation.

Tom paced back and forth by the foot of the bed, gesticulating wildly. "On my way home, as I was passing the lumberyard, I almost hit something!"

"Oh my God! Did you run someone over? I told you a thousand times not to drive drunk!"

"No. I didn't hit anybody! But on my way home, coming from the direction of the lumberyard, in the middle of the street stood an animal, must have been eight feet tall, with brown hair or fur, and big teeth! And it looked right at me! Then it took off into the woods. Just like that," he snapped his fingers, "it was gone!"

"It's called a bear, you asshole. I can't believe you woke me up in the middle of the night to tell me you saw a bear!"

"No Sherry. Not a bear. A monster!" Tom's eyes were as wide as cherry tomatoes.

"I think you should sleep it off. Take a shower. Have a cup of coffee. You're drunk, and I bet you also smoked some weed. Well, that's what you get. A big, fat, hallucination! Now leave me alone." Sherry turned over pulling the blanket over her shoulder.

Tom tried to believe that it was just a bear, and that the rum had exaggerated what he thought he saw. He pictured telling the guys his story, and then he imagined being the laughing stock of the bar for the next few weeks. Slowly his mind began to calm and he rationalized away some of his excitement. "Yeah, you're probably right. I had too much to drink. And by the way, I did not smoke any weed tonight. Good night." He turned the light switch off, yanked off his jeans and got under the covers. And while it was true that Tom hadn't been doped up that night, unknowingly he had told a lie. He actually *had* struck something with his car that night, and the evidence dangled out there on the grill of his truck, waiting to be found.

Chapter 2

Steve Bettis was busy shoving duffel bags into his wife's Nissan Pathfinder, but like any seasoned New York City Detective, his mind was back at work. It would take a few days of fishing and breathing in fresh air before his mind would begin to settle. The tension would unravel slowly at first, but would gain momentum, like a tiger slowly trailing her prey before building up to a break-neck sprint. His wife Maureen wanted him to take the shortcut to less stress: find a job on Long Island with fewer dangers and less hassle. To Steve that also meant fewer challenges and less excitement. It was simple for her to say. Maureen never understood the allure of New York City. All she saw were ominous buildings and dark alleyways that hid a rancid assortment of shadowy miscreants: junkies, creeps, bums, and whores. Every door led to triple-X porno or a sticky-floored bar. To her the city was cramped and noisy, filthy and vile—and nothing else. Steve couldn't deny all that, but he would deny that that was all that the city offered. While Steve dealt with the worst of it and gazed upon the pallid hue of death on New York's streets more than most, there was the other side as well, the side he meant to protect. If there wasn't an aspect of beauty, something worth saving from all the slime, he might have very well taken a job on Long Island long ago. But for every threat there was an antithesis: young mothers slowly strolling through wintry city parks with their children wrapped snugly in blankets, a surprisingly calm view of the Hudson revealed with one magical turn around a corner, the stately façade of the Met protecting centuries of the world's greatest genius, the brilliance of the world's finest architects found at every turn of the head, or the awesome power of Wall Street, toward which the world's ear was always turned. Steve's daydreams weren't always pretty, but it was this beauty and strength of New York

City that always allowed him to make it through the ones that weren't.

His grandfather found the property long ago, when he made a wrong turn somewhere trying to return to his Schroon River campsite. It was a cute little farmhouse with five bedrooms, two living rooms, three porches, a kitchen and a back dining room with a large bay window facing a perfectly leveled back yard with a beautiful view of two acres of trees, grass, and mountainside. He noticed it was for sale and did not waste any time deciding it was the perfect vacation home for him and his family. The Schaefers seemed eager to sell. Apparently, there had been an accident, which resulted in the death of one of the children, and the parents felt that selling the house would give them some closure. Steve's grandmother named it the "Farm" because, while it wasn't a working farm, it had all the subtle touches of a 19th century farmhouse: antique white exterior, green shutters, and a metal roof that allowed for heavy snowfalls to melt and slide gently off to the side of the house.

But that's not all it had. The Farm had a darker side as well that deterred many guests from returning. Steve's mother was the one who had perhaps the most dramatic paranormal experience. She would often recall the story of when the twins were infants, and Steve and Maureen had them set up in separate playpens to put them to sleep. Steve and Maureen fell asleep early on this particular night, preparing for the 2:00 A.M. feedings that was sure to disturb their sleep, and a good portion of the following morning.

Steve's mother slowly rocked in her reading chair, quietly turning the pages of one of those cheap romance novels you find on spinning racks in souvenir stores. She usually read more literary material, but the title had caught her eye: *The Final Flower*. And something about the hero's face painted on the cover reminded her of her late husband. After a time her eyelids drooped, her vision slowly faded, and her breathing slowed to the steady pace of the branches brushing against the old windowpanes of the house.

She opened an eye. An hour had passed? Two? Across the room was a door, behind which were the stairs that led to the second floor. The door was just closing, and she could hear slow, steady footsteps ascending to the top of the staircase, pausing at the top step. Strangely, she could hear breathing, but it was not her own. She tried to wake herself, sure that she was trapped by some awful dream, but her body remained heavy and still. The footsteps began again, descending this time. Thump. Thump. Thump. Thump. A dim light illuminated the edges of the door. She perked up at the edge of the chair. The glow became brighter, and slowly the creaking door swung open. There was nothing there but the old stairs and an eerie luminescence. She turned her head, averting her eyes from the strange light. She caught her reflection in the window. There she sat, eyes wide with terror, her knuckles white as she clutched the armrests of her chair. She felt a cold wind passing over her right shoulder. No, a steady, rhythmic, cold wind: breathing. As she focused more closely on her image in the window, she was amazed to see a phantom form beside her: the ghostly image of her late husband, his soft eyes and warm smile there to comfort her through this sickening moment. She breathed a small sigh of relief and awe, then turned to greet him. But instead of her husband's loving face, she saw beside her the chiseled face of man she did not recognize, a man with dark eyes and a fierce expression that she could not decipher. The phantom moaned and grasped her shoulders, provoking her to let out a stifled scream. As her panic surged, the scream grew louder and louder until Steve came rushing down the stairs to investigate his mother's distress. As Steve barreled through the heavy, wooden stairway door, the window burst apart and sent shattered glass across the entire living room. Steve jumped across the room to shield his mother from the flying debris. His mother refused to let go of the chair for the remainder of the evening.

Steve made breakfast for his journey to the Farm with his wife Maureen and their now thirteen-year old twins, Devin and Becka. The twins were yearning to visit the Farm since the weather became warm a few weeks ago. By 7:00 A.M., they were fully packed and already shooting a few hoops in the driveway to pass the time. Their dog Spike knew they were going somewhere, since she saw Becka tuck her leash away in the back seat. Spike suddenly had the same spring in her step that she had had years ago. She was ten years old, but Steve kept her in good shape by taking her jogging every night with him. Physical fitness was a big part of Steve's regimen. He took full advantage of the gym at his precinct, showing up for work an hour early to work out and staying an hour late to scamper on the elliptical. And even after his rigorous workouts, which were more to relieve the stress of the job than to keep his lean swimmer's build, he would still take the dog out for her exercise if the twins failed to do so. Over the years, Steve had a hard time keeping up with Spike, but lately, the both of them had been slowing down. She was a medium sized mutt of indeterminate breeding. She had the long shaggy hair of an Afghan, the height and build of a Labrador, and the intelligence of a Border Collie. But who really knew what she was? All Steve cared about was that she was good with the kids and she was loyal: the perfect family dog.

Steve walked out the back door with a buttered roll in his hand and saw his kids playing *Around the World* while Spike danced around them. "You guys ready to go?" he asked with a smile. "Make sure you go to the bathroom before we leave, 'cause I'm not stopping for a while. And Devin, take Spike for a walk!"

"Already did, father," said Devin. Devin was the soft-spoken wise-ass of the family. His politeness always seemed to belie a subtle sarcasm. Becka ran into the house to use the bathroom.

Within minutes, Maureen and Becka came out the back door, locked up, and got into the truck. "Let's rock and roll!" said Maureen as she pounded the passenger side dashboard with her fists. She put on her sunglasses and some lip-gloss, then tilted the seat back and found some tunes on the radio. They were flying up Interstate 87 in no time!

As they pulled the car into a rest stop in Albany, Becka felt the urge to empty her bladder. Steve and Devin walked Spike around the parking lot of the fully accommodating fast food mobile while Becka and Maureen used the ladies' room. While walking Spike, an older gentleman walking with his toy poodle on the grassy area designated for pets approached Steve briefly, then wandered off. Spike had squatted to pee, so Devin could not hear the conversation. When Spike was ready to go, Devin scuttled up to Steve.

"Who was that guy? Did you know him?"

"He's a retired cop from Brooklyn. And no, I never met him before."

"What did he say to you?"

Steve pointed to his .38 snub nose Smith and Wesson revolver on his hip. "He spotted my gun."

"Why did you bring your gun with you?"

"Force of habit. You never know when you're going to need it."

"I don't think I ever noticed." Devin looked innocently at his father. The boy was smart as a whip, but it bothered Steve that his son was not at all street smart.

In the meantime, Becka was once again pestering her mother for a new dog.

"Mom, can I get a puppy?"

"No Beck."

"Why?"

"Because a puppy is a huge responsibility. You're going to start dating in a few years and you'll have nothing to do with the dog. Then who do you think will be stuck taking care of it?"

"I'm not going to drop everything just because I *might* get a boyfriend. I'll take care of it. I do a good job with Spike, right?"

"Sure Beck, you're great with Spike. But you were just a baby when Spike was a puppy. You don't remember the furniture getting chewed, the holes dug in the yard, the pee on the carpet, the training, teaching the dog to walk on a leash. You don't have the time to do all that. You have school, your schoolwork, your friends, your sports. It's just not a good time."

"I'll make time."

"Becka, please drop it. No dog, no cat, no iguana, no chinchilla or whatever that thing was you wanted last month. No more animals! We all have a full plate. Enough."

Becka decided to ease up on her mother for the moment. She'd discuss the issue with Devin and they would double-team her at another time. She thought to herself, "But really, what full plate did Mom have? Getting up in the morning and putting on make-up? Gimme a break."

Chapter 3

Tom woke up fairly early on this particular Saturday morning. I guess you could say he had had a rough night. He was awake by 6:15 A.M., two hours earlier than his normal weekend routine. He re-thought last night's occurrence over and over again. He woke up at least twice during the night dreaming about this creature. In any case, he was awake so he figured he might as well go about his day. He poured a cup of coffee, put on his boots, and left a note for Sherry to let her know that he would be at the lumberyard, feeding the animals. Tom never worked on weekends, and never asked his employees to work weekends either. Besides, most of them did side jobs on weekends and he didn't want them coming in to steal his lumber. Jesse Luongo, the manager and Tom's most trusted employee, took inventory every Friday of all the remaining wood. Sherry kept some barn animals in the rear of the lumberyard, mainly for the kids to play with when their daddies dragged them to the lumberyard. Every Saturday morning, Tom made a trip to the lumberyard to feed the little buzzards. Tom used to think that Sherry kept the barn animals there to check up on him, and the idea of that flattered him. So when Jesse told him that it was his own girlfriend Justine convincing Sherry to use the animals as an excuse to spy on Jesse then report back to Justine, Tom came to the reality that his wife couldn't give a rat's ass about him. That's when his mind started shifting to Margo Gargan, a divorced woman across the bridge who was way too attractive and way too young for Tom, but good for daytime fantasies to make the days go by while at work. There was nothing better than imaginary sex with Margo then going home to Sherry, Sherry was by far the best cook in Warrensburg. And Tom had been selfishly eating her recipes for twenty-five years.

Tom walked out the front door and around the front of his truck when he noticed something out of the corner of his eye. Hanging from the grill of his truck was a tuft of long, reddish-brown hair. He stood there staring at the hair for a moment. Flashes of the creature from last night sprang into his mind. Twisting and contorting his body, his eyes scanned his property. He was seemingly alone. He set his thermos on the hood of his truck and bent down on one knee to examine this strange chunk of hair. Once at eye level, he immediately smelled something foul. It was a familiar smell. A few years ago, Sherry went on a cruise with her sister for a week. She had stocked up on fruits and vegetables so Tom would be forced to eat healthy while she was away. Tom never ate the broccoli, even though he reassured Sherry that he had eaten every ounce of it. A few weeks later, a nasty smell began to emanate from the refrigerator. Sherry found the culprit while Tom was at work, so she took the rotten broccoli and put it under his pillow. That was her way of letting him know that he was caught in a lie! "Rotten broccoli," thought Tom. He could recognize that smell anywhere! He chuckled to himself, admiring Sherry's quirky sense of humor, gratified to see she still had one. He knew that after revealing his story to her last night, he had opened the floodgates for a torrent of jokes about his "creature of the night." He just didn't think she would be this quick! Tom untangled the hair and brought it inside the house, wrapped tape around the end of it, and stuck it to the back of Sherry's bathrobe, which was hanging from the bathroom door. He planned to tease her later for having a big "tail" when he got home from feeding the animals.

The lumberyard felt eerily empty when Tom arrived. At first he was confused as to what was missing. He walked past several pallets of stacked lumber and moved down towards the barn. It suddenly dawned on him exactly what was missing. He couldn't hear the animals. No squeals, no clucks, no baying or howls. Tom quickened his pace, from a slow walk to a jog, and then to a run. As his stomach began to churn he broke into an all out sprint towards the barn. He got within ten yards of the pen when he saw one of Sherry's precious sheep lying on its back on the ground with its insides shredded apart. *Colonel Moynahan lay motionless covered with blood on the side of the road.* Knowing this possibly wasn't the worst of it, he didn't stop running. Tom headed straight for the barn. As he had feared, the door was wide open. He stepped into the barn and all he saw was blood. There was blood on the walls, the floor, and on the hay. With all the spattered gore, it was hard to distinguish the lifeless bodies of three pigs, and three more sheep. *The remaining men in his platoon all shot by snipers.* The pigs were almost unrecognizable, with only their heads and hooves remaining. Tom never saw the bodies of the roosters, but there were feathers everywhere. A chill raced up Tom's spine from the middle of his back to the neatly layered hair on top of his head. Horrified, he stood motionless. His thoughts immediately shifted to the sighting of the creature from last night. The beast had been coming from the direction of the lumberyard, and they had come into contact in the middle of the street. The creature then continued to move across the street and into the woods. Tom suddenly had a disturbing thought: the killer could still be in the barn. Trying his best to remain calm, so as not to alert the intruder, Tom's eyes scanned the perimeter of the barn. He took a few backwards paces while trying to limit the noise of crackling hay and then turned to leave. But before he had a chance to fully exit he heard a faint noise coming from the far corner of the barn. Tom swallowed hard and found the courage to follow the noise, forcefully denying all his notions that this might be a sadistic creature's ploy to lure him in. He squinted his eyes as a barrage of images from his days in Vietnam flooded his mind. His panic rose as he recalled how a small Vietnamese child turned on him moments after he saved the young boy's life. Tom had only moments to react to the grenade that tumbled towards his feet before the explosion ripped apart a village hut and most of Tom's faith in humanity. Forcing the bad memories out of his mind, he found the strength to investigate the sounds. Tom lifted up several broken boards and breathed a small sigh of relief. Sherry's lone piglet lay helpless in the corner, shivering and shell-shocked. He quickly looked over the animal and concluded that it had escaped the bandersnatch that had wreaked havoc in this once safe haven.

Tom carried the little guy to his truck and placed the tiny, quivering body neatly in his lap. The thirty-second drive home stretched into what felt like hours. The flashback he had experienced in the barn had been the first in years, but anxiety had been sneaking up on him for several months now, causing him to drink more than ever. He knew it was coming, his anxiety proportional to the increase in army recruiting commercials in recent months. He'd also spotted some uniformed soldiers posted outside the Grand Union, drawing the attention of young kids right out of high school by promising them a fast-paced career with no student loans attached. Unlike most retired Army soldiers, he didn't want his son to follow in his footsteps. He knew the outcome, despite what they tried to sell you on. He wanted more for Marc, and Marc had more to offer than he did at that age. Tom never engaged in war stories from the jungles, or bragged about how easy and cheap the women were in that part of the region. He even dismissed the idea of carrying a gun since he had come back from the war, contrary to what others in his area were doing. When his son developed an interest in skeet shooting, he taught him how to shoot, but never encouraged him further. As it turns out, his son was an excellent marksman. Still, Tom didn't possess any real firepower other than a basic rifle which hadn't been shined in years. But after walking into a bloodbath in his own place of business, he was reconsidering.

He darted to the bathroom and grabbed the hair off Sherry's robe. Sherry was still sleeping, but he woke her to fill her in on what was happening. Sherry anxiously listened to his story while caressing the piglet in her lap and trying to hold back tears. As upset as she was, she could tell her husband was losing it and had to once again be the strong one. "But Tom, it still sounds like a bear to me, or a moose. There have been moose sightings lately. Justine said she just saw a moose a week ago, coming down from the mountains onto her property. Besides, you were drunk last night. If you start telling people you saw Bigfoot, people will think you're a loon."

"I may have had a few drinks, but I was still alright to drive. And I know what I saw. And what about this hair? Look at it! This did not come from a goddamn bear, or a moose! So, maybe I did hit that thing last night, but it wasn't human and I wasn't about to pull over and ask it if it was alright!"

Sherry threw her hands up in the air. "I don't know what to think. I'm going to the lumberyard to see my animals!"

"Sherry, no. You don't need to see this. You have the only survivor in your lap. I'll call Bob and we'll get to the bottom of this. But do me a favor, and stay home. Don't leave the house 'till I get back." Sherry studied Tom's face as a quizzical expression passed over it and then vanished. He stood up abruptly. "I got to go."

Sherry silently observed as Tom placed the clump of hair in a Zip-lock bag and stuffed it in his pocket. She also noted that he left with his .22 rifle, which had been in the closet of his home office for years. Tom's vivid nightmares and shouting in his sleep had not gone

29

unheeded by Sherry, either. She knew that was why he had been drinking so much, but decided to stay out of it. Well, this was the final straw for Sherry. The barn animals were her only retreat in her lonely life, and the intimacy she shared with them was genuine. Now, they're gone. Just like Allison, just like Marc when he left for college, and just like Tom since he started drinking again. Sherry lifted up the piglet, placing him on the floor and walked into the dining room. She picked up an apple from the fruit bowl on top of the table and tossed it to the pig. As she watched the tiny piglet nibble on the apple, she decided she had enough. Warrensburg had nothing left to offer, and she needed to get away. She had tried lengthy vacations in the past, such as cruises and trips to The Caribbean with woman she could only go so far as calling them acquaintances, but she now saw clearly that she needed to leave, permanently. "Sorry pig," she said genuinely, "but I can't stay here another ten years just to raise you, and then watch you die. I just can't. But I will find a good home for you. I promise. As for me, I don't know where I'm going, but I know I can't stay here. I was expecting 'Bigfoot' for some time now. Goes all the way back to the Vietnam days, when Tom and his war buddies were so psychologically damaged from that agent orange they dropped on them, that they believed their mission in the jungles was to find Bigfoot. Because we had no business being in that war. I don't know if that story is true or not, but that's what Tom says when he's sleeping. So I knew this was coming. And I knew that when this day came, I'd have to get the hell out of here." She knelt down beside the pig and stroked his back as he munched on the apple, scattering little chunks all over the floor. "So, you see why I can't keep you? My husband is crazy. And I'm afraid, well, he might be capable of just about anything. Hell, he might be 'Bigfoot' who killed my barn animals. I have no psych training. But I've seen a few episodes on Oprah about this stuff. And I've done my research at the library and on the internet. I got to leave. He's been going crazy for some time now. And I've been alone for too long now, that I think I'm going crazy." Sherry walked over to the screen door, staring out onto the porch. "I've lowered myself to a conversation with a piece of bacon."

Bob lived about four miles west of Tom, on the other side of Schroon River. Tom pulled his truck off to the side of the dirt road and allowed another vehicle to pass over the old, one lane-bridge spanning the river. The vehicle slowed to a stop as it came alongside his truck.

Spencer Gargan leaned out his window and shouted a cheerful hello to Tom. "When is Marc coming home?" Spencer asked of Tom's son.

"He's just finishing up his finals. He'll be home in a few days."

"Can't wait to see him! I miss my butt brother!"

"What about that little girlfriend of yours? She dump you yet?"

"Yep. Just three weeks ago she said she doesn't want to be tied down for the summer."

"That's too bad, son. But it is the summer, and the tourists will be here soon. You should enjoy it while you can," said Tom remembering a time when he was a teen, cruising the village for tourist chicks wearing short shorts and loose tops.

"That's just what my mom said."

"How is you mother?"

"Fine. She's at work."

"Tell her I said hello, and if she needs anything done around the house, tell her to come by the lumberyard."

"Well, see ya Mr. Blake!"

Tom saw that Spencer had his quad in tow on the trailer. "You better not be trekkin' all over Henkel's

31

property. Last time you guys rode your quads through their yard, you two bozo's nearly got shot!"

"Yeah, that was great!"

Tom waved his fist in the air. "You rotten kids! I swear you're going to give my wife a heart attack one day." Tom shook his head disapprovingly as Spencer drove off with a stupid smirk on his face.

Spencer was a childhood friend of Tom's son, Marc. He was a good enough kid, but when he and Marc got together, they always found a way to get into trouble. Sherry and Marc's football coach had been the driving force behind Marc's decision to go away to college. Spencer's mother didn't have the money to send him to college, but he wouldn't have gone if he could have. Marc was always a little more mature than Spencer, and Sherry thought it would do Marc some good to be away from him. Now that Spencer and his girl broke up, he would be up to no good again. And somehow that meant Marc would be involved.

Tom continued on his drive to Bob's house. He was glad that it had been a clear morning with no fog and the promise of a sunny day ahead. Bob was some years younger than Tom and lived in a trailer atop five acres of trees and shrubs. Although he had waterfront property, he kept his trailer far away from the river near the road. Tom would always nag Bob about not taking advantage of his land and setting up a dock with a canoe or a kayak. Bob would just shrug it off and claim that the mosquitoes were too much of a nuisance to enjoy the river. A few months ago Bob was offered a good chunk of change from Blumenfeld Development Corporation, which wanted to turn the property into a fishing lodge. Flat land was a big selling point in this area, mainly because it cost so much less to simply knock down a few dozen trees than to add leveling the property to the equation. Bob never wanted to sell. He'd rather bust his back all day delivering Pepsi throughout Warren County and go out and spend money he didn't have. Bob lived mainly by the barter system. "You scratch my back, I'll scratch yours" was the motto with which Bob sealed most deals. No money exchanged whenever possible. Tom tried to explain to him on a number of occasions that if he sold his land, he wouldn't have to work anymore. His property had been a great investment and he should cash in while he could. Bob wasn't known for being smart, and I guess on some level he just couldn't understand how the market worked. Either that, or he was the most stubborn son-of-a-bitch that one could ever meet!

Tom pulled up next to the ridiculous looking Pepsi truck that was bigger than Bob's home. He rolled his eyes and walked up to the door and knocked three times before letting himself in. "You should lock your door at night, and I mean it."

"Tom, is that you?" said Bob as he lifted the pillow up off his head and glanced at the fluorescent green clock on the VCR. "What the hell are you doing here at eight in the morning?"

"Bob, get up." Tom kicked the side of the couch. "You're never going to believe what happened last night!"

Bob sat up and looked around the room. "I guess I didn't make it to the bed last night. What the hell time did we leave the bar anyhow?" He got up off the couch and headed towards the kitchen while scratching his ass. "You want some coffee or juice?"

"No thanks. Bob, what I'm about to tell you stays between me and you. Last night, after I left the bar, I think I hit something in the road by the lumberyard. I slammed on the brakes and there he was!"

Bob removed the Folgers can from one of the cabinets. "Who?"

"Bigfoot!" Tom took a seat on the kitchen table while Bob made coffee. He pulled the Zip-lock bag out from his pocket, opened it, and handed the hair to Bob.

"This smells like shit! What is this?" questioned Bob.

"It's Bigfoot's hair!"

"I didn't think you were a believer," stated Bob as he adjusted his eyes to the bright sunlight shining through his kitchen window. He shut the curtains before turning back to Tom.

"Let's just say that now it is falsifiable," said Tom as he lifted himself off the table.

Bob opened his eyes wide and tried to focus them and understand what the hell was going on here. "You have one chunk of hair, Tom. What's to say that you didn't pull it off a horse?" Tom was acting out of character, and he wasn't sure where Tom was going with this.

"I have more evidence, other than seeing it with my own eyes and having a piece of hair! It slaughtered my barn animals. Every single one of them! Well, except for a small pig. Grab your camera and boots and let's go!"

Bob tried to make sense of Tom's unusually childish behavior and quickly came to the conclusion that Tom was going through a mid-life crisis. He waited for his coffee to brew, then filled his own thermos and decided to be there for Tom, as ridiculous as his story was. He went into his bedroom and found his camera, which he hadn't used since his girlfriend left him over a year ago. He smiled at the thought of Jeanie and glanced at the photo of her that was still in a wooden frame on his dresser. Checking to make sure the camera had film, he met Tom out on the lawn.

Chapter 4

Steve, Maureen and the twins arrived shortly after noon. They climbed out of their sport utility vehicle and onto the overgrown mesh of grass, pine needles, and crabapples to find a way from the driveway to the front door. Steve and Maureen made their way past the well to the screen door. Once inside the screened in porch, Steve lifted up the rabbit statue and found the skeleton key that unlocked the door. The house was exactly as they had left it, minus some of the warmth, charm and cleanliness. The air felt like cool liquid as the Bettis' flowed into the house. All around them was a damp chilly feeling that would take a day or two to dispel. Not that this bothered Steve in the least. He dropped his keys on a small buffet table and then smiled at the puff of dust that erupted off it. Visually skimming both living rooms, he announced to the Farm, "We're back!" Not that Steve had any supernatural experiences of his own; his tongue-in-cheek banishment of spirits was his sardonic acknowledgement only of everyone else's beliefs, especially his mother's. The idea that his family's vacation home was haunted was incompatible with Steve's logical and scientific approach to the world. But he hated to argue with and deflate those whose sense of mystery in the world overrode their better judgment. He especially hated the look his mother gave to him whenever he expressed his doubts, for she was dead set on what had happened to her years ago. And he often found himself in the minority to the many others who backed up his mother's claims.

When Devin was younger, he would sit-up in what the family called "the ghost room," a corner bedroom that could only be accessed through another bedroom, and have lengthy conversations with "the Indian". To Steve and Maureen it appeared that Devin had created another imaginary friend, but Steve's mother believed Devin was making "connections to the other side." The ghost room had earned its name well before the twins were even born. Steve's brother, George, was in there with his girlfriend one night, when she swore that George became temporarily possessed by an evil spirit. She let out a piercing scream and her dog ran up the steps to come to her aide. As if an invisible wall was built in the doorway, the dog barked at the entrance of the room, refusing at all costs to enter into the room, even at the expense of his owner. George eventually married this woman, but she insisted he cut off all ties to the Farm. Steve had had no bad experiences with the Farm, and Maureen loved it just as much as Steve did, so he bought it from his mother when she couldn't afford to keep up with it anymore. He was not superstitious like his brother and his sister lived in California, with no interest in the Farm at all.

Although the property wasn't fenced in, the Bettis' dog Spike never ventured far. She sprang out of the truck and quickly marked her territory, letting the others know that this land was hers.

Steve went straight to work by mowing the lawn, while Maureen swept and dusted the house. The twins were given the task of cleaning up the fallen crabapples so Steve wouldn't send out a barrage of missiles with the mower like he did last year. Devin bent over to pick up some apples, and Becka couldn't resist the urge to chuck the biggest crab apple she could find at his ass. As a pitcher on her school's softball team, Becka's aim was dead on. Devin retaliated with a handful of crabapples tossed right at her head. Becka ducked and took off in the direction of the woods. Spike trailed behind, trying to take the lead. Devin was used to running the 200 meter dash in track, and it did not take him long to catch up to Becka. She was trapped in a headlock before she could think of her next move.

"Maureen. Could you come out here for a minute?" said Steve as he approached the back porch.

"What is it?"

"That tree. It looks like it's on its way out. I have to cut that thing down."

"Right this minute? I thought we were going to go food shopping when you were done with the lawn?"

"You guys go without me. I'm worried it's going to crash into the window." Just as Steve said that, two chipmunks chased each other down the tree trunk to the ground.

"I think they heard you."

"Yeah, cute little guys aren't they?"

Maureen smiled and retreated into the house. She saw Becka and Devin sitting in the living room, both of them flushed and out of breath from wrestling and racing each other back to the Farm. "What's wrong with you two?"

"It's so buggy," said Becka. "We need bug spray."

"There's got to be about ten cans in the cabinet."

"Yeah, and they're all empty," said Devin.

"Alright. Let's go. Your father is going to stay here and chop down a tree. Becka, don't tell me that's a giant mosquito bite on your forehead?"

"No. That's just a mark from Devin the Retard."

"Don't mess with the bull if you can't take the horns," laughed Devin.

"You're such a loser," said Becka as she punched him in the arm.

"Enough, you two! We just got here and you're already acting like a bunch of animals!"

They drove the seven miles down Schroon River Road and headed towards Main Street. Maureen noticed that some of the houses on the road had slightly changed. Yet despite the development of some of the local properties, the changes were relatively minor. The population was still a fraction of any Long Island town, and Warrensburg hadn't lost the tranquility and charm that attracted her in-laws here years ago. Maureen pulled into the Grand Union parking lot and gave the usual speech to the twins. "You guys can walk around town, go to the pizza parlor, whatever, but stick together and meet me at the car in forty five minutes."

Devin and Becka had been saving their allowances for several weeks prior to their vacation. Immediately, they both saw the yard sale on the local Presbyterian Church lawn and headed in that direction.

"I bet I can find something really cool for Erica," said Becka.

"Yeah, I think she's getting tired of the same souvenirs from Lake George every year."

"Besides, I bet we can haggle with the prices," said Becka. Her best friend Erica was famous for her overseas travels and outrageous gifts, (courtesy of her rich parents, of course.)

Upon their arrival onto the church property, Devin bypassed the old ladies selling baked goods and the elderly men displaying antique-like novelties and trinkets as if he was driven by a higher force to reach the church on top of the hill. Becka had stopped to admire the artwork and didn't care much that Devin did not shop at her side. This year was a big turn in the twins' battle for independence, which began upon entering Junior High School. Devin made new friends upon joining the soccer team, and Becka entered the cruel world of jealousy and deception that develops between thirteen year-old girls and continues throughout college. Her naivety about the world was eroding only slowly, hardly keeping up with her demands for freedom.

Passing the silver jewelry and hand-carved bears, Devin found what he unconsciously had been searching for. An immensely tall, copper-skinned man with long dark braids and stoic features stood near the rear of the church, playing a rhythmic tune on a wooden flute. Shoppers smiled in his direction but only one stayed to hear the end of the one-man symphony. Devin admired the talented individual and browsed through the man's collection of Native American instruments and jewelry while listening to the music.

The dark, indomitable man sensed the presence of an old spirit and allowed the excess wind to flow out of his lungs. He slowly lowered the flute and scanned the yard sale, hoping to come into contact with this powerful life source when Devin entered into his peripheral vision. A smile spread across his face as he approached the adolescent.

His voice asked the question but his eyes were subliminally saying something else. "Do you see something of interest?"

Devin looked up and returned an awkward smile, then tried to look away, but his mind drifted and he stood in front of this stranger, his thoughts in a flurry.

The size difference put Devin's gaze at the height of the man's chest, whose shirt bore a picture of an elk.

The man tugged on the corners of his shirt, flattening out the image.

"It's an elk," he said. "The elk is the symbol for pace, stamina, and equilibrium of energy."

"I'm sorry," apologized Devin. "I did not mean to stare." Devin put his hands in his pockets and shrugged his shoulders. "I was deep into your music. I hadn't noticed that you stopped."

"Ah, you have just experienced the power of the cedar flute."

"What?"

The man extended his right hand. "Allow me to introduce myself. They call me Loudbear."

Devin took the man's hand and gratefully shook it. "Devin, that's me." He smiled and pointed to himself.

"What did you say about the flute?"

"The cedar flute is empty, not full of itself. The pure spirit of one who plays the flute can empty him, allowing for The Great Spirit to come and fill his emptiness. As voice is offered to the wind, hidden power can fill the emptiness of any who listen and hear."

"You played, I heard." Devin picked up another cedar flute off one of Loudbear's folding tables. "How much is this?"

"Ten dollars. I make them myself." Loudbear took the flute from Devin's hands and placed a red feather in one of the holes, then wrapped it in tissue paper. "For you, it's a gift." Loudbear handed back the wrapped flute to Devin. "I want you to have it."

"That is very kind of you, thank you. What is the feather for?"

"It's my tribe's version of a card."

"I studied Native Americans in Social Studies this year." Devin looked over Loudbear and contorted his face. "By process of elimination, I'm going to guess that you're Mohican."

"I'm impressed."

Devin began a diatribe that he had memorized almost verbatim from his eighth grade Social Studies teacher. "I picked your tribe because I know that most Mohicans who originally lived along the Hudson were devastated by warfare and European disasters during the early colonial period, then forced to leave by the Dutch. The remaining Mohicans went to Massachusetts. I didn't know there were any left here." Devin turned slightly red. "Then my teacher had us watch *The Last of the Mohicans* to finish off the lesson."

"Then I should go down in history!" Loudbear turned away from Devin and kneeled down to grab a bottle of water from his cooler. He reached his hand behind his back and handed one to Devin. He then sat down on a small folding chair.

Devin accepted the water and looked around and found a small bench. "I'm embarrassed to say that I thought that was a true movie. Is it true that it was filmed here in Lake George?"

"That's what I hear. Who are you here with?"

"My sister."

Loudbear looked south and spotted a young girl wearing white shorts with a yellow tank top. "She's right there," he said, pointing to Becka.

Devin stood up and looked in that direction. "You're right. How did you know that was her?"

"Same aura," Loudbear said as he sipped his water.

Devin was amazed. "Are you a psychic or something?"

The man smiled at Devin's question. "No, I have learned to sense auras. You have a very wise aura surrounding you. I sense that you are very powerful." Loudbear winked in the boy's direction.

Devin felt a little scared and looked away. "I don't think so," he said.

"Your sister, she's your twin, right?"

"Yes, how'd you know?"

Loudbear ignored the boy's question. "It is true that all twins have an extra sense? Close your eyes and let your mind drift to nothing. What do you feel?"

Devin closed his eyes and started to concentrate.

"No, no, no, Devin. Don't think about it. It's not a thought. What is the first thing that comes to mind?"

Devin let his mind drift elsewhere and blurted the first thing that came to mind, "a red collar."

"A red collar. Powerful."

Devin nodded, not sure of what he should say.

When a customer came over to Loudbear's table, he excused himself and got up to assist her. Devin walked over to Becka. He told her about his strange interaction with the Mohican and Becka insisted on meeting him. They made their way back to Loudbear's area and her eyes fixated on one particular piece of jewelry, a choker made of leather with a bear claw dangling from the turquoise centerpiece. "This necklace. It's beautiful, is it real?"

"That is no ordinary necklace. And I'm afraid it's out of your price range." Loudbear picked up the choker and caressed it with his fingers. "This is made with deerskin, antler and bear claws. The hair-pipes are made of white bone."

"I thought you made them yourself?" asked Devin.

Loudbear nodded his head.

The animal rights activist in Becka came out without pausing. "You killed all these animals just to make one necklace!" scolded a disgusted Becka.

"This necklace is not for fashion. It is for awareness, power, abundance, and healing powers. It is to be worn by someone who needs it. Someone who understands it, and someone who believes it."

Becka looked at Devin. "Let's go. I've heard enough."

"Sorry," said Devin to Loudbear as he was being dragged away by his angry sister.

Loudbear smiled and called out, "It's O.K. She's driven by instinct. I like her."

Devin and Becka reached the sidewalk in front of the church. "You were so rude to that man! I'm so mad at you right now," yelled Devin.

"Whatever," shrugged Becka as she walked towards the supermarket, leaving Devin at the church.

Devin ran up behind her. "Not everyone is a die hard vegetarian like you. Maybe you forgot, but we nearly wiped out an entire race whose only means of survival was by killing animals. They didn't have medicine, or Bibles. This is how they lived. If they got sick, they wore a necklace for strength. There is nothing wrong with that. They worshipped animals. They're not like the models who wear a fur coat 'cause they think it looks good. And he wasn't going to sell it to someone for fashion."

"Alright. I'm sorry," admitted Becka, a bit taken aback by the forcefulness of Devin's defense.

"You should apologize to Loudbear."

"He doesn't care. He was laughing as we walked away. Come on, let's get back to the car."

Chapter 5

Jesse Luongo enjoyed his days off. He made a decent living drawing up blueprints for contractors at Tom's Lumberyard during the week, but on summer weekends he fished the local rivers for trout and bass. There was little in the world as relaxing as the sound of the reel spinning as he cast into the cool flowing waters of Schroon River. "A man with a fishing pole and a beer isn't looking for much else," he had always said, "except for a nice piece of ass, of course." When Jesse wasn't snagging fry from the river he cast his net over the local ladies. He baited the line with his naturally strong build and piercing green eyes. It didn't take long for him to reel them in, especially when the stock was summer tourists looking for a short weekend of fun.

Being a perpetual ladies' man didn't deny Jesse the joys of fatherhood. His first born, Danielle, was a product of high school lust without the nuisance of condoms. Jesse had been dating Danielle's mother throughout high school, and when she found out she was pregnant they decided to keep in touch and raise the baby with one hundred percent involvement on both ends. It seemed easy enough: Claudia lived off of Main Street while Jesse lived in the more rural section of Warrensburg, beyond Schroon River Road. Danielle would have the privilege of growing up on both sides of town.

Jesse fathered his second child, Austin, with a tourist from Queens who hadn't planned on living out her life in Warrensburg. She was just a few years out of high school and certified in the dead end career of "medical transcriptionist." Within the first few days of missing her period, she got into her Ford Focus and drove right up Interstate 87 to Jesse's exit with a pregnancy test kit in her pocketbook. The bleached blonde took the test into the bathroom of Jesse's trailer and shoved the proof in his face.

To her surprise, Jesse was thrilled by the outcome and insisted she move in with him immediately.

Justine developed a good life in Warrensburg. Jesse supported her financially, so she could stay home and raise Austin. They had no intentions of marrying, but in this neck of the woods, marriage was considered highly overrated at best. Jesse was undeniably good looking, and she was still a very attractive woman, even though she never fully lost the baby weight. There didn't seem to be the desire for woman up here to be a size two, and Justine fell victim to rich, home-cooked, oversized meals and fresh blueberry pies. She became close with Sherry, more out of courtesy for Jesse because her husband was Jesse's boss, but she adored Danielle. She couldn't wait until the summer time, when the Bettis' would come up from Long Island and tell them how crowded the place had become. After an evening with Maureen, Justine always reassured herself that she had made the right decision by relocating. The Bettis' owned a summer home next door to Jesse and Justine. As young boys, Steve and Jesse were inseparable in the summers. As they grew older, their friendship drifted. But they never had any problem picking up where they left off come July.

Jesse heard the familiar sound of the ancient lawn mover left behind from Steve's grandfather and ran inside the house. Justine was pulling a tick off Norma's back with a pair tweezers on the back porch.

Jesse walked towards the front door and braced himself on the newly painted moldings. "Summer is officially here. The Bettis' have arrived!" he said as he made his way to the back of the house. "Norma get another tick? I knew that flea and tick treatment was just a gimmick!" He grabbed the tweezers from Justine's hand and got to work.

"Guess what, Norma? Your friend is here! Yeah, Spike is here! You can go play with her!" Justine always talked to Norma as if she were a person. "I think Norma knew that Spike was coming soon. She has been sniffing around their house for days!"

"Don't speak too soon. I didn't see them yet. I don't even know if Spike is still around."

"Jesse, don't you dare speak like that!"

"I'm just saying, with Long Island traffic, it's not the safest place for dogs. O.K. Norma, good girl." Jesse patted Norma's ass and stood up. He looked to Justine, "You know the drill."

"Yeah, I know. The first night the Bettis' are here, we have a big barbeque that I alone, prepare and cook while you revert back to your childhood days with Steve. But you know, it would be nice if they called for once, to tell us when they were coming."

"They come the same time every year, you know that!"

"That's not true! Two years ago, we didn't see them until August! You were so pathetic. Waiting by the window like a kid on a rainy day!"

Jesse smiled at her. She was absolutely right! He couldn't even argue that one. They both burst out laughing. With that thought, he ran out the door and into the shed where he hopped on his John Deer and headed towards Steve. Norma ran out after him.

After making sure Jesse was off the property, Justine went into the bathroom and criticized herself in the mirror for the third time that day. Jesse had done away with the scale, but the numbers never meant anything to Justine anyway. Maureen and her perfect body were in the house next door, and Justine was stuck here with a spare tire around her mid section that seemed damn near impossible to deflate. She pulled her hair back and shoved her finger down her throat, forcing whatever food she'd eaten during the day to come back up and disappear into the toilet. She preferred vomiting outside, but occasionally did it in the house during the day. The only problem with puking inside the house was that she could never get all the vomit to flush down the toilet, and that would make for more arguments between her and Jesse. He knew that she was bulimic, but that didn't mean he understood the disease or knew how to support her emotionally. Justine couldn't help but think once again how lucky Danielle was to have her to talk to. Jesse was a good guy, but never got the concept of how women felt or thought. His expertise in gratifying women never went further than the bedroom. And that was no lesson to pass on to their beautiful young daughter.

From the bathroom she could hear the phone ringing, causing her to quickly wash her hands and run to the phone, her only exercise for the day. "Hello? Hi Sherry. No, I'm not busy. I was just about to head out to the garden to pick some vegetables for a salad. The Bettis' are here, and we're having a barbeque. You and Tom should come over. What's that? Tom thinks he saw Bigfoot? Uh-huh. Well, I'm sorry about your barn animals. Like I said, I saw a moose recently. And I hear they are vicious. I am not letting Austin out alone. Yeah, I bet it was a moose. It startled me, too! But I was sober when I saw it! O.K. Thanks for the warning. Talk soon. Bye."

Chapter 6

Bob stared at the long line of black trash bags that now contained the remains of Sherry's animal farm. Tom wiped his brow and tossed the bags into the back of his pickup. The two men left the truck in the lumberyard for a moment and walked across the street to where Tom's encounter with "Bigfoot" had taken place. Bob squinted his eyes and puckered his lips, perplexed. In his simple mind, Bob pondered the situation. "Those animals were definitely butchered. A bear would kill one animal, maybe two, but the whole damn bunch of them? The likely suspect would have to be a pack of wolves. But how could they open the barn door? Was it left open? Jesse locks up every night. In his fifteen years at the lumberyard, Jesse had never forgotten to lock the door to the barn. He cared for those animals. Could Sherry have gone there after Jesse locked up? Sherry had been acting rather odd lately..." Bob's mind was racing, but in circles. Tom quickly discredited every possible scenario that Bob presented as if he had already thought of the possibility himself, which he had.

"I know, Bob. I want to believe it was one or all of those things, but trust me. It's just not possible. And there's no need for you to remind me of my wife's peculiar behavior. I live with her, remember?" Lately Sherry had been walking around the house reporting sightings of their dead daughter. Tom was not the let's-discuss-your-feelings kind of guy, so whenever Sherry mentioned Allison, Tom found an excuse to retreat into the garage with a few beers or a bottle of vodka. It's not that he dismissed the idea of ghosts entirely, but having his wife run around the house like a mother playing hide-and-seek with a dead baby just didn't sit well in his psyche.

"Did you call Jesse?"

"No. I told you. I don't want anybody to know about this. At least not until I get to the bottom of things."

"Why don't you want to ask him? You don't have to give him an explanation, just bring it up in conversation."

"Two reasons," said Tom. He held up two fingers but kept his eyes on the bushes in front of him. "Number one, if I ask him if he locked up, he'll know that the barn wasn't locked and he'll think I'm accusing him of something. You know how paranoid that guy gets. Number two, he will start an investigation of his own, wanting to know why I asked him. Then he'll tell Justine, and then the whole town will know."

"The whole town will know what? Sometimes I just don't get you, man. And I wouldn't worry about Jesse telling Justine a thing. I bet your wife is on the phone with her as we speak."

Tom knew that Bob was acting rationally, and that's exactly why he had asked him to come along with him. But Bob wasn't saying anything that Tom hadn't already thought…

"Wait a minute! I am on to something!"

"What?" Tom was eager to hear what Bob had to say. Bob was by no means a rocket scientist, but what he lacked in intelligence he made up for in common sense. Tom knew he was missing something, but was beginning to doubt that Bob would pick it up.

"Kankro and Demitres. This is exactly the kind of stunt they would pull. Maybe they even dressed up as a Bigfoot to make you think you're nuts. The whole thing was staged!"

Tom stopped walking, turned around and sucker-punched Bob across the chest. "That is the dumbest thing I have ever heard you say, and I have been witness to much of your stupid nonsense."

Bob punched Tom in the upper arm. "And why is that so dumb?"

"Why the hell would they go through all that trouble to piss me off? You know what, just don't even answer that. I regret ever telling you about this whole thing." Tom picked up the pace and put a few yards between them.

Bob didn't answer him. In his head, it sounded reasonable, but when he heard himself say it aloud, he knew it sounded rather silly. Feeling slightly embarrassed, he started to laugh. Tom heard him and he started to laugh, too. "Do me a favor, Tom. When you find your Bigfoot, and you sell your story to the tabloids, don't mention that I came up with that stupid idea."

"Believe me, I won't. As funny as it would sound, I'd have to admit that out of everyone I know, I chose you to take along with me. By the way, do you have a gun on you?"

"No, a hunting knife. You really think we're going to need it? I never saw this side of you. I thought you were anti-gun since Vietnam?"

"I've reconsidered." Tom stumbled across something very peculiar. "Bob, check this out." Tom pointed to a patch of large, green lily pads that had been previously plucked and dropped there.

"These are lily pads, from the pond. They still have the stems on them. Somebody must have picked them and brought them over here." Bob bent down and felt them. "Somebody was definitely here. You can almost see an imprint. And there is that damn smell again!"

Tom kneeled down beside Bob. He retrieved the hair from his pocket and smelled it again. Then he smelt the patch of lilies. "Identical." Tom and Bob took some more pictures, just as they had at the lumberyard.

*   *   *

Steve was ten feet up the tree when he glanced down at the pine needles beneath him and felt queasy. The ladder had been in the garage for about forty years, and the wood was starting to rot. He could feel the rungs bowing under his weight. He decided the tree dilemma would have to wait, and started to climb back down to earth. With only a few more steps to go, he heard Jesse's voice coming from the shrubs which separated their properties.

"Yee haa!" Jesse screamed as he jumped the slight incline in his lawn mower.

Steve laughed and thought to himself that only Jesse could pull a wheelie in a John Deer.

"If it isn't the city boy himself! How you doin', man?" Jesse stepped off his vehicle and gave Steve a nice hug with a few pats on the back. "You look great, man."

"Long time no see. You look good yourself. How did you get your lawn mower to jump like that?" asked Steve with a huge smile on his face.

Jesse was also glowing with excitement. "What are you talking about? My ride? I didn't do much, just put on some different tires and straightened out a turn or two in the gas line. You know what they say, "No matter what you do, you gotta have fun doin' it!" Jesse laughed and lifted up the seat to his mower. He pulled out two cold Budweiser's and handed one to Steve.

"You're a trip. That's what I like about you. You're always the same ol' Jesse."

"If you were the same ol' Steve, we'd be getting high in my barn right about now!"

Steve laughed, feeling slightly awkward for acting his age. When Steve was sixteen, his parents were going through some marital turmoil. Apparently, Steve's mother had been having an affair with the next-door neighbor.

One night Steve came home earlier than usual and found his mother embraced in a good night kiss with Danny from next door. Steve didn't confront her directly, but he knew what her pleading eyes were asking him to do. He found himself in a mental battle of right and wrong. Steve's mother came home and pretended that nothing had ever happened. That only made matters worse. Steve saw a side of his mother that he never knew existed. In his mind, she was the backbone of the family. She had always been at home raising three children while her husband spent countless hours working for the N.Y.P.D. At sixteen, Steve could not have imagined the loneliness that she felt. Steve distanced himself from his father, afraid that he might slip up and tell him the truth. He and his father had always had a close relationship, and this secret was tearing him apart inside. The guilt he was feeling was unbearable, and after three weeks, he ran away.

He aptly stole Danny's car and drove straight up the interstate until he reached the Farm. He didn't pack more than one week's supply of clothes or food. It was about 2:00 A.M. when he reached his destination. He walked next door to Jesse's parents' trailer and tapped on the window to his bedroom. Jesse opened up the window and saw a figure standing there.

"Who goes thar'?" he asked like a drunken pirate.

"It's me, Steve. Come out here."

Jesse crept out of his window in order not to awaken his parents. "What's going on? You guys aren't supposed to be here for another few weeks."

"I came alone. It's a long story."

Jesse and Steve started walking towards the Farm. "Wait a minute. The magic dragon should be here for this." They walked over to Jesse's barn and headed up the ladder to the second story where the haystacks were stored. Jesse lifted up a bundle and removed a wooden slat from the floor and retrieved his stash. He replaced the bundle and the floor and headed for the Farm. They wasted no time and lit up before they reached the front door. Since the electricity was turned off for the winter season, Steve lit a lantern for light.

"You just missed Claudia. She stopped by for a little action before bedtime."

"Seems like everybody is stopping somewhere for a little action before bedtime," sighed Steve as he took another hit.

"What's going on? Why are you here alone?" asked a stoned and confused Jesse.

"My mom is having an affair with the neighbor."

"How can you be sure?"

"'Cause I saw them making out!"

"Oh, shit! Well, your mom is pretty hot."

Steve shot Jesse a nasty look. "I'm serious. My dad has no idea. If I see my father again I'm going to tell him. That's why I ran away."

"How did you get here?"

Steve laughed and pointed to the driveway. "I stole that bastard's car! My neighbor, Danny!" Steve was hysterical at this point, and Jesse started to laugh also.

"You're crazy! That is something I would do!" Jesse clapped his hands twice and fell over laughing. "You're unbelievable Bettis! But don't you think that tomorrow morning they will be here looking for you?"

Steve unlocked the old wooden front door with the skeleton key and pushed his way in. "No way. Why would they think to look here?"

"'Cause it's an obvious place to look."

"Nah, they'll never find me. I'll hide out for a week or two, then go home when things settle down. My Dad is a detective. He'll put two and two together when he realizes whose car I took."

"No offense, but if your Dad was such a great detective, I think he'd see that his neighbor is bagging his wife."

"Shut up! My father is a great detective!" Steve was upset by that comment. His father had received countless awards for solving cases that many others had deemed unsolvable. "But wait a minute, you may have a point. Maybe my father already knows. Maybe that is why my mother was not so inconspicuous. Maybe that is why my father is always working overtime. Maybe they are going through a divorce and they just don't want to tell me!"

"You're a real genius, Bettis. I think you should be a detective," said Jesse as he passed Steve the joint. They sat down on the couch and Steve set the lantern on top of the coffee table.

"Maybe," Steve took another hit. He did not feel anxious anymore. He felt very comfortable, stable.

That is why Steve loved the Farm so much. It could have been Jesse, the marijuana, the Farm, or a combination of the three that always put Steve at ease when he was there. Steve recalled that later that night they planted marijuana seeds in the backyard, under a clear sky and with the full moon as their guiding light.

Steve came out of his daydream and remembered that Jesse was just ribbing him about not getting high anymore. "That's funny you say that," he retorted, "'cause if I recall, it was your idea that I become a cop!" Steve laughed and he suddenly felt confident again.

"And you're a damn good cop, too. I wish cops around here had your brains."

"You still having problems with those two knuckleheads?"

"Not really. I've lived here my whole life and it still baffles me that two cops, who aren't even from

Warrensburg, can be so corrupt and get away with it for years."

"If they are as bad as you say, I would start my investigation from the top. They most likely have connections higher up. What are their names again?"

"Kankro and Demitres. Two big, bad apples in one small basket."

"You said they're not from here? Where are they from?" Steve was in detective mode again.

"Fuck it, who cares!" Jesse shook it off and changed the subject. That was typical Jesse. If he ever had a worry, you'd never know. Steve couldn't help but wonder what event had taken place between Jesse and these guys. Working in law enforcement himself, he found it hard to believe there was truth in Jesse's stories about these cops. In the NYPD, each officer had to take an oath to "serve and protect those who can't protect themselves." And those who didn't follow the code were typically exposed by the Internal Affairs Bureau. Dirty cops had a hard time escaping scrutiny in the city. Steve had difficulty understanding that it was not the same everywhere. On one hand, Jesse still behaved like a sixteen year-old. He still drank until he vomited, smoked weed, slept with random girls and handed them fake phone numbers, even rode his quads on anyone's property with a little jump. He could see Jesse driving home drunk or stoned from somewhere and the cops doing what they had been paid to do. But on the other hand, Jesse was responsible. He had worked steadily for fifteen years at Tom's Lumberyard, was a good disciplinarian with the kids, coached his son Austin's baseball team, built his house by himself, and was always there when a friend needed him. It wasn't that Jesse had told Steve about any particular incident with the cops in Warrensburg, just a few passing mentions of how ass-backwards they were.

Chapter 7

After dinner, Steve and Jesse walked back to the Farm to set up the fire pit. The twins played with Austin on the trampoline while Maureen and Justine cleared the outdoor picnic table. Austin was nine years old, but hadn't had much contact with other kids since school ended for the summer break. His sister Danielle was eighteen, and her schedule was just starting to free up since her prom and finals were over. Danielle was eager to attend Syracuse in the fall, so she planned to make this summer her best one yet! That meant spending as little time as possible at her father's house, with her pesky little brother. Although her mother was married, her stepfather was never able to have kids. Since they already had Danielle, they accepted it for what it was instead of opting for other solutions. Danielle lived like a princess at her mother's house. But when she was at her father's, he put her to work. She was too young to appreciate the integrity of doing things for your self. Justine had called her and invited her to dinner with them, but she declined the offer. Her stepfather Don, (also Jesse's cousin,) had recently bought her a brand new fire engine red Jeep Cherokee for graduation. Jesse was dead set against the idea of his unemployed daughter driving around in a new car, but in the end he lost the battle. Jesse knew that Danielle had no intentions of getting a job this summer, and he tried to impress this truth on Don and Claudia, but they went ahead and bought the truck anyway. In the end, Don and Jesse had come to an agreement: she would pay for her own gas and insurance. Needless to say, there had been a lot of tension between Danielle and Jesse over the last couple of weeks.

"Mom, we're going back to the Farm," said Becka as she climbed off the trampoline.

"O.K. We'll meet you over there in a minute," responded Maureen as she carried the remaining silverware into the house. "Bring Austin with you."

"Come on, Austin. I'll race you to the swing," said Becka.

"Hold on." Devin had gotten his shorts caught on a spring in the trampoline.

Becka and Austin glanced over at Devin and started laughing at him.

Devin had a great sense of humor. His strongest asset was his ability to find humor in any situation. At this point, he was hanging upside down underneath the trampoline. "You can help at any time!"

Becka walked over to him and held up the trampoline while tugging on the spring. As expected, Devin fell on his head. "Come on you retard, let's go."

"Thanks Beck," he said while laughing at himself.

Maureen and Justine had been watching this ordeal from the kitchen window. "Devin is such a goofball. He always has been," remarked Maureen as she chuckled out loud. "If there is a crack in the sidewalk, Devin will trip over it. Becka on the other hand, is the complete opposite. She's definitely more coordinated, and I think a bit stronger emotionally as well."

"It must be great, having twins who look out for one another," said Justine, who couldn't give a rat's ass about the twins, or Maureen for that matter. She tolerated Maureen for Jesse's sake, but inside was ridden with jealousy. Maureen, although eight years older than Justine, was a poster board for the perfect mother and housewife. And Jesse didn't make it any easier when he reminded her how he and Maureen had kissed before she was engaged to Steve. She was in great shape, her husband was successful, her kids were wonderful, she had a house in Warrensburg and a house in Long Island, and she obviously had a close relationship with Steve. When asked how long she and Steve had been dating before he proposed, she would give the cockiest smile ever and say six months! It was so nauseating. Maureen headed for the door and Justine looked her up and down. She even shook her hips when she walked! Who does that? She cursed Jesse in her head, for not marrying her even after she had his baby! She also resented the fact that Jesse showed a warm, affectionate side to Steve. He listened when Steve spoke. Almost as if he looked up to him. It had been years since he responded to her that way!

"Are you ready, Justine?" asked Maureen in her cheery voice.

"I'll meet you over there. I need to freshen up a bit," responded Justine, barely able to disguise her disinterest.

Justine went into the bathroom and examined herself in the full- length mirror once again, waiting for her mid-section to evaporate on the spot. "Why am I so fat? No wonder Jesse doesn't love me anymore! All I do is cook for his majesty all day long. And how can I help but pick at all the food?" Justine started to sob, then rushed for the toilet and made herself puke. Her disease was progressing rapidly, but unfortunately no one had cared to notice. Vomiting made up for her bad choices. She felt instant gratification. And in her head, she felt she looked a little thinner. She brushed her teeth, changed her clothes, and was out the door. A few beers and she wouldn't even notice Maureen. Hopefully, Jesse wouldn't either.

As the sun started to fade into darkness, Steve and Jesse set up a ring of stones behind the Farm to create a fire pit. Steve sent Devin to gather wood and kindling to keep the fire going, while Becka and Austin searched for marshmallow sticks. After the stones were in place, Steve went to the garage to grab some chairs to place around the fire pit.

"Hey Becka, let me see that stick."

Becka walked over to Jesse, who was sitting on a bench in front of the fire, and handed him her most perfect marshmallow stick yet. "I know, it's perfect," she said with the famous smile that she inherited from her mother.

"You ain't kiddin' kid," said Jesse, already half buzzed from his earlier brewskies with Steve. "How did you get the point on the end so sharp?"

"I carved it with my knife," said a proud Becka.

"Good job. Let me borrow that knife to make a stick for Austin." Jesse smiled at Becka as he rested his beer can next to the bench. Becka was Jesse's goddaughter, so she always held a special place in Jesse's heart.

"Can I have a sip?" asked Beck.

Jesse looked around, mainly for Steve who, at the moment, was nowhere in sight. He could see Austin and Devin skulking around the side yard and that Maureen was in the house. "O.K., but just one sip. And don't tell your father!"

Becka looked around, double-checking that the coast was clear. She could see Justine heading up the property. She bent down, grabbed the beer, and took a long sip. "Thanks Jesse," she said as she rested the beer can back in its place and stood up to find another stick for her brother.

Jesse pointed his finger to his cheek. "Who's your favorite Godfather?"

Becka kissed his cheek then headed off into the back field.

Roasting marshmallows over the fire was a family tradition at the Farm. Earlier in the day, Maureen had bought graham crackers and Hershey's chocolate for creating "S'mores." They did this every night while visiting the Farm, with the exception of a rainy night. In that case, they'd set up for a tournament style series of Yahtzee, equipped with bowls of barbeque and onion and garlic potato chips, puffy cheese doodles, and cans of soda to fuel the marathon of family competition.

Maureen kicked open the back screen door with her foot, letting it hit her in the shoulder as she attempted to carry the cooler from the back dining room into the yard. Jesse saw the door fly open and Maureen's sandal smack into the tree by the back porch. He jumped up to assist.

"Let me give you a hand."

"Thanks." She handed over the cooler, then reached behind her to grab the bottle of wine on the plastic end table on the porch. Realizing she forgot her wine glass, she retreated into the kitchen. Standing on tiptoes, she tried to reach for the glass on the second shelf in the cabinet. She had just grabbed the stem of it when she heard a loud thud from beyond the window. Startled, she jumped back and lost her balance, forgetting she was only wearing one shoe. Her head smacked hard against the door and she found herself falling backwards into Jesse's arms.

Jesse caught Maureen before she tumbled onto the floor and helped her to her feet. She turned around slowly, her face flushed, her cheeks suddenly warm.

"Thanks," she said as she brushed her hair behind her ears. "I must have lost my balance. I heard a noise outside. It sounded like it came from the root cellar." She held her hand against an itchy spot on the back of her head and felt something warm and sticky. Jesse saw the blood trickling off her fingertips and lifted her up, carrying her into the living room. He placed her on the couch in a sitting position.

"Let me take a look at that." He sifted through her thick brown hair and found the open wound. "It's not too deep, nothing a few stitches couldn't fix."

"That's just what I wanted to do, hang-out in a hospital all night," said Maureen as she tried to laugh it off.

"Hospital? We're talking three or four stitches. I'll do it myself."

"You're kidding, right?" She looked up at him, halfway knowing he was being totally serious. "Steve is not going to allow you to stitch up my head."

"Alright, but the closest hospital is over thirty miles away, and you will be there all night. Or, you can trust me and get this taken care of before anyone even knows about it."

Maureen glanced over towards the front door, then back at Jesse. "O.K. You win. Can you run upstairs and grab my flip-flops by the foot of the bed?" Jesse retrieved the rubber shoes, then walked her over to his house.

"Sorry I wasn't there a second sooner, so you wouldn't have hit your head."

"I guess we know who Devin gets his clumsiness from," joked Maureen. They walked into Jesse's house and he led her into the bathroom. Maureen straddled the toilet seat backwards to give Jesse full access to the back of her head.

"Wait here just a moment, just stay right there." Jesse left the bathroom and came back with a bottle of Absolut Vodka. He opened the bottle and handed it to Maureen. "This will only hurt for a moment, but you might want to take a gulp before we start."

Maureen grasped the bottle and chugged it down like she was in a college sorority.

Jesse shaved a small section of Maureen's head, then applied the necessary stitching until the blood stopped. The whole process took less than five minutes. She hadn't realized that the stitching was complete so she stayed in the same position on the toilet. "How come you never got married," she asked him.

"You never asked."

"Ha, ha," laughed Maureen as she reached for the alcohol again.

"You're all done." Jesse tapped her on her shoulder.

Maureen got up off the toilet bowl. "Thank you."

"No problem. C'mon, we should get back." Jesse held the bathroom door open for her. "Ladies first."

Maureen sauntered through the living room and headed towards Jesse's bedroom.

Jesse watched her suspiciously. "What are you doing?"

"Oh, relax. I need another mirror to see the back of my head." She set herself up in front of the full-length mirror and grabbed Justine's make-up mirror from the nightstand, holding it up behind her.

Jesse waited in the doorway with his hands resting on the top molding above the door. Maureen smiled at him through the mirror, not sure if his pin-up pose was deliberate or not. Jesse disappeared for a brief moment, then returned with the bottle of vodka. He stood behind Maureen and took the mirror out of her hand, replacing it with the vodka bottle. Feeling like a bizarre version of Adam and Eve, she sipped the bottle while he brushed her hair away from her neckline and tugged on her shirt. He landed a small but intimate kiss on the sensitive curve of her exposed left shoulder. Maureen closed her eyes and turned around to face him. When she opened her eyes, Jesse was gone. She turned to see the back of him walking into the living room. Then she heard the front door shut and wondered how far she would have taken it if Jesse hadn't had the sense to walk away from temptation.

Justine made herself comfortable in one of the vinyl camper's chairs that Steve set up around the pit. She reached into the cooler next to her and cracked open a beer. Hearing unfamiliar footsteps, she looked up to see

Steve making his way towards her with arms full of firewood. "You want me to roast you a marshmallow?" she asked him.

Steve laid the wood next to the bench. "No, but you can toss me a beer."

Jesse came up from behind Justine and put his fingers to his lips for Steve to stay silent. He grabbed the back of Justine's chair and yanked it backwards, causing her to spill her beer all over her shirt. "Ahhh!" Jesse then set the chair back in its place.

"You asshole!" Justine fussed to wipe the beer off of her shirt.

Jesse found this amusing while Steve handed over a rag to Justine, feeling embarrassed for her. Devin also felt awkward so he diverted the attention by positioning two marshmallows on Austin's stick then stuck one onto his own. "O.K. Austin, don't put it in the fire, just wave it around the top of the fire."

"Got it," replied Austin.

Maureen came out of the front door with her glass of wine and joined them at the fire pit.

"You got some great kids, Steve, honestly," complimented Jesse as he tried to avoid eye contact with Maureen.

"Yeah. They're great. And Austin, he got so big" replied Steve.

"Yup, Austin's put some meat on his bones recently. Justine too." Jesse looked towards Justine and smiled.

"Fuck you, asshole!" said Justine.

"Whoa. Slow down there, chugger. We're all just playing around. No need to get so upset." Jesse motioned with his hands for Justine to take it easy.

Maureen and Steve exchanged a quick glance and then got up from the fire pit and started walking towards the dark, open field.

"Justine, I think you're really pretty. And you look fine the way you are," said Devin with a sincerity that was made even sweeter by his youth.

"Thank you Devin. I'm sorry I cursed in front of you." It had been so long since someone told her she was pretty that she didn't care that it came from a thirteen year old kid.

"It's not like I haven't heard those words before," laughed Devin. Maureen and Steve made their way back to the fire pit after giving Jesse and his girlfriend time to wind down.

Having caught the disapproving look from Steve, Jesse decided to make peace. "Justine, I'm just kidding. I promise, no more fat jokes for tonight." Jesse got up and put his arm around her.

"No more fat jokes at all, or I'm out of here." She lightly tapped Jesse on his head.

The night was dark and the only visible light was the orange glow of the fire and the electric blue of the bug zapper. Steve took his flashlight and walked to the garage. "Becka, Devin and Austin! Get your butts out here for some Kick the Can!" Steve appeared out of nowhere with an empty coffee can in his hand. "Put your potatoes in, and we'll see who's it." The kids and Jesse ran over to Steve and held out their fists in a big circle. "One potato, two potato, three potato four...." Maureen stumbled over to the fire pit next to Justine and sat down with her wine. Kick the Can was another upstate tradition for the Bettis'. They only played at night, and never with fewer than five players. This made it especially difficult for the "it" person, who spent most of the game groping blindly through the darkness in vain attempts to locate the kicked can. Even when the can was located and the chase began in earnest, it was hard to tag the players who darted in and out of the tree line--faint shadows in a gray mist.

While the men and kids played their game, the women chatted by the fire pit. Justine had downed at least a six-pack by this time, and Maureen was pretty drunk herself. In the distance, Justine heard a soothing noise and focused her attention in the direction of the sounds. It sounded like it was coming from the back porch, but the area was not lit and she did not feel like getting up. Very relaxing, she thought.

Maureen also heard the sounds. She looked at the back porch and said to Justine, "Do you hear that? I bought the most beautiful set of wind chimes this afternoon at the church yard sale. Wait until you see them in the morning. It's two birds, a bright red cardinal and a blue jay sitting on a perch, with dangling flowers in all sorts of colors. Absolutely gorgeous! And for only eight dollars!" Norma didn't seem too interested in the wind chimes and headed to the back field in the direction of the kids.

During the third round of kick the can, Becka was "it". Devin kicked the can so hard, it actually landed in the woods. Becka took her time fetching the can, for she knew it would take her a while in the darkness. She thought she heard it hit a tree, so she headed in the direction of the only sound she heard. In the faint distance, she heard Devin shout, "Take some of that!" She made a mental note to focus on catching Devin first when she made it out of the woods. An impenetrable gloom settled over the area as she crossed the tree line. She was only about ten feet into the woods when she realized she could barely even see her hand in front of her face. Becka was forced to get onto her hands and knees to feel for the can. It couldn't have gone any further than this, she thought to herself. Suddenly, she heard the rhythmic sound of twigs and pine needles getting louder as if someone were coming towards her from behind. Although slightly frightened, she said out loud, "You don't scare me Devin. I know it's just

65

you." After saying that, she didn't hear anything. She stood up and still didn't hear anything. She took a few steps further back into the woods. She heard it again. She paused and heard nothing but silence. Becka was frightened at this point, and couldn't see which direction was the field and which way were the woods, but she knew she had to rationalize in a situation like this. It couldn't be Devin, she thought, because Devin would never venture into the woods at night. My Dad wouldn't do this to me, neither would Jesse. Austin would be too concerned with finding the best hiding spot. Her eyes swept the surrounding darkness, but nothing appeared besides her own frantic mental images. Dogs. It's got to be the dogs. Just as Becka was trying to calm herself, she smelled something foul. "Eww, gross! Spike, Norma, is that you?" She turned around and began heading in what she hoped was the direction of the house. As she fumbled in the darkness, the horrible smell grew stronger. She had almost become entangled in the low branches of a large pine tree when she heard the sound of the can crushing about two feet away from her. She screamed for her father and ran as fast as she could, bouncing violently off of the many trees in the dense woods.

Steve, hearing his daughter scream, immediately retrieved his snub-nose from his hip and ran towards the woods. "Becka, are you alright?"

"Daddy help! Something is chasing me! Help!" screamed Becka, her shrill voice echoing through the woods.

Maureen heard her daughter crying and ran into the house to let Spike out. Spike ran out the back door and darted straight for the woods. She bypassed Steve and let out several very loud barks as she entered the many rows of neatly planted pine trees beyond the back field.

Becka felt Spike's fur brush against her leg and instantly felt relief. To her disappointment, Spike didn't stay with her and instead, she kept on running. Becka knew this was bad and screamed for her Dad again. Steve followed her voice and had to have been within five feet of her, but couldn't see a thing. "Becka. I'm right here. I'm reaching my hand out. Grab my hand and keep talking to me."

"Dad! I'm right here! I'm stuck on something. I can't go any further!" The footsteps were getting closer and she could now feel the warm breath of another being closing in on her. "My shirt is caught on something." She thought, "The grip of a killer?" Her cries became ferociously desperate, "Please help me, Daddy please!" The assailant paused, sensing something was off, and then retreated into the woods.

It had been years since Steve had heard Becka cry. She was not a child who was easily frightened. The last time Steve had heard Becka cry was when she was nine years old, when she had broken her ankle after getting hit by an off-course softball. Steve took another step and found Becka's hand. "It's me, Beck. It's me. You're going to be alright. I'm gonna go behind you and untangle your shirt." Becka was shaking with fear and didn't respond. Steve almost had the shirt loose when they heard a loud yelp from Spike. Immediately following the yelp, they heard a loud growl not more than ten feet from them, possibly closing in. Steve raised his gun to the sky and shot off three rounds. As he did that, he saw a light. Jesse approached with a flashlight.

"Don't shoot! It's just me!" Jesse shined the light on Becka and Steve. Steve pointed behind him and Jesse focused the light in that area. "It's gone." Jesse cut Becka's shirt with a switchblade and quickly released her from the tree. Steve carried her back towards the house. "Is she alright?"

"It was a close one." Steve still had one more kid to protect. "Where are the other kids?"

"Everybody's safe and in the house.   Where's Spike?"

"I don't think she made it."

"I'm going to find her. C'mon."

Steve saw that Jesse still had his knife out and was ready to jab at the enemy.   "I'm going in with Becka. Whatever's out there, can stay out there."

"Steve, I understand what you're saying. But both our dogs are out there, and I'm not leaving them."   With that, Jesse took off into the woods. Jesse had an uncanny loyalty to his dog that Steve wasn't about to dissect in this time of crisis.

Chapter 8

Sherry and Tom were just finishing up breakfast when the tune of "Walk this Way" came blasting through the living room window. Tom got up from the table and walked to the front door where he saw Marc playing air guitar and smoking a cigarette while he leaned up against his red 1983 Firebird. Tom was shocked to see just how much Marc had filled out since college. When he was home for Christmas, he looked a little taller, but because of the winter clothing, Tom hadn't noticed that Marc put on a good twenty pounds of sheer muscle. Marc was wearing blue jeans with a black tank top that accented his biceps and broad chest. Even his legs appeared to be thicker.

"Welcome home, son!" Tom's greeting fell on deaf ears.

Sherry ran towards the door and pushed Tom aside. "Marc! I'm so happy to see you!"

Marc flicked his cigarette to the ground and walked over to his mom. He gave her a big hug. "Hi Mom. Hey Dad."

Tom walked down the steps and shook his son's hand. "You look like you've been working out."

"Yeah, my football coach has been kicking my ass!"

"Does he know you smoke?"

"I don't smoke. Only when I drink coffee, which is hardly ever."

"Coffee and cigarettes. Any other bad habits you picked up at college?"

"No." Marc smiled and walked back to his car. "Are you going to help me unpack or you gonna stand there and be a pain in the ass?"

Sherry went inside to heat up some oatmeal for Marc while Tom helped unload the car.

"We weren't expecting you home until Tuesday."

"I didn't plan on leaving until Tuesday, but my Anthropology professor was supposed to have some type of surgery on Wednesday, so he gave us the final early."

"Is it anything serious?"

"I don't think so."

"I bet it sucked for all those wait-till-the-last-minute-to-study kids. And please God tell me you're not one of them!"

"No. Dad. I think I did alright on the final. I actually like that class. My guidance counselor picked it for me to fill in my schedule, but it's interesting stuff. They will post the grades online next week."

During breakfast, Marc could not help but think he was involved in a game of twenty questions. He had been living on his own for a year now, and had forgotten how nagging his parents could be. "Enough about me. What's been going on around town? I miss anything?"

Tom shot Sherry a dangerous look from the corner of his eye. Sherry caught the look and talked about her new hairdresser. "His name is Frank, and I think he's gay, but look at the job he did on my hair!"

Marc also caught the look. "What? What's with that look?"

"What look?" asked Sherry trying to sound smooth.

"The look that Dad gave you. The 'keep your mouth shut' look."

"Well, Marc, now that you mention it, we need to discuss your curfew," said Tom in a successful attempt to change the subject.

"You got to be kidding me. I'm nineteen years old. I'm in college. I'll help out around the house, but that's it."

"Marc, it's just that we worry about you. We're still your parents. I know a curfew at your age sounds ridiculous, and we're not saying that you have to come home when it's dark, but a little phone call goes a long way." Sherry was the voice of reason in this parent duo.

"O.K. I'll keep you informed of my whereabouts." Marc excused himself from the table. "I need to sleep. I drove straight home from West Virginia without stopping."

Marc was fast asleep within five minutes. Sherry had gone into his room to make sure he was sleeping. "He's out like a light," she informed her husband.

"Good. Sherry, I'm sorry about the way I've been acting lately. I'm just so confused as to what I saw the other night, and with the barn animals, and with the hair on my truck. There's something out there. I'm not going to go looking for it anymore, but whatever this thing is, I want you to be cautious when you're outdoors."

Or indoors, she thought to herself. Seeing how in shape her son was, she didn't have the slightest fear for him. And on some level, knew that he would always be safe, and on his own way out of Warrensburg.

Tom heard the phone ring and hurried to pick it up before it woke Marc. "Hello?"

A sobbing Justine was on the other line. "I need to talk to Sherry."

"Justine? What's the matter?" Tom was not a big fan of Justine's, but he was genuinely concerned.

"What is that thing you thought you saw the other night? Bigfoot?"

Tom mentally cursed Sherry for opening her big mouth. Bob was right. Now everybody knew. Damn Sherry!

"It was nothing, just a moose," said Tom feeling more annoyed than he'd been in a long time.

"Yeah, well your moose killed my Norma! And hurt Spike!" Hearing herself say that Norma was killed instantly made her cry again.

"Who is Spike?"

"Steve Bettis' dog. Steve is at the vet with him right now. Jesse found him in the woods last night, about ten feet from Norma's body. Right on Steve's property!"

"Where is Jesse?"

"He's in the yard. Digging a hole for Norma. Right next to the hole he dug for Shelby."

Tom covered the phone and asked Sherry, "Who is Shelby?"

"Jesse's horse," she whispered back.

"Sit tight. Me and Sherry will be there in two minutes." Tom hung up the phone and aimed his thumb towards the front door. "Let's go."

Tom and Sherry argued the entire two-minute car ride to Jesse's house. Sherry apologized for telling Justine, but argued that it was a good thing she did tell her. Justine met them at the front door, trying to wipe her tears away.

"Oh Justine. I'm so sorry about Norma. Is everybody else O.K.?" Sherry hugged Justine while Tom stood behind her, feeling completely useless and somehow responsible.

"Everybody is fine. Becka was within inches of losing her life." She raised her voice towards Tom. "Your 'moose' was creeping up behind her when Steve and Jesse cut her loose."

Tom had been staring at the ground. When he heard about Becka he looked up towards Justine. "Where is she now? You didn't tell me about the girl over the phone. What exactly happened?"

Sherry cautiously eyed her husband as he questioned Justine.

Justine filled Tom in on all the details. Then, almost as an afterthought, she added, "But I was drunk. I don't know exactly how or what happened."

Tom was all too familiar with that story. He walked around the house to see Jesse covering Norma with soil. "Wait a minute, Jesse. I need to see her body."

"What for? It was a bear. She didn't stand a chance. Did her job, though. She must have protected Becka, or she'd be the one in the ground now." Jesse was leaning on his shovel, looking only at Norma as he spoke.

"I disagree. What I didn't tell you, and maybe I should have, is that I think something other than a vicious bear is roaming around these woods."

"What are you talking about?" Jesse stared Tom straight in the eyes. "Was that a cheap shot at my Uncle?"

Tom shook his head, wondering what Jesse was talking about, but figured it could wait. "Friday night, on my way home from the bar, I ran into a large creature coming from the lumberyard. At first I thought it was a bear, but it was walking on two feet, and it had long hair. It stopped and looked at me and I nearly shit my pants! In a flash, it was gone. Now I had been drinking rum that night, so I guess I thought I was hallucinating. But yesterday morning, when I went to the lumberyard, all the barn animals had been butchered. I found a long piece of hair on my truck, which had to have been from that animal that I may have hit. I called Bob to help me clean up the mess, and we retraced the scene from Friday night, where I saw him crossing the road. We found a patch of lily pads on the ground, and the same smell from the hair was on the lily pads."

"What the hell are you getting at, Tom?"

"I'm not sure exactly. But it sounds a lot like Bigfoot to me." Tom wasn't sure how Jesse would react, but he did catch on to the fact that Justine never told Jesse about his Bigfoot tale. Maybe Justine was all right after all. He didn't have a reason for not liking Justine, she was just different, a city girl. And everybody knew how city girls were. They definitely weren't like girls from upstate.

"And why didn't you tell me this yesterday? I have kids, you know." Jesse was livid, raising his voice to his boss and tossing his shovel into the air.

Tom put his hands out in a friendly gesture, how a stranger should approach a dog. "I didn't know exactly what it was. I'm sorry. Why did you mention your uncle?"

Jesse saw now that Tom meant no harm, and truly believed that Tom did have his own encounter with Bigfoot. "My Uncle Tony saw Bigfoot in this area some sixty years ago. He was young, about Austin's age. He and his friend Ben Schaefer were riding on a double bike, with Tony in the front seat. They rode all the way up the hill on Rock Ave. into where the moffits live, where the road, along with civilization, ends. They couldn't ride the bike uphill, so they walked it a good mile around the bends. When they reached the dirt road, Tony had to take a leak. Ben didn't have to pee, so he waited by the bike. Tony walked about ten feet into the woods and turned around to piss, when he smelled shit. He thought he stepped in it at first, so he lifted up his feet one at a time to check for shit. Both feet were clean, so he looked around the immediate area so he wouldn't step in it. When he looked in Ben's direction, he says he saw Bigfoot. It came right up behind Ben and snatched him off his feet. Ben screamed for help, but Tony's instinct was to hide behind a nearby boulder. This ape-like creature threw Ben over his shoulder and disappeared with him into the woods on the opposite side of the road from Tony. Bigfoot must not have seen my Uncle, or he wouldn't be here today."

"Holy shit! You never told me that! Your Uncle Tony never told me that! What happened to the boy?"

"Nobody knows. Tony waited until they were out of sight, singing a lullaby to himself to drown out the sounds of his friend screaming. He jumped on the bike and coasted all the way down to his house at the bottom of the road. Said he was going faster than a Camaro. He ran inside and told his Dad, but it was too late. An entire search and rescue team went out looking for Ben. The only thing they could find was his right shoe in a tree about twenty yards from where he was last seen."

"I never heard that story. Was it in the papers?"

"It was a little before your time, Tom, but sure. It hit the papers. Everybody said it was a bear. Wasn't too uncommon for a bear to attack a kid in the woods. Still isn't. But to this day, Uncle Tony will tell you up and down that it was Bigfoot. So if you ask me if I'm a believer, I'd have to say 'yes.' And why didn't you call me when the barn animals were killed? Were you just going to wait until work Monday and say, 'Oh yeah, I think Bigfoot ate the animals.' What were you thinking?"

"I was thinking that I was going crazy. I didn't want you guys teasing me for the rest of my life!" Tom was not a selfish man, but this entire episode made him feel selfish. "And your girlfriend is already calling this thing 'my moose'!"

"Well, if I were in your shoes, I'd probably do the same thing. But I don't think I'd run to Bob!" Jesse bent down and unlatched the red collar from Norma's neck and tossed it onto the picnic table. "Don't worry about Justine, she just feels guilty about Norma and is looking for someone else to blame."

"I told Bob because he doesn't work with us, and I was with him at the bar the night it happened. So, did Ben's family just assume it was a bear? Did they believe Tony at all?"

"Shortly after the incident, they moved. Steve's grandfather bought the house for a vacation home. The freaky thing is, the double bike is still in the garage. I don't even remember how old I was when I met Steve. Seems like he was always here -in the summer that is. But what I do remember is Steve bringing me into his garage and showing me this double bike. We could not balance on that thing to save our lives! Steve always insisted in riding in the front seat. It wasn't his fault he couldn't steer. The front rim on that bike was so warped, it's a miracle we made it across the street to Uncle Tony's house alive! You could actually see the tire wobbling underneath the frame. You felt like at any minute, the thing could fly off! The trick to the bike was, the faster you went, the smoother the ride. Anyhow, we made it to Uncle Tony's house and he freaked out upon seeing the bike. He sat us down in these two huge Adirondack chairs and started to tell us about his Bigfoot story. We nearly wet our pants!"

Tom looked down the road and saw the Adirondack chairs on Tony's front lawn, no doubt the same ones Jesse was talking about. He heard footsteps coming up from behind him and turned around to see Steve. "You scared the crap out of me!" Tom's heartbeat sped up a few beats. "How long were you standing there?"

"Long enough to hear about Uncle Tony's Bigfoot tale."

Jesse tried to read Steve's body language, but he could tell that Steve was in cop mode: emotionless and searching for answers. "How's Spike? Is she gonna make it?"

"Yeah, just some cuts and bruises."

"Did the vet say it was the wounds of a bear," asked Tom.

"He said it doesn't look like it."

"What animal did he suggest could inflict such types of wounds," asked Tom who shared a look with Jesse.

Steve looked around and saw Austin on the swing set. "Let's take a walk."

Jesse tossed in the remainder of the dirt and the three of them headed towards the barn. It had only been a few months since Jesse buried Shelby, and he found himself having trouble concealing his pain. "You have to see Uncle Tony's new dog, Rip. Spike will enjoy him, I know Norma did. Steve, do you remember where I used to keep my stash?"

"Sure. Under the wooden planks in the second floor of the barn, under the haystacks."

Jesse laughed. He was happy to see that Steve shared the same memories of their childhood together. "Guess where it is now?"

Tom, feeling left out of the male bonding session, decided to chime in. "Under the wooden planks on the second floor of the barn?"

Jesse looked at Tom and laughed. "How'd you know?"

"How'd I know? You show up at work at the same exact time every day. You go to the bathroom the same exact time every day. You even tune-up your car the same day every year! Nobody's more predictable than you. That's how I know you would never forget to lock my barn door at the lumberyard."

"Did you have a break-in?" Steve seemed concerned.

"Uh, no. Not exactly." Tom repeated the series of events from Friday night. "I'm so sorry, Steve. Looking back at it, I should have called Jesse. I didn't know you and the kids were coming up. I really didn't know."

"What's the protocol around here when there is a large bear sighting? Do you report it to the police? Do you call the local news? How does it work?" Although Steve had been going upstate since he was a kid, he still couldn't understand how different the police were. In some parts of Long Island, if you saw a raccoon in your yard, you could call the police and demand they remove it from your property. When you pay over twenty thousand dollars a year in property taxes, you can tell the local police to take out your trash! If a dog in the city or in Long Island were butchered while in its doghouse, it would make the headlines on the evening news! Up here, people and animals disappear and nobody seems to be bothered by it.

"We don't send out a blimp to alert all the neighbors. It's common sense that up in these areas, you have to expect a bear. It's like swimming in a lake in Florida. You don't always see alligators, but you better believe that there is at least one in every lake."

The three men walked into the barn. Jesse went right for his weed while Tom glanced around the barn, focusing on the stage-like setting featuring a drum set and microphone. Even in his late thirties, Jesse was still the rock star in his own little fantasy. Usually Steve wouldn't mind that Jesse smoked a little marijuana around him, but this time he was annoyed.

Tom made sure the barn doors were closed tightly, then took up a sitting position on a nearby haystack. Jesse and Steve sat on a long wooden bench facing Tom.

Jesse inhaled a large quantity of smoke before passing it to Tom.

Tom took a hit, exhaled, then looked at Steve. "What did the vet say?"

"There are no claw marks, indicating that it couldn't be a bear. Spike's injuries are from her being tossed into trees, and puncture wounds caused by sticks. There were no bite marks on her. The vet pulled sticks out of her body."

"What are you saying?" asked Tom. "I know what I saw. And it was not a fucking bear."

Jesse reached behind the haystacks and retrieved a crushed up coffee can and handed it to Steve.

Steve took the can, observed its twisted form and handed the can to Tom. "There's only one animal out there that can do this to a can, and attack two dogs without clawing at them. A sick, twisted individual that we detectives like to call a sociopath. I'm sure you've heard of them."

Tom took another hit and passed the joint back to Jesse. "You thin a *man* did this?"

"I'm a homicide detective in New York City. We don't have many woods there, but we do have Central Park. Rapists, muggers, all the skels hang out in the dark areas waiting for their next victim. And after they commit their crimes, they run in there to hide. It's not easy with a team of men in Manhattan hunting for a creep in the woods. So out here, a man can easily hide-out till it's clear. Even with a flashlight, the visibility is next to nothing."

Jesse's head was down as he rolled another joint. Jesse's silence could only mean that he was deep in thought. "I thought you believed my Uncle when he told us about Bigfoot."

"Yeah, when I was ten years old. Let's get serious. If it was a bear, which it wasn't, both Spike and Norma would have claw marks in them. The vet confirmed this."

"Tom saw Bigfoot Friday night."

Steve could not believe the insanity coming from Jesse's mouth, and shook his head vehemently.

Jesse always got annoyed at Steve's cop attitude. "Steve, listen up for a moment. Don't say anything, just hear me out."

Steve nodded.

"I'm 5'11". I weigh 210 lbs. I'm in better shape than the guys my daughter brings home. *I* don't have the strength to crush a can like this."

"I'm sorry, I'm not just going to sit here and listen to you two try to convince me that Bigfoot exists. It's one of those upstate urban legends that I don't buy for even a minute. And you wonder why we call you people…" Steve cut himself off when he realized what he was about to say, and the repercussions that were sure to follow.

"You're the only guy I know that smokes weed with his boss!" Steve walked out the barn doors slamming them as he left.

Tom slowly took the joint from Jesse's hand and they both smiled. "Do you think he was going to call us Rednecks or Hicks?" They found themselves in a hysterical laughter, and Tom had to stand up to get back to business.

Tom made sure that Steve was long gone before asking his next question, "Where was Maureen while this was happening?"

Jesse got serious again. "The girls were drinking beers around the fire. Steve and I were playing with the kids in the field. Norma was sitting right by Justine's side around the fire! She never leaves Justine's side!" He took another hit of his drug of choice and handed the joint back to Tom. "She must have gotten excited when Maureen let Spike out of the house, and ran off into the back with Spike."

"You're avoiding the question. I asked, where was Maureen?"

"I just told you- sitting at the fire with Justine."

"Was that awkward?"

"If you have something to say Tom, just spit it out."

"Everything about this tells me to stay the hell out of it, but here it goes. Sherry was at the lumberyard the other day. She said she overheard you talking to someone on the phone. She heard you say, I'm still crazy for you, Maureen."

"She must've heard wrong. I might have been talking to Maureen, we are friends." Jesse was fumbling for the right words. "But I wouldn't say something like that, unless we were joking around and your wife took it out of context."

Tom motioned it off. "Like I said, I'm staying out of it. But I will tell you this: Steve Bettis is a good friend of yours, a true friend. They don't come by often, so don't fuck it up. No broad is worth a real friendship."

Chapter 9

Marc awoke peacefully from his long nap. The drive home from West Virginia had been the longest distance he had ever driven alone. While on his ride home, he couldn't help but think of all the truckers, wondering how they stayed awake for such a long time without drifting off into oncoming traffic. He must have drifted off himself for at least two seconds a few times while on the interstate, having been jolted back into consciousness by the rumble strips along the side of the road. Frequent stops along the highways for purchasing hot cups of coffee allotted him some much- needed energy just to stay awake. He was about five hours from home when he decided that he would never again try to drive home alone. Even the loud, heart-thumping music he blasted through the stereo was hardly enough to keep him alert.

He was happy to be home! And the homemade oatmeal was definitely a bonus compared to the campus chow he'd been eating for the last ten months. Stepping out of Warrensburg and into a new environment was like opening the doors to another dimension. He had made new friends, met new coaches, new girls, and had even picked up a touch of a Virginian accent. While it was a great experience to go away to school, the longer he was there the more he found himself wishing he were back home. He had an untold connection to the town he was always talking about getting away from. There was something about the river, the woods, the camping, hiking, privacy, and, perhaps most of all, his longtime friend Spencer, that made Marc homesick. The fact that Spencer had had a girlfriend this time last year made it a little easier for Marc to leave home. Spencer's demeanor had evolved while he had a girlfriend. He pretended he enjoyed doing girly things and all the shenanigans that go along with becoming a couple, but most of all, he wasn't always available for Marc anymore. He was always with Debbie. Marc never had a steady girlfriend, although he could have had his pick of the litter. He was too involved with football. Always thinking of the future. If he hung-out with a girl for more than a few weeks, his football coach would get on his case about it and hold more practices. He got the hint. Football now. Girls later. That didn't bother him. What irked him was that Spencer had a girlfriend. But girlfriend or not, Marc was going to enjoy his summer with Spencer, so he headed over to his place.

He was about to write a note on the message board hanging on the side of the refrigerator for his parents when he noticed one for him: MARC, WENT TO JESSE'S HOUSE. DON'T GO ANYWHERE. WE NEED TO TALK TO YOU BEFORE YOU LEAVE. LOVE, MOM AND DAD. And here it starts, he thought. What are they going to do, remind me to brush my teeth? Marc could just hear his mother saying, "Marc, before you leave this house you must brush your teeth!" With that thought, Marc went into the bathroom to brush his teeth.

He pulled up to Jesse's house and saw a brand new fire engine red Jeep Cherokee in the driveway. He laughed to himself thinking that Jesse must have got caught cheating again and had to win Justine over big time! He walked up the steps to Jesse's front door half expecting Justine to answer wearing diamond earrings and a new wardrobe. He was shocked to see a captivating smile with a body to back it.

"Hi Marc!" Danielle took two steps forward and pressed her breasts firmly against Marc's chest. "I haven't seen you in so long! Come inside!" She disengaged from the provocative hug and motioned for him to follow.

Marc was taken back. Although Warrensburg was a considerably small town, he couldn't remember when he had last seen Danielle. "Danielle, right?"

"Don't you play those games with me," she scolded in a sultry voice. "I know you remember who I am. You think that because you're in college now that you're too cool to socialize with a measly little high schooler?"

"If you were in college, you would know that 'high schooler' is not even a word," grinned a cocky Marc.

"Well, I see you're still a prick."

"I'll give you a dollar if you can give me the definition of a prick." Marc smiled, folded his arms, and cocked his head to the side. "I'm waiting."

Danielle squinted her eyes and let out a small smile. "Touché".

Justine and Sherry stepped into the living room. "Marc, I thought I heard your voice. I'm glad the both of you are here. We need to talk to you two."

"Mom, what's the matter? You look nervous. Is everything alright?" asked her concerned son. Sherry's usually calm demeanor had become visibly disturbed by something. Marc immediately sensed his mother's anxiety.

They all walked toward the dining room table and took seats. Justine and Sherry sat next to each other and Marc and Danielle sat across from them. "There has been something going on around here that has shaken up the town quite a bit. Well, only in the wooded areas, and only at night. We may have an angry bear on our hands. And he is blood thirsty," Sherry explained with a careful choice of words.

"So? What's the big deal? The weather is heating up and the bears are coming out of hibernation. This happens every year. If you don't bother them, they don't bother you. Mom, it's elementary." Marc stopped short of accusing her of being a "worry-wort," she had always hated that term. But it seemed obvious to him that she wasn't handling the anxiety of letting her son go very well. Danielle chimed in, agreeing with Marc. She was leaving for Syracuse in two months, and hadn't really thought how it might affect Justine and Jesse.

"Maybe not a bear. We may be talking about a moose. We're not sure. But over the last few nights, there had been a few incidents. First, our barn animals at the lumber yard are all dead. They were brutally attacked and killed by a large animal. Secondly, last night," Sherry grabbed Justine's hands as she mentioned this last part, "Becka Bettis was chased in the woods behind her house. Spike was injured and Norma was killed."

Danielle looked at Justine and immediately her eyes swelled up with tears. "No. Please no. Please tell me it's not true!" Danielle jumped up from the table and ran into her stepmother's arms, knocking over one of the dining room chairs. Marc stood to pick it up.

"Yes, baby. It's true. Your father buried her this morning. I'm so sorry Danielle." Until this moment, Justine hadn't even thought about how Norma's death might affect Danielle. Those two practically grew up together. Justine remembered a few years back, thinking how cute it was that when Danielle went back to her mother's house, she'd bring Norma with her. Jesse would bring Norma back home when Danielle was in school, and return her to Claudia's before Danielle got home. Claudia lived in "town." It wasn't much different than Queens. The streets had numbers instead of names, and there was little privacy between houses. Claudia preferred this type of lifestyle to living in the rural part of town. She had always been more social than Jesse.

"How is Becka?" asked Marc. "How old is she now? I think the last time I saw her she was in diapers."

"She's thirteen, and she's alright. Jesse and Steve got to her before the beast," replied Justine, trying to hold it together for Danielle as she stroked her step-daughter's long hazel-brown hair.

"So what was it? A moose or a bear? If Becka was in the woods, she had to have seen it."

"It was dark. She didn't see anything, only heard it. The poor girl. I just feel awful," answered Sherry.

"Where is she now?"

"She is at the Farm, with her mother and brother. The poor girl must be traumatized!" Sherry had raised her voice a few notches, before her eyes filled with tears again.

"I have to see Norma." Danielle let go of Justine and ran out the back door. One look at his mother and Justine and Marc could tell there was more to the story than what was being told.

"Mom, what really happened?" demanded Marc.

"What are you talking about? We just told you."

"No offense Mom, but it's just not adding up. I have never seen a moose in Warrensburg."

"I have. A few actually. Seen them coming down from the mountain." Justine pointed to the mountain behind the Bettis' farm. "Only recently though. This is the first I've seen of them. When I told Jesse, he didn't believe me at first either. Not until I brought him to where I seen it and showed him the footprints- or hoof prints I should say."

Marc looked at Justine, then suspiciously eyed his mother. "So you asked me to come down here to tell me there is a killer moose on the loose?"

"Something like that. Marc, your father has been drinking again since you left for college. And not just at functions and parties, but a lot. Practically every night. I didn't want to distract you with this stuff while you were at school. That's why I didn't tell you."

"Mom, I hate to tell you this, but Dad has been drinking since before I left for college. He stores his liquor in the garage. I thought you knew. I figured he was hiding his liquor from me. Ironic, huh?" Marc let out a small chuckle. If this is what married life is like, remind me never to get hitched, he thought to himself. I don't care how hot she is. Then his mind shifted to Danielle.

"Marc! This is not funny. Your father may be having alcohol- induced hallucinations. Although we have no concrete evidence that a moose has been killing animals in the area, your father is convinced that he saw Bigfoot!" Sherry was starting to raise her voice again, a rare occurrence for her.

"Take it easy! So Dad got drunk and claims he saw Bigfoot. What's the big deal? Just last week, my friend Corey at school got drunk and swore he saw an elephant on his roommate's bed. We all laughed and teased him about it the next day. I think you forgot how to have fun, Mom. You too, Justine."

"Did you think it was funny that your mom's barn animals got killed too? You arrogant, insensitive bastard!" Justine left the room and stormed out the back door, slamming it as she went.

"I hope you're happy," yelled Sherry.

"Mom, I'm sorry. That's not what I meant. What happened to your animals?"

"We're not sure exactly, but we do know that they're dead."

"I'm sorry to hear that. I'll be careful. I'm going to Spencer's." Marc was about to leave, when a distant thought caught his attention. "Mom, do you remember last summer, when Spencer and I were camping along Schroon River, and I told you that Spencer went outside the tent to take a piss, and he found himself staring a large mountain lion in the face?"

Sherry vaguely recalled the story. "Yeah, now I remember. I'll mention it to your father. Marc, we really don't know what's out there. If it is a moose, I heard they are very aggressive, especially during mating season. Please, just stay out of the woods."

"And mating season it is," Marc leaned in towards his mother and kissed her on the cheek. "I'll check in with you later."

Marc's sarcasm had always made Sherry smile. "Just get out of here, you pig."

Marc was walking towards his car when he saw Danielle getting into the red Cherokee. "That's your ride?" he asked shaking his head in a disapproving manner.

"Graduation present. You like it?" she asked as she smiled proudly towards him.

"Yeah, it's nice. Do you know how to drive it?"

Danielle flung her hair back and lightly bit her lower lip. "It's not stick, although I've been told I handle them real well."

Marc was not expecting that answer. He gazed back at her, not knowing if she meant what she had just said, but he suddenly got a mental image of her sucking his dick in that new graduation present. He decided it would be best not to respond and acted like he wasn't fazed by teases like her. "I'm sorry about your dog."

His response took her by surprise. Maybe college girls talk like that every day. He's so hot, maybe he's accustomed to girls giving it up to him on a daily basis. If that's the case, maybe playing hard to get would interest him. "Thanks. See ya around."

"Whatever." Marc smiled at her at got into his Firebird and headed towards Spencer's.

"Danielle, wait up!" Sherry came out the front door and ran towards Danielle.

"Marc just left."

"That's O.K. I wanted to talk to you, not him. Listen, I know you're upset about your dog, and you have every right to be. I know exactly what you're going through right now. Sort of, I mean, barn animals can't possibly compare to a family dog you've had for years, but....I'm rambling. Sorry, I do that when I'm nervous."

Danielle looked at Sherry. "I loved Norma, but she saved Becka." Danielle was unaware that Sherry had given up on God a long time ago when she said, "God works in mysterious ways." Sherry looked at the floor as Danielle continued, "I was just going to meet up with Marie, but I think I'll say hello to Becka first, see how she's doing. I didn't even know they were here."

Sherry looked up and observed Danielle's movements, envisioning what Allison would have looked like if she were still alive. "I think that's a good idea, but I have something for you at my house. A piglet of mine survived the attacks of this weekend, and I think you could use a companion right now."

"That's really sweet of you, but don't you want it?"

"It's not a good time for me. I'm going through my own issues and with my husband's drinking... I'm just not in the right frame of mind."

"I don't think I can Sherry, I'm starting college in the fall. But I'll ask Becka if she wants it, she loves animals. Maybe I'll bring her by your house this afternoon so she can meet him."

"That would be great!"

*   *   *

Maureen, Becka and Devin sat around the table in the dining room in the back part of the house while sipping tea and playing Yahtzee. Becka sat furthest away from the back door, near the door that separated the kitchen from the dining room. Maureen and Devin both noticed her glancing out the back window across the long field and into the dark and distant woods. Becka was not always one who displayed her emotions. She appeared calm on the surface, but was internally plagued by a hyper-vigilance over what had occurred the previous night. Like Sherry, she was an atheist, but unlike her, Becka's non-belief was the result of her education and reliance on scientific reasoning. She wasn't jaded; she simply saw God as man's creation, not the other way around. But she did feel that luck was definitely on her side in the woods last night. Or maybe it was karma. Like many teenagers, her beliefs were a hodgepodge of many ideas, not all of which were in synch. She believed strongly that 'what goes around comes around,' so she spent some of her spare time dishing out food to the homeless at the town shelter, or stood outside of Pathmark every Friday night in December dressed as an elf, collecting money for Toys for Tots. She was a good person, and she believed her good deeds had contributed to her escape from what could have been a horrific ending to a girl with so much life left before her.

Devin rolled the dice while Becka once again stared through the window. This time, she did not look away. "Mom, did the vet tell Dad what made the marks on Spike?"

"No. Beck. I don't know. Don't you worry about Spike. She's fine."

"Did he say it was a bear?"

"I don't know."

"I want to know. Where is Dad?"

"He's at Jesse's. You can ask him when he comes back. But I really don't think you should worry yourself about it. Everyone is fine."

"Everyone but Norma," said Devin. Maureen tightened her lips, straightened her back and narrowed her eyes towards her outspoken son. He knew he should shut-up. But that wasn't his style, and she knew that.

"Devin, not another word. I mean it." His mother was serious, but so was Devin.

"Why not? Becka's the one that brought it up. I think she wants to talk about it. It's not good to keep emotions bottled up. Isn't that what you always tell us?"

"There are times for everything. And right now is not the time for it!"

"It's O.K., Mom. I want to talk about it," said Becka as she looked at her mom and brother. "I want to know what wanted to eat me. I want to know what I did to attract the animal. If it was a bear, maybe she was looking for her wounded cub. Maybe I was too close to the cub."

"Becka, you did nothing wrong. You just happened to be at the wrong place at the wrong time. Justine said it was most likely a moose. She has been seeing them around here lately."

Devin scrunched his eyebrows together. "Yeah, sure Mom. A moose. A moose has antlers that are five feet in width. The trees in that part of the woods are all no more than three feet apart. Don't you think Becka would hear the antlers clanging on the trees? Better yet, don't you think a moose would get stuck between the trees? And last time I checked, moose weren't exactly carnivores."

Devin was too damn smart. He was the self-proclaimed animal expert in the family, always glued to the Discovery channel, Animal planet, and any other station that showed animals all day long. There wasn't one animal out there that Devin didn't have all the facts on. Marine animals, land animals, reptiles, insects: if you named it, he knew of it. "So then it was a bear, Devin. What difference does it make?" Maureen couldn't have been more annoyed.

Becka brought her mug of tea up to her lips. "Whatever it was, it smelt like shit." She looked at Devin and the two of them burst out laughing. Maureen let this curse word slide. Anything to change the subject, she thought. She looked at the twins and smiled. They were so lucky to have each other. A sudden knock on the back door startled Maureen, and she turned to see it was Danielle.

Chapter 10

Sitting at the Brew N' Stew bar in Bumfuck, New York was the last place Jack Whittaker expected to be since announcing his retirement two weeks ago. He had recently purchased a quaint, three -bedroom condo situated on a small man-made lake in Sunrise, Florida. With his two kids now all grown up, and his divorce finalized, he could finally start another life in another state. No nagging, cheating, slutty ex-wife calling twice a week for money to keep her pathetic dog grooming business afloat. Why should he *still* owe her money? The kids could fend for themselves. She didn't need child support anymore! She had already taken half his pension! He had worked for twenty years as a customs agent in JFK airport. What a waste of a life, he thought gloomily. There he stood, day after day, inspecting the grimy luggage of suspicious persons trying to enter and exit the airport, stripping them naked and watching them shit out bags of cocaine. And for what? To put his kids through college? His daughter dropped out of her sophomore year at Stony Brook to marry her English Professor, and his son failed all but one course in his first year at SUNY Farmingdale before deciding to quit school and become an unpaid "professional" skateboarder! And at the same time his wife was "fucking some nigger" who sold electronics two doors down from where Jack rented a shop for her to trim the balls of indecorous little poodles! And now he owed her money to maintain the lifestyle she had become accustomed to? When the Suffolk County judge ruled that he had to relinquish forty percent of his earnings to his wife, Jack decided to sell his pathetic, one-man investigation firm that he had started in the wake of his retirement from customs.

He was getting burnt out from the private sector anyhow. At fifty-two years old, you can only sit in the car for so many hours before your back starts to ache. At least that was the case for Jack. He didn't enjoy exercise, and he loved fried food. He was built of a tall stature, but it still couldn't hold his weight. The last time Jack stepped on a scale it wavered over the three hundred mark. He didn't think that was possible, but nonetheless did nothing to change his habits. Jack Whittaker was many things, but health conscious was not one of them. So there he sat, in the dumpy little bar, sucking on the bone of a spicy buffalo wing for whatever meat he may he have missed on his first bite, while slurping on a cold Bud and trying to act nonchalant — as if he were a steady patron.

When Jim Healy hired him to investigate a few cops who didn't play by the rules and Healy agreed to pay in cash, Jack was intrigued and decided to take on the job. After all, he was a fellow officer and had seen his share of tainted government officials. He knew their profile all too well. Back in customs, Agent Molloy, who Whittaker frequently worked with, was indicted on charges of sexual assault for his eager and rigorous pat downs of female passengers whom he profiled trying to board the planes, mainly the big-busted ones wearing the under wire bras that would occasionally set off the sensors on the metal detectors. He would take them aside and unabashedly graze his thumb over their nipples during a routine check for concealed weapons. Most victims were too embarrassed to report the incident, or naively thought it an accident, but Molloy got carried away like a pedophile behind the wheel of an ice cream truck and finally felt up the wrong person. This large bosomed chick attempting to board a flight back to San Francisco had no doubt that Molloy's patting was intentional and made a scene at the airport. Her clever attorney informed the media and, as intended, other victims and even a few non-victim opportunists came forward with all sorts of accusations on a number of security and customs agents. Jack was called in to testify about his co-worker. He had secretly caught Molloy doing this over a dozen times, but had always kept to himself about it. Before the trial Whittaker was called into his boss' office and reminded that he didn't see anything of that sort. He was also "reminded" that major personnel changes were already in the works and that the company would hate to see the expenditures of a costly lawsuit affect the employees' generous pension benefits. That was when Jack mentally gave up on the job. It wasn't long before he retired early and sought out his own business venture. This Healy case gave him an opportunity to vicariously get back at Molloy and his supervisors.

Mike's bar typically did not do well on a Sunday night in the summertime. Occasionally a few tourists who couldn't afford to party in Lake George came in, but his regulars usually bought cases of beer from the supermarket and stayed at home with family and friends. Maybe late in the night they'd stop by, but Mike expected business for him to be slow. He took Tom's advice and hung a sign on the window that read, "10 cent wings." Tom told him it may catch the eyes of customers on their way to the diner across the street. Mike looked at Jack Whittaker gorging himself on bar food and smiled to himself.

"Hey, big guy. Can I get you another beer?" Mike picked up Jack's empty glass and gently rotated it in front of him in a way that made the beer foam at the bottom of the glass rock back and forth like the ocean's waves creeping up on the shore and slowly fading back. Mike learned this technique from his father. His dad used to tell him that a working man could never ignore the subconscious visual this move implanted in his mind.

"Yeah, sure. Why not?"

Mike opened a fresh bottle and poured another one for Jack. "I'm Mike." He reached over and shook hands with his new patron. "Are you visiting the lake?"

"Yeah. Retired. I'm looking into buying property in Warrensburg. Any areas you can recommend?" Jack loved role-playing. Something he and his ex used to do while they were dating. He would pretend that he was the big bad wolf and she was little red riding hood. He'd chase her through her parents' house when they weren't home and sexually attack her on the staircase. This game always exited him until one day she wanted to be the wolf. Jack never felt comfortable as the submissive one, and this feeling of vulnerability eventually brought their role-playing adventures to an end.

"Sure. What are you looking for? Waterfront, farmland, secret hideaway type?"

"That's a good question. My wife would like something dark." The unconsciously spoken double entendre wasn't lost on Mike and a small smile escaped his lips. "I mean, hidden. Privacy, mainly. We're from the city and would just like to be left alone. No nosy neighbors, no noise, no sirens."

"So you're city folk? We got a lot of them retiring to these areas lately. I hear the taxes and expenses are a killer! What did you used to do, if you don't mind me asking?" Another trick from Mike's father is to pretend you're interested in the customer. Act like you give a shit even if you hope to never see him again.

"I used to sell watches. I had a store in a mall."

"Wow. You must have done real well for yourself." Watches? Mike noticed this guy wasn't even wearing a watch.

"Yeah, I did O.K. So, uh, I'm staying up a few miles from here. How are the cops around here? Are they going to hassle me 'cause I'm not from around here? How strict are they with drunk drivers?" Since there was

96

nobody else in the bar, Jack thought he'd start with the bartender.

"I see. You're one of those paranoid city folks. Trust me. You'll be fine. The cops don't bother with the tourists. They got enough problems with the teenagers' cow tipping."

"Are there a lot of cops in this area?"

He didn't bite at the cow-tipping comment. This guy is looking for something, thought Mike. "Why are you so concerned with the cops? Are you hiding a body in the trunk or something?" Mike was trying to be nice, but this guy was just plain annoying. If there was anything that annoyed Mike it was someone beating around the bush. He was accustomed to drunken guys being blunt about just about anything, right down to their bowel movements.

Jack was obnoxious and impatient. He never left a place without getting all the useless information he could possibly think of. The truth was that he had never been a good private investigator. He had the contacts, and could sell a rotten tooth to a dentist, but undercover was just not his specialty. His friend and only employee, Eddie, used to make jokes that Jack got made every time he opened his mouth. Eddie was the surveillance expert. He was an undercover narcotics officer for years before he began working for Jack. Even when Jack was made, Jack would argue that he wasn't. This used to piss off Eddie to no end. Jack was also cheap. He paid Eddie by the hour instead of a salary. If they worked in the field together and they got made, Eddie couldn't get a full week of pay while Jack was still profiting from the thousand- dollar retainer from the client. They argued relentlessly about this until Eddie quit. After three months and going through a half- dozen employees, he gave in to the salary idea and Eddie came back to work. After that, Eddie found the humor in how fast Jack got made.

Once again, Jack stood out like a sore thumb, although he didn't think so. "No. I don't really care about the cops. But I," Jack looked around the room and up towards the window, "was at the diner earlier and heard a few people talking about how corrupt the police were, said something like they were fed up with being bothered by them. If I'm going to move up here, this concerns me. My wife is a knock-out, and I don't need some perverted police messing with her."

Mike took one look at this guy and figured there was one truth to this story. He probably did eat at the diner earlier. But there was no way this guy had a wife who was a looker. He hardly looked rich. The green Saturn in the parking lot undoubtedly belonged to him. "Listen man, around here, people don't go snooping around on the cops. I don't know what you're up to, but you'd be best to take my advice and quit while you're ahead." Mike stood firmly behind the bar with his arms folded and made it known that he was not fucking around.

"Hey, hey, hey. Slow down there, buddy. I'm not snooping on anyone. I don't really care what people do. I guess I heard wrong at the diner. I'm sorry. Are you related to any of the cops? I mean, why else would you get so offended?"

"I think it's time for you to pay your bill, and be on your way." Mike was smart enough to know that if Demitres and Kankro suspected he was talking to a snoop, his business would be doomed. A young couple entered the bar just in time to divert his attention and sat at a small table across the room. "Hey guys, what'll it be tonight?" Mike walked out from the bar area and over towards the nice-looking couple.

Jack wasn't sure what had just happened, but he was not about to stop here. He left a twenty- dollar bill on the bar to cover his nineteen dollar tab, and walked past

Mike, making sure to check out the woman occupying the small table. "Have a good day, pal."

"Yeah, you too. And good luck with the house hunting," Mike smiled to Whittaker as he pulled a notepad from his apron. Jack exited the bar as Mike peered through the dark windows and jotted down the tags on his car.

Chapter 11

Marc was thrilled to see Spencer, and the sentiment was shared by Spence, who had been eagerly awaiting Marc's return home from college. When he walked into Spencer's room that afternoon to awaken him from his previous night's beer fest, Spencer kept his head under his pillow and said, "Hello, Marc. You still have the same walk." Then he lifted his blanket, cocked the pillow slightly to the side and said, "Come over here and spoon me."

Marc took off one of his sneakers and threw it at his head. "You gay son of a bitch!" he shouted and then ran over to the bed and jumped on Spencer, pinning him with a full nelson.

"Uncle! Uncle!" screamed Spencer. Marc released his friend and took a seat at Spencer's desk. He still couldn't figure out why Spencer even *had* a desk. They exchanged drinking stories for a few minutes while Spencer's mom cooked them up some burgers. Marc was like a second son to Ms. Gargan, so she enjoyed catering to his every need when he was around. The conversation turned from drinking and girls to a comparison of home life to that beyond Warrensburg.

"West Virginia is O.K.," Marc explained, "but the woods around there are so creepy. Missing people, men and women, are reported every day. Eventually their bodies show up with missing pieces and shit. Usually found in the woods by hunters with dogs or whatever. Some crazy people down there. It's not like here. So, what do you say? You want to leave tomorrow, go for a few nights camping? We'll get some beers, a few bottles of Captain Morgan, a little ganja. Who's around these days? We should rally up the crew." Marc's face was wildly animated and his speech was racing, as if speaking quickly would help him catch up with everything he'd missed

100

while at school. He hadn't felt this out of the loop until he saw his friend again.

"I don't know who's around anymore, Marc. I mean, Chuckie works with his father full-time now. Matt made some new friends in Glens Falls since he started community college. He's never around. I don't even think he lives here anymore. I heard he moved in with those guys from the Falls. Eric went to trucking school or some bullshit like that and he's on the road all the time now. And me, well Debbie called it quits last week. But I got another one in the works.

"Who? Anyone I know?" Marc did not like where this conversation was heading. He didn't mention a girl earlier today. He felt like he was in an episode of the Twilight Zone, watching his friend slowly slip away from him.

"You know her. Marie. Marie Healy."

"No way! She's got an ass like an onion! You think you have a shot?"

"I think so. I saw her father at the supermarket. He's got one of those remote control wheel chairs now. It's kinda cool. Anyway, he was waiting for Marie to pick him up, so I waited outside with him and helped him with his groceries. She pulled up and thought it was cool to see me helping her father. She asked what I was doing later on so I gave her my number. I took her to the movies and she was all over me."

"How are the Healy's doing? Aren't there like five kids or something?"

"It's Marie and three little kids, boys I think. Since she graduated, Marie stays home and takes care of all of them while her mother works during the day. It's sad and all, but I think it's cool the way they all stand by each other in these bad times. Not like my dad. When things got rough, he got out."

A grin appeared across Marc's face. "So you're taking advantage of her 'cause she's vulnerable?"

"No. I ain't taking advantage of anybody. She's cool, man. Actually, she's gonna be here soon. I told her I'd take her to the arcade tonight. Maybe grab a slice of pizza or something. You should come."

"I don't know. I don't want to be a third wheel. Maybe I'll pass."

"Don't be a chump. Come on. You can always hook up with a tourist."

Marc made Spencer pull his arm to see if he really wanted him to tag along. "Alright. Fine. I'll go." Marc heard footsteps coming from down the hall and the sound of a female giggling. "I think your prized package is here."

Marie opened the door to Spencer's bedroom and held it open behind her for her unexpected friend. "Hi Spencer." She walked over and gave him a kiss on the cheek. "This is my friend Danielle. I hope you don't mind if she comes out with us tonight. I forgot we made plans." Danielle waved in a friendly motion towards Spencer and turned to smirk at Marc.

"The more the merrier. That's what my pal Marc was just saying, weren't you?" Spencer looked towards Marc for a pleased reaction.

Marc got up from the computer chair and offered his seat to Danielle. "Here, have a seat. I know how uncomfortable you must be after driving around in that brand new Jeep and all." Marie walked over to the bed and sat down next to Spencer.

"Thanks Marc. Come to think of it, my ass does kind of hurt. Want to rub it for me?"

"You wish." Marc went into the dining room to grab another chair, returning with a bottle of Pepsi and four plastic cups.

When Marc entered the room Spencer got up from the bed, walked over to his stereo and retrieved a bottle of Captain Morgan from behind his speaker. "Ahy Ahy, Captain! For this occasion, I am going to lavish ye with some fine pirate booty."

*   *   *

Bob had just gotten off the phone with Tom when he noted the clock on the VCR showed 9:13 P.M. He agreed to meet Tom and Jesse at The Brew N' Stew at ten o'clock. Bob lifted his right butt cheek from the couch and pulled out his wallet. To no surprise, only a ten dollar bill and a few singles were left. Tom will pay, he thought to himself as he changed the channel. *Goodfellas* was on HBO. It had just started, too. He briefly thought about calling Tom to tell him he'd catch up with him another time, but soon got too wrapped up in the film to make the call. Just when Henry Hill was eating a late dinner with Jimmy Conway at Tommy's mother's house on the big screen, Bob heard what sounded like a car door slam. He got up and looked out the window towards his truck, but didn't see anything. He looked out the kitchen window facing his Pinto, but didn't see anything there either. Checking the VCR display, Bob realized he was late, and figured Tom and Jesse didn't feel like waiting all night, so they came by the trailer to pick him up.

Bob lived alone, and he definitely preferred it that way. He wasn't exactly a lady's man, but at six foot two and with a muscular build from lifting cases of Pepsi all day long, he could catch a date with a woman when he wanted to. Occasionally he would have the guys over to watch a football game and he'd put out some chips, but his trailer wasn't exactly accommodating for guests. With a ten by fourteen living room, an eight by ten kitchen and a tiny bathroom, friends weren't exactly breaking down his door to relax in his lapse of luxury. Besides, most of his acquaintances had their own houses, and wives who would cater the occasion with sandwiches, wings and dips. Bob thought about this for a moment and took a good look at his trailer. Maybe Tom was right. A slightly bigger place wouldn't be so bad after all.

His thoughts drifted to Jeanie, a woman he was serious with until a year ago. They had a lot of fun together, but his lack of ambition eventually drove her away. Her career as a wildlife conservationist took priority over partying with Bob, and when an opportunity came to study Polar Bears up close and personal, she packed up and headed to the Arctic without even a phone call to him. He received the break-up letter a few days later, and thought she was just playing head games with him. It took him a week to get off his ass and go over to her cabin. He was amazed to see it was completely empty, decorated only by a large "FOR RENT" sign in the window. Jeanie McLaughlin would forever be "the one that got away."

Getting up to look for Blumenfeld's business card, Bob heard the thud again. This time he was positive it was coming from his truck. With dignified anger, he headed out his front door and down the steps, taking long strides towards the direction of the sounds. "You kids better get outta here! I'll break your scrawny little necks if you try to steal my sodas!" Bob walked around to the driver's side of the truck but didn't see anybody. He then bent down and looked underneath the carriage: nothing. "You rotten kids!" Noticing the driver's side door of his delivery truck was open, he reached up in an effort to slam it shut. Suddenly the door hinges seemed to burst loose and the heavy panel came crashing down on him. "What the hell!" Bob fell backwards on his right shoulder as the door landed on his upper torso and the window knocked him in the forehead. He quickly tried to lift the door off of him, and had it about halfway up when his right arm went lame, causing the door to fall on him again, this time partially crashing down on his legs. "Son of a bitch!" He grabbed the door with his left hand, and by using his hips and thighs to thrust the door up, he managed to roll out from underneath. Struggling to his knees, Bob hoisted himself up to his feet, favoring his left leg.

He looked around, but all was darkness. Sensing he was not alone, he thought about his adventure through the woods with Tom the previous afternoon and his heart began to beat faster with each passing second. Quickly, he started making his way towards his trailer when he heard footsteps coming towards him. A gust of wind blew past his face and there it was: *that smell*. That god- awful smell of the hair Tom had been holding. Bob prayed this was one of Tom's sick pranks, but knew it wasn't his style. As the pain surged throughout his body, he forced himself to turn in the opposite direction of the scent and run as fast as he could towards the street. His shoulder ached and a searing pain radiated throughout his body with each pounding step of his feet on the pavement. It was dark, but soon he felt the blacktop under his feet. He ran in the direction of his closest neighbors: the Henkels. Their motion light turned on and he ran up the steps, screaming for help. Once he reached the door, he saw a note tacked onto it for the mailman, letting him know they were on vacation. Wasting no time, Bob turned and headed for the bridge leading to the rest of town. His breath flowed in and out in a deep series of wheezes, his weak cardiovascular system pushed to its limits. His bruises and broken bones couldn't handle the pressure much longer, and he was about to collapse when he heard breathing coming from behind him. Faster, he thought. *Come on Bob! Faster! Faster!* He pumped his legs as fast and hard as he could down the dark, deserted road. Visions of him and Jeanie danced through his memory in an attempt to ignore the pain he felt as a raging fire seared though his right shoulder. He was about to look back and gauge how much of a lead he had on his assailant when he saw headlights coming towards him from across the bridge. *Please God. Help me now. Please save me*! He ran awkwardly towards the approaching vehicle, an endless fifty yards away. He waved his left shoulder in the air, as quietly as possible, not knowing how much distance lay between him and his attacker.

Marie clenched onto Spencer while he rode his quad down the road in an attempt to beat Danielle and Marc to the bridge. "Faster Spence, faster!" she screamed, as she looked to her left and saw Marc's quad sneaking into view.

Danielle poised herself upright and licked Marc's neck while she squeezed his hips and gently tugged on his belt loop. Marc would have been into it if he hadn't been trying to get Spencer's attention.

"Spencer! Slow down! Someone's on the bridge!"

Danielle leaned to her right, looked over Marc's shoulder and saw what appeared to be two people running over the bridge. "Two people! There's two people on the bridge!"

Marc looked up and saw the second figure. "Spencer!" Within a minute, Spencer and Marie would surely hit and most likely kill the people on the bridge. He released his right hand from the handlebars and removed his helmet. Chucking it directly in front of Spencer's quad, he slammed on the brakes, spraying mounds of dirt beneath him.

Bob reached the foot of the bridge when he heard a girl scream, followed by a powerful crashing sound. He stopped running and instinctively crouched down and held his arms over his head to escape the flying debris, momentarily forgetting why he was running in the first place. One of the headlights he had seen had just gone over the side of the bridge. His attacker, which sounded as if he were no more than twenty feet behind him, let out an ear-splitting roar that resembled a combination between a bear's growl and a wolf's howl.

Spencer's front left tire hit Marc's helmet and his quad flipped instantaneously, flinging both him and Marie into the air. Marie screamed as she tumbled off the edge of the bridge and down the cliff leading to the river. Spencer sailed ten feet into the air before crashing down onto the metal hull of the bridge with a thud that was still audible over Marie's screams. The quad flipped three times before plunging into the cold river.

Danielle screamed, "Marie! Marie!" She jumped off the quad and ran towards the cliff. Marc turned his quad so the headlights were facing Danielle and ran after her. "Danielle. Get back here!" He caught up to her and grabbed her by the waist as she thrust herself back and forth. "Marie!" She cried as she clenched her hair in her fists and pulled as hard as she could. "Oh my god! Somebody help her!" Marc spun her around and she dug her face into his chest. "She's dead, Marc. She's fucking deeeeaddddd!"

"Shhh! Be quiet, Danielle. Don't panic. I need you to stand right here. I'm going to bring the quad around so we have some light. Stay right here so I don't go over the edge. Can you do that for me?"

Danielle's body was trembling uncontrollably. "OooooKKKAAYYY. OOKKAAAAYYY." Marc ran to his quad and was turning it towards Danielle when he saw Spencer lying on the bridge. He ran over to his friend. "Spence. Buddy. Please answer me! Spence!" Spencer was lying on his back and blinked his eyes. He was winded and in bad condition.

"I, I, I, I, I."

"Spence. If you're alive, please say something."

Spence tried with all his breath to make any sound he could. "EEEEAAAYYYY."

"Spence! Did you say something?" Marc put his head on Spencer's chest and tried to feel his heartbeat. On the opposite side of the bridge, he saw a man crouched down covering his head. With only the dim light from the quad, Marc couldn't make out who it was. Based on their location, he figured it could be Bob. "Hey! You! Don't just stand there. Fucking help us!"

Bob stood up to see the two young men as silhouettes in the headlights, one lying on the bridge, the other on his knees next to him. He took a step towards them when he was grabbed by the neck and thrown down on the ground with a force that knocked him unconscious.

Marc froze in disbelief. In slow motion, he saw his mother talking about how his father saw Bigfoot. Her speech was slurred, like playing a KISS record in slow motion. B-I-G-F-O-O-T! That's not how she really said it, but it's how she said it now. He jumped to his feet and ran to the quad, hopping onto it in record timing. "Danielle!" He steered the quad back towards town, kicking up dirt as the tires spun wildly on the unpaved road. "Get on the fucking quad! Quick Danielle!" He revved the engine and reached his hand out towards her.

"No! I'm not leaving her here!"

"Get on the fucking quad or you die, bitch!" He yanked her by the elbow, threw her onto his lap, and drove off. "Stay still. I think I just saw your stepmother's moose!"

Chapter 12

Jack Whittaker sat in his parked car at the diner across the street from the Brew N' Stew bar. With the bartender getting so defensive about the cops, Jack felt he was a man to be watched. He picked up his cell phone and dialed Jim Healy, alerting him of Mike. Jim told him to bark up another tree, that Mike was only protecting the officers to save his own ass. Kankro and Demitres could easily wait outside the bar and follow home all Mike's patrons, causing him to lose his business. Jim said he wouldn't be surprised if the cops were also on Mike's payroll. Jack insisted he get Mike to talk, that it would be stellar for the case, to which Jim replied, "No. No locals involved. That's why I hired you, and if you can't follow my orders, you're fired!" Jack agreed, but thought he was on to something and stayed put. "One more thing," Jim added, "you're off the clock for the evening. Start billing me again in the morning." Just like that, he hung up. Jack was too curious to call it a night, and, not for the first time in his private practice, he worked above and beyond without pay. If he had a social life, he reminded himself, he'd be doing something more interesting with his time.

He turned on his audio recording of *Great American Short Stories* and pulled out his stubby little car pillow and fell asleep for a few hours. Eventually, a commotion outside the bar woke him up, and he lifted his head to see two men run out of the bar and jump into a Ford flatbed pick-up truck, heading north up Horicon Ave. Jack sped out after them up the windy road. There were no streetlights, and the fog was getting thicker. Since they were the only cars on the road, it wasn't hard to keep up. About four miles into the chase, the pick-up made a right hand turn onto a dirt road then stopped the engine, leaving the lights on. The two men got out of the truck with shotguns and one of them walked up to Jack's car,

109

which was no more than twenty feet behind them. Jack was sure these two hicks were going to kill him, and instinctively pulled out his gun and laid it on his lap.

Tom walked up to Whittaker's driver's side window. "Listen man, there's been an accident, and I think it's best if you turn around and find another route."

"What type of an accident? I'm a retired officer, do you need some assistance?" Jack pulled out his badge and extended his hand out the window to properly greet this armed gentleman. "Jack Whittaker."

"Tom Blake. And that over there is my friend Jesse. Is that gun loaded?" Tom shook his hand.

"Yeah. It's always loaded. I'm from New York."

"Well, a few kids were involved in a bad accident on the bridge. A bear of some sorts may have been involved. So be ready to shoot." Tom was not ready to exploit his Bigfoot theory, not yet at least, and not to someone from out of town.

"Tom, I got Spencer over here," yelled Jesse. "He's breathing. I don't want to move him. Call an ambulance."

Spencer looked up at Jesse. In barely a whisper he moaned, "Please take me."

"Just stay put. Don't try to talk. Help is on the way."

Tom and Jack rushed over to Spencer's aid. Tom did a quick introduction and instructed Jack to stay with the young man. Jesse and Tom ran back to the truck to grab a few flashlights. Living in this neck of the woods, flashlights were a necessity and every truck was equipped with at least one. "How is he?" asked Tom.

"I don't know. I don't want to move him. I don't know if he broke his neck or what. But I'll tell you one thing, he can't move."

"Shit. Did you check the other side of the bridge? Marc said it may have been Bob."

"Let's look for Marie first. She might still have a chance. Grab me some rope." Jesse and Tom hurried to the end of the ravine and called for Marie. No answer. Jesse picked up a rock and tossed it down. "Marie! You got to say something! It's Jesse, Danielle's father. I'm going to come down there. If I'm getting closer to you, please make some noise." Jesse and Tom headed down the slope trying their best to keep their footing.

"Hang in their, buddy. A helicopter is on the way." Jack held the flashlight up to his face so Spencer could see him.

"Please," moaned Spencer. "You have to get me out of here. Bob is dead."

"What are you talking about, son? What happened?"

"It just crushed him. Picked him up. Threw him."

"What? A bear?" asked Jack.

"No. Bigger than a bear. He looked at me. Then bit Bob's stomach. Ripped his liver right out of him. And ate it! Get me out of here!" Spencer tried to lift his head up off the ground then it crashed down hard onto the bridge. "Why can't I move," he cried out in frustration.

"I think you hit your head real bad, kid. Just try to relax. I'm here with you and I have a gun. I used to be on the job. Trust me, you're in good hands. And I tell you what, it's a good thing you're still drunk right now, or you'd be in a lot of pain. You reek of booze."

There was something soothing about Jack's voice. Spencer laid still, allowing himself to relax. "Did you see my girlfriend?"

"No. Those guys are looking for her though. They seem like they know what they are doing."

Spencer tried to smile. "I hope she's lying on her stomach. With her ass in the air, they won't miss her."

111

Jack laughed aloud. He admired this boy's sense of humor in a crisis. "You know what they say, if you can't laugh, you might as well be dead."

"Can't say I ever heard that." Spencer rolled his eyes back and began to pass out.

"Spencer! You've got to stay awake, son. Look at me. Keep your eyes focused on my face."

Spencer slightly opened his eyes, but his voice was also slipping away. "You're one u-ggggg-ly dooood." His eyes rolled back inside his head and he passed out again.

Jack Whittaker did not look up, but could hear the sounds of the police sirens pulling onto the dirt road, making their way to the bridge. He'd seen injuries like this before, and fainting was never a good sign. He held Spencer's hand and squeezed it tightly, letting him know he was going to be alright, even if he didn't believe his own words.

Two cops got out of separate vehicles and proceeded to make a large X in the road with white paint surrounded by a few flares. Jack's greasy hair flew around his head in four different directions, so much so that he had to pull it back and out of his eyes to see the helicopter preparing to land. Within two minutes, Spencer had been strapped to a gurney and taken away by three medics in the chopper. Jack raised himself and was met by none other than Officer Demitres.

"I'm going to need a statement from you," said this colossus of a guy who looked like he could banish you into oblivion without breaking a sweat.

Jack's luck could not have gotten any better. He reached into his right pocket and turned on his tape recorder. "I don't know, Officer Demitres, is it?"

"Yeah. Who are you, where are you from, and what are you doing here?" asked this huge figure who was standing about a foot away from Jack and blocking his view of the rest of the planet.

"Jack Whittaker." Jack held out his hand but Demitres just stared blankly at him. "I'm vacationing here. I headed up the road over there and made a right turn, only to find two men blocking the bridge. Being a fellow officer, I pulled over and offered to help."

"Fellow officer. I like the sound of that. Where's your jurisdiction," demanded the cop in a sarcastic tone.

"JFK Airport, New York, Customs." Jack reached for his wallet when all too soon Demitres had his arm twisted behind his back.

"Not so fast, tough guy," he said as he yanked Jack's arm up a notch.

"Get the fuck off of me! I'm going for my badge!" In a split second, Demitres had Jack's gun and wallet in his right hand while holding him with his left. He released Whittaker, knocking him to the ground.

"I think you broke my arm, you crazy bastard!" Jack rubbed his elbow, checking to see that it was still intact.

"Then you got away easy. Why were you in the bar asking about cops?" Demitres now had both his gun and Jack's pointed at Jack's head.

"I wasn't. I was inquiring about real estate." Jack sat up on the dirt road. Coming up from behind Demitres was his partner, who Jack was relieved to see was a bit smaller than the terminator standing before him.

"Well, well, well. If it isn't Mr. Jack Whittaker, P.I.," said Kankro in a matter of fact kind of way.

Kankro stood beside Demitres, holding a manila folder. "Private Investigator, I thought you were a customs agent?" asked Demitres.

Before Jack could answer, Kankro opened up the folder and shined his flashlight on the papers inside. "Says here you were hired by a Mr. Jim Healy, for a payment of three thousand dollars plus expenses, to conduct an investigation on an Officer Pat Demitres and Officer Alan Kankro."

"There are two guys down there looking for an injured girl," squawked Jack who felt his heart drop into his stomach. "She needs help." Jack rose to his knees, awkwardly trying to get to his feet.

Demitres did not seem phased. "What is it you would like to know about us, Jack?"

"Nothing! I was fired this evening! I swear!"

"Did you get the money," asked Kankro.

"Yes. It's in my wallet. You can have it, just don't kill me, please." Jack's life flashed before his eyes and he knew if those two hicks under the bridge did not come up soon, these pigs would blow him away.

Demitres fished through the wallet, retrieved the money, then tucked the wallet into his pants. Feeling confident that Whittaker wouldn't dare try to manipulate the situation, he tossed the gun back to him. Jack let the gun remain on the ground for a few moments, knowing all too well that Demitres would not hesitate to shoot him in "self defense." The look on Demitres face proved Jack correct, and unloaded his weapon in front of the officers before tucking it away in the back of his pants.

"Is it all there?" asked Kankro.

"Seems to be. There's just one problem," replied Demitres.

Kankro turned around to see Tom and Jesse walking towards them. Jesse was carrying Marie in his arms.

"Where's the chopper?" asked Tom.

"We didn't know there was someone else involved. What the hell went on here?" Kankro lied.

Jesse laid Marie down in the back seat of Tom's truck and started the engine. "You guys got to drive in front of me to give me some assistance. This girl's in bad shape."

114

"Wait! Bob is somewhere around here," cried Tom.

The two cops locked eyes for a moment. Without saying anything aloud, Kankro got into his vehicle to escort Jesse to the hospital, guiding with his lights and sirens. As Kankro pulled his police car around, he rolled down his passenger side window and addressed Whittaker to leave town immediately, or he wouldn't last till sunrise.

Demitres starting walking over the bridge. "Where did Marc say he saw Bob? Across the bridge?"

"Yeah, I'll meet you over there in a minute."

Tom walked over to Whittaker. "What was that all about?"

"I don't know," he lowered his voice. "But I have it on tape that the officers threatened my life."

"Who are you, and what's your story?" Tom could not fathom what he might have missed in the fifteen or so minutes he was searching for the girl, but he figured these two parties met previously and there was some bad blood between them. "You know what? I don't really care. Those two bozos have a problem with everyone. Want to know why Jesse didn't hand her over to them and let them take her to the hospital?"

Jack, still haunted with the thought that he was going to be shot and pushed over the bridge like damn road kill, looked blankly at Tom. "I give up. Why?"

Tom gazed at Jack intently. "That Kankro is a pervert. That's why. That was a beautiful young girl left unconscious in the middle of the woods. Kankro would have her panties down and around her ankles before bringing her up to the road. And nobody would have even known about it. Welcome to fucking Warrensburg."

"Yep, we got another one over here," yelled Demitres from across the bridge.

Jack felt nausea creeping up his esophagus and tasted old hot sauce. He turned from Tom and threw up

115

everything he'd eaten during the course of the evening. Being in the same area as Demitres made him feel as if he was walking into a lion's den, and his gut feeling told him to run away, far away.

"I thought you were a cop? You sure don't have a cop's stomach, that's for sure."

Jack hesitated for a brief moment, then, against all instincts, scurried with Tom over to Demitres. Tom shined his flashlight on the wooden planks as they crossed the one lane bridge to the other side of the river. They came across a pool of blood halfway to the other side. "This must be Spencer's blood," Jack noted and felt suddenly ashamed for thinking of himself in a time when two kids were fighting for their lives under the big bright light at this very moment.

Tom ignored the blood and made his way towards the end of the bridge. More blood. This must be Bob's, he thought. He focused on a blood puddle and a small drip line, like a search for the pot of gold at the end of a rainbow. But this was no rainbow, it was what was left of his long-time pal. The trail of red led into the bushes on the side of the road. He brought this to Jack's attention and they searched as best they could with the little light they had. He turned to Demitres, who had stepped away to make a private phone call. Tom tried to remain calm given the situation, but it was clear that Demitres did not seem overly concerned that Bob had been murdered, and although he couldn't think of any particular incidents involving Bob and the police, he didn't think the tag team favored Bob much. He recalled Bob saying that Demitres showed up with a beer when he called the police a few weeks ago to report a break-in. "Strange," considered Tom who thought it was best to leave Demitres alone with his call, as there was a chance that it could be urgent. He called out to Jack, "Go bring your car around, and shine your brights over here."

Jack did as he was told. Even with the brights on, it was still hard to make out blood spots on the bushes, but they were there. Drip. Drip. Drip. Splat. Drip. Splat. The sound caught their attention before their eyes, two sets of which frantically looked up and down for the unmistakable sound. Jack was hoping it was the ambient noise of the river below, but his own fears told him otherwise. Turning his attention to the left, he saw the empty upper torso of what was left of a grown man.

Bob's carcass looked like a buck who had just been shot and gutted by a master hunter. He was bleeding from the inside out, with his loins dangling out from under him. Tom focused on the beam from Jack's flashlight. "Bob, why the hell didn't you meet me tonight?" He screamed at Bob as if he could reply, and sifted through the bushes and trees in search of the rest of his body, without having any luck. "Demitres, did you see all this?" The officer was still on the phone, most likely calling for a bus.

Jack looked at the remains of Bob's body then gestured in the direction of Demitres. "I don't know what the fuck is going on here, but I'm not staying around for that lunatic over there to gut me like he did this guy." Jack backed up and headed for his car.

"Wait a minute," Tom tried to grab Jack's arm, but Jack moved too fast. "The cops didn't do this."

"Fuck this. I'm out a here." Jack jumped in his car and rolled up the window as fast as he could. "I'm sorry for your friend, really I am." He apologized through the window and drove off, heading south down Schroon River road towards his cheap motel in Diamond Point. A few miles into his drive, he flicked his interior lights on to see the mess Kankro left in his car. The glove box was open, and his notes were all over the place. Jack was cursing the son of a bitch cop when he heard a noise. He looked at his passenger side floor, noticing the clasp was open on his camera bag. He tried to lean over to open it, to see if his camera had been stolen, but couldn't reach. Shifting his weight to his right glute, he grabbed the handle with his middle finger. His left hand jerked on the steering wheel and sent the car crashing into a telephone pole on the right side of the road. His airbag exploded, thrusting his neck back into the headrest and leaving him with a nasty bloody nose. The front end of the car crumbled like a wet piece of cake and his right front tire popped off. Jack felt the heat of the airbag and thought his car was on fire. Frantically, he tried to kick the door open and escape, but his left leg was wedged between the seat and dashboard. He quickly unbuckled his seat belt and tried to puncture the airbag with his fist in order to assess the damage done to himself.

Whittaker rolled out of his car and stumbled around to the passenger's side. It was so dark, he didn't even know what he hit. He reached in the window, grabbed his flashlight with his uninjured arm and shined it on the front of his car. "God damn telephone pole!" Reaching into his pocket he grabbed his cell phone.

"Hello?"

"Jim! It's me, Jack. I wanted to let you know that..."

Jim cut him off mid-sentence. "Not now, Jack. My daughter has been in an accident and I'm waiting to hear from my wife on her condition."

"Is it your daughter Marie?" asked Jack.

"Yeah. How'd you know?"

"I was there! Well, not at the time of the accident, but I found her friend Spencer lying there on the bridge. Two guys, uh, Jesse and Tom I think found her in the woods."

"Jesus fuck! How did she look?"

"I don't know. It was dark. I know she was breathing, I'm sorry I don't have more info. Jesse drove her to the hospital."

"What about her boyfriend? How is he?"

"He couldn't move, but he was talking to me at first. Then he went unconscious and they airlifted him. I just left the scene when I hit a pole on Schroon river road. I'm stuck. Can you send one of your friends to get me, maybe that guy Tom? Anyone but those dirty cops."

"You met Kankro and Demitres?"

Jack couldn't help but feel proud at this moment. "Met them? I have them on tape threatening my life." And the proud moment suddenly fled as quickly as it came on. "They went through my car. I was made. And they know you hired me."

"Shit!" In any other situation, Jim would demand his money back from this moron. But all he could think of was Marie.

"Look, I have enough evidence to bury these two. Just help me get out of here before they come back, kill me, and discard of the evidence. They already stole my wallet and emptied my gun! Hang up with me and call someone."

"O.K."

"Jim, as a precaution, I'm going to call you back in five minutes. Don't pick up the phone- let the answering machine pick up and I'll play the tape into the machine so you have proof in case something happens to me." Jack looked down the dark, windy, deserted road and got a bad feeling.

"Alright, but make it one minute and no later cause I'm waiting for my wife to call. I'll call Tom now. Which direction are you heading?"

"You tell me where I should go. All I see is darkness."

"Head north, away from town. You'll see a lumberyard on your right. That's Tom's. He owns it. Wait there and Tom will pick you up soon."

Jack reloaded his gun, gathered his cameras, keys, flashlight and tape recorder and headed towards the lumberyard. Luckily he had a spare pillow in the trunk so he used the pillowcase as a carrying bag. He picked up his night vision goggles which were also in the trunk, and adjusted them to his face. Within a few minutes, his eyes had adjusted and he could see somewhat clearly. Jack was a small time private investigator, and he recently found a site on-line called Spies R' Us, that sold all sorts of illegal gadgets to surveil a subject. The night vision goggles were expensive, and he knew he would have no purpose for them other than to spy on the teenagers who would frequent his dead-end block and make out. Sometimes they would fully undress, and this was enough reason for lonely ol' Whittaker to make the purchase.

Whittaker had not walked such a long distance since the police academy, and was starting to experience difficulty in breathing. From the density of the air, he sensed the late night mountain fog had made its way to the road. He squinted and was relieved that he couldn't actually see the haze through the NVG's, for the atmosphere combined with the reality of the situation at the moment, would have surely pushed him over the edge.

Dragging his feet, he saw a glimmer of light coming towards him. In the distance, he could see small shapes hopping on and off the road. As the car closed in, Jack was able to make out the petite toads trying to get to their destination on the other side of the street. Not sure if he should attempt to grab the driver's attention or hide himself in some shrubs, Whittaker made a last minute decision to steer off into the shadows of the night reminiscing about those who didn't make that choice in 'The Texas Chainsaw Massacre.' As the car passed by, Jack saw what must have been the Lumber Yard and picked up his pace, hoping to find protection from the two cops on their way back to the bridge. He then made the all important phone call and transferred the incriminating recording onto Healy's answering machine.

*   *   *

"Well, this is Bob alright," said Demitres in a compassionless tone. He grabbed Bob's arms and began dragging him over the bridge.

"What are you doing!" yelled Tom, unable to cope with the site of his friend's body being manhandled by this beast.

Demitres cracked a smile. "Relax. He can't feel a thing."

"Shouldn't you wait for someone to take photos or something?" He was about to get nasty with Demitres when his own cell phone rang. As he spoke to Jim Healy, he watched in silence as Demitres let Bob's body carelessly drop to the ground. He ended his short phone call and was about to question Demitres again when he was cut off.

The officer had no problem picking up the conversation where it left off. "I'm here, I saw him dead. And the missing body parts speak for themselves. You don't need to be here. I think I can fill in the details without an eyewitness."

"But this is a crime scene, and he's my friend!"

"And the medical examiner is going to need to see the body, so I'm bringing it down to the morgue. I don't think we need to drag the coroner out of bed at this hour for his expertise on whether Bob is dead or not. Go home Tom."

Tom might have tried to argue with the officer, but was suspicious of Demitres' behavior and thought that maybe, possibly, the cops already knew about Bigfoot and were covering up the evidence in some type of government conspiracy. The kind that innocent witnesses get killed over. And now Jack was waiting for him at the

121

lumberyard. Reluctantly, he left on foot and started to walk home, his house being less than a mile from the bridge. He knew if there was any evidence of Bigfoot surrounding that crime scene, that idiot of a cop surely ruined it by now. He seemed to be trampling all over the place, almost intentionally making it harder for the Forensics Unit to uncover any evidence. It was too dark to notice any extra large footprints, but it wouldn't matter come morning. Everything would be disheveled from the chaos.

After a half mile of random cars driving up and down the road, Jack's goggles picked up the shape of a small shed-like building at the Lumber Yard and decided to sit on the steps facing the opening of the property to wait for his ride. Unfamiliar sounds started to fill in the silence, which is to be expected when one is alone in the inky blackness of an Adirondack night. Jack looked to the right of the shed. Nothing. The chirruping sounds of crickets sang their incessant songs, but there was little else he could decipher in the mesh of background noise. He looked to the left. Nothing.

As he sat in the still of the night, he could hear movement coming towards him. Jack sensed the sounds were coming from his left, and they were growing louder. These were not the sounds of the crickets, but rather that of the ground being stepped on: branches breaking, wooden planks hitting together, and the unmistakable rhythm of someone breathing heavily. Jack stood up and quietly walked to the right side of the shed. He listened again, but didn't hear the sounds anymore. "Either the animal, human or not, stopped because he heard me move," he thought, "or went off in the opposite direction." Just as Jack had consoled himself with the thought of the thing leaving, he heard it again. Twigs breaking. Snap, crack, snap, crack. It was definitely getting closer, and it was definitely a pair of feet making this noise, not the sounds of a four-legged animal. Jack traced the perimeter of the shed and only moved when it moved. "One of those crooked cops," he thought. They had been so close to killing him on the bridge. If those locals hadn't appeared when they did, Jack knew he wouldn't be here right now. He laughed to himself on that one. "Be here?" He asked himself, "Would I rather have gotten killed on the bridge or here in a dark lumberyard by myself?" Jack was trying to stay positive, but feelings of despair were overshadowing the mood.

The sound of a horn made Jack perk up for a brief moment. Maybe it was Tom looking for him, or maybe the partner of the cop on the other side of the shed. Staying still for the time being seemed to be the better move. Within a few seconds, he saw light coming from the driveway, then he heard the sound of someone running right past him into the rear of the lumberyard. With his night vision goggles, he saw a tall blur run past the shed at a tiger's speed and seemingly disappear into nowhere.

Tom got out of Sherry's Ford Focus. "Jack, are you here?"

Was this a set-up? Jack couldn't remember what Tom's voice sounded like. The intense ring of his cell phone startled Jack and he backed up, stepping on something sharp. "OOOwww!," he yelled uncontrollably. He opened his phone but did not say anything.

"Jack? Where are you?"

"How do I know you're really Tom?"

"Jim just called me to pick you up. I'm standing in the driveway. Are you here or not?"

Jack didn't recognize the voice, but knew it wasn't Kankro or Demitres. He hung up the phone and stepped out from behind the shed. The silhouette standing in front of the headlights was not big enough to be one of the cops, or as big as the thing that just ran past him. He took off his NVG's and limped his way towards the car. "Thanks for coming for me. I just cut my foot on something behind the shed. You got insurance?" he joked. He sat in Tom's passenger seat with the door still open and removed his shoe and sock. Blood was making a red puddle under the car door.

"You want me to take you to the hospital?"

"No. I'll be fine." He took off his other sock and wrapped it around his wound. "Who was that who just ran into your lumberyard?"

"I came alone. You can't see shit in this darkness, so how did you see someone?"

Jack pulled his night vision goggles off of his neck. "With these."

Tom took the goggles. He positioned them on his face and looked around, seeing a green version of his lumberyard. He handed the high-tech spy wear back to Jack and got into the car, then slowly turned to Jack.

"I know what you're going to say," said Jack, gagging. "Sorry about the smell. I think I might have stepped in shit."

Chapter 13

Marc and Danielle sat in a small office room just beyond the emergency room in Glens Falls Hospital and gave their statements to Officer Kankro. Kankro looked at Marc and said, "Now, I'm gonna have to ask you to please step outside a minute while I finish up with her."

Danielle looked at Marc and grabbed his wrist.

"Why do I have to leave? We were both there, and both saw the same exact things," said Marc.

"Because this is official police work, and this is how we operate. Now do what you're told and step outside."

Marc gripped Danielle's shoulder. "I'll be right outside the door. Shout if you need me." Marc got up and left the room, keeping his eyes locked on Kankro.

Kankro was not intimidated by the kid, and stared back at Marc until he left the room. His eyes then honed in on Danielle's C-cup breasts. "So tell me, were you guys drinking tonight?"

She looked up at him and their eyes met. "You know we were. We already told you that."

"Tell me exactly what happened at Spencer's house, and don't say you already told me. I know yous were drinkin', but was there any sex going on?"

Danielle's face twisted upwards in disgust. "I don't know what sex has to do with the accident." She pushed her chair away from the table and stood up.

Kankro grabbed her wrist. "You're done when I tell you you're done. Sit your pretty little ass back down!"

Danielle wrapped her foot around the leg of the chair and kicked it backwards, allowing it to slam into the door. Marc heard the thud and swung the door open.

"Get your hands off her! She's a minor and needs her parents in here or she tells you nothing!" Marc grabbed Danielle's free hand and yanked her out into the hallway. "Just walk fast," he told her. They made their way into the waiting room, went right into the bathroom and locked the door. "You stay here. I'm going to get a security guard. I don't trust that dirty cop. What did he do to you?"

Danielle's eyes started to tear as she wiped them away with her fingers. Marc handed her some toilet paper. "He asked if anyone had sex at Spencer's, and stared at my tits the whole time!" She began to cry.

"That fucking pig!" He pulled Danielle's head into his chest. "It's alright. I don't think he'll try anything that stupid again."

"Where's my Dad? Doesn't he know we're still waiting here?" Danielle locked her fingers around Marc's waist.

"He knows. He's talking to the doctors and Marie and Spencer's mothers."

"How do you think they are?"

Marc ran his fingers through Danielle's hair. "I don't know. Spence may have a few broken bones. Marie's head was bleeding pretty bad when your Dad brought her in here. She was completely knocked out. But I'm not a doctor, what do I know? Danielle, what exactly did you see on the bridge?"

"I saw two people. What did you see?"

"I saw a big fucking ape come out of nowhere and tear that fucking guy to shreds! Then I left my best friend lying there to die just to save your ass! If I hadn't thrown my helmet at Spence's quad, that thing would have killed all of us!"

Danielle pulled away from Marc. "If you hadn't thrown your helmet, Marie and Spencer wouldn't be in the condition they're in right now!"

"Fuck you! How could you say something like that!"

"It's the truth! Why did you do that?" she yelled.

Marc's face turned beet red and he was so angry he talked through his teeth. "Why? Why did I do that? 'Cause if I didn't they would have run over that fuckin' idiot on the bridge! That's why! Do you think I knew they were going to run off the fucking road? Spence is my best friend, and right now he's lying in a fucking hospital bed fighting for his life! So I think now's a better time than any other to grow the fuck up and stop acting like you're the only one involved in this! Our friends may be dead, and I may be on my way to jail for drinking and driving. By the way, thank you very much for mentioning that to officer asshole back there! And here you are, standing here without a fuckin' scratch on your precious fuckin' head, and you're crying over some cop staring at your tits, which are completely covered by a padded bra, a T-shirt and a denim jacket! I never met a more shallow human being in my life. And don't forget, I've lived outside of Warrensburg!"

Danielle crumpled up the toilet paper and threw it into the toilet bowl. "So what? You think you're better than me because you moved out of Warrensburg? You wouldn't have made it to the bus stop if it wasn't for your father's money!"

"*My* father's money?" Marc stabbed himself in the chest with his pointer finger. "Who's the one driving around in a brand new thirty thousand dollar truck?"

"It was a gift! Same as the Firebird that *your* father bought for you!"

Marc opened the bathroom door. "I don't need this shit right now." He stormed out, leaving Danielle in the tiny bathroom by herself. He was about to leave when he saw Jesse standing by the vending machines.

"I ought to beat the shit out of you right now! Where's Danielle?" screamed Jesse.

"I wasn't drinking. Danielle is fine. She's in the bathroom."

"Bullshit!" Jesse pounded on the bathroom door, demanding that Danielle come out.

Danielle emerged and threw herself into her father's arms. "Dad! How is Marie?"

"Well, they gave her twenty three stitches on her head and sent her in for a CAT scan. Her vitals are good but her head was hit pretty hard. She's in a coma. They don't know for how long, if she'll be brain damaged, or if there is swelling on the brain. These next twenty-four hours are crucial. Danielle, this was a serious accident. Be prepared for the worst."

Danielle started to tremble. "How is Spencer?"

"He'll live. He broke four ribs and has a collapsed lung. Danielle, this could have been you." He grabbed her elbows and started to shake her. "What the fuck were you thinking getting on a quad with someone who'd been drinking? Haven't I taught you anything? You never fucking listen! You're killing me, Danielle!" Jesse wanted to give her a good ass-beating, but managed to hold back. "Let's go. Your mother and Don are waiting for you at your house. You too," he said, motioning for Marc to get in the truck with him. Marc took a seat in the back of the truck, forcing Danielle to sit up front with her father who also had a few beers under his belt. Jesse pulled out of the parking lot like a bat out of hell. "And you, Marc! You think 'cause you to college that you're smarter than everyone around here. Well let me tell you something! That stunt you pulled tonight was about the stupidest thing anyone has ever done!" He looked towards Danielle. "Almost as stupid as you getting on the quad with him! Your truck, your fucking brand new truck, it's gone! This is not open for discussion!"

"I know! I never should have got on the quad! But Dad, Marc wasn't drunk! Spencer definitely was, but Marc only had one drink." She turned her body to face Marc in the back seat of the truck. "Tell him, Marc. Tell him you only had one drink."

Marc knew enough not to argue, not now anyway.

"Oh, that's great Danielle. He didn't seem drunk. And when did you start drinking? Does your mother know you drink? You're not even of age to fucking drink! You moron!"

Danielle pulled her knees up to her chest and started to cry again. "This has been the worst night of my life! Please don't say another word! Not right now!"

Chapter 14

Steve Bettis was going head to head with Andy Roddick in a tennis match when he was awakened by the sounds of Spike barking, an unusual response from Spike, and one which, given her recent injury, alarmed Steve. Instinctively, he grabbed his gun off the nightstand and tiptoed out the bedroom door and into the hallway, taking a quick glimpse towards Maureen to see if she was still asleep. Her mouth was cracked open with a slither of drool slinking down her right cheek, a good sign she wouldn't wake for another six or seven hours. He walked down the stairs into the main living room and saw Spike ripping apart an old, oval braided rug on the floor. "Spike! Stop that!"

Spike looked up at Steve but continued to tear apart the rug with her uninjured paw. Steve grabbed hold of it and pulled it out of her mouth. He dropped it on the floor and a cloud of dust filled the area. The noise had woken up Devin who was now at the top of the stairs, calling for his father. "Everything's alright. Spike is just chewing on the rug. Go back to bed."

"Chewing on the rug? I guess she's feeling better." Devin came down the stairs rubbing his eyes. He kneeled down and patted Spike on the head. "What's wrong Spike? What's the matter good girl?" Spike licked Devin's face and pawed under the green couch sitting caddy-cornered in the corner of the room. "Dad, I think something's under the couch. I think you should see what it is."

"Scaredy cat." Steve poked at Devin's side.

"I'm not looking under there! You can't peer pressure me."

Steve laughed. "Fine, you big baby. I'll do it." He pulled the couch out a few feet towards the center of the room, revealing at least a hundred mouse droppings and a mountain of cobwebs and dust.

"That's gross," said Devin, as he reached into the kitchen for a dust- pan and broom. Spike stuck her nose to the floor like a bloodhound and sniffed around the newly opened area. Steve swept the mess while Devin held the dustpan. "What is that line on the floor?"

"That's the trap door leading to the basement."

"The same crawlspace that leads to the cellar doors outside?"

"Yep. Same one."

"That doesn't make any sense. Why would someone build this house with a staircase to the basement from outside and not inside? What do you have to do, open the door and jump down? There are no other stairs inside the basement, only the ones that you walk to from outside."

"It's an old house, like in the Wizard of Oz. People run down into the cellar to protect themselves from the tornadoes."

"This is upstate New York. There are no tornadoes in this area."

"It had other purposes. I'm going to make myself a cup of tea, since I'm awake now. You want some?" Steve was never the scholar. The fact that his kids were so god-damned bright challenged his ability to speak with authority. It also reminded him that those useless facts he never paid attention to in school could come back to kick ya' in the ass at any time. But of course, Jesse would know the answer to that question. Was there anything that guy didn't know?

"Sure." Devin sat on the couch while his father boiled water in the kitchen.

After a few minutes, Steve walked back into the living room with two mugs and handed one to Devin. "Papa loved this house. Grandma too. Every year on their anniversary they would come up here for a night or two without us kids. I remember one summer we were here, I must have been your age, and my Dad, Papa, went out for a ride by himself. He was gone all afternoon, and your Grandmother was pissed. She was hanging laundry on the clothesline in the back when he came walking up through the yard. Your aunt Peggy was on the tire swing, and I was pushing her, real high. It seemed like she was going higher than the trees. Anyway, we heard them arguing about something when the ground beneath me seemed to change colors. I thought I was seeing things, but my parents saw it at the same time and immediately stopped bickering. Peggy was in mid-air when she yelled out, "The sky fell onto the ground! Look out!" Steve laughed. "She was about six years old at the time. My parents came running towards me and dropped to the ground at the same time right beside my feet."

"What was it?" asked Devin.

"Blue flowers. Everywhere. Seems they popped up instantaneously. It was the weirdest thing I'd ever seen. Grandma looked at Papa and said, "You did it! I don't know how, but you did it."

"I don't get it. He did what?"

"Every year, on their anniversary, my Dad would hunt all over the property for these blue flowers for my mom. It was her birthstone color, so when he first presented them to her, she fell in love with them. He never found them outside of the Farm, which made them even more special to her. Well, on this particular day, I don't know if it was the sun or what, but they grew! I don't know what kind of flowers they were, but they were real neat to look at. They were in full bloom when we left that summer, but they never grew back. Nothing in that area now but pine needles."

Devin shared a similar image with his father. "Were they tulip shaped with a white center?"

"Yeah, they were. How'd you know that? Did you see them?"

"No." Devin felt an uncomfortable feeling trickle down his spine. This must be what Loudbear was talking about, he thought. "Becka was painting a picture of a blue flower before she went to bed tonight." Something about that painting was unsettling to Devin, but he couldn't pin point it. And now that his father brought up this bizarre story, he knew they were of some significance, but to exactly what extent he was not sure.

"That's neat. Maybe she saw them. Maybe they're back. I'll call Grandma tomorrow and tell her that her pets are back. That's what she called them. Her precious little pets."

Devin sipped his tea and rested his cup on the end table. "Dad, can I ask you something?"

"Sure, what is it?" God, please let me know the answer to *one* of his questions, thought Steve.

"Is it true that this house is haunted?"

Steve didn't like where this was going. "Yeah, there were some stories, but every house has its stories. Who told you a thing like that?"

"Grandma. And Aunt Rachel. And Jesse. And I remember a Native American here when I was younger. And Uncle Tony said a kid died in this house. Is that true? Also, last year when we were here, I bought a book at a local garage sale, *The Hauntings of Warrensburg*, that said a lot of houses around here are haunted."

"Devin, not everything you read is true. And no, a kid did not die in this house. A kid who lived in this house wandered too far into the woods and was attacked by a large bear, and yes, unfortunately he did die. As for your Grandmother, she misses your Grandfather very much, and if she wants to believe that she awoke from a dream here one night and saw him standing beside her, I don't see anything wrong with that. Your Aunt Rachel,

133

now she is just cheap. She used the excuse that this house is haunted to get out of the upkeep that comes with owning a second house, and your Uncle George, who is also cheap, went along with it. And you were four years old when you saw that Indian. At the time you were obsessed with cowboys and Indians. You had the guns, the action figures; it was only normal for you to create an imaginary friend. Becka never saw him. And don't forget, this house is old. It creaks, rattles and shifts. People can believe whatever they want. But nobody has ever gotten hurt in this house. Am I right?"

"You're right. But Dad, I met this guy at the church yard sale the other day. He looked just like the Indian ghost from here. He's a Mohican Indian. His name is Loudbear. We got to talking, and he said I was a psychic. He gave me a cedar flute."

"What do mean, he gave you a cedar flute? People don't just give things away, Devin. What did he want from you?"

"Why do you always have to be so paranoid Dad? Why can't you believe that some people are just nice?"

"Because people aren't nice, Devin. When are you going to learn that?"

Devin let out a yawn. "I'm getting tired. I think I'm going to hit the hay."

"Yeah, me too. Put your cup in the sink or your mother will have a heart attack in the morning." Steve waited for Devin to get to the top of the stairs before turning off the living room light. As the light went out, he had a sudden flashback of his last image of the blue flowers. He remembered something happened that night. It was so long ago, he wasn't sure if it had really happened or was part of a dream. A bear and a wolf were fighting further up the hill. A guy from one of the houses up there was getting home from work late and didn't see the animals on the other side of the road. He must have startled them slamming his car door, and was mauled to death by one of them. Steve remembered the car ride back to Long Island, where he heard his parents arguing which one it was. His dad believed it was the wolf. His mother, the bear.

Chapter 15

DRUNKEN TEEN'S TALL TALE MAY HAVE MERIT

Police anticipated a stroke of good luck when they heard that 19-year old Spencer Gargan witnessed the murder of Robert Murphy, 42, until the teen revealed his impression of the killer. As far as bizarre claimants go, Gargan has placed himself in the ranks of P.T. Barnum. "Bigfoot killed Mr. Murphy," insisted the obviously shaken boy. "I swear, I've never seen anything like it -- the monster tore Murphy apart with his bare hands!"

The claim is made even less reliable by the circumstances surrounding Gargan's approach to the bridge where the murder took place. Driving a four wheeled all terrain vehicle, Gargan was speeding blindly onto the one-lane bridge off of Schroon River Road when he lost control. Girlfriend Marie Healy, 18, was sent hurtling down the embankment where she came to rest just before the river. Initially suffering from severe head trauma and multiple abrasions, she has since been upgraded from critical condition to stable as the swelling on her brain decreased dramatically during the evening. This is according to sources in the Intensive Care Unit of Glens Falls Hospital, where she was admitted late last night. Gargan claims he witnessed the murder as he lay on the wood and metal bridge.

Although officials seem skeptical of an actual Bigfoot sighting, police have revealed to reporters an ongoing investigation into a satanic cult who may be disguising itself as the mythological creature to terrify the public and elude capture by the police. "These delinquents are

136

going to get what's coming to them, believe me," was the official statement offered by Officer Patrick Demitres, who was the first one at the scene.

Murphy's body was badly disfigured in the attack. A source from the medical examiner's office indicated that several internal organs had been removed from the body. Funeral arrangements will be made pending the conclusion of an official autopsy. Gargan's all terrain vehicle has been retrieved from the river and impounded for inspection. A blood sample taken soon after his arrival at Glens Falls Hospital revealed Gargan's blood-alcohol level to be .13. The legal limit in New York State is .08.

While sipping coffee, Tom sat quietly next to Spencer's bed reading the "Adirondack Journal". He had told the nurses that Spencer would no longer be speaking to officials without an attorney present. An aide walked in to bring Spencer his breakfast, and the sound of her accent awakened him.

"Good morning, child! Time to wake up and have some food," she said in a loud Guyanese accent.

Spencer opened his eyes, trying to focus on the robust, black female standing before him. Out of the corner of his eyes, he saw Tom sitting there holding up the cover of the local newspaper, which showed a drawing of a gorilla-like animal hovering over a bridge.

"Mr. Blake, if you're here to kick my ass, you're too late," said Spencer in his usual sarcastic manner. The aide left them alone in the room, placing the tray of mush on his bedside table.

"That's not why I'm here. How are you feeling?"

"I'm O.K. Any news on Marie?"

"She's hanging in there. Her reflexes are responding to outside pressure, which is a good sign that her brain is still functioning. The swelling went down. The doctors are very optimistic."

"I feel so bad. You know, they won't even let me in there to see her."

"Don't take it personal. Nobody's allowed in there. Your mom is at her house now, helping with the kids."

"Yeah, that was my idea," said Spencer.

"Was it also your idea to call the paper?"

"I didn't call anyone. When they brought me to my room, the press was already there. The only reason I'm not in jail is because I'm in the hospital."

"Well, the doctors tell me you're going to be alright."

"Yeah. Hospital or jail, I don't care where I am as long as I'm not outside." He stared intently at Tom. "What I told the paper, I wasn't kidding. I saw it. After it killed Bob, it ran right past me! I was sure it was going to kill me, but it didn't. It just kept on running."

"What do you mean, it ran past you? Did it stop, sniff you or anything?"

"No. It was like it didn't even notice me."

Tom thought about his own experience with the creature from the road the other night, not even a mile from the bridge. This thing didn't try to attack, just kept going. Afterward, it killed the barn animals. "Maybe Bigfoot fills up on one meal, then goes home to rest." Tom pondered.

Spencer interrupted his thought process. "It looked like it was running towards Marc, but I don't remember the exact sequence of events. All I remember after that is some ugly guy talking to me while I was still on the bridge. Then I woke up, and I was here, in this hospital bed."

Tom smiled at his son's friend. "I believe you. I believe you saw Bigfoot, because I saw him too. Like you, I also was drunk. I was on my way home from the bar

Friday night, three days ago. For more reasons than you can imagine, I want this thing to be Bigfoot. But it may be a hoax. So I think we should sit back and gather some concrete evidence. That ugly guy from the bridge, he's lending me some of his equipment. He's a private investigator and he's got some really neat gadgets."

"Why is a private investigator here?"

"Your girlfriend's father hired him to take down Kankro and Demitres. Trust me, after this lawsuit that Jim Healy brings upon the cops, he and his family won't be hurting for money anymore. He's already speaking with an attorney who is digging behind the scenes to get more evidence on Kankro and Demitres in order to guarantee a sure case."

"I had no idea. Marie didn't tell me anything. But how is the cops being dicks going to prove what they did to Jim Healy a few years back?"

"Leave it up to the lawyers. They'll bring down the whole police station to get a point across. After hearing any indecent acts concerning one of their own, they'll most likely settle out of court. The Healy's will get their money, which is all they really want anyway."

Spencer liked the idea of that, the idea of Marie leading a normal life. "Mr. Blake, why are you getting involved?"

"Trust me, I was not part of the plan. But at the bridge last night, I watched how carelessly Demitres handled Bob's body, and it ticked me off. I also thought that the cops knew more about Bob's assailant then they let on. You, me, and Marc are the only ones who saw Bigfoot, and we may be in danger."

Spencer tried to sit up. "What are you talking about?"

Tom pushed Spencer's shoulder back onto the bed and pressed a button on a small remote, causing the mattress to incline a little. "Trust me on this one. This is what you're going to do: when the cops get here, and they'll be here soon to question you again now that you're sober, tell them you must have made up the story, because you don't remember seeing anything from last night. And tell them you won't speak to them without your attorney present. And don't worry about that either, I'll retain one for you."

"But Mr. Blake…"

"Then, you're going to ask them to leave. Tell them you don't feel good, and act as if you're going to throw up. They'll be at my house later, and Marc is going to tell them the same thing. Understand?"

Spencer hadn't a clue as to what Tom was up to, but he trusted him and agreed to go along with the plan.

After leaving the hospital, Tom picked up a dozen assorted bagels, a half pound of cream cheese, and a gallon of fresh orange juice before heading over to Jim Healy's house. As expected, he saw Margo Gargan's truck parked in the driveway, and he made a point to brush his hands through his thick hair before getting out of the truck. He carried the bag of goodies up to the front door and knocked loudly.

Jim Jr. answered the door and let Tom in right away.

"Hey, little guy." Tom could not tell the kids apart. "You boys hungry? I brought some bagels with cream cheese!"

Margo was in the kitchen brewing some coffee for Jim when she heard Tom's voice. "I'm in the kitchen, Tom. C'mon in here. Is Sherry with you?"

"No, sorry, just me." Tom brought the bagels into the kitchen and heard Jim's wheelchair making its way down the hallway. "Jim, I just came from the hospital. They wouldn't let me in to see Marie, but the doctor's tell me they expect a full recovery."

Jim shook Tom's hand. "I don't know how to thank you enough, Tom. You saved her life. Hell, if I wasn't stuck in this damn chair, I could have saved her life."

"Don't beat yourself up about it. Me and Jesse were there, and that's what friends are for. I brought bagels. Let's eat. I'm starving."

Margo set the kids up at the coffee table in the living room in front of the T.V. so the adults could talk in the kitchen. "Tom, you didn't need to hire an attorney for Spencer. He was drinking and driving. He should pay the consequences."

"I agree, Margo," said Tom. "But not with these cops. You don't know what his blood alcohol level was, or if it was manipulated. He didn't crash 'cause he was drunk. He crashed because Marc threw his helmet at his tire to get his attention. Marc saw someone at the other side of the bridge. Alcohol or not, it was an accident."

"I have to agree," said Jim. "And it was my daughter who suffered the most."

"Let's not forget about Bob," reminded Margo.

"Trust me," smiled Tom. "That will never happen. I'm in his will. He left everything to me. I encouraged him to write a will a few years ago, after he got into that car accident when his stupid little Pinto flew into the river. Since he had no family, he left everything to me. There's a developer, Josh Blumenfeld, who's willing to pay top dollar for Bob's property. I'm going to call him today. He wants to turn the place into a fishing lodge. If he's willing to call it 'Murphy's Lodge', he can have it at a good price. He liked Bob. I'm sure he'll want to be at the funeral. Bob will be missed, but at least he won't be forgotten."

"That's a great idea!" yelled Margo, bringing tears to her eyes. "You know, Bob and I had a thing once, or twice. I'm going to miss him. He was a great neighbor, great friend."

"Yeah," said Jim. "But what do you think killed him?"

"I don't know. I really don't know. But we owe it to him to find out," said Tom.

Chapter 16

Marc did not sleep much during the night, and was surprised to see that his alarm clock said 10:54 A.M. The last time he checked it read 6:48 A.M. Four hours. That would to have to be enough for now. He rose from his bed and headed towards the bathroom when he almost bumped into his father in the hallway. Stumbling backwards, he banged his head on the corner of a wooden picture frame holding a photograph of Sherry and Tom's wedding day. As Marc paused to straighten out the picture on the wall, an unfamiliar image stared back at him: his mother smiling.

"It's alright, son. It's just me."

"I didn't hear you."

"I didn't want to wake you. Did you need to use the bathroom?"

"Yeah," said Marc as he passed his father in the hallway.

Tom poured a cup of coffee for himself and a glass of orange juice for Marc. He heard the sound of the toilet flushing. "Marc? Come in the kitchen please. I think we should talk."

Marc knew this was coming, and since he didn't hear his mother's voice, thought he might as well get it over with before she got home. He sat down at the table across from his father and sipped the juice, trying to avoid eye contact.

"For starters, I know you were drinking last night. And I expect that. You're in college now, and it's perfectly normal. The part about you driving in that condition is what disappoints me."

"Before you go any further, I was not drunk. I had one drink. My stomach wasn't feeling right, so I only had one. But I did know Spencer was fucked up, and I shouldn't have let him drive. I'll take the blame for that."

143

"It's not about taking blame, Marc. You know, we're getting off the subject. Here, read this." Tom tossed a newspaper across the table.

Marc picked it up and read the title. He looked up at his father, and at that moment, they both knew something was out there. "Dad, Mom told me yesterday that you saw Bigfoot coming home from the bar. *From the bar*. Which means you were drinking, and you drove. So don't lecture me anymore."

Tom was embarrassed. "You're right. How about we make a pact right now that we will never drive drunk again?" Tom reached his hand across the table.

Marc shook his hand. "I saw it too. I can't believe Spencer talked about it to the press."

"Son, do you really believe it was Bigfoot? You actually got a good look at it?"

"Dad, I took an anthropology class this semester and my professor is a believer. I can't say I ever was until I took the class. But after last night, I know it was Bigfoot. By the way, I sent an e-mail to Professor Ramsey yesterday for some more Bigfoot info. Every characteristic my professor talked about, this thing had. It's size, the sound it made, the fur. I have to admit, though, when Mom told me you saw Bigfoot Friday night, I didn't think anything of it. I thought you were just drunk."

"I spoke with Spencer on that subject. I just came from the hospital, and he's going to be back to his normal self again soon. There is a private investigator in town, and we are going to get to the bottom of this Bigfoot thing. He's here for another reason entirely, and I'll get to that later. But he can still help us. Son, I want you close to home. This thing seems to come out only at night, so we have to bait him to catch him. This P.I. has night vision goggles, and he agreed to lend us his equipment."

"Night vision goggles! Cool! Where are they?"

"They're in the garage. I'll show you them later."

"Why do you want to bait and catch Bigfoot so bad?"

"For starters, it killed my friend. And second, I'd like to be able to sleep again. When I tell you I've had only five hours sleep since I saw this thing, I'm not exaggerating."

"Dad, I didn't realize it was Bob. It was dark, you know?"

"I know. What matters now is that we catch this thing before it strikes again."

Marc poured what was left of his juice into the sink. "You're not going to believe this, but I have all my notes on Bigfoot in my car. My friend at school, we call him Tits Mcgee, he told me to never throw away any notes. Said his sister was cramming for a final using only her text, and all these stupid answers were from another professor's class. I didn't quite get it at first, but then I noticed that in both my psychology class and my marketing class we discussed Maslow's hierarchy of needs, and one professor explained it a lot better than the other. It clicked and I knew exactly what Tits was talking about."

"I know I shouldn't, but why "Tits Mcgee?" asked Tom shaking his head.

"'Cause he has tits. You know, man boobs. I'll go get my notebook."

Just as Marc was walking through the living room, he turned back to his father. "Why aren't you at work today?"

"Jesse is handling things. I wanted to see Spencer and talk with him before he spoke to anyone else. You know, while the image was still clear in his mind. I'm going back to work in a little while." Tom cupped his hands around his coffee mug. "Marc, this isn't a joke. This thing saw you last night."

"Dad, it doesn't go after people with a vengeance. This isn't Orca."

"Tell that to Bob." Tom waited patiently as Marc went outside to his car and came back with the notebook.

Marc and his father sat at the table going over Marc's notes word for word, absorbing everything they could about the alleged Bigfoot. Tom toasted a bagel for Marc while Marc fried up some eggs.

"Did you know that Bigfoot is attracted to wind chimes?"

"No, Marc. I guess I skipped over that page. But I did see that it hibernates in winter."

"That makes no sense to me. Where could this thing possibly hibernate?"

"Anywhere. Down the road for instance, where the moffits live. You know how many abandoned cars and huts there are in that area?"

"Moffit area," laughed Marc. "That's where old Tony saw Bigfoot as a little kid. You might be on to something, Dad. And down the road from moffit land is the Bettis' Farm, where it came after Becka."

"You knew about that Tony story with the double bike? I just heard about it the other day. How did you know it?"

"Spencer told me years ago. His grandfather was friends with Tony, or something like that."

"Doesn't sound like a story anymore, does it?"

"No," said Marc. "Maybe we should talk to Tony."

"I agree. I'll pay him a visit later. Did I ever tell you about the men from Oregon who served in 'Nam with me?"

Marc never heard his father mention Vietnam before, and his mother never talked about it. He knew his father fought in the war, but when Marc was younger and asked questions, Tom's response was always the same: "It's not something you talk about."

"There were these three men, con-artists actually. They would talk to us about Bigfoot, how he was real and they'd seen him and knew how to locate him. When you're out in the jungle, and you're being shot at by children and things you can't even see, you hang on to words in your head. Hopes, dreams –anything to keep you from thinking that you're not going to live to see the next day. So when these idiots were talking about us troops getting together after the war and camping out in Oregon, it got us thinking we were gonna make it, make it through the war. We actually planned the whole trip: who was going to bring the liquor, who was going to bring the food, who would bring the women. It gave us all hope. Not that any one of us ever wanted to camp out again after the war, but at least we would all be alive and together again. So anyhow, these jerks asked all of us for three thousand dollars a piece for professional cameras, and Bigfoot tracking devices and a bunch of nonsense. Three grand was a lot of money back then, and still is today, but we didn't care. I don't think anyone of us actually had the money, but we all agreed to go on this Bigfoot adventure. This little myth is what kept me alive." Tom looked down, took a deep breath, and got up from his chair. "You feel like having a shot of whiskey?"

Marc was aware that it was still rather early in the morning, and the thought of a shot of whiskey after fried eggs made him want to vomit, but he knew his dad needed it. "Sure."

Tom walked over to the cabinet and laid out two shot glasses on the counter. Marc joined him and they held up their glasses.

"To Bigfoot," toasted Marc.

"To Bigfoot," smiled Tom.

Tom placed the shot glass on the table and looked at Marc, who was still cringing from the liquor. "So this professor Ramsey, how does he know all this stuff about Bigfoot?"

"They're facts. Documented facts, I guess."

"Documented facts. How are these documented facts if Bigfoot himself hasn't been documented?"

"A girl in my glass, I think she's pre-law or something, she brought up the same question, saying that this evidence is circumstantial at best."

"What was Ramsey's response?"

"He said she was right. But one day, it will be proven, because the truth is always discovered, no matter how deep it's buried. Are you having second thoughts?"

"Your pre-law girl has a good point. I think you should ask her out when you get back to college."

"Did I mention she's fat?"

Tom rolled his eyes at the comment, although dating fat chicks was never his forte either. "My point is that if there are Bigfoot facts out there, then anybody can create the illusion of Bigfoot. It's been done before, Marc. That famous footage of Bigfoot strolling through the woods has been ripped apart by scientists and every other expert out there, some of whom swore that it was the real deal. Years later, the confession was made that it was a hoax. Some guy's girlfriend made a costume out of cheap material."

"Dad, they did it for the money, which I'm sure they made a lot of. They weren't using it to kill people and get away with it."

"But someone may use a similar costume for another purpose."

Marc grabbed the whiskey off the table and poured himself another shot, and one for his father. "Then the question is 'why'?"

"Then question number two is, was Bob the target?"

"I guess we should be open-minded about our creature being nothing less than a sick human being. Steve Bettis is a NYC homicide detective. He's certain it's just some psychopath."

Marc and Tom chugged another shot. Marc took the empty shot glass from his father's hand and rinsed both out in the sink. "O.K., but did he see the 'costume'?"

"No, son, he didn't."

"Bigfoot is one of those things you have to see to believe. Steve Bettis is from Long Island. I bet you he's never even seen a deer outside of The Bronx Zoo.

Tom nodded his head in agreement. Marc had brought up a good point. The detective from New York City only knows about New York City.

"Hey, Dad. I have an idea. Why don't you call your war buddies and tell them about Bigfoot? I'm sure they'd want to know that it exists! Maybe you can have them over and we can all go on that mission. I'd love to meet your friends. You never talked about them before." Marc turned around, expecting to find Tom wearing the same look of enthusiasm that he was. Instead he was met with a frown.

"I can't."

"Why not? It sounds like your friends would be up to it!"

Tom walked to the back sliding doors and gazed out the glass into the backyard. "'Cause they're all dead."

Chapter 17

Sherry parked her car behind the Grand Union parking lot and opened up her cellular phone. Scrolling down the alphabetical list of numbers on her two inch screen, she stopped when the name Ramsey was highlighted. On the third ring, a man's voice answered. Scratchy, yet dignified.

"Hello? My name is Sherry Blake. My son Marc is a student in your Anthropology class."

"Yes. I tried to reach him last night. I received an e-mail from him, regarding Sasquatch, and I am not quite sure if I'm being fooled or not. I wouldn't waste my time if it were any of my other students, but Marc didn't come across to me as a prankster." Sherry raised an eyebrow and wondered if he had Marc confused with some other student.

"He mentioned he has some evidence, such as hair. I'd like to collect the hair and take it to the lab. That will clear up any questions Marc may have."

Sherry's eyebrows made a large arch on top of her forehead, the expression startling herself in the rearview mirror of her own car. She turned the mirror away from her and leaned back in her seat, thinking now that erasing the nutty professor's message from the home answering machine and calling him behind her family's back wasn't such a great idea after all. "You know, I think it is just a prank. My husband, he's been drinking a lot. And I think he got Marc all worked up over nothing..."

"Mrs. Blake, I know you must think this is ridiculous, hearing yourself say these things out loud. But Marc, he is my top student. He did not believe in Bigfoot when he entered my classroom. He strongly argued against it with the best law students in the University. Something made him believe what he saw. I already booked a flight upon receiving the e-mail. Do you have this hair or does Marc have it?"

Sherry remained silent, contemplating on what to do. Could Tom be Bigfoot? The lab tests would prove if it's him or not. But if it's not him, would she have any other reason to leave him? She needed to believe that Tom was crazy. "Oh, I don't know."

"Mrs. Blake, Sherry. May I call you Sherry?"

"Yeah."

"You don't have to make up your mind now. I will be in Warrensburg at five o'clock this afternoon. Perhaps we should discuss this over dinner? I have never been to Lake George. Maybe you can choose the restaurant and I can pay the bill?"

Sherry smiled, trying to remember the last time she went out to eat in Lake George. Tom hated the Village. *Filled with too many tourists.* "O.K. I'd like that. Well, this is my cell number. Call me when you arrive. I look forward to meeting you." She shut her phone and readjusted the rear-view mirror to see her face. Her eyes sparkled and a childish smirk spread across her lips. "Do I have a date tonight?" Feeling energetic for the first time in years, Sherry decided to hike the trail behind the Grand Union. She and Tom used to hike this trail back when they were dating, and some half mile into the trail, she wondered if their names were still engraved in the heart shape of an old oak tree, or if the tree itself had died, yet another symbol that her marriage was dead.

The trail was used often, but looked just the same as the last time she hiked it. That was when Marc was six years old. He made it all the way to the top of the mountain, which offered a breathtaking, panoramic view of Warrensburg. This wasn't a very long trail, no more than three miles, but Sherry remembered every last detail of every turn. She spotted the old oak tree, still alive, green leaves still flourishing from every branch. Well, that doesn't mean anything, she said to herself. She approached the tree, half hoping to see it had some funky tree disease upon close inspection, but it didn't. It appeared to be in good health. Old, but healthy. She caressed the tree as she rounded it to feel for the carving, which to her surprise, was faded away to almost nothing. New bark had started to grow over the scars they made in the tree, healing itself from old wounds.

Sherry backed away from the tree, admiring the resilience of this beautiful oak tree, when another marking caught her eye. It was on another tree, six feet behind the oak, but at the same eye level as 'Tom loves Sherry'.

"Kids are not romantic anymore," she said, and headed back down the trail. On the way back to her car she thought about the way her world had changed. Not just her world, she realized, but the entire world. The difference in generations. Tom couldn't get over Vietnam. Sherry wanted to move on. The oak tree had even moved on. Marc was on his way out of Warrensburg. Tom would never dream of leaving Warrensburg. Back then, boys carved in trees how they loved their girlfriends. Nowadays they carved things like "Lucifer's Seeds" and "Ozzy Rules!"

Chapter 18

Jesse had come over to the Farm on his lunch break to warn Steve about Bob's death and another possible Bigfoot attack. While Steve and Jesse differed on who they believe to be the killer, they agreed to tell Maureen that is was a bear. The perfect couple had been arguing all morning, and Jesse's arrival was like being saved by the bell. Steve hated arguing with his wife. He hated arguing in general. The twenty minutes Steve spent with Jesse in the driveway shaved about four layers of anxiety off his chest, even if it was bad news he'd received.

After Jesse left, Steve snuck in through the back door, hoping to avoid Maureen.

The screen door hadn't even fully shut when Maureen's mouth went running. "I don't think we should leave just because there was a bear on the property," said Maureen who was wiping down the cooler in the kitchen. She picked up exactly where they'd left off. Women were strange like that.

"A bear on the property! Becka was almost killed! It wasn't like we were in the dining room eating breakfast and a bear strolled across the back lawn! It came after her and in the process killed a dog! It could've been Becka!"

"I know, it was bad. But it was an isolated incident. I believe this is one of those times when you have to get back up on the horse."

Steve stared at his wife in disbelief.

Maureen felt his eyes burning through her shirt and stopped tidying up to look him in the face. "You know what I mean. If we take them home, they will be afraid of this place. You don't want that to happen, do you?"

Steve knew Maureen brought up a valid point. What Maureen didn't know, was there was a killer prowling these woods, not a bear. And if Steve told her the truth, it would make her never feel safe here again either.

Steve bit his tongue. It's how he rose through the ranks in the police department and kissed ass to some of the dumbest sergeants he ever worked with. And it was no different with his wife. "You're right, honey." He kissed her on the forehead and headed for the kitchen.

He was reaching for a can of soda when he heard his wife call his name. "Yeah?"

"Did I see Jesse outside a little while ago? What did he want?"

"Uh, nothing. He just came by to say hello. He had to get back to work, though. He said Tom took the morning off. One of his friends died last night."

Maureen walked into the kitchen. "That's awful. How?"

"Listen, Mo. We just talked about this. So don't get all exited. He was out late at night---alone. He was attacked by a bear."

Maureen's hands came up by her mouth. "Oh my god! Do you think? Do you think it was the same bear?"

Steve rested his soda on top of the stove and grabbed Maureen's shoulder's. "It doesn't matter, 'cause I have my gun. And nobody is leaving my sight. You understand? Nobody!"

"Oh yeah, your gun came in real handy the other night," shrieked Maureen.

"You're damn right it did! If I hadn't shot my gun off, the bear wouldn't have run back into the woods!"

"I thought Jesse shot his gun," questioned Maureen.

"No, baby. Your knight and shining armor did not save the night that time. It was *me*." Steve jabbed his thumb against his chest.

"Oh, I see! So you're still mad about that! Well let me remind you that it was fifteen years ago and we were drunk. Not to mention you and I weren't even married! And if you had been behind me on that hike, instead of pissing into the wind, maybe you would have caught me."

"I bet you didn't even fall. You were flirting with him the whole afternoon! 'Jesse, what kind of work-out do you do? Jesse, I can wash my bikini on your stomach!'"

"I never said that!" shouted Maureen.

"What, you think I didn't hear you? I dropped back on the trail because I thought you wanted to be with him. We must have hiked for two miles before you noticed I hadn't been involved in the conversation. I saw you and yeah, I was pissing into the wind. That's why Jesse stopped walking. He saw me go off the trail. Did you even notice I left?"

"I turned around to look for you and I lost my footing. Jesse grabbed me and broke my fall. Maybe I was gracious to him for saving my life! Did you ever think of that?"

"So what you're telling me is, and correct me if I'm wrong, that when you lost your footing and Jesse grabbed you, you felt so gracious five hours later when we were setting up tent that you walked over to him while I was fetching water and jabbed your tongue down his throat. Now that is gratitude! Shit, I've been a cop for fifteen years, saved numerous lives, put murderers and rapists behind bars and nobody ever came up to me and so graciously stuck their tongue down my throat for all my troubles!"

"I can see the logic in this conversation left about five minutes ago. I'm going upstairs and painting my toenails." Maureen stormed out of the dining room and headed for the stairs.

As a last retort, Steve yelled to his wife, "Jesse didn't even have a gun the other night!"

"Mom. Me and Beck are going to ride the double bike into town to get some pizza," shouted Devin as Maureen walked passed him.

"No you're not."

"Why?" asked Devin.

Maureen ignored him and continued up the steps, slamming the stairway door between them.

"You heard her," Becka teased, "she's painting her toenails. You know what that means."

Beck went into the back dining room and up to her father, who had traded in the soda for a Budweiser. "Mom's painting her toenails. What'd you do now?"

Steve looked at Becka, who was a spitting image of Maureen, just a few inches shorter. "Your mom's just in one of her moods. Let's give her some alone time. I think it's a good idea that you and Devin go into town. Go to Jesse's and see if Austin wants to go with you."

"Dad! He's so annoying! Do we have to?"

"Yes. Now get out of here before I change my mind."

Beck and Devin went into the garage and filled the double bike's tires with air. Devin hopped in the front seat, while Becka took the rear. They pedaled across the field and into Jesse's yard. Devin spun the front tire on the gravel rocks and they both hit the brakes. They came to a full stop and Becka jumped off the bike first.

"You wait here," she told him. "I'll go get Austin."

"Great," sighed Devin. He got off the bike and turned it around to face the road when he saw something on the picnic table. He put the bike down and walked over to the table. He felt his heart flutter. There it was, lying there in broad daylight with the sun glimmering off the buckle: The red collar.

Devin looked up to see Becka walking down the shaded path that extended from Jesse's front steps. "Good news! He's shopping with Danielle."

"That is good news. You see that collar?"

"Yeah," said Becka. "It was Norma's."

"Really? Are you sure?"

"Yes. That's what she was wearing. Sad, isn't it?"

"More like scary. That Indian, Loudbear, he told me to close my eyes and picture something when we first got here. I don't know why, but I pictured a red collar." Devin pointed to Norma's collar. "That red collar."

"That is weird. But maybe someone was walking a dog at the flea market with the same collar and that's why you saw it." Spike came running across the yard with a dirty, beat-up old shoe in his mouth.

"No. It was that collar. And it was lying on this picnic table."

"So maybe you're a psychic!" Becka's words dripped with sarcasm.

"Whatever Beck. I thought you'd see the connection. When we get into town, I want to see Loudbear."

"Well I don't. That guy is creepy. Follow me back to the Farm. I'm going to bring Spike back. Come on girl!" Beck ran back to the farm and Spike beat her to the front door, laying the nasty shoe on the doormat. Beck picked it up and tossed it in the house, quickly shutting the screen door after Spike ran in.

"Ahhhhh!" Devin had crashed the bike into the well in the front yard. Beck knew what had happened without looking. "Oh yeah, only the brakes in the back are working!" He got up and brushed the dirt and leaves off his shorts. "Thanks for letting me know, Beck." Devin gave the bike a push with his feet. "Ready, go!" They began pedaling the seven miles down Schroon River Road and into town. "Why don't you like the Indian again?"

"I don't know. That guy gives me the creeps. Like he knows something."

"I got that same feeling, and that is why I need to talk to him," said Devin.

"Fine, but I don't want to be near that guy. He scares me."

"Beck, you hardly met him. He's not a creep, he's just a bit different than most people we know."

Steve got into his car and kept a loose tail on the kids as they pedaled down the only road leading to Main Street. As he passed the lumber yard, he saw Jesse's truck parked by the gate and suddenly felt rage run through his body. So Jesse made-out with Maureen almost two decades ago. That wasn't it. Deep down, Steve was always a little jealous of Jesse's care- free lifestyle. Jesse treated girls like used gym socks, so he certainly didn't think it was a big deal to make out with your best friend's girl. But it was. It was to people who had scruples. Jesse's tough guy ways always attracted women. At forty, his body looked the same as it did at twenty. Maybe even bigger now, more muscular. Even though Steve had a gun and a badge, he always felt like less of a man around Jesse. The lumber yard was miles behind when Steve finally made up his mind. He was not leaving Warrensburg until he caught the bastard that came after his daughter. He had a hard time believing it was an animal in the woods that night, stalking his daughter like prey. Every instinct told him it was a deranged man, possibly even a serial killer after hearing the story of Bob Murphy. Steve told himself that his detective instincts would kick in and he would catch this guy, if he was still in the area, and prove to Maureen that he was more of a man than she'd ever thought. If she only knew of all the women in Manhattan hitting on him, begging to be cuffed and frisked. City women have blue fever. "And I never even thought twice about it", he thought to himself.

The twins turned the corner onto Main Street and passed by Stewart's convenience store and Potter's Diner.

"Do you want to do a scavenger hunt when we get back?" asked Devin.

"O.K. We can stop at the five and dime and pick up some materials," replied Beck. "Don't look now, but I think Dad is following us again. I saw him ducking behind the car when you crashed into the well."

Devin laughed. "I didn't know the brakes didn't work!"

"I can't believe Dad still follows us into town. We're thirteen now," complained Becka.

Devin did not agree with Becka on this subject, but to entertain her he responded, "I'm practically a man."

"Let's ditch him," said Becka. They parked their bike next to a pillar in the small strip mall outside the dollar store.

Ever since entering Junior High School, Becka developed an overwhelming longing for her sense of autonomy. She now walked to school, instead of taking the bus, and sometimes she would wake up early and go jogging before anyone in the house stirred. She never told anyone she was leaving, but she just left. Late at night she would even sneak out of the house and walk to Erica's and throw rocks at her window to wake her. Erica, however, was not impressed, and would secretly inform Devin of Becka's whereabouts. They lived in a decent enough neighborhood, but recently the riff-raff from neighboring towns were coming in to spread their wanna-be-gansta attitudes and cause trouble. Devin and Erica both worried about this, but agreed it was just a rebellious phase that Becka was going through, and decided it was best to ignore it.

Devin on the other hand, was just the opposite. Junior High to him meant more homework, stricter teachers, more chores at home, and witnessing kids who used to be innocent turn into jerks practically overnight. He didn't like it, and wished he could go back to elementary school. He didn't grow much physically over the last few summers either. He was now the smallest one on his soccer team, and his playing time could practically be measured in seconds. He also felt Becka slowly slipping away from him. Until recently, the two were practically sewn together at the hip. When their parents would announce "lights out," Becka used to turn off the lights in her room and run down the hall to Devin's room to play board games by candlelight. Now when it was lights out, Devin would run to Becka's room only to find the door locked. To make matters worse, boys in school were now looking at Beck in a whole new light. "Since when is it alright to make a comment about my sister? These idiots would never have said anything a year ago! What makes them think they can say it now," he wondered.

While in the store, Devin peeked through the window and saw Steve's car in the parking lot. He and Becka walked across the street to Marco Polo's, a little pizzeria next to an old bookstore, and had lunch. The pizza place had a back entrance, out of which the twins snuck before heading towards the church to find the Indian. The locals had daily yard sales on the church property in the summer, and it wouldn't be hard to locate Loudbear.

While the kids were eating pizza, Steve guessed it was a better time than any to buy cold-cuts from the butcher, who was located across the street from where the twins were. As he was waiting for his order, he glanced around the store at the never-ending rack of potato chips. "Things sure have changed," he thought. You used to have the choice of plain or barbeque. Now, there's salt and vinegar, pickle, ketchup and sour cream and cheddar flavored chips. Maybe because he wasn't a junk food fan he hadn't noticed it before.

"Steve? Steve Bettis?"

Steve turned around to see a middle-aged man he did not recognize calling his name. Instinctively, he cupped his gun. "Do we know each other," he asked.

"F.D.N.Y. Gerard Higgins. Engine 409. I saw your picture in *The New York Times* last week."

"Oh, yeah? Thanks." Steve reached out and shook his hand.

"That was some job you did nailing those Russians," announced the fireman, a little more loudly than Steve would have preferred.

Cops and firemen worked hand in hand during most events in Manhattan, and every time one of them exceeded at their profession and made the headlines, they were treated like celebrities; their heroic acts were the talk of the station houses until something else exciting happened. Recently, Steve was working on a case where the body of a Russian teenage girl was found floating along the Hudson River. After following many dead leads, the unlikely arrest of an infamous drug-dealer from Coney Island took the case in another direction. Although his captain told him to move on, that the Russian body in the river was no longer a priority, Steve's intense interrogation and an exchange for a plea bargain led him to a suspicious customer with connections to the Russian Mafia. During an unauthorized surveillance, the thug led Steve to an underground amateur pornography studio where young Russian women were told that sex was the way into American modeling. Most of the women complied, but the others found themselves drifting along the cruel currents of the Atlantic with a cinderblock attached to their ankles. Steve's persistence paid off and his captain was now re-opening closed cases of missing illegal Russian immigrants, the media putting Steve back in the limelight. "Yeah, well it's all part of the job. You know how it is." Steve felt embarrassed and did not like the attention of the locals in the store, who were now staring at him.

"Are you vacationing in Lake George?" Steve asked the fireman to change the subject. Back from his rookie days doing surveillances on drug dealers and illegal arms sales, he knew the first rule on a stake out was not to loose focus. And he *was* on a surveillance, observing his kids' actions. This guy was distracting him. "Politely say goodbye," he told himself.

"No, I'm an electrician on my days off, and I'm doing a job up here. Nice place though. Me and my boss partied in Lake George last night. A little pricey, but we had a blast."

Steve's order was up. "Alright, it was nice to meet you." Steve took his cold cuts and walked over to the register where a buxom blonde with perfect teeth rang up his tab. As Steve reached into his wallet and sifted through his larger bills to find a ten, he found himself wondering if Jesse had slept with the check-out girl. The ringing of the cash register broke his concentration and he quickly dismissed the thought and hurried out of the butcher's shop, grabbing a free copy of the *Warrensburg Herald* on the way out. He was relieved to see the double bike still parked outside the Five and Dime. Sitting in his car, he read the article about the accident on the bridge, every aspect of which confirmed his instincts: a psychopath on the loose. What stuck out in his mind though was the notion that a satanic cult may have been behind the gruesome killing. It just didn't add up that such a cult could exist without any suspected members. Then again, Steve reminded himself that he was out of his jurisdiction, and maybe cults were a serious problem up here. He saw how desperately these hicks wanted to believe that Bigfoot existed in their hometown, even if he was killing people. Pretty sad, he thought, that his best friend Jesse was one of those pathetic believers.

Devin and Becka crossed over Main Street towards the church. They didn't see Steve's car in the parking lot of the shopping center, but only because they didn't have time for a thorough search. "You know Beck, Dad's just doing this because of what happened the other night."

"Well I got over it. And so should he. Listen, I think I'm going to run over to the bait shop and get us some stuff for fishing. Want to go fishing tomorrow?"

"Yeah, I'll go fishing. But just come with me. I'll only be a minute." Devin did not like the idea of them splitting up.

"No way," said Becka. "I told you, that Indian friend of yours scares me. I'll be like ten minutes. If I'm not back by then, you *and* Dad can come look for me."

"Fine, Beck. But you've got *ten* minutes. Not eleven, and not thirteen," said Devin mocking his mother. Becka laughed and took off as Devin walked up the hill towards the back of the church and was relieved to see Loudbear resting on a bench playing the flute. At least it sounded like a flute.

"Loudbear. I need to talk to you."

The sight of Devin brought a genuine smile to Loudbear's face. "Hello, again. Good to see you."

Devin was unaware that he was even the slightest bit angry with Loudbear until he heard his own tone. Loudbear stood up and offered his benched seat to Devin. "Here, please take a seat." Loudbear sat down in a folding chair adjacent to the bench, and positioned his palms on his knees, leaning forward to embrace each word the child had to say, as he sensed trouble.

"Relax. Tell me what troubles you."

"You troubled me the other day. Remember when you told me to close my eyes and picture something?"

"Yes, I remember."

"Why did you tell me to do that? What did you think was going to happen?"

"Devin, I just sensed that you had a psychic power and taught you how to use it. It can be used to your advantage, you know. It can make you more aware of your surroundings."

"Are you a psychic? Can you see events in the future?"

"Everybody sees what may come to pass every day. But only a true psychic can make sense of these visions, perceive the meaning behind them. It is a little scary, I know. And I could have explained myself better, but we were interrupted by your sister, Becka, right?"

"Yeah. How come you can't predict the lottery?"

"You are not the first one to ask me that. Lottery is a drawing. There is nothing natural about numbers. They have no significance in life. If you see a cat under a table across the yard, and for whatever reason this cat catches your eye, now that is a sign. If it is meaningful, something will come to you. The cat would trigger your powers. Are you following?"

"Sort of. Well, not really."

"If my memory serves me correct, you saw a red collar when you shut your eyes. How did this red collar come into effect?"

"We were playing kick the can, a game in the backyard of the Farm. It was dark. I kicked the can into the woods and Becka ran after it. She was chased by some large animal and started to scream. My Dad and his friend ran into the woods to help her, and that man's dog was wearing a red collar!"

"My interpretation of that would be to warn your sister not to enter the woods alone at night again."

"A little too late for that. The dog is dead. Becka is fine. She got away. My dog Spike got hurt pretty bad, but the dog with the red collar is dead. What do you and your psychic powers have to say about that?" Devin's eyes were bulging and he was now trembling.

"I'm terribly sorry for the loss of the dog. But did you ever think that it may have happened for a reason? If the dog wasn't killed, maybe your sister would have been. And let me remind you, that was your psychic feeling, not mine." Loudbear leaned back in his chair and folded his legs.

Devin was beginning to realize that the Indian caused him no harm. "I'm sorry. This stuff just freaks me out. I don't think I can handle it."

"I think you're doing a fine job. I have a book for you. Not here, but at my house. I will give it to you. It explains how to use your powers and how they work. And most importantly, how to recognize them."

"I was just starting to forget about it. Then, when we left this morning, there it was, the red collar, sitting right there on my neighbor's picnic table. I thought I should talk to you."

"You mean the red collar never left your mind?" Loudbear looked across at Devin and met his eyes. Devin tried not to look away, but Loudbear's appearance suddenly changed and he felt like he was in some sort of a trance. Loudbear spoke in a low, monotonous voice. "You are in grave danger. I feel this incident involving the red collar is not over. You need to go back home. Not this farm you speak of, but home."

Devin could not handle this feeling without his brave sister, and stood up to go find her. His peripheral vision clouded with purple dots as he rose from the bench. "I have to go now." He nonchalantly crept away from the Indian, attempting to ignore the fact that his own body temperature was rising. Loudbear sensed Devin's feeling of vertigo and grabbed his arm, leading him back down onto the bench. As he sat down and tried not to black-out, Devin heard Becka's voice. His eyeballs barely managed to shift to the right when he saw Becka standing there, in the same shade of gray as he must have been in.

"Devin! Something's going on!" Becka was flushed and out of breath. Loudbear released Devin and took hold of Becka's shoulders, directing her towards the bench next to her brother. "You look like you need some water. Devin, under my table is a cooler with a bottle of water. Get it for your sister. And there is a rag in there, dab it with some ice and hand it to her!"

"Becka. I'm here. Nobody's going to hurt you in my presence. You look like you saw a ghost." Loudbear pushed her hair back and felt her forehead.

Becka tried to catch her breathe. "I, I, I, hold on." Becka held up her finger and took another large gulp of water. "Spike. She was chewing on a sneaker before we left the Farm today." Becka paused and caught her breath again. "It was Pat's husband's sneaker. I think he's dead!"

Devin looked at Becka in disbelief, wondering if he had passed out and was having a bad dream. "What the hell are you talking about?"

Loudbear interrupted. "Pat, from the Bait N' Tackle shop. Her husband Dale went fishing a few days ago, and never returned. Pat hung a sign on the door saying she's closed until they find her husband."

"Yeah, and there's a picture of him in the window. And the sneakers he's wearing in the picture match the one Spike had today! I *know* it's him. I bet you he's dead!"

Devin tried to say something when he heard a loud crackling sound, followed by the screams of other bargain hunters. Loudbear and Becka looked to see a large oak tree no more than twenty feet away from them split in half as people scattered to get out of the way. Loudbear's eyes did a quick search for Devin who had thrown himself into the fetal position on the ground covering his head. Loudbear reached down and pulled him up by his elbow, before leading the twins towards the rear of the church. Thunder struck, and lightening hit again as another tree on the property caught on fire. Glass shattered through the

166

church windows as the large oak tree crashed through the side of the building. Loudbear changed directions and led Becka and Devin to his white '79 Buick Skylark, shoving them into the passenger seat. He leaped over the hood of the car and jumped into the driver's seat, quickly taking them away from the fire.

Steve heard a rather loud *thud* and reached for his gun. He looked towards the bike and felt only slight relief to still see it there. In his peripheral vision he caught a flash of light coming from the direction of town and immediately started the engine. He drove up to the church and saw people running for safety. The tree took down a cable wire and set some live ones loose. An elderly lady in a typical flowery dress waddled down the hill towards Steve's car. Steve hopped out and opened the door, helping her into the back seat. "It's O.K. ma'am, I'm a police officer. Let's get you out of here." He drove up to Stewart's, where fire trucks were already making their way to the scene. "I'm Steve Bettis. Are you hurt?" he asked the old woman, as he made eye contact with her through the rear view mirror and turned into the parking lot.

"Madeline Totten. And I'm fine, thanks to you. Just a little frightened, but I'll be fine."

"Were you alone?"

"These days I'm always alone. I hope everyone's O.K., but that's the most excitement I've had in years. That's terrible to say, isn't it?" Madeline clenched her purse and looked out the window, ashamed of the ugly truth.

"I'm a New York City Detective. I think I can understand."

"Well, I won't take up any of your time. I'll just get out here."

"Nonsense. I'm taking you home. Where do you live?" There was no doubt in Steve's mind that this

167

woman had some history to share, but now wasn't the time or place for a lengthy conversation. "Mrs. Totten, I'll take you wherever you need to go, but I'm going to have to ask you to tag along while I find my kids who are at the shopping center."

"Alright. I see no harm in that. But let me get into the front seat. I'm not Miss Daisy, you know." He tried to conceal his nervousness by forcing a smile and got out of the car to open the door for Madeline. As she was slightly struggling to get up from the back seat, Steve looked away, knowing she felt embarrassed for acting her age.

He turned his head toward towards the street, as a white Buick crawled into his view and he saw his daughter in the front seat. "Becka! Becka!" He ran to the driver's seat and started to turn the car around as Madeline slammed the passenger door shut. "He's got my daughter! He's got my kid," he screamed as he punched his horn for the rubberneckers to move out of his way. The traffic was not moving out of the parking lot and the Buick just made its way past the only traffic light in town. It was heading east: an unfamiliar route to Steve. "Hold on!" he screamed.

Chapter 19

Marc was eating lunch in the kitchen when he saw a blur of brown pass by the living room window. Pulling into the driveway, he saw Kankro and Demitres making their way past his Firebird. "Shit!" He wasn't sure if they had seen him through the screen door, so he dropped onto all fours and crawled to his bedroom, locking the door behind him. "Like a fuckin' fire drill."

Knock Knock Knock. Knock Knock Knock. "Your car is here Marc. The front door is open. Your parents' cars are not here. We know you're in there. Now open the fucking door and let us in," said Demitres in his usual manner.

Marc picked up his cordless phone and dialed the number to the lumber yard. "Dad. Dumb and Dumber are here. They're knocking at the door. What should I do?"

"Pretend your sleeping. I'm on my way home. I'll handle them." It took no more than two minutes for Tom to get home. "Officers. What can I do for you?" He asked as he got out of his car.

"This doesn't concern you, Tom. We just want to have a word with Marc," said Kankro in his passive-aggressive politeness.

"Do come in and make yourselves comfortable. Would you like a cup of coffee, a soda?" said Tom. "Marc is probably still sleeping. I'll wake him up for ya. Have a seat." Tom directed them towards the living room. Kankro and Demitres exchanged looks, but decided to sit down anyway. Marc came out of his bedroom wearing sweatpants and a white tank top, with Tom in tow.

"Marc. We want you to know that we just spoke to Marie," said Kankro.

"That's great! So she's in the clear?" Marc hadn't slept that well during the night, his thoughts drifting to Marie every time he closed his eyes.

Demitres looked at his partner and chuckled. "Funny that you used that term, 'in the clear'. 'Cause you're not. She confirmed that you were drinking and driving that night. What do you have to say for yourself?"

Tom came strolling in from the kitchen with a tray of shot glasses and a bottle of vodka. "Sounds like you got a tip of the story from someone with head trauma. Let me ask you, did you give my son a breathalyzer at the hospital? As I recall, you didn't. I can tell you that I saw Mr. Peterson drinking a beer at the bar, and two hours later he was food shopping. Are you going to run down there and arrest Mr. Peterson? No. You know why? 'Cause you can't. Now what is it you really want?"

"Demitres was thinking of putting an extension on his house. Sure could use some lumber for that project, couldn't you?" said a smug Officer Kankro to his partner.

Demitres scratched his head. "Come to think of it, I could use a little help with supplies." He reached out his hand and grabbed a shot of vodka, then handed the other one to Kankro. Tom took a shot himself and they all smiled, each for different reasons.

"Bob Gargan was killed last night. You have any leads on that?" asked Tom.

"Yes. We believe that *Lucifer's Seeds,* a satanic cult, is responsible for the murder," replied Kankro.

Other than the mention of it in the paper this morning, this was news to Tom. "Who are they?"

"For one, Bob called us in just a week ago to make a report that some kids were stealing sodas from his truck. We didn't think anything of it at the time, but it is our job, so we checked it out. The locks were pried open, and a high school ring from Carmel, New York was found not far from the truck. Turns out a recent graduate from Carmel had been reported missing. When we spoke with detectives on the Carmel end, we learned that they had visited the girl's home and found numerous e-mail correspondence with a member of *Lucifer's Seed* on her computer. The girl, Tara, was interested in a boy from the group. We found her car a few days ago behind McDonalds. Nothing left in it, and the doors were unlocked. We called in the hounds and traced her scent through the woods behind the restaurant, about two miles down and leading to the hook not far from Bob's house. We crossed the river and the dogs lost the scent. We then called in the divers and they found the body. Well, most of it. Strange thing was, the organs were missing. Could have been fish, but not likely. The medical examiner says they appeared to ripped out, with what device he couldn't tell 'cause the body had been sitting in the river, and the fish got to the real evidence. We had our computer geek do some investigating and he discovered these satanic cults use the organs for some kind of ritual. The medical examiner believes Bob's organs were taken the same way as the missing girl's. So, I believe we have a match. You see, your tax dollars at work," explained Kankro. "With Bob's body, we'll be able to come up with more answers, since it hasn't been tampered with."

"And many farm animals in the area have been mutilated, again, their organs missing," added Demitres.

Tom glanced over at his son, not knowing if he should mention his animals. Maybe these cops were actually on to something. Maybe these disturbed kids made up some kind of costume like a Bigfoot to throw people off. It was all starting to make sense now. "Do you have these freaks in custody?"

"Not exactly. It's not like the movies, Tom. These weirdoes look just like you and me. They blend in. They don't wear black and walk around looking like Marilyn Manson. If they did, shit, our jobs would be real easy," said Demitres.

Marc had been standing in the kitchen not saying a word, but thought this was a good time to intervene.

These dirt bags were showing some sign of humanity. He walked into the living room. "You said you have some exchanged e-mails, right?" The cops nodded. "Can't your geek run a trace back to where the computer sending the e-mails was?"

"He did. All exchanges were made right from our very own computers in the Warrensburg library," said Kankro.

"There is a sign in sheet, and you have to leave your I.D. at the desk to use the computers. Did you guys check that out?"

"You have some brains kid. Maybe you are studying down their in West Virginia and not just getting drunk and having sex with underage girls with perky tits. But these miscreants are a little smarter than you. They use fake I.D.'s. I'm sure you're familiar with them. I mean, how would you purchase liquor if you didn't have the proper I.D.?"

"I didn't buy the liquor. Spencer had it. I didn't ask him where he got it."

"Right. You just helped him drink it," said Demitres.

"Yes. I did have a drink. But I wasn't drunk. Hell, I wasn't even buzzed."

Tom interjected. "Let's get back to the *Seeds,* if you don't mind. Bob didn't have any family, and I'm handling the funeral. When are your guys going to be done with the body, so I can put him to rest."

"We're done. We've concluded that it was the *Seeds,* and we're doing all we can to catch these guys. But Marc, if you feel you could help out in any way, you're welcome to join the investigation. I mean, you were there last night. What exactly did you see?" asked Kankro.

"I saw Bob. But it was dark, real dark. I wasn't even sure that it was Bob. I just saw a man at the other end of the bridge. He was being chased by something. I couldn't see behind him. Like I said, it was real dark out. The only light I had was from the quad. I saw a shadow behind him, but it looked too big to be a person. I'm sorry I can't be of much help, but that's all I saw."

"Then why did you bail? You left your best friend laying limp on a bridge with someone, or something coming straight for him! You're a real pal," said Kankro.

"I know enough not to move someone with a back injury. He said he couldn't feel anything. Yeah, I left. But I got him help. I called you guys, didn't I? And besides, it didn't come after Spencer. Why don't you ask Spencer what he saw?"

"That fool was so drunk he says he saw Bigfoot. Then he reported that to the paper. So let me ask you, Marc. Did you see Bigfoot?"

Marc looked at his father and caught the slightest shake of his head. "No. I didn't see Bigfoot."

"Guys, I think there is something I should tell you," said Tom. "My barn animals were attacked also. Happened Friday night. I found them Saturday morning."

"Why didn't you report it," demanded Demitres.

"Let's be serious. You guys aren't exactly legit cops. You came over here today to blackmail me for some of my lumber. Which you're not getting by the way," he added while looking at Demitres. "You guys blew this one. If you had done your job that night at the hospital, instead of focusing on Danielle's bust, maybe you'd have something on my son. But you don't. And you may have a clue or two on Bob's murder, but you still don't have a suspect in custody. So, I think you have a long day ahead of you, and we don't want to take up anymore of your valuable time. My barn animals are dead. Three pigs, three roosters, and three sheep. You can add them to your pile of evidence. And Jesse's dog. He's at my lumber yard if you want to talk to him about it."

Realizing they weren't going to get any fringe benefits from this case, they decided to leave. Tom walked them to the door and watched them pull out of his driveway. Turning to his son, he asked, "Did we get it?"

"Yep." Marc retrieved the nanny cam from the mantel and rewound the tape, starting it from the beginning.

Chapter 20

The rain was coming down hard and the loud claps of thunder made Devin nervous as he sat with his head tucked between his legs in Loudbear's back seat. Loudbear drove the kids through town and turned down a slim, winding road that lead to what appeared to be nothing but shacks tucked in the brush off to the side of the road. "Where are we going?" asked Becka. The shacks were not much more than the ones the moffits built up the road from the Farm, only these ones had windows.

"I'm taking you guys to my house and out of this stormy weather. Unless you want me to take you back to your house?"

"Where do you live?" asked Devin as he lifted his head up to see out the window. "Just up the road. You might not have known this but Schroon River runs far south and eventually feeds the Hudson River. Well, I live on the bank of the Hudson."

"I did know that," bragged Devin. "We just never drove through this part of town with our parents. I've never seen it lightening like this before. And the thunder is crazy loud!"

"It's just a typical summer storm, caused by the heat. But yes, they can be very dangerous this time of year. No time to be riding your bike in a storm like this. Don't you get summer storms on Long Island?"

"Not like this!" Devin eased up a bit, acknowledging that it was a temporary storm. "Thank you for the ride. I'm curious to see your house."

"It *is* a house. Built many years ago. Not a tee-pee."

Becka laughed, "Awe shucks! I've never been in a real tee-pee."

"I do have a real outhouse, though. Have you ever been in one of those?"

"Why do you have a house without a toilet," asked Becka.

"Like I said, it is a very old house. My ancestors built it over a hundred years ago, when they didn't have the plumbing available for inside. I'm used to it. Here it is." Loudbear pulled into a long path that was hidden from the rest of the road. If you didn't know it was there, you'd be sure to miss it. The path was about a half mile long, covered in pine needles and rocks and shadowed by hundreds of coniferous trees. It led upwards to a small cabin on top of a hill. Outside the house were perfectly carved wooden statues of bears, moose and geese. The house itself looked like it had been hand carved, then dowsed with lacquer for extra shine. A few yards away there was a rustic little outhouse with a large round slate walkway leading to it.

"This house is beautiful. Definitely does not look a hundred years old! Our house, the Farm, now *that* looks a hundred years old!" Becka was amazed at the sheer beauty of this house. "My mother would die for something like this! She's always been interested in exterior designs and architectural structures from other centuries."

"You can bring your mother here anytime," welcomed Loudbear, surprising himself with his unusual hospitality towards white people.

The path of trees shielded the driveway from the downpour. Devin and Becka hopped out of the car and took a few steps before suddenly stopping in their tracks. "Wolves!" they screamed simultaneously and jumped back into the car. Seven canines came running towards them. "Halt," said Loudbear as he held up his hand. All seven dogs stopped in unison, some of them sat down while the rest remained standing. Loudbear tapped on the car window. "They're not wolves. They're my dogs, and they won't bite you. They just want to say hello."

"Holy shit Dev! This guy has wolves as pets."

Devin carefully studied the body language of the dogs from behind the safety of the car, noting seven tails wagging and that none of them were showing teeth. "I know. But they seem nice. I'm getting out." Devin climbed over Becka and got out of the car. "Hi pups," he said, holding out his hand and trying not to sound nervous. The largest one walked over to him.

"His name is Okeano," said Loudbear. Okeano was a male, sporting a thick coat of black, white, and grey, with big, blue, intimidating eyes, standing twenty nine inches at the withers and weighing one hundred and twenty pounds. "Okeano means 'bringer of death', or 'killer whale' in English." Devin let the wolf sniff him and then patted his head, as Becka watched from the car. Okeano looked back at the other wolves who then joined him in meeting this new person. "He is the alpha male of the group. They are not wolves. They are Native American Indian Dogs, or NAIDs."

"But they look just like wolves." Devin was disappointed in himself for lacking the knowledge of this particular dog breed. He made a mental note to research them when he got back to Long Island.

"I know. But they're not. They are descendants of wolves, yes. Great companion dogs who lived with the Native Americans as family members. They are great with children, and it is said that they used to baby-sit the kids when the parents were hunting and gathering. Don't let their gentleness fool you, though. If betrayed or left hungry these dogs can track and kill a bear in less than ten minutes. Let's go inside now," said Loudbear.

Becka slowly got out of the car. One of the smaller dogs jumped on her, licking her face while still in the air. Becka petted the dog and kept walking. Loudbear gave them a tour of the house, which wasn't big, but still impressive with its mostly hand-made furniture and display of gadgets scattered throughout. Some of the dogs came inside with them, and one of them even hopped onto the stone mantle and perched herself there like a statue. "I wish I had my camera," said Becka.

Loudbear smiled at the girl. It had been a long time since he had company. "That is Hammerhead. She likes to sit up there. Here is my camera. You can keep the roll of film when you're done, just bring the camera back before you return back to Long Island."

"Thanks!"

"See Becka, I told you he's not a creep." Becka was embarrassed knowing full well that Loudbear heard Devin's comment. Loudbear led them into an adjoining room in the house.

"Devin, here is my library. You can have the psychic book I told you about. But first, you have to find it."

Devin looked around the room at what had to have been over two thousand books, neatly tucked into built-in shelves that covered all four walls. He could hardly believe that they were all in alphabetical order, and found the "P" section on the north wall. He climbed a small wooden ladder up to the seventh shelf. "Psychic minds? Is this the one?"

"Yes. You're very good with your letters. I think you'll like that one." Devin sat down in a cushy chair in the corner of the room and began flipping through the pages. "Do you have a phone," he asked.

"No," replied Loudbear. He walked up to Devin and lit a large candle on the adjacent end table. "No electricity." Devin smiled and kept reading.

Loudbear then walked over to Becka and handed her a candle. "That is an old map of Warrensburg, before it was called Warrensburg." Becka had opened a treasure chest in the middle of the room and found various maps in that tinted orange color which one assumes had once been

178

white. Loudbear took it from her hands and laid it out on a coffee table. "This is the church." He pointed to the map, drawing an invisible line with his finger. "Here is my house. This is where Stewart's is now. This is the elementary school, which back then was just a forest. And this path is Schroon River Road, or Horicon Avenue."

Loudbear brought a kerosene lantern to the coffee table, adjusting it so that the flame was at its brightest.

"This is so cool," said Becka. "Devin, you have to see this." Devin walked over to Becka and knelt down in front of the coffee table next to Becka and Loudbear, who were also on their knees. Becka traced her finger up Schroon River Road, and recognized the pond on the left. "This is now the Lumber Yard," said Loudbear, pointing to the other side of the road on the map.

"This curve, right here. This is near the Farm." She ran her finger up and down the area. "I guess there was no road here."

"That's not the Farm," said Devin pushing himself towards the center of the map. "Loudbear, where is Pucker Street," he asked.

Loudbear looked at the map. "Pucker Street?" He looked confused and took a closer look at the map. He ran his finger up Schroon River, following it around a bend. "I can't say I ever heard of that street. Some of the roads up in that area are somewhat new. Either way, your street was not a street in those days."

"Rock Avenue," interjected Becka. "It used to be called Rock Avenue."

"Oh yes. I do know that street. There is a lot of unspoken Mohican history surrounding that area. Moffits up that way, too." Loudbear thought for a moment about the real events that took place during the war. The events the history books don't mention: ones that shine upon the shear brilliance and spirituality of the Native Americans. How the Indians lost the battle, but won the war. Did they win, he wondered? Were they winning now? Were the whites finally going to pay for what they did? The kids seemed to know about the moffits. Loudbear thought most people forgot about them. Did anyone really know who the moffits were exactly? Did they know that they were descendants of the white men who tried to eradicate the Indians? That they were the prisoners whom the Indians had captured? Did they know that the moffits were the white man's own people whom they willingly left behind to avoid being slaughtered by Chief Ta Ta's men?

"We know all about the moffits. But they're further up the road. We're down here, close to Schroon River Road," lectured Devin. The moffits were a group of people who had not conformed to civilization. They didn't work or pay taxes, but by right owned a small portion of land just north of Pucker Street. Some believed them to be Indians, but upon closer inspection, their brown skin was actually white, covered in layers of dirt. People believed they were into incest, but nobody got close enough to study them. It was assumed that they didn't bother anyone so long as they were left alone. Devin pointed to another part of the map. "If this were a road, this is where the Farm would be."

Becka looked at where Devin was pointing, "Oh yeah." Loudbear looked at the map, afraid of the property they were referring to, if indeed they were correct. Loudbear thought it was better not to mention the curse, although his intuition was already confirming his worst fears. He made a mental note to check out this Pucker Street.

"Why is there a big ring where the Farm is? This map is very confusing. Maybe it's upside down," said Becka. Hammerhead snarled from the mantle and showed her teeth to Mako, who was passing by.

"Those two are always at it," said Loudbear, looking into the other room at the dogs. "Looks like the storm passed. You two better come with me now and I'll bring you back to town." Loudbear looked down at Becka. "I'm sorry, but the maps stay here. However, I do have something for you." Becka followed Loudbear into a separate room. To her astonishment, she saw a small workshop with tons of beads and jewels. Loudbear picked up a bear claw necklace. "Please, I'd like you to wear this. It will give you the strength you're going to need to combat any demons. I feel you and your brother are in grave danger. I've told your brother this."

"That is real sweet of you, but I don't even eat dead animals, yet alone wear them around my neck."

"I wish you'd reconsider. If I lend you a book I have on human and animal connections, perhaps you'll change your mind." He led her back into the library and quickly found the book he was looking for. "Devin, you can borrow any book you'd like, but bring it back to me before you leave town." Devin grabbed a few books and they got into the car.

The brief summer storm had passed, and Becka again took the front seat, while Devin made himself comfortable in the back. Loudbear put the car in reverse, and was about to back out of the driveway when Becka stopped him.

"Wait! I must take a picture of your house for my mom!" Becka yanked the old door handle and jumped out of the car, snapping pictures of the old log cabin. "When I get this film developed I'm going to paint a canvas of your house. It'll be my gift to you," she offered as she got back into the car.

"Becka's the best artist I know," bragged Devin from the back seat.

Loudbear smiled towards Becka, then put the car in reverse.

"Loudbear, what do mean that we are in danger? Do you think whoever killed Pat's husband is still out there?"

"I do. And I believe you are correct in thinking Pat's husband is dead."

"Do you think the killer was after me in the woods?"

"I believe you got lucky that night, Becka." He looked at her out of the corner of his eyes. "Real lucky. And that is why I think you should wear my necklace. People are only lucky once."

Becka pulled the necklace out of her pocket, thumbing the smooth bones of some unfortunate animals.

Steve was waiting anxiously by the double bike. From the description he gave to Madeline, she assured him his kids were in good hands. But unfortunately, she did not know where Loudbear lived. Madeline offered to stay with Steve until the kids got back, but he wanted to be alone and dropped her off at her house. Normally he would have enjoyed some friendly small-talk, but at present his mind was racing too fast to listen to Madeline's soft voice. "Think positive," he told himself. But negative thoughts crept into his mind as he recalled his conversation with his son the previous evening. Devin mentioned that he met a Native American. This man tried to befriend him by giving him gifts. Now he has my kids! Devin and Becka are together. Aren't they? He hadn't seen Devin in the car, only Becka. The kids would not split up. Would they? Maybe this Furbear character is a decent guy. Madeline said from my description he was with Furbear, and he's a good guy. But who knows what he's into behind closed doors. It's not like pedophiles announce it to the world! He knew he had to get out of cop mode and think like a rational man. Paranoia had been a side effect of the job. Maureen and Jesse had been years ago, and it never went further than a kiss. And yet, he still harped on it. He still harped on many things. He decided he would give it five more minutes then go to the cops with what information he had. 'Could this Indian be the serial killer?'

"The bike's still there," said Devin. "And so is Dad," said Becka. Loudbear turned into the parking lot and drove up to the bike. Loudbear closed his eyes tightly. He kept a tight grip on the steering wheel and began to breathe heavily. Devin's head started to ache and Becka felt the discomfort in the car, asking them if they were alright. Loudbear did not answer her. A disturbing image was racing through his mind. Steve ran up to the car and pulled open Loudbear's door. "Dad, what are you doing?" Becka yelled as she climbed out of the passenger door. Loudbear lost his premonition and suddenly opened his eyes to see Steve waving a fist in front of his face.

"What are you doing with my kids! Devin and Beck, get out of the car now!"

"Dad, he got us out of the storm, relax. Sorry, Loudbear, my Dad's a little paranoid," explained Devin, losing touch with his premonition also.

"I understand," said Loudbear as he stepped out of the car. He reached out his hand to Steve, "I am Loudbear. You have good kids. They tried to call, but I don't have a phone. I'm sorry if I worried you. Storms up here can get real bad, and I didn't want to leave them at the church. The big oak had fallen down, barely missing them."

Steve looked at the kids and saw there was nothing wrong with them. "I'm sorry. I've had a crazy week. Steve Bettis." Steve took Loudbear's hand and shook it genuinely.

"I know," said Loudbear. "Devin told me all about what happened in the woods."

"We're not used to running into large wildlife on Long Island. This has definitely heightened my worries some bit."

"Dad," said Becka. "Loudbear has dogs that look like wolves."

"Oh yeah," said Steve still pumped with adrenaline but trying to conceal it. "That's great. What are they, Huskies?" he asked Loudbear.

"No. They're NAIDs. Your kids can explain it. It's been nice meeting you. And Devin, don't forget my books. I'll be at the church all week. You and your father should come say goodbye before you leave for home. Becka, when you develop that film, make sure you put Hammerhead in a nice frame. She's a real beauty!"

"I will." They waved and Loudbear drove off.

When Loudbear was no longer in sight, Steve grabbed Devin and Becka and smacked their heads together. "Ooouuchh! What was that for?" asked Devin as he rubbed his head.

"Cause you two idiots almost got yourselves killed again today! How many times have I told you never to get in cars with strangers? How many times? And getting in a car with a guy who doesn't even have a last name! 'Furbear.' You two idiots got in a car with a guy like that!"

Becka giggled. "Loudbear Dad. Loudbear."

"What?" Steve asked.

"You said Furbear. It's Loudbear."

"Get in the car!"

Devin threw the double bike in the trunk and got into the back seat. "Is this because he's Indian? Are you prejudiced Dad?"

"I don't care if he's black, white, yellow or orange! You don't get in the car with people you don't know!"

"Red. You didn't mention red," said Becka.

"Becka! Another word from you and I swear I'll slap you so hard you won't see daylight for a week!"

"Watch out Beck. Thems is fightin' words," laughed Devin from the back seat.

184

"That's it! We're going home! You've done it this time. You've really done it this time! Do you know that right before you left on your bike I was arguing with your mother about going home? And now this! When we get to the Farm you better pack, 'cause we're leaving tonight!" Becka did know about the argument. In the last two years she had perfected the art of eavesdropping. She also now knew it wasn't a bear in the woods. She couldn't pinpoint it, but sitting in the car with Devin and Loudbear, she had picked up on another conversation, although this one was without words. It was full of images. She looked in the back seat at Devin who was rubbing his temples with his eyes closed, and thought she smelt the blue flowers she found in the field.

Chapter 21

"I have to go to Bob's trailer," announced Tom. "I haven't been there since Bob was killed. If he was the target, the answer is in the trailer. But I can't see how anyone would want to hurt Bob. The break in was just kids trying to steal his sodas."

"I'm with you, Dad." Marc followed his father out the door and into the pick-up truck. The thunderstorm didn't last long, the black clouds disappearing as the cops left the Blake residence.

Tom looked over at Marc and laughed about the coincidental change in the weather. "If that wasn't a sign that these guys are bad news, I don't know what is."

"Yeah. Did you see the two black crows following their police cruiser?" joked Marc.

They two drove past the lumberyard and turned left at the one-lane bridge leading to Bob's property. The rain had stopped, but water was still dripping off the top of the bridge frame, reminding Tom of Bob's blood, as it dripped from the bushes. He closed his eyes momentarily to get the image out of his mind, but Marc's own memories of the bridge came flapping out of his mouth, bringing Tom back to that unfortunate night. Within a minute, Tom was pulling up next to Bob's Pepsi truck, with the driver's side door lying on the ground next to it.

Marc opened his passenger side door and commented on all the mosquitoes the rain let loose. "In West Virginia, we don't have mosquitoes like this." He slapped the little buggers as they attempted to suck blood from his exposed neck.

Tom walked in the door first, which of course was not locked. He wondered if the cops had even checked this place out. The T.V. was on, dirty clothes covered the floor, and there was a half-empty beer can on the end table next to the couch. Every thing appeared to be normal, except for this can of beer. Bob was never known to walk away from an unfinished drink.

The sound of the television was starting to annoy Marc, and he went over to turn it off. He picked up a business card from on top of the set and asked, "Who is Blumenfeld?"

Tom was holding a picture of Jeanie in a wooden frame. "Do you remember Jeanie?"

Marc shook his head.

"Bob was in love with this woman. She wanted to get out of Warrensburg and study Polar bears in Alaska. She was real smart. Educated. High ambitions. Nobody knows what she ever saw in Bob. He was a good-looking guy, but by no means was he a scholar. I don't even know how the two of them held a conversation. But as they say, love works in mysterious ways." He put the picture down on the end table. "I'll have to contact her and let her know what happened to Bob. I can't recall if they were still in touch, but I think she should know."

"Dad, who's Blumenfeld?" Marc asked again and handed the card to Tom.

"That's another Bob story. I have to call him." A smile slipped out of Tom's mouth as he recapped the story and legacy of Bob to his son. "We were drinking beers one day, about a month ago maybe, and playing horseshoes by the trailer. Bob was so good at that game. Damn, I'm going to miss him." A tear swelled in the corner of Tom's eye, but he dabbed it out before it could form. "So this black Mercedes shows up out of nowhere, and this conspicuous, dark- haired, dark- eyed man wearing designer jeans and a collared polo T-shirt gets out of the car and approaches us. I mean, the guy smelled of money. Bob and I looked at each other and we immediately thought he was lost, and most likely, an asshole. So Bob wanted to have fun with this guy. Also, I think Bob's manhood was a little threatened."

"Why? 'Cause this guy was rich?"

"Well, Bob was used to being the good looking guy in the crowd, and I think this hot shot brought him back down to earth, so to speak."

"I thought Jesse was the stud in your pack?"

"He is, and Bob accepted that. But this guy was sophisticated, an Ivy League type, and obviously not from around here. Jesse and Bob are attractive in a rough kind of way, so to speak. But this guy looked like he just stepped out of a G.Q. magazine."

"Was he big?"

"Yeah, I'd say 6'2", maybe 6'3". Anyway, he walks over to us with his hands in his pockets, but full of confidence too, not putting his hands in his pockets because he was shy or nothing, but maybe to show us that he was not a threat. So he walks over and asks us who owns the property. Bob picks up his beer and asks who the fuck wants to know? The guy puts out his hand and introduces himself as Josh Blumenfeld, obviously not intimidated by Bob or me. We all shake hands and Bob says it's his land then offers him a beer. Blumenfeld accepts the beer, pops it open and starts to drink. I could tell that Bob was annoyed that this guy had a beer with us. He assumed this yuppie wouldn't dare drink beer from a can out in the open. It was quite funny, actually, that Bob couldn't piss off this guy or make him feel uncomfortable. But boy did he try! After a few minutes of Bob's mental abuse, Josh picks up a horseshoe and he wraps it right around the stake. Bob thinks Blumenfeld is showing off, and tries showing him up, but misses the stake. Finally Bob gives up and says to the guy, "So what do you want from me?" The guy smiled and said that he wanted to buy his property and turn it into a fishing lodge. Bob immediately dismissed the idea, and I tried to intervene. Blumenfeld is a developer from Long Island whose friend has a place in Lake George, and he was scouting the area with business on his mind. He offered Bob a lot more money that the land was actually worth, and I had been hounding him ever since to take the offer."

"Why didn't he want to sell it?"

"Pride, I think. He didn't want this businessman buying off little guys, or something like that. Stupid, and I reminded him of that every time I saw him. I think he was tossing the idea around though, when he realized Josh was someone he could actually see himself hanging around with. I have to admit, this guy was hard to hate."

"So do you think Bob was going to call him last night?"

"I don't know. Maybe. I know he had called him about a week ago. I think they spoke a few times over the phone, 'cause Bob had been mentioning him lately. I think he kind of envied the guy or something. I remember teasing him about that."

"Maybe Bob told him no, so Blumenfeld killed him for his land."

"It's my land now, and I *am* going to sell it to Josh." He took the card from Marc's hand and put it in his wallet, along with Jeanie's new address in Alaska.

"For how much?"

"Enough for your kids to go to college."

"If I don't have kids, do I get to keep the money?"

Tom thought about Marc's earlier comment for a minute. "Blumenfeld's an aggressive businessman, but he's no killer. He liked Bob. He's going to be upset about this." Tom looked around for anything that might be suspicious or out of order, but didn't seem to know what he was looking for. He was waiting for some big clue to jump out at him, but nothing did. The business card in his wallet was the only lead, and having met the man himself, he knew it was a dead end. But did the cops know this?

Chapter 22

Marc arrived at the hospital in a good mood, knowing Marie and Spencer would eventually recover from their injuries. The afternoon spent with his father put Marc in positive spirits. He made his way off the elevator when he spotted a curvy nurse bending over the counter to retrieve something from the other side. He walked up behind her and asked if she needed help.

"Oh," she looked him over quickly, and he caught her checking him out. "Could you get that pen for me?" He briefly studied her face, noticing she was much better looking from behind. "Here you go, ma'am." He handed her the pen and walked to Spencer's room, deciding he wasn't interested.

He heard voices inside the room and looked in to see Marie in a wheelchair. He thought he'd give them a moment alone and headed to the vending machine, passing again by the curvy nurse.

"Hi," she cooed.

Marc did not want to mingle with the nurse, and pretended not to hear her.

"Marc," someone said in a familiar voice.

Keeping his head down, he turned it to the left, and saw a pair of leather flip-flops with neatly polished red toenails. His head followed the feet up to a mini-skirt, revealing very toned thighs. He skipped over a sleek mid-section and met Danielle's eyes. "Hey. How are you doing," he asked her.

"I'm O.K. I can't believe all this happened just twenty- four hours ago. It feels like I haven't seen Marie in weeks."

"I know. Listen, I'm sorry about what happened. I knew Spencer was drunk, and I let him drive." Marc didn't know how guilty he felt until he saw Marie.

"It was my fault too. Don't take all the blame, Marc." Danielle sounded sincere, not like the victim she'd been acting like yesterday.

"Is your Dad still pissed off at you?"

"He's always pissed off at me."

"Are you in a lot of trouble?" he asked her.

"You can say that. My mom dropped me off here. He took my car away."

"Ouch. You need a ride home?"

"That would be nice. But let me just tell you that he's a dick! I can't count how many times he came home hammered driving his truck. If you look up hypocrite in the dictionary, you'll see his picture."

"My Dad, too. I called him on it this morning. We made a pact never to drink and drive again."

"But you weren't drunk last night!"

"I know. Want to go in? Marie's in there with Spence."

"I know. I just came from her room."

Marc noticed that Danielle had a package with her and felt stupid for not bringing something himself. "I forgot something in the car. I'll meet you in there." He ran down to the gift shop and bought a blue teddy-bear with a bandage on its head, complete with a hospital gown and a get well balloon. He was now officially broke and knew why his father had insisted he take the summer position at the lumberyard.

"Spencer." Marc came into the room and patted his friend on the head, tying the balloon to the bed rail. "How are you doing, Marie?" he asked as he handed her the teddy bear.

"I'm going to have a full recovery. My brain swelled a little, but they got it to go down. I have a huge headache, and I'm only allowed to sit up for ten minutes a day. But other than that, I'm fine." She held up a pink

191

nightgown that could almost pass for lingerie. "This is from Danielle."

"What are you waiting for? Put it on. Let's see how it looks," said Spencer.

The curvy nurse came into Spencer's room. "Sorry Marie, but if I don't get you back to your room, you're going to turn into a pumpkin." She grabbed the handles of Marie's wheelchair and began carting her off.

"Goodbye. Thanks guys. See you tomorrow," said Marie, who looked and sounded like the Vicodin they had given her was starting to kick in.

The nurse looked at Marc and whispered, "Come by my station before you leave." Marc just smiled and nodded.

"Look at you! You're in here five minutes and you've already scored with a hot nurse. I'm in here for twenty hours and I can't even get some rice pudding!" Spencer grinned.

"She is not hot. You fell harder than I thought if you want to hit that," Marc said.

"Hello! You guys want to tone down the testosterone while there's a lady in the room," snarled Danielle.

"Lady? Marc, do you see a lady in the room," asked Spencer.

"No." Marc looked under the bed. "No lady under the bed." He looked around the room, "No lady in here."

"Ha. Ha. Ha. Real funny. Well, I'm off to help Marie into her new sexy nighty. Too bad you're stuck in bed, Spence!" Danielle got up from the visitor's chair and started walking towards the door. "Don't leave without me, Marc."

"I won't."

"Dude. What's up with you two?" whispered Spence once Danielle was gone.

"Well, let's see. The night started off pretty cool. She was getting all liquored up and was all over me, and then, oh yeah, you crashed your fucking quad and you and your girlfriend ended up in the fucking hospital! Therefore, I didn't get laid!"

"Hey, I didn't get laid either! And by the looks of it, I won't be getting any for a long time. At least you and Danielle can go off and do it tonight!"

"Seriously, Spence. I never should have let you get on that quad. I knew you were fucked up. I feel like this is my fault."

"It's not the first time we got fucked up and rode the quads. We do it all the time, remember?"

"Yeah. But usually we're just stoned. You were drinking heavy last night man."

"I know. And I paid the price."

"You were lucky. We all were. Did you hear that the cops are saying a satanic cult killed Bob?"

"Yeah," said Spencer. "Bunch of crap. I'm telling you, I saw Bigfoot."

"I took a class in West Virginia on anthropology. I learned a lot about Bigfoot. I had this professor, Dr. Ramsey. He is a huge believer. He's been to the Bigfoot museum in California. It's not that I wasn't willing to believe him, but I just wasn't truly convinced. Not then, anyway. I don't know about my Dad. I think he's falling for the satanic cult story."

"Satanic cult? Funny. I never heard of a satanic cult around these parts. Whatever man, I'm going with my gut on this one. I saw the fucking thing. And you saw it too and then fucking left me there to get my balls ripped off! That reminds me, I'm really fuckin' mad at you!"

"Bro, I'm really sorry. I thought you broke your neck. I didn't want to move you."

"Fuck you. You thought you saw a beefed up gorilla coming your way and you left for cover. If it had been me in your place, I'd have taken you with me. I never would have left you there. Never."

Here came the guilt again. "I'm sorry. You're right. I shit my pants. Fight or flight. I flew."

"Fight or flight? What is that, some college bullshit?"

"It's true. When you get startled, your survival instinct just kicks in. You run, or you fight. It's not something you choose. You're body just does it."

"Oh, I see big professor," said Spencer. "So what you're telling me is that on the outside, you're a big tough guy football player chick magnet, but on the inside, you're really just a pussy?"

Marc laughed, liking the idea of being called 'professor'. "Yeah. Something like that."

"I'm alright with that. As long as you admit it," said Spencer.

"Do you still want to have butt sex with me," asked Marc trying not to laugh.

"Yeah, but I think it's fair to say that you'll be on the receiving end," joked Spencer.

"Oh, alright," said Marc.

Spencer's mother walked in to catch the tail end of the conversation. "Is this a bad time, lovebirds?"

Marc blushed and stood up to greet Margo Gargan. "No, come on in. I was just leaving."

"Don't leave on my account," she said. Spencer looked up to see a man waiting in the doorway.

"Jack, come in. Mom, this is Jack Whittaker, the guy who *didn't* leave me lying on the bridge," he looked over at Marc and winked. "And this is my best friend Marc, who did."

"Spencer! Marc did exactly what he should have done! If it weren't for him, you'd still be lying on that bridge," snapped his mother.

"Yeah," agreed Marc. "Nice to meet you, Jack. My father, Tom Blake, was just telling me about you this morning. And thanks for lending us your equipment. We've got something good for you."

"I know," said Jack. "I just met with your father." He shook Marc's hand.

"Alrighty then," said Marc. "I'll see you tomorrow Spence."

Marc walked out of the room and headed for the elevator when the curvy nurse ran up to him. "Hi Marc. My shift ends at midnight. Want to go for a drink?"

"He can't. He promised to take me to the movies tonight," said Danielle. She grabbed Marc's ass and then put her arm around his waist.

"I'm sorry, I didn't know you two were a couple," said the nurse.

"It's true. She's my bitch," said Marc, putting his arm around Danielle's shoulder. Danielle pushed the elevator button and smiled at Marc. "You owe me."

"Thank you. I hate turning women down, it's such a sad thing."

The doors opened and Danielle walked into the elevator. Marc followed and pressed the lobby button. He looped his pointer finger into the top of her skirt and pulled her towards him, kissing her on the lips. She took his tongue into her mouth and let him seduce her. They reached the lobby floor. "Now we're even," he said and left her standing in the elevator speechless for a moment. Then he extended his hand behind him without looking back. She took it and they walked towards the exit doors. "You need a ride?" he asked her.

Chapter 23

Nighttime. My time. Hunt time. Watch. Listen. Go. Out the door. Through the trees. On the path. Stay close to the path. Which way? This way. Horses. Many horses. Easy kill. Eat some. Bring back some. Go. Stay on the path.

His mind was getting stronger, as well as his physical condition after being imprisoned for what felt like ages. *Ages. Could have been ages.* Things looked different, yet familiar. How long had it been? He had been released for a reason. His head ached. *Water. Need water. Stop. Listen. Hear it. Must go this way.* He found his way to the stream, which wasn't far off from where he started. He made his way through the shrubs and found footing on the rocks. Having the ability to see in the dark, he bent down, grabbing the water in his hands and bringing them up to his mouth as he let the water slide down his throat. A nearby dog began to bark, slowly making its way towards him. He looked up and momentarily forgot about the horses. *Come to me. Come to me.* The dog was barking louder now, running in his direction. Suddenly, it stopped and made a 180 degree turn before running back to the house from which it came. *No! Come here little creature!* After the trauma his body had just been through, he was tired and lacked the energy to run. It became obvious this dog was not going to make it easy for him. It ran up onto a porch and a bright light came on, causing him to close his eyes. *Stay still.* A decent sized man came outside with a shotgun in his hand.

"Bo! What is it boy?" Johnny walked across his backyard with his weapon, searching for the scent Bo had picked up. Bo led him to the stream.

"Johnny!" His girlfriend stepped onto the porch wearing a pink bathrobe with her long, wet, blonde hair in a towel on top of her head. "Come back here. I swear if you shoot another deer, I won't have sex with you for a month!"

Johnny ignored his girlfriend and followed Bo towards the pond. The shrubs were getting thick, and he cursed himself for allowing them to grow so out of control. What had once been a beautiful pond with decorative shrubs leading into a functioning stream now looked like a dirty swamp with overgrown weeds, misplaced rocks and a hideous access trail that couldn't even be recognized as a path anymore. "I'll put it on the list, he mumbled to himself."

Bo ventured into the pond area, leaving Johnny to clear his own path. He was no longer barking, but sniffing profusely with his nose to the ground. The porch light could barely be seen in this area, and Johnny cursed himself again, this time for not bringing a flashlight. He heard Bo splashing in the water a few yards in front of him, so he rolled up his pants and took long strides to keep up.

Dina walked into the kitchen and grabbed herself a bottle of beer from the refrigerator. After snorting a few lines, she liked nothing more than a cold beer. She heard the screen door slam shut while fiddling with the bottle opener at the counter. "I knew you couldn't turn down sex," she said without turning around. She unloosened her robe and let it fall to the floor, revealing her naked body.

He knew he didn't have much time. His purpose was to kill, and she was easy pray, but when her robe hit the floor, he suddenly had mixed feelings. He had never done this before. *Or had I?* His head still ached and things were somewhat of a blur. He took two large steps towards her and placed his left hand on her lower back, forcing her upper torso onto the counter. The pain in his head seemed to triple now, and his mind went blank again. *Screaming.* He heard screaming. He dropped her naked body to the floor and watched the blood run down her backside. Taking what he needed, he left just as quickly as he entered. His headache was gone, and he gained speed as he ran up the hill towards the horse farm.

"You givin' up on me, boy? What kind of huntin' dog are you?" said Johnny as he followed his dog away from the pond. Bo darted out of the bushes and ran back towards the house, barking. "You ain't gettin' no bone for this one, you lazy dog!"

Bo ran up to the porch and barked at the screen door. "I'm coming," said Johnny. He walked up the steps and opened the door, allowing Bo to enter first. "Don't worry, Bambi's still alive," he said as he pulled his muddy boots off and left them on the porch to dry. He walked into the kitchen and saw Dina's lifeless body lying on the floor surrounded in blood with her intestines dangling from what used to be her stomach.

Chapter 24

Becka was standing at the bathroom sink, wearing her flannel pajamas and brushing her teeth while Devin sat on the edge of the tub reading Loudbear's *Psychic Powers* book.

"Dev," Becka spit the toothpaste back into the sink.

Devin didn't bother to look up. "Yeah?"

"What did Loudbear mean when he said that we're in grave danger? What is he talking about?"

"I'm not sure. But it sounds like he feels that the Farm is dangerous."

Becka rinsed off her toothbrush and placed in on the shelf next to the sink. "I think we need to find out why he feels that way. I saw him freak out when I pointed out where the Farm is on the map. I mean, O.K., this place is dark at night. There are no streetlights, and it's crawling with wild animals that we can't even see. But in the daytime, I don't see any harmful animals. Do you?"

"That's 'cause the killer carnivores are nocturnal!" Devin slammed the book shut for an extra scary effect.

"I'm serious." Beck popped open the bathroom window and unlatched the old screen.

"Maybe he senses that the Farm is haunted. I had a conversation with Dad about it, and he completely denies it."

"What do you think?" asked Becka.

"Oh, it's definitely haunted. I remember seeing and talking to that Indian ghost. I think that's why I started talking to Loudbear. He reminds me of him. I've been reading this psychic book, and it's teaching me how to recognize things. And those flowers you drew, they're bad news. I get a bad feeling from them, and I'm going to show them to Loudbear.

"O.K. I'll show you them tomorrow. But take a look at this tree here. You can't even see it at night, but in the morning it's crawling with chipmunks. If there were carnivores creeping around here at night, don't you think they would eat the chipmunks?"

"Why settle for an appetizer when the big meal is just beyond the door! Mouuuuwwww!"

"I'm serious. Let's do an experiment. Wait right here, and don't let Mom or Dad in." Becka tiptoed downstairs and grabbed three hot dogs from the refrigerator.

Re-entering the bathroom, she said, "I'm going to drop these hot dogs out the window, and in the morning, we'll see if they're still there. If there are little nibbles out of them, then we will know it's just little animals out there. If they are gone, we try another experiment tomorrow night." She dropped the hot dogs out the window. It was already pitch black out and she couldn't see where they landed, but heard one distinctively hit the cellar doors below.

Chapter 25

ANOTHER VICTIM: SAME M.O.

Johnny Adam Walker, 26, of Warrensburg is cooperating with the Warrensburg Police, hoping to be cleared as a suspect in the brutal slaying of his girlfriend. Police say they received a phone call around 10:00 P.M. last night from Mr. Walker stating that he followed his dog into his nearby pond in search of a deer before returning to find his naked girlfriend, Dina Puglesi, 24, of Lake Luzerne, lying on his kitchen floor with her "insides missing." Police are still investigating, but believe the incident to be linked with the recent murder of Bob Murphy, whose entrails were also ripped apart. Ms. Puglesi's body was taken to the morgue for an autopsy. Cocaine was found on the premises and Mr. Walker was "heavily intoxicated" when police arrived. Mr. Walker denies the cocaine was his and said that Dina was an occasional user. Police are still searching for the weapon used in the slaying of Ms. Puglesi, and say they are planning to drain the pond in the morning. Mr. Walker's attorney, Paul Brookstone, is confident that the autopsy results will clear his client. "The prime suspect here is 'Lucifer's Seeds,'" says Officer Kankro, "but Mr. Walker was the last person to see Ms. Puglesi alive." Charges have yet to be filed.

Tom handed Sherry the paper. "Would you look at this," he said, shaking his head as he tossed the paper over the kitchen table.

Sherry picked it up and carefully read the article. "Lucifer's Seeds? Why does that sound so familiar?"

"The cops believe them to be the suspects, a satanic cult of some sort that Demitres is on to."

The carving in the tree from yesterday's hike struck in Sherry's mind like a freight train. "Oh! I remember where I saw that! They're nothing but a bunch of kids who listen to rock music. They carved their sign in the tree behind the Grand Union. On the trail. I saw it yesterday. Any idiot would know it's nothing but stupid kids with nothing to do. They hang-out behind the shopping centre if the cops are really looking for them."

Tom looked at his wife suspiciously, "What were you doing on that trail?"

Before she could answer, Marc walked into the kitchen wearing a suit and tie that had been tucked in the back of his closet for years. "Marc, you look so handsome," Sherry commented, reminiscing that the last time she saw him in a suit was for his high school graduation.

"I feel like a goon. This suit does not fit me at all!"

"I know, and we'll definitely buy you a new one for graduation, but who knew you'd grow three inches and gain twenty pounds in a year?"

Marc sat down at the table and picked up an apple, taking a big bite out of it. Noting his mother was still in her pajamas, Marc asked, "Mom, aren't you coming to the funeral?"

"You know I'm no good at those things. Besides, I am going to stay here and help the caterers set up. I liked Bob. He wasn't the smartest man in the world, but he sure was a looker. I really am going to miss him." Her eyes welled up with tears and she quickly left the room.

Marc glanced over towards his father, who was sitting at the kitchen table with his arms folded across his chest. "Dad, are you O.K.?"

"Yeah, I'm hanging in there," responded Tom, keeping his suspicious eyes on his wife as she fled the room. "I'll feel a whole lot better once we find Bob's killer." He reached across the kitchen table and poked the newspaper with two fingers. "Read this. Inspector Clusoe over there just said she knows who Lucifer's Seeds are. Says they're nothing but a bunch of kids who listen to loud music behind the Grand Union. If your mother has seen them, does it sound like somebody who is keeping a low profile?"

Marc picked up the paper and read the headline. He quickly browsed through the article. "Then why would the cops try to sell everybody on that story?"

"I don't know, son. I really don't know. Maybe the cops know it's Bigfoot and it's a government secret at this point, like Roswell. Or, we have to consider that it is someone in a costume."

"Yeah, but the way it moved, Dad. I don't think someone can fake that. Like Spencer, I'm going with my gut on this one, and my gut says Sasquatch. As a matter of fact, I sent another e-mail to my Anthropology professor last night. I'm still waiting to hear back from him. He's a true believer, and a pretty convincing one. I'm a little disappointed that the cops got you thinking it might be something else. They'll say anything. You know that."

"I'm glad to know you actually listen in the classroom." Tom heard the sounds of someone pulling into the driveway. "Let's go. The limo's here." He picked up his suit jacket from the back of his chair and put it on, walking towards the bedroom. "Sherry, we have to go." Sherry was sitting on the edge of her bed and Tom walked over to her, kissing her on the forehead. She didn't look up when she said goodbye.

The death of Bob, or anyone for that matter, brought back bad memories for Sherry. She and Tom had just been married when Sherry became pregnant. Estimating the time of conception, the child qualified as a honeymoon baby. Sherry had an easy pregnancy, with no complications, and was ecstatic about becoming a mother. Tom stayed up all hours of the night carving a wooden cradle to perfection for the newest member of the Blake family. Sherry spent most of her days during the pregnancy at church, praying for her unborn child's safety. Her friends and family planned a beautiful shower at The Georgian Hotel and Restaurant. Sherry had gained forty-two pounds and hand stitched her dress for the occasion, since it was of no surprise thanks to her sister Ella.

On the eve of Sherry's first contractions, she packed her bags and Tom drove her to the hospital, trying to keep her calm during the drive by telling dull stories of the events of the lumberyard during the week. When they arrived at the hospital, the doctors took Sherry in right away and began the birthing process. Tom, dressed in scrubs, was the fist one to see his daughter enter into the world. She had the most perfectly round head you could ever imagine, and a perfect button nose identical to Ella's. The doctor pulled her out and Tom thought she was sleeping so peacefully, and wanted to hold her right away. The doctor, however, quickly handed her to the nurse and they both fled into another room. Sherry had started to scream, knowing by the commotion that this was not a good sign. Tom didn't know what was going on, and told Sherry that everything would be alright. Moments later, but what seemed like a lifetime to the Blakes, the doctor came into the room and said that the baby had been strangled by the umbilical cord during delivery, or while still in the womb. She had passed before she had lived. Events immediately following Sherry's living nightmare were fuzzy, but the one thing she does remember is that God let her down, and she would never forgive him. Tom and Sherry didn't hold a Christian funeral for the infant. Sherry did not want God to have *her* baby. She hadn't been to church since then, and although Tom fought for Marc to be baptized, Sherry had won that battle too. Sherry knew that Tom still went to church on Sundays, but it was never mentioned.

She sat there on the edge of her bed, listening to Tom and Marc's footsteps as they left the house and heard the limo pulling out of the driveway. God took another one. She snuck into the garage and stole the night vision goggles, along with a few more strands of Bigfoot's hair, stuffing them both into her pocketbook. Carrying it back into her bedroom, she heard a loud crash that came from Marc's bedroom. Assuming this was another one of Allison's ways of letting her know she was with her, Sherry felt a comfortable chill rise from her body. She slowly walked down the hall to Marc's room and put her hand on the doorknob, taking a deep breath, and quickly opened the door. Her emotions quickly turned from excitement to anger and then disappointment when she saw Danielle trying to climb out of the window. "What the hell are you doing?" she shouted.

"I'm sorry. I know this looks bad, really bad, but I fell asleep here last night and I wanted to leave quietly so you wouldn't get the wrong impression. The window made a weird noise when I tried to open it. I'm really sorry."

"Well you should be! You scared the living daylights out of me!" Sherry looked over Danielle, who was wearing a pair of Marc's sweatpants that were disgustingly too big for her slim body and one of Marc's old T-shirts. It didn't take much to assume what went on the night before. Danielle still had one leg over the windowsill, the other dangling over Marc's bed.

The look of embarrassment on Danielle's face was cause enough for Sherry to crack a smile. "Get back in here and have a seat. It's about time we had a talk." Danielle crawled back in the window and followed Sherry into the kitchen, taking up the seat across from where Sherry usually sat. "You must be hungry. Let me make you some breakfast. I still have some fresh pancake batter in the fridge. You want blueberries in it?" asked Sherry.

"Um, okay. Sure. I'll have some tea, also, if you don't mind. I'll put the water up. Do you want some?"

"That sounds nice. To tell you the truth, it feels nice to have some estrogen in the house. I'm with Tom most of the time, and now that Marc's home, well, it's just nice to have another woman around."

"You're not mad at me?" asked Danielle while filling the tea kettle. "I can only imagine what you're thinking!"

Sherry looked over at her from the counter where she was mixing blueberries into the batter. "I was once your age too, you know."

"I wish my Dad understood that. He doesn't even want me to *see* Marc again. You can't tell him you saw me here. Please! He'll kill me!"

"Your father always liked Marc. What is his problem?" asked Sherry feeling herself becoming defensive of her only child.

"It's because of the accident. And I think my Dad has a problem with anyone who went to college. He's only allowing me to go because my mother and Don are paying for it."

"Was Marc drunk?"

"No. And I'm not just telling you that to get Marc out of trouble. I was drunk. So were Marie and Spencer. But Marc wasn't feeling too good. He spent most of the night hanging out with Spencer's mom."

"Margo Gargan is crazy about him. I used to be jealous of her. Not just for being close with my son, but also because I'm pretty sure Tom had eyes for her at one point. He'd stop by her house whenever it snowed to shovel her car out of the driveway, and then go inside for some hot chocolate, or whatever. I can tell you that his spirits were always uplifted after spending an hour at Margo's!"

"Maybe he was just helping her because she didn't have a husband?"

"That would be nice of him, but the old Henkel's next door to her had no help either, and I never saw Tom shoveling their driveway. Do you really think he'd be helping her out if she wasn't 110 pounds with D-cup breasts?"

"Now that you mention it, I think my Dad has been over there to 'hang some picture frames'," admitted Danielle.

Sherry pursed her lips and raised her eyebrows. Normally the thought of Margo Gargan flirting with her husband made her furious. This morning, however, she was laughing about it. Sherry dished out the pancakes and Danielle poured the water into the mugs. Thoughts of her and Ramsey sharing a candlelight dinner from the previous night filled her memory. Looking at Danielle, she knew Marc would be alright without her. And if it didn't work out with Danielle, she was confident that Marc would pick another winner.

"So, did you and Marc hang picture frames?"

Danielle nearly choked on a blueberry. "What? No!" Her face turned beet red.

"Come on, you can tell me. I wasn't kidding when I said I was once your age."

"Alright, alright. I'll share the news. We kissed, and you know, a little other stuff. But we did *not* have sex. We watched a movie then fell asleep."

"Oh yeah? What movie?"

"Trading Places."

"How'd you end up wearing Marc's clothes if you *fell* asleep?"

"He leaned over me to put his drink back on the end table just as I was sitting up and spilled coke all over my clothes. So I changed into his 'cause mine were wet. If you want, I'll show you the coke stains."

"Easy there Monica Lewinsky. I don't need to see the dress." They both started laughing. "Seriously though, are you a virgin?"

"That's kind of personal. Why do you want to know?"

"I want to make sure you know what you're doing if this is going to continue with my son. Tom and I are paying a lot of money to send him to college, and I don't want him to get you or any other girl pregnant and drop out. And you have a future too. Don't throw it away for one lousy night. Trust me, you don't want to end up living in this town for the rest of your life. There's a whole 'nother world out there."

"I know all about sex. This is Warrensburg. What else is there to do in the woods?" She started laughing and Sherry chimed in, wondering how long it's been since she had sex. 'Could she still perform?' She wondered. She'd soon find out.

"Tell me about it!" They both started laughing again.

"Alright Allison, I hate to cut it short but I have to get going. The caterers are going to be here soon and I still have dishes to do." Sherry stood up and gathered the plates before heading to the sink.

"Danielle. It's Danielle."

"What honey?"

"You called me Allison. My name is Danielle."

Sherry turned around and saw Danielle standing there with her coffee mug in her hand, wondering what Allison would look like at her age. Would she have long chestnut hair like Danielle, a slim waist, a matching bright smile? "I'm sorry. I don't know why I called you that."

"Is that one of Marc's ex-girlfriend's?"

"No. Don't be silly," she said, waving her hand in the air like it was nothing.

"Okay. You're not going to tell Justine about this, are you?"

"No. You have my word. Women always keep secrets. Remember that."

Danielle nodded, knowing she trusted her best friend Marie with everything. She grabbed her clothes and walked out the front door, looking back at Sherry who was suddenly moving in high speed. She thought Sherry was acting rather odd all of a sudden, and wondered if Marc had a girlfriend at college that he wasn't telling her about. "Son of a bitch," she told herself. I was too easy. That asshole made me think he really likes me! I'll show him!

Sherry watched as Danielle walked north on Schroon River Road, heading towards Jesse's house. After she showered, she dialed Professor Ramsey at Motel 8 and let him know that she had more hair for him, as well as the night vision goggles they would use on their own quest for Bigfoot. She assured him she would be there shortly.

Chapter 26

Steve and Maureen had just finished breakfast. The kids were in the living room playing Parcheesi, acting on their best behavior. Becka tiptoed into the kitchen and tried to eavesdrop from behind the vintage refrigerator.

"You're awfully quiet this morning. Are you still not speaking to me?" Steve hadn't told Maureen about the disappearing act the kids had pulled, let alone getting into a car with a strange man. And he *was* strange.

Maureen got up from the table, wrapping up the bread and storing it in the bread box. "No. But I want to spend less time in Warrensburg. I want to go antique shopping in Bolton Landing. Maybe rent a boat and spend the day on the lake."

"Wow! I wasn't expecting that answer! Why the change of heart?"

"I think we should move on and enjoy the vacation. You work hard, you deserve a break. But no more talk about the Jesse incident, and no more talk of the woods incident either. Do we agree?"

Becka gave Devin the thumbs up sign and ran back into the living room. "They're talking again. We're going to Bolton Landing today. She said something about a Jesse incident. Did he get hurt in the woods that night?"

"Not that I know of. Maybe she meant Norma."

"Yeah, maybe."

Steve came into the room and told the kids of their plans for the day. Maureen walked past them, reminding them to pick up all the Parcheesi pieces, then went upstairs to get dressed. Steve tilted his back into the stairwell to make sure Maureen had gone into the bedroom and shut the door. "Remember," Steve said in his best Robert Deniro impression, "I got my eyes on you." The kids laughed, acknowledging the first sign that their dad was starting to relax again. Truth be told, his mood always depended on Maureen's.

Devin slipped into his sneakers as Becka searched for her flip-flops. "C'mon, Beck! Let's go see what happened to your wieners."

"I can't find my flip-flops." She bent down to look under the couch, feeling for her footwear. She felt the outline to the trap door and traced it with her finger.

"You're so lucky Dad and I swept under there the other night. There were thousands of mouse turds right where you hand is!"

Becka was about to mention the lining she found, when she felt a slap on her back. She turned and saw her flip-flop lying next to her on the floor, then looked up at Devin, who was laughing.

"I found your shoe."

Becka slipped the rubber shoe onto her foot, then kicked it in the air, letting her flip-flop fly off. It smacked Devin square in the face.

"Ouw!" He squealed.

Becka grabbed her flip-flop and put it on before Devin could hit her again. "Let's go." They went through the front door and around to the side of the house just underneath the bathroom and kitchen windows. "I don't see them, but I don't know where they landed," said Becka as she searched for the hot dogs.

"Let's check the area. They're hot dogs. They can't have gone too far," advised Devin.

"I'll check the bushes." Becka moved away from the cellar door into the small side yard while Devin searched around the root cellar, directly below the window. He stepped on top of the wooden doors and applied some pressure.

"Dev, I found one! Over here! I think a rabbit got it. I see rabbit rounders!"

Devin turned towards the side yard and fell on his face. He looked back to see his shoelace caught in the cellar doors. "Beck! I need some assistance!"

Becka picked up the nibbled hot dog and brought it over to Devin, who was sitting on the doors trying to get his lace out.

"What happened?" Becka saw that Devin's knee was bleeding.

"My lace got stuck, and I tripped."

Becka laughed at her clumsy brother. "What else is new?" She bent down to untie the sneaker. "The plastic part is stuck. I can't get it."

"You're going to have to open the door."

"Well I can't open it if you're sitting on top of it!"

"Go into the living room, under the couch. There is a trap door leading to the basement. Go down there and lift up the door a little, and I'll pull it out."

Becka momentarily forgot about the outline under the couch. "Oh, that's what I felt. Have you ever been down there?"

"No, I just noticed it the other night. But bring a flashlight. I bet it's dark."

"Thanks Dev."

"Or get Dad if you're too afraid."

Becka was always up for a challenge, or a dare. "I'm not afraid. I'll do it."

"O.K. Beck. Watch out for the killer carnivore!"

Becka ran up to her room for her flashlight. From the hallway, she could hear her parents having sex. "Gross!" She tiptoed down the stairs and moved the small couch to reveal the trap door. There was no handle on it, so she went into the garage and retrieved a flathead screwdriver. She could see Spike was down the road near Uncle Tony's house, already playing with another dog.

Becka wedged the screwdriver into the planks of wood and the door opened, exposing numerous spider

212

webs filled with the remains of unfortunate insects. With her left hand she lifted up the door, aiming the flashlight with her right hand. The old wooden steps were visible and she started to go down them, propping the trap door open so she wouldn't get locked in. Goosebumps began to rise up Becka's legs, for the temperature dropped at least five degrees as she entered the hidden space. There must have been dozens of cobwebs in her hair by the time she reached the bottom step. Shining the flashlight around, she noticed what looked like the frame on an ancient bunk bed. Hearing something crunch under her foot, she quickly looked down and found a bunch of huge lily pads on the dirt floor. She picked one up and shoved it down the back pocket of her shorts. Across the cellar was another set of steps leading up to the wooden doors. She had to bend down as she ascended them so as not to hit her head. "Dev, can you hear me?"

"Yeah. What's it like down there?"

"It's really cool. I feel like I'm in a dungeon. It's cold and smelly." Becka took a brief moment to shine the light around the place. There appeared to be a wall of cinderblocks cemented together, partitioning off a separate section of the space. A few of the cinderblocks were missing, as if the wall had not been completed. "Looks like there is a whole 'nother room in here." Beck shined the light upon the wall, focusing on the missing pieces. "Looks like it's under the kitchen." She set her back against the wooden doors and pushed up from a squatting position. The door barely budged, but it was enough for Devin's shoelace to get free.

"Got it. Thanks Beck."

Becka stepped down from the stairs and tucked the flashlight between her thighs so she could brush off her back. She saw a spider fly off through the light and her back instantly became itchy. Scratching it, she followed the spider with the light, and thought she saw fur on it.

"This better not be a frigin' tarantula! Dev, are there tarantulas upstate?" The spider ran towards the wall and into the other room under the kitchen. Becka trailed it as and it climbed up the cement wall, disappearing into a crack. She started to feel dizzy, and purple dots crept across her field of vision. Her brother's explanation of tarantulas was fading out, the words sounding like a distant monotone recording of a weather report. *Tarantulas live in the Southwestern United States, typically in mountain foothills and deserted slopes...* With her legs feeling oozy, she sat down on the floor and leaned against the wall. Her right hand fell to her side and the flashlight rolled along the ground, which was made up of a mix of dirt and cement. She brought her knees up to her chest and tried to take deep breaths. Her thoughts drifted to the frightening event in the woods. "If Devin hadn't kicked the can so far into the woods that night..." she mumbled. She closed her eyes and rubbed her hands over her face, knowing this must be an allergic reaction. She tried her best to come out of it. Her heart was racing and she squeezed her eyes shut real tight and counted to ten. At ten, she opened her eyes. More lily pads were in the room, and there appeared to be a small ape-like animal lying on top of them. As her eyes regained focus, her heart rate started to stabilize. She controlled her breathing and reached for the flashlight. Feeling the spider bite on her back starting to swell, and the dizziness come back again, she called out for her brother.

Devin opened the outside cellar doors just in time to grab Becka's hand before she passed out again. He dragged her limp body to the well and splashed water on her face, causing her to regain consciousness. "Wait right here, Beck. We have some Benadryl in the house. I'll go get it." Her vision started to fade out again, but not before she saw a large figure walking down into the cellar. Her eyes rolled back inside her head and she blacked out again.

Chapter 27

Things had gone smoothly for a weekday funeral service. The temperature was in the mid seventies, the sun wasn't too bright, but the sky was neither overcast, and since Bob wasn't a wealthy guy, there were no family members fighting over what they thought rightfully belonged to them. In fact, there were no family members. Josh Blumenfeld attended the ceremony, and Tom introduced him in the eulogy, informing the congregation of how he agreed to name the establishment "Murphy's Lodge". Josh also agreed to keep Bob's belongings and use them as décor in the rooms of the lodge as another tribute to Bob. Ironically, Bob was laid to rest in a small cemetery not far from where he lived. Most of the townsmen showed up to pay their last respects to Bob, and then moseyed on over to Tom's house for some fine, catered food. Mike had closed the bar for the day, and put up a $1000 reward for anyone with information leading to the arrest of Bob's killer. He wasn't handling Bob's death very well at all. Earlier, Sherry had heard someone in the bathroom sobbing as she quietly awaited her turn. She was taken aback when she saw Mike emerge from the room. "Mike, are you alright?" she asked gently, placing her soft hand upon his shoulder.

"I thought I'd be, but, I don't know. Bob would never hurt anyone. Who would do something like this to him? It just doesn't make sense."

"I can't answer that. But from what I've heard it's a cult of kids. That's the talk of the town anyway."

"Yeah, well then why can't these cops bag 'em if it's just a bunch of stupid kids?"

"I don't know, Mike. I never thought of it like that. I suppose you're right."

"Well I'm not going to just sit back and let the cops think this is some kind of joke. You want to know what I

215

did? I marched right into Sheriff Farley's office and demanded something be done! I own the only bar in town! I have dirt on everybody, including Sheriff Farley. Hell, I have a little cousin who's afraid to leave the house! I let it be known that shit will hit the fan if he doesn't call in some help from another department. We need some real detectives on the case!"

Sherry saw an opportunity to find out exactly how much the town knew. "Do you think it was Bigfoot?"

"Some drunk kid reported it to the papers. I'm a bartender, remember? Enough alcohol could make even the smartest guy in the world make some pretty ridiculous allegations. I've heard them all. You want my opinion? I think it is a satanic cult. But I don't think it's kids. I think it's some sick adult fucks. Maybe in their thirties even. Misfits. No jobs. No women. Ugly fuckers. Charles Manson wanna-be's. I think they started out killing animals, then escalated to killing humans."

Satisfied with one less Bigfoot crusader, she glanced across the room and saw Mrs. Gargan and took that as her cue to end this testosterone infused conversation with Mike, who was so drunk that he was going to start repeating the entire conversation again. "Excuse me, more guests have arrived," she interjected before Mike could get another word out.

Sherry made her way to the front door. "Margo, how are you doing?"

"Fine. Thank you. Spencer will be home soon, and I'll will be busy tending to him. I've been caring for the Healy kids the past few days, and boy am I exhausted! I don't know how that poor little Marie keeps up with them! They're good kids, but a handful."

"That is so nice of you," admitted Sherry, finding herself feeling somewhat guilty for not helping out. "But in my own way," she thought, "I'll be helping Warrensburg more than anyone if all goes accordingly."

"And it's nice of you to hold the gathering at your house. I'm going to miss Bob. You know, we used to have a thing, Bob and I. It never amounted to anything, but I always enjoyed his company. This is just so awful. And to think that the people responsible for this are still out there!"

Sherry had her suspicions about Margo Gargan and Bob Murphy. Both were slim and attractive, and lived close enough to walk to one another's house for a little nookie before bedtime. All the men in town would love to spend a night with Margo, if they hadn't already, including Tom. Although he denied having any attraction to Margo, a giddy grin would consume his face whenever she was around.

It was apparent that the entire town was going to come together and get to the bottom of this. Sherry had to play her part too, she realized. "I know! What does that make it? I mean first you have Bob, then Pat's husband is nowhere to be found, then Jesse's dog, my barn animals, that girl from Walker's cabin...When is it going to end? Enough is enough!" Although she felt bad about the recent incidents in town, somehow it shed some light on what had happened to Allison. At least she wasn't the only one prone to misfortune.

As Bob's mourners reminisced about the kind of man he was, Tom slipped into his garage to mourn in silence. He removed a red milk crate from the top shelf of his work bench, lifted the dirty paint canvas, and retrieved his own private bottle of Absolut. Taking long slugs from the bottle, he circled his garage, searching for something that would jolt his memory of the late Bob Murphy. All he could think of was walking with him in the woods the other day, discussing the possibility of Bigfoot. Tom grabbed a cardboard box from under his workbench and began sifting through his "Bigfoot evidence." He recalled that Bob mentioned something about some kids stealing his sodas from the truck, but it didn't make any sense. Why would kids steal sodas from a guy and run scared when he came after them, only to return wearing a costume and kill him weeks later? For sodas? No, no way. While the cops were sure it was these same kids, Tom knew it had to be something else, something big. After all, he'd seen it, and kids couldn't mimic the size of this thing, nor the smell of it for that matter. Tom lifted a lily pad from his evidence pile and brought it to his nose, taking in the putrid scent once again. Upon hearing the side door to the garage open, he shoved the plant back into the box and kicked it under the workbench.

Marc was standing in the doorway, looking ill.

"Marc, what is it?"

"I just checked my e-mail. When I didn't hear back from Professor Ramsey, I sent an e-mail to that fat law student I argued with all semester long. She sent me some of her highlighted notes from her thesis. There's strong evidence to support the theory that Bigfoot isn't a rogue predator. She says they are rarely alone.

"What are you talking about?"

"They hunt in packs."

Tom and Marc both heard the front door slam, and a chaotic march of footsteps scampering down the driveway. Tom lifted the bulky garage door in time to see all the guests leaving. "Where is everybody going," he called out.

Margo Gargan ran over to Tom with her large breasts bubbling out of her little black dress. "Bob would have appreciated this moment," he thought to himself.

"Mike just got a call from Sheriff Farley," explained Margo. "He arranged for the F.B.I. to come here and solve these murders. The agent in charge has apparently just arrived in town. We're all going to town hall to give him the facts. We're going to get Bob's murderer!" Margo reached for Tom's elbow and guided him towards her flatbed Ford parked on the side of the road.

Tom briefly hesitated, feeling a side of him awaken like a bear coming out of hibernation. Somewhere between Bigfoot and Margo Gargan's cleavage, Tom felt alive again. A feeling of hope coursed through Tom's body. He turned towards his window and saw his wife staring at him. She, too, had a lively look in her eyes. As she cradled the phone against her ear with her shoulder, she smiled at him as she waved him off, signaling him to go without her.

"You're going with them?" asked Marc.

"Yeah, what's the problem?"

"Dad, do you believe Kankro and Demitres?"

"No. No I don't. But the F.B.I. is here, and I want to hear what they have to say. They might know something that we don't. By the way, where are the night vision goggles?"

"What are you talking about? You had them."

"Shit!"

Mike beeped his horn and waved Tom over.

"I'll be home later. Please look for the goggles for me. I imagine they're expensive and Whittaker may be leaving tomorrow. We'll talk about this later. The hunting in packs thing, interesting." Tom was obviously distracted.

"But Dad," Marc implored as Tom joined the rest of them like a pathetic follower. "Dad! There's more!" he screamed as his father followed after Spencer's mother. "You suck, Dad!" Marc yanked his baseball cap off his head and threw it to the ground.

"C'mon," urged Margo.

Tom looked to Margo, who was already trotting down the driveway, kicking up her dress with every step. Without hesitation, Tom put one foot in front of the other and caught up to Margo, jumping in the passenger seat of

219

her truck. She smiled at Tom, pushed her foot down on the accelerator, spun the tires, and followed the caravan to Town Hall.

Tom looked out of his window, almost hoping his comment would get lost in the wind of the moving vehicle. "You look nice today."

"Are you saying I usually don't look good?"

"No, not at all. I uh, I heard you have a date with Jack Whittaker tonight."

"Are you jealous, Tom?"

"Me? No, I'm a married man."

Margo gave Tom a devilish grin. "That's too bad."

*   *   *

For two hours the townspeople tallied up the death toll and reviewed the turn of events. Pat made a tear-jerking speech and blown-up newspaper articles were tacked to the walls. Special Agent John Galvin absorbed every detail of the case, waiting for some clue to jump out at him. He did what he had been trained to do, noting the townspeople uniting as one, while the deputies retreated in their own corner of the room, alone. Galvin squinted his eyes as he read the body language of the larger of the two cops: cornered.

Kankro and Demitres watched the nightmare unfold in front of their faces: an entire town rallying against them. Demitres knew this was bound to happen, that one day the two of them were going to push the envelope too far and bring all of their good times to an end. They both looked to Sheriff Farley, who was playing along with the townspeople, encouraging everyone to report any suspicious activity.

One local who had recently lost his girlfriend was getting out of control, bringing unwanted attention to Officer Kankro. Johnny Walker's voice was raspy and loud, and his accusations gave Agent Galvin a good starting point for his investigation.

"Somebody snuck into my house, and killed my girlfriend," screamed Walker, "and I immediately called the cops." Pointing at Kankro and Demitres. He continued. "Those two meatheads over there took over forty minutes to get to my house. And when they got there, they assumed I was the killer! I had to lay out three thousand dollars to hire an attorney to prove my innocence! Now, I'm out three grand and Dina's murderer is still out there! This is bullshit!"

Sheriff Farley didn't give the locals enough time to destroy the reputation of his two finest officers. He screamed to the crowd, "Now that's enough! My officers are dealing with a very delicate matter, and it's police procedure to consider everyone a suspect at this point. Dina Puglesi was a victim of a heinous crime, and she paid for it with her life. So, Mr. Walker, my apologies if the town doesn't see your three thousand dollars as a top priority." Skillfully taking the attention off of his officers, he introduced a young recruit from the Federal Bureau of Investigation. "Now, I'd like to introduce you all to Federal Agent Galvin. He will be taking over the cases of the recent homicides in the area, and he expects full cooperation from everybody."

Agent John Galvin took the podium as he addressed the crowd. "At the present time, I will be conducting my investigation from the Sheriff's office. I urge everyone to come speak to me directly with any information regarding the recent homicides in your humble town. Now, from the information provided to me about the case, I strongly believe that the killer is still amongst us, possibly even in this room as we speak." The locals stared at each other with distrusting eyes, trying to recount strange behaviors from their neighbors. "As Sheriff Farley said earlier, everyone is a suspect at this

221

point. All the evidence collected thus far suggests that the perpetrator of these crimes is someone quite familiar with this area. I understand that the children of Warrensburg have been given a curfew of nine o' clock. For the time being, I'm going to extend that curfew to the adults as well."

This statement was met with loud jeers and more than a few slanderous remarks. The quiet town was beginning to feel like a penal colony. Galvin continued, "All businesses are to close by nine, giving no one an excuse to be out. This curfew will be strictly enforced, and anyone not abiding by the rules will be fined for interfering with an official, federal investigation." The agent left the podium and walked across the street to the police station, ignoring the raucous bellowing from the furious townspeople.

Kankro and Demitres watched Galvin leave as the locals argued amongst themselves. Farley slithered away from the crowd and met his officers on the steps outside Town Hall. "Why'd you call the Feds," demanded Demitres.

"I had to, politics. Look, this guy is a trained professional, and once he finds the killer, he'll move on, and we'll have our town back. For the time being, I need you two to stay low. No more bullshit until he leaves, understand?"

Demitres was not comfortable with the Feds taking over. "Trained professional my ass! That little fuck is right out of the academy!"

Kankro chimed in. "I agree. How much experience can he have anyway? Besides, we know it's Lucifer's Seeds. We just need a little more time, then we'll nail them."

"I'm sick of hearing about Lucifer's Seeds! You guys have a name of a cult, a name that you saw engraved in a tree, and you made a real connection to a murder downstate, but you still don't have any clue as to who these supposed satanic worshippers are! My job depends on how I keep this town safe, and we'll all be out of a job this time next year if these murders don't stop!" With that said, Farley lit a cigar and walked back to his office.

Chapter 28

The Bettis' piled out of the Pathfinder, shaking sand off of their clothes in the overgrown driveway of the Farm. Steve went to the front door to let Spike out of the house. She pranced around Steve running toward the street, with barely a limp left in her. "Alright. Let's go for a walk. Maureen, want to take a walk up the hill with me?"

"Sure." Maureen sprayed herself with more bug spray, then handed the can to Steve who made sure Maureen's back was covered. Becka and Devin were in the garage gathering their badminton rackets for one last game before the sun went down. Maureen peeked her head in and announced to the kids that they would be back in a few minutes.

Devin peered through the garage window as his parents walked hand in hand up Rock Avenue towards the moffits. "O.K. Beck. This better be good."

"Come to the root cellar with me."

Devin followed his twin to the cellar and helped her open the heavy wooden doors.

"You wait here, and don't lock me down there. I'll be right back."

Becka disappeared down the old concrete steps into the cellar and appeared a minute later. "O.K. Here it is!"

Devin turned around to see his sister holding what looked like a baby gorilla in her arms. "Holy shit, Beck! Where did you get that?"

"I found it in the root cellar this morning. I think it lives in here."

Devin took the baby into his arms and inspected it. "Smelly little thing!"

"I know. I want to keep it. What kind of monkey do you think it is?"

"I don't know, but it's a female."

"What do you mean, you don't know? You've studied every kind of monkey on the planet since you were in third grade! You even designed what a space monkey would look like if monkeys lived in outer space. How could you not know?"

Devin handed the baby back to his sister and scratched his head as he paced back and forth on the rough grass in front of the cellar doors. "I can honestly say I have no idea what species of ape that is." He took the little monkey from Becka's arms again and thoroughly inspected the hands and feet. "The feet are throwing me off. They're too close to human feet. Take a look at this." Devin held the monkey's foot in his hand, then pointed to the structure of Becka's exposed foot. Look at the toes. This monkey cannot hang from a tree, or curl its feet. In fact, her feet appear to contain the exact bones of human feet. This is not an ape, Beck." He gave the creature back to his sister.

"So, what are you saying, it's some kind of a hybrid? Who's desperate enough to mate with an ape? The moffits?"

Devin shook his head at his twin sister's accusation as a scary thought entered his mind. The touch of a headache was starting to come back, but he pressed on his temples, fighting it off. He allowed his eyelids to shut and his mind to clear, following strict directions from Loudbear's book. Becka was talking, but he managed to tune out her voice. A breeze blew past him, and he felt as if he was riding the ripples of the wind, then saw a quick flash of blue. In the blur of color was an image. Blue flowers. And in the blue flowers he saw a vision: Bigfoot.

Devin opened his eyes and stared at his sister who was now walking away from him carrying the little monster. "Where are you going with that?" He called out.

"I know what you're thinking. I can hear your thoughts when you get those headaches, and I won't let you hurt her." Becka hugged the infant in her arms. "She's just a baby. She's never hurt anyone."

Devin did not share Becka's concern for the little terror. "Beck, that means it has parents, or at least a mother. Think about what has been going on around here! People have been reporting that they have seen Bigfoot! The papers are reporting missing people and dead animals! I can't think of any other animal that could have matched the criteria of what was chasing you in the woods. And you said it yourself, it smelt like shit." He sniffed his own hands and motioned to the animal.

"What do you think we should do?"

"Beck, this thing and its family live under the Farm! We need to tell Dad."

"Are you crazy? He'll think this thing's mother is what tried to attack me in the woods! He'll kill it!"

"Becka, this things mother *did* try to kill you in the woods." Devin paused to think for a moment. "O.K., I'll hold off on telling Dad for a little while. We'll talk to Loudbear. He'll know what to do."

"Alright," agreed Becka. "But let's take a picture of it first." After taking a picture of Devin holding the baby, the twins carried the beast back to the root cellar and fed her milk and instant grits as the sun quickly faded into the night. As they locked the root cellar for the night, Devin had an idea. "We have to move her. We can't keep her here."

"Why?"

"Because we are here, and if her mother comes back to feed her she just might end up killing us."

"Dev, the baby's been here, and the mother hasn't killed us. If we move the baby, the mother will want to know where we moved her, and then she really will kill us. I saw her go into the root cellar this morning when you went into the house to get the Benadryl. She could have killed me, but she didn't. She could have come in the house any night this week and killed all of us, but she didn't."

"I suppose you're right. Tomorrow morning, we find Loudbear. This has to be what he's talking about. Promise me you won't go into the root cellar alone to feed her?"

"Promise," lied Becka.

Chapter 29

Whittaker had just gotten back from the thrift shop and was trying on his new horrific suit jacket in front of the mirror in his dingy little motel room. Jack had brought with him a dark brown pair of dress pants, a common garment in his travel suitcase, and a yellow dress-shirt that somewhat matched. He always brought this outfit on overnight surveillances, convinced of its value as a disguise. Tonight, he was pretending to be sexy. Since it was summertime, he hadn't brought a jacket with him. The last thing he was prepared to do was go out on a date! He hadn't been on one in years, and was worried he had forgotten what to do or how to act. The finality of funerals makes some women feel exceptionally generous, and Jack was hoping Margo was one of those women. If Bob Murphy hadn't died, Jack would not be going on a date tonight. There was no doubt about it, Margo Gargan was an attractive woman. But usually attractive women didn't go for guys like Whittaker. He was burly, overweight to put it correctly. And he almost never made it to a second date with anyone. He supposed it was because he talked too much. One woman said he even bragged too much about cop stories. He looked in the mirror, sucked in his stomach and warned the reflection staring back at him, "Mental note to self: keep conversation down to a minimum. Let her do most of the talking." Beads of sweat were starting to form on his forehead. He went into the bathroom and pulled a few strands of toilet paper off the roll and wiped his face. He still had twenty-five minutes before he had to leave, so he sat on the edge of his bed and played around with the remote. Margo had picked the restaurant. It was called The Jaagar House, she had said, known for its variety of foods and friendly staff.

Jack's heart began to beat faster as he tried to kill time until his big date. "I feel like I'm fifteen again," he said to himself. The anxiety piling up inside of him forced him to want to exercise, an activity as rare to him as declining a dessert after dinner. The Forest View was actually a quaint little motel, the entire building consisting of one floor with white siding and blue trim, a wooden deck covered with a porch roof to protect guests from bad weather, and an unattached main office on the adjacent side of the unpaved gravel parking lot. Beyond the lot, there was a welcoming little dirt trail covered in pine needles. Other than Jack's blue Suzuki rental and one other car, the lot was empty. He guessed it had to be the front desk personnel's vehicle. "The Forest View motel isn't that much of a dive," he thought. They didn't offer housekeeping so he picked up his room as best he could. Not that he thought Margo would go back to his room with him, but, then again, he never thought she'd agree to go out with him either. "Things sure are strange in this neck of the woods," Jack mumbled to himself.

He stepped out of his motel room and onto the wooden deck. The outside temperature was just below eighty degrees, and the wooded path into the forest appeared very inviting, with squirrels scurrying about the treetops. Jack walked around the motel and headed for the trail. The forest was not as quiet as Jack had expected it to be. Birds were chirping, squirrels and chipmunks were running up and down trees, jumping from branch to branch. Their playful acrobatics made a considerable amount of noise as the branches shook and crashed into one another. Although he knew there was nothing in the forest but animals, he felt as if he were being watched, possibly by those dirty cops. They were bound to have some info on him by now and were probably setting a plan into motion that would send him back to Long Island in short order. But no, he hadn't seen any unusual cars in the lot. And they would not have any idea that the rental belonged to him. Unless Margo was setting him up.

"Why would a woman like that want to go out with a guy like me?" he thought. Paranoia was a feeling all cops developed on the job: for many it was a matter of survival. Paranoia kept a cop alert without allowing his fight or flight response to overtake him in a crisis. But fear was something else. The tension it created was nearly unbearable and it could make a cop edgy, dangerous. Sure, the job made most cops paranoid, but Jack wasn't most cops; he hadn't even started as a beat cop. He had never worked outside of Customs for J.F.K. Airport. He had never been out in the field where he could have been shot at, or run over, or stabbed for a bag of H while acting undercover as a drug addict. He was fortunate enough to work in a comfortable environment, and always indoors. So when a situation became tense, Jack's usual response was a mixture of panic and confusion. The feeling he was picking up now, in the woods, was well beyond any other bad feeling he had experienced. A sickening sense of fear was welling up inside of him and he couldn't figure out its source. To try to shake off the feeling, he picked up a rock and tossed it into the woods. After waiting a few seconds and listening to the rodents scamper from behind the shrubs, he decided to walk back to the lot and pick up Margo, even if he was a little early. As he turned towards the lot, he felt a sudden pain in his head, then watched as the rock fell to the ground. He turned around but did not see anyone. Picking up his pace, he practically ran to his car, cursing himself for not having his gun on him. He had left it in the nightstand drawer, having decided that a gun might not be the best thing to bring on a first date.

Margo was applying the last of her aqua net hair spray onto her rollers in her hair when she heard a knock at the door. "That's odd," she thought. "He's fifteen minutes early. A little too eager. What a turn-off." She took her hair out of the rollers and walked to the door. Opening it, she saw Jack standing there holding a small bouquet of flowers. "Hi Jack. Come on in, I'm almost ready. Are those for me?" she asked as she held out her hands for the flowers.

"I'm sorry I'm early. You finish getting ready. Do you have a vase?"

"Yeah, under the hutch in the dining room. You didn't have to. That was very sweet of you, Jack."

"It's no problem. I'm not used to the woods, you know. So I apologize in advance if I'm a little jumpy. I'll explain when you get out of the bathroom."

*   *   *

Dinner went smoothly, Jack thought. They had just placed a dessert order and Margo was talking about Spencer's recovery.

"You're son has some sense of humor. As beat up as he was, he was still cracking jokes to me. He seems like a good kid." Jack meant it, comparing Spencer to his own good-for-nothing wastoid who was probably lighting up a blunt at this very moment back in Jack's Long Island living room.

"Oh, he is. Don't get me wrong, he has his faults. I'm just so happy he's all right. Marie too. They had just started dating, you know, but I think she's the one."

"She's the one? How can you possibly tell? My son goes through at least two girls a month, and everyone is 'the one' to him. This generation is different. Back when we were young, we had maybe two serious relationships before we tied the knot. Not these kids today. That's why AIDS is so rampant right now. Kids are clueless nowadays."

"I disagree. Maybe where you're from dating is like that now, but not here. The population isn't all that much in this county. And it's more convenient to date someone from your own town. I think these two are good together."

"Maybe they are, for now. But who knows? I'm sure when Spencer goes to college he'll find ten more Marie's."

"Spencer isn't going to college. There's more work around here if you can learn how to work with your hands."

"Now that is something I think we can both agree on. Same on Long Island too. Carpenters make more than grad students these days. I have a friend whose son graduated from Hofstra University a year ago. He's now a male secretary, although his title is "Administrative Assistant." They started him at twenty six thousand dollars. The market is so bad these days. Spencer should try to get into civil service. The pay is merely tolerable, but the benefits and pensions are better than anywhere else. Maybe one day he can replace these two jerk-off cops reeking havoc in your town."

Whittaker was not an exceptionally good-looking man, but he did have some good qualities about him, Margo thought. She's been through dozens of men since her husband left her sixteen years ago, but none of them meant anything to her. Maybe because most of them were married, or too young to consider much more than a glass of beer and a one-night stand. Jack was a good conversationalist, so far, at least. And Spencer seemed to like him. Maybe this one was a keeper. Nah, who was she kidding. As Jack was going on about his career as a customs agent, which was impressive to this woman who made professional waitressing a career at The Georgian, she made a conscious decision to allow this date to blossom into a friendship, and marked sex off the agenda to gain this man's respect.

"She's giving me the eyes," thought Whittaker, "I'm definitely getting lucky tonight. How long had it

232

been?" he wondered to himself, as he pretended to listen to Margo speak of her boring nights as a waitress while he discreetly tried to imagine what she looked like without her clothes on. Jack was thinking about how he should approach her when the check came. Without hesitating he whipped out his American Express Card and placed it inside the leather sleeve and tapped on it twice, grabbing the waitress' attention.

"American Express? Is this business or pleasure," asked Margo, fully aware of how those words can easily be misinterpreted. Mischievously she thought to herself, "There's nothing wrong with some friendly flirting, right?"

Whittaker blushed but saw this as his opening move. "My presence in your humble town is business, but tonight has been my pleasure," he smiled as he lifted up her hand and kissed it gently.

Jack and Margo held hands as they walked out of the Jaager House. He walked her to the passenger side and opened the door for her. She turned around to smile at him then found his tongue being jammed down her throat. "Down boy," she said as she pushed him away.

Jack was taken back. "I'm sorry. You just look so beautiful and I couldn't resist. Was I out of line?"

"No, not really. You just caught me off-guard. I was not expecting that."

"Yeah, well, I've always felt that the element of surprise works best for me. If a woman doesn't want to kiss me, well, too late. Already done!"

Margo laughed, finding his sense of humor appealing. "It's O.K." She got into the car and closed the door, leaving Jack standing there, pondering his next move. The ride back to Margo's wasn't complicated, but Jack had to pretend he was lost to find out if she wanted to go back to his motel with him.

"I'm not sure where I'm going, so you're going to have to help me out with directions. Am I taking you home or is there somewhere else you wanted to go?"

"My philosophy has always been, why rock the boat? I had a good time tonight, so you can take me home now."

"I didn't mean I was expecting anything else from you. I'm just a little creeped out about what happened to me back at the motel."

"Are you afraid to go back there? I thought you were a cop."

"I was. And yes. I am somewhat afraid. Sounds ridiculous, right?"

Margo glanced over at her new friend. "I'll tell you what. If you promise to be a gentleman, you can spend the night. You can sleep in Spencer's bed."

"I appreciate that. Thank you. Do you mind if we take a drive to the Forest View so I can check out and gather my stuff? In the morning I plan to collect my gear from Tom and drive home."

They pulled into the barely lit parking lot and were surprised to see that no cars were there.

"That's odd," said Margo. "This is tourist season. You usually get the poor families lodging here because it's so cheap. I don't see anyone around. No wonder you're freaked out, this is like the Bates motel."

"I noticed most people left on Sunday. With soaring gas prices, most people aren't doing much traveling these days."

"Yeah, the Georgian slowed down somewhat too."

They got out of the car and walked up to the checkout desk, where they weren't all that surprised to see a sign that read, "FOR CHECK-OUT, DROP KEY IN SLOT. THANK YOU." They walked to Jack's room and let themselves in. Margo jumped onto the bed while Jack went into the tiny bathroom to pack his toiletries.

"The bed's comfy," she called out as she positioned herself provocatively on it. Acknowledging why they stopped at the motel, Margo knew she'd never see him again and decided to sleep with him after all. It wouldn't be her first one night stand, or her last.

Jack peeked his head out of the bathroom and looked at Margo, who smiled warmly at him. Without hesitating, he strutted over to the bed and jumped on Margo, passionately kissing her lips. She wrapped her legs around his large frame and started to tug on his shirt. He paused momentarily to pull it off and cupped her breasts while his mouth made its way down her neck. Her blouse was almost opened when she stopped him. "Did you hear that?" she asked.

"No," he responded as he pulled her bra back to reveal her left nipple. She strained her neck to listen for the sound while losing her momentum. He slid his right hand up her abdomen and reached for her right breast, pulling the bra up over her chest this time.

"Jack, stop. Somebody is at the window." The curtains were closed and the outside could not be seen from the motel room.

"Nobody is there," he said as he reached behind her to undo her bra. It had been a while, and he had always found unclasping a bra more difficult than untangling a Slinky.

Margo slipped out from under him and stood next to the bed, pulling the bra back over her breasts. "Would you please check? I definitely heard something."

Jack looked her over as she stood beside the bed. "You are so sexy! You're driving me crazy! Alright, I'll check if you promise to get back into bed." Jack walked over to the window facing the parking lot. "And I expect that bra to be off by the time I turn around."

Margo bent down and picked up her blouse. "I think the moment is lost." She slipped the shirt over her head as she walked into the bathroom, locking the door behind her.

Jack ran to the bathroom, sensing sex was no longer going to happen. "Margo, what's the matter?"

"Nothing! Would you please see if someone is outside?"

"Yeah, O.K. Fine." He walked passed the bed and opened the curtain. With his eyes scanning the parking lot, he noted that no cars were in the lot. "There's no one there. The parking lot is still empty." He put his shirt back on and opened the front door. The outside temperature was comfortably warm for Diamond Point. The humming of the vending machine a few doors down made him crave a soda. Buttoning his shirt, he stepped onto the rustic, blue, wooden planks of the running deck and stopped at the machine. Reaching into his back left pocket, he clumsily yanked his wallet out of his pants, spilling change all over the deck. He bent down to pick up his change when he heard the planks creaking behind him. Without looking up, he asked Margo if she wanted a soda.

Bigfoot stood over him, as if observing Jack's human behavior. Jack put his hands on his knees and began to stand, causing the monster to suddenly feel threatened. Bigfoot grabbed Whittaker in a head-lock and dragged him towards the woods. Jack tried to scream but the choke-hold was cutting off his air supply. Desperately, he tried to dig his heels into the gravel lot as he was being hellishly dragged into the bleak darkness of the deep woods. Remembering moves from the police academy, he kicked his right leg back and sank his heel into his assailant's shin, applying pressure as his foot forcefully made its way down the lower portion of Bigfoot's leg. This did not seem to affect the creature, and it showed no sign of slowing down its pace. Jack then tried to hold onto the monster's arm and lift his legs off the ground, allowing his body to be carried as dead weight. This move proved to work as Bigfoot released her grasp on his neck and Jack fell to the ground. Jack had no time to get up so he crawled as fast as he could while trying to lift his knees up off the ground. He was almost up when the creature threw herself on top of him, knocking him to the ground again. Whittaker managed to roll onto his back and kicked his legs violently into the monster.

"Margo," he screamed out. "Get my gun! It's in the nightstand!"

Margo peered through the dark motel window when she heard Jack scream. She jumped over the bed and pulled the gun out of the drawer. Unlocking the safety on the weapon, she stepped onto the decking of the Forest View and watched in horror as Bigfoot stood up to face Margo, standing only twelve feet from her. Jack was still on his back kicking at the beast. "Shoot it," yelled Jack!

Margo aimed the gun at the beast and pulled the trigger. The bullet ripped through the thick flesh of the monster and blood spattered out of its chest. Bigfoot leaped over Jack and ran towards Margo. Margo shot two more rounds into the creature's abdomen, its blood raining down upon the deck. She ran into the motel room and locked the door. The beast wavered for a few seconds before falling backwards, knocking Whittaker to the ground as he tried to rise to his feet. The animal was now lying on top of him, and was too heavy for him to lift off. He squirmed and rolled until he finally got out from under it. "Margo?"

Margo opened the motel room door and poked her head out. "Jack, is it dead?"

"Yeah, I think so." Jack sat next to the beast, breathing heavily as he examined the animal. "Call that F.B.I. guy." As she dialed the sheriff's office, she heard a loud growl, half howl, coming from outside the motel room. Dropping the phone, she ran to the window. From the light of the vending machine she saw another creature, a larger Bigfoot right behind Jack. Before she could grab the gun, she heard Jack's scream ascend into a high pitched wail that was then suddenly silenced. She watched in horror as the larger of the beasts dragged both Jack's decapitated body and the smaller Bigfoot into the woods. When they were no longer in sight, she ran to Jack's rental car and drove to Sheriff Farley's office, where Agent John Galvin was stationed.

*   *   *

Bigfoot brought Jack's body to a clearing in the woods beyond the motel. He ripped out Whittaker's heart and handed it to his female companion, sensing her pain and knowing that this would be her last meal. She coughed out what appeared to be pints of blood as she gnawed on the fresh flesh of Jack's heart. Had they stuck together, she never would have gotten shot. But feelings of guilt were not very prevalent in the psychology of the Sasquatch, so he watched her eat and waited for her to die. As her eyes turned from weak to empty, he ate some more of his prey.

After eating enough to hold him over for a few days, he carried his mate's body to a nearby bear cave and left her at the entrance. His own survival instinct taught him that remains of his kind must never be found, and bears have always taken care of the dirty work. He knew he needed to lay low for a little while before he went back to his young one, who still fed on lily pads.

Bigfoot's mind was starting to expand, his brain forming the ability to absorb information. The female was much smarter, and he had been learning from her. She had been following humans, learning from them. He had been killing them, for the curse. *Why didn't she kill the human in the woods? Why did she kill the human by the river?*

What was different about the kill I did in the cabin? Why did it feel different? Emotions were a new and vague sensation for this Sasquatch, so he felt confused and disoriented more than anything else. Back to basics. *Survival. Blood.* He ran back to the front of the Forest View and found Whitaker's head, eyes bulging out of his fat face. He picked it up to eye level and stared at it a few moments, but nothing came to him. He glanced around and saw *her* blood. *Evidence. Must not be there.* Her blood was on the exterior of the Forest View, where she had been shot. Blood was dripping from the head in his hands. He took the head and cracked it open, much like a coconut, and smeared it all over the walls, covering *her* blood. He then went into the motel room and found the weapon that killed *her.* He picked up the strange object and beat the head with it several times, until the face of this creature was indistinguishable. He placed the gun and the head on top of one of the vending machines, and then retreated back into the woods when he heard the sirens approaching.

Chapter 30

Kankro stood with his back to a tree in the late hours on The Sagamore's waterfront resort. He waited patiently as the wealthier tourists walked hand in hand for a romantic stroll across the manicured lawn, with the moonlight reflecting off enchanting Lake George. Moving ever so slightly, he kept his body out of sight when the couples changed direction. One particular couple in their early thirties walked down the dock, heading to the west side of the resort. It would be O.K. with Kankro if they stayed there for some time. With the nighttime temperature stable in the low seventies, no clouds in the sky, and the moon at its peak, he saw no reason for the couple to traipse indoors. Wearing black sweatpants with a black hoodie, he blended into the brush more inconspicuously than a chameleon. Several minutes had gone by and the couple had still not returned. He was sure they would be at least another twenty minutes, if he was lucky, and he had to choose his latest triumph in the next few moments, or call it a night.

"Hi honey. I just got out of a meeting. I'll be staying at the Sagamore Hotel. It's beautiful up here. Wish you were here. I was hoping I'd catch you, but I guess I'll talk to you in the morning. Goodnight. I love you."

The woman was pacing across the great yard, talking on her cell phone when she walked passed Kankro. She ended the phone call and turned back towards the hotel when she was hit hard in the head from behind.

Kankro positioned his victim in a headlock and dragged her into a wooded area. He threw her onto her stomach and yanked at her fitted black slacks. The woman tried to adjust her eyes, then felt warm blood trickling down her face. Kankro saw his prey waking up, so he clubbed her over the head again with his nightstick. He looked around and saw that besides the distant couple at the edge of the lake, the rest of the property was vacant. With the bitch's pants already off, he pulled her thong underwear to the side and inserted his meatstick into her wet little hole. It took all of thirty seconds to reach climax: the real foreplay had been the hunt, the feeling of total domination over his unsuspecting victim. Violating her was just one, final act of violence that asserted this monster's control over his victim. He pulled out just in time to squirt his semen away from the body, leaving no evidence behind. Making sure all was in place, he dressed the woman and sat her up against a nearby tree, as if she had fallen and hit her head. When she came to, she wouldn't even know she had been raped and humiliated.

Now that the night was complete and all was in order, Kankro shoved his ski mask into the front pocket of his hoodie and proceeded to jog on the open path. He ran down past the dock by the young couple and off to a sandy beach area, where he untied his jet ski and headed back to his own waterfront property in Bolting Landing. All things considered, it was a good night for Officer Kankro.

Chapter 31

Steve's internal clock was still on the job, and he instinctively woke up at 6:00 A.M. The wildlife outside the Farm was already awake, the crickets chirping and roosters crowing. He put on yesterday's jeans and strapped his hip holster in place before walking across the hall to the bathroom. The morning sun was rather bright against the yellow walls of this cottage-styled bathroom. As he was washing his hands, he recognized the chipmunks playing in the tree. He was sure it was the same couple from the other day, and felt a sense of relief that they'd found a new tree to inhabit.

Waiting for his coffee to brew, he opened up the front door and stepped onto the porch. Spike was already at his side, waiting patiently to be let out. He opened the door and Spike limped towards the well to do her business. Steve walked down the white rock path leading to the street and waved to a bearded male in a gray suburban. The man nodded and slowed down as he approached.

"You don't live here year round, do you?"

"No," said Steve. "We've owned the house for years, but usually only make it here for the summer. But we have someone maintaining it year round."

"Well, there's a large brown in the area," said the bearded man. "Seen him on my front lawn just now, snooping around."

"You mean a bear," assumed Steve.

"Yeah. Probably won't bother with you. But be careful. He's a big one!"

"Thanks. I'll keep that in mind. Hey, let me ask you. Is that normal, to see a brown bear up here?"

"They usually stay in the woods, but for some reason they've been venturing out more than ever lately. Some say it's because of global warming. As you may know, we bring our garbage to the dump, so I don't think that's the reason. A few weeks ago, one was spotted in the dumpster behind McDonalds. That makes sense, but when it comes to residential properties, I'm not sure what they're looking for."

"My daughter was chased through the woods the other night, and my neighbor's dog was mauled. Do you think that could have been the bear on your property?"

The man in the truck looked wearily at Steve. "Oh, I don't think so. If it was a hungry bear, your daughter wouldn't stand a chance. But you never know. Strange things have been taking place over the last couple of weeks. I'm sure you've read the papers."

"I know. I'm a New York City Homicide Detective. My theory is that it's a serial killer."

The man with overgrown facial hair looked back towards the road. "Well, whatever it is, I hope they catch it real soon." He pointed to a shot-gun on his passenger seat, adding, "Before I do."

"Thanks again," Steve said as he tapped on the door of the man's truck and nodded. He looked down the road at Uncle Tony's house and felt brave enough to walk to the bottom of the hill in the cold chill of the morning. He got his coffee and called for Spike, who always seemed to show up out of nowhere. He wasn't at all surprised to see the two, blue painted Adirondack chairs positioned in Tony's front yard with a small table between them. An ashtray containing a half-smoked and still burning cigarette rested on its edge. Steve sat his coffee mug on top of the table and took a seat. Hearing the sound of Tony's screen door, he turned to greet him, surprised to see that the old man was carrying a shotgun in his hands this early in the morning.

"Uncle Tony, how are you?"

Steve began to stand up out of respect for the old man, but Tony motioned him to sit back down. "You've been here almost a week, and you come to see me now at six o'clock in the morning!"

Is it *that* early? "I'm sorry. But it looks like I didn't wake you."

"Don't worry about it. When you get to be my age, your body wakes up at the butt-crack of dawn, whether you want to or not."

Steve smiled. "We've had a hectic week."

"So I've heard. Jesse told me all about it." Tony looked over towards Spike, who had apparently met Rip. "My new dog. Just four months old."

Steve looked across the field and saw Spike trying to keep up with a young bloodhound. "Cute dog."

"His name is Rip. Named him that, 'cause he's a rip!"

Steve chuckled, then remembered the conversation with the bearded man. "A neighbor of yours from up the hill just drove by and told me there is a large brown bear in the area. Are you worried about the puppy?"

"Now what's a bear want with my dog?"

"I don't know. To tell you the truth, I don't really know that much about bears. I hear there's been moose in the area, too. I figured that's why you're armed."

Tony sat down next to Steve. "Bears, moose, and blue flowers. There's just one more piece to the puzzle."

"Blue flowers? What are you talking about?" asked Steve.

Tony looked at Steve and his expression turned serious. "When you were just about eight years old, if you remember, I sat you and Jesse down right here in this exact spot and we had a little chat about the last time I rode that double bike."

"Are you kidding? How can I forget? I think you gave me nightmares 'till I was twenty-five!"

"So you remember that I saw Bigfoot. What you probably don't remember, is that summer when Bigfoot

244

was here, so were these damn blue flowers. They're back, you know. And it's no coincidence that things are going wrong around here."

"Blue flowers? They're my parents' anniversary flower, or something like that. I thought they symbolize romance?"

"You can think I'm just a crazy old man, most people do. But I know what happened to Ben Schaefer. And it wasn't a bear. Now, you can believe me or not, I don't really care. But sure as shit, when the blue flowers arrive, Bigfoot is not far behind."

"I think my daughter saw a blue flower. Devin was telling me something about it the other night."

"Rip came home covered in them last week. Ever since then, I've been on high alert." Tony pointed to the barrel of his shotgun which was now lying next to him, halfway concealed under the snack table. "That's about when Pat's husband disappeared. Man was fishing on Schroon River. Just like he does every morning. But this day, he don't return." Tony turned his attention to the woods beyond his property. "I don't believe in coincidences."

Steve pretended to believe that the old man was onto something. "You may have a point, Tony." He stood up and looked at the Farm across the street, south of Tony's house. "Maureen and I came by last night, but you weren't home."

"That's 'cause me and Rip were out looking for it last night. Only comes out at night, you know. But it comes home in the morning, wherever its home is. That's why I'm out here with my gun. Hoping to get it on its way home."

"I've got to get back before Maureen wakes up. She's on edge lately. Stop by later, the gang would love to see you."

Uncle Tony nodded.

Maureen was making eggs when Steve came in through the back door with Spike and his new friend Rip. The twins jumped up to see the puppy while Steve introduced Rip as Uncle Tony's new dog. The smile that Rip brought to Becka's face made Steve want to run out and pick up a puppy at the shelter.

As if Maureen could read his mind she stared at him with clenched lips. "Don't even think about it!"

"I don't know what you're talking about, Mo."

"I know that look. Just think. In five years our kids will be off to college. We can travel, book cruises..."

He knew she was right. She was *always* right. "Listen up guys. There is a brown bear up the road, so I want everybody staying in, or we all go out together."

Devin's eyes lit up with excitement. "You saw a bear!" Outside of the Bronx Zoo, he had never seen a bear.

"No, not me. Some guy I saw this morning told me he saw one skulking around his property for food."

"Why do you call him Uncle Tony if he's not your uncle," asked Becka.

"That's how we were introduced, I guess. That reminds me, Becka. Did you see any blue flowers lately?"

"Yeah. In the back field. I drew a picture of one of them. Want to see it?"

"Becka, no!" yelled Devin.

Steve looked at Devin. "What's the matter?"

"I don't like them. I get a bad feeling about them, Dad."

Becka ran upstairs to get her drawing, coming back down with it and a camera. "Here. I also took a picture of them. I don't know what it is-was about those flowers, but it was like I was drawn to them. They aren't even that pretty. But Dad, it's like I was mesmerized when I saw them. I can't explain it." She snapped a photo of Rip and Spike sharing food from the same dish. "Can we go into town to get my film developed? I can't believe I forgot my camera at home. I have to give this one back to Loudbear."

"Who is Loudbear, and where did you get that camera?" demanded Maureen.

"Oh shit," Steve thought. He hadn't told Maureen about the twins' expedition the other day, and he felt another fight brewing. In a desperate attempt to save his vacation, he informed Maureen that they all met a nice man in town when they went for pizza. Catching his wink, Becka spiced up the story with some minor fictitious details.

Becka obviously had the story under control, and Steve took advantage of the moment by sneaking out of the house. Picking up a large stick, he poked around the pine needles on the side of the house in search of the blue flowers.

"And what are you doing outside by yourself, father?"

Steve looked up quickly, startled to find Devin peering out of the bathroom window. "I wanted to pick some blue flowers for your mother," he replied.

"They're over there, but I really don't want them in the house." Devin pointed Steve in the direction of the field, through the ATV driven path. Steve turned but didn't see anything.

"I'm coming down," shouted Devin. He ran down the stairs and hit his head on the slanted ceilings as he turned to enter the staircase. "Auhw!"

Steve heard the front screen door swing shut and saw Devin coming towards him while holding his head. "What now?"

"I hit my head on that frigin' low ceiling by the stairs. Did midgets live here before us?"

Steve checked for blood. "No blood. You'll live." Devin led the way to the blue flowers as Steve explained the best he could about the design of the house. "From what grandma told me, the Farm was built years ago. That cellar you asked about the other night, your mom told me it's a root cellar. That's where the farmers would store excess crops so they wouldn't spoil. Since the floor of the cellar is dirt and the walls are made of cement, it kept the vegetables cool enough that they wouldn't spoil during any season."

A lot of things had changed since Devin first inquired about the root cellar. Now all he wanted to do was change the subject until he got another chance to speak to Loudbear. "There're the flowers." Devin pointed to a small patch of the blue flowers underneath a crab apple tree when all of a sudden he got a vision of a large Bigfoot, much bigger and more vicious than the one in the cellar. It was killing a woman, a woman was screaming, screaming loudly!

Steve knelt down and picked a couple of the flowers. "These are the anniversary flowers!" He lifted them to his nose. "Strange smell for a flower," he said as he brought them up to Devin's nose.

Devin wanted nothing to do with them and tossed his father's hand aside. "I bet they're actually weeds."

As Devin was speaking, Steve remembered a conversation he had with Madeline Totten about her being some kind of flower expert. "Devin, I forgot to tell you. The other day, when you took off with that Indian, I met a botanist who lives in Warrensburg. I want to bring these flowers by her house today and find out about them. I've been hearing some conflicting stories concerning them. Uncle Tony shares your feelings about them." Steve tucked the flowers into his shirt pocket.

"I think that's a good idea, Dad!" Devin took hold of Steve's arm and pointed to the Farm. Steve lifted his head in time to see the large brown bear sniffing around the side of the property, near the cellar. Slowly lowering his right hand to his hip, he retrieved his gun and held

Devin behind him with his left hand. He cursed himself for not seeing the animal first. His receptors were somehow not working properly, and this made him extremely anxious.

"You're not going to shoot him," whispered Devin.

"I don't want to, but if he comes after us, or tries to get into the house, I don't have any other choice."

Devin knew exactly what the bear was after, and knew his family would be safe from *this* predator.

From inside the house Spike started to bark and Maureen told Becka to let the dogs out. Becka got up from the table when, through the back window, she saw her father with his gun drawn. Her first thought was that her father found the baby Bigfoot, that somehow it had crawled out of the root cellar. She ran to the kitchen window for a view of the root cellar, where she saw the bear and felt instantly relieved.

"I don't think so Mom."

Maureen followed Becka to the kitchen window and quickly decided she was not comfortable with only two feet and a sheet of glass between her family and a full grown bear. Pulling Becka away from the window, she urged her daughter to follow her to the upstairs bathroom, where they could watch from the second floor window. Becka began snapping pictures of the bear with Loudbear's camera.

"He's so cute," said Becka.

"Not when he's trying to eat you!"

"Bears don't eat people, Mom."

"Oh no? Devin and I saw a special on Discovery Channel where a couple were hiking and a bear attacked and killed the wife. And I think he ate her, but they didn't show that part on T.V." The bear started to claw at the cellar door, then suddenly jumped back as if it knew the old rotted wood couldn't support its weight. Sniffing around the area, he proceeded towards the front of the house. Spike was still barking, and Rip was just starting to join in on the noise. Steve and Devin remained where they were, standing erect and still so as not to startle the bear if it turned towards them. Luckily, it went in the opposite direction. Becka and Maureen went into the kids' bedroom, where they could visibly see the garage. They still had no visual on the bear, and Becka asked her mother if they could go downstairs into the living room in order to locate it.

"O.K. But stay close to me." Maureen went to the front door and spotted the bear sniffing around the well. "Is that a *hot dog* in its mouth?" Becka pushed Maureen aside and took several more pictures. From the ground floor they got a better perspective of the bear. "He's huge," said Maureen.

Becka reached into her pocket and pulled out the necklace that Loudbear had given her. Something inside of her told her to put it on. "Mom, this is from Loudbear. It's a real bear claw."

Maureen felt the tip of the claw and rubbed the necklace. "This is beautiful, and looks very expensive. I'm shocked you would wear such a necklace. Why did he give it to you?"

"He said it's for protection."

"Your father's a cop. You don't need any extra protection."

"Devin told him about the other night. He's a psychic, you know. He says Devin's psychic too. I think he knew this bear would come here." Becka knew why the bear had really come to the Farm, and rubbed the necklace once again.

"That's a bunch of bologna. I hope you don't believe him."

"I do. He told Devin when we first met him to close his eyes and picture something. Devin shut his eyes and saw a red collar. Then Norma got killed. She was wearing a red collar, Ma." Becka purposely left out that that Loudbear had warned them to go home. Becka fondled the claw between her fingers. She wondered if Loudbear already knew about Bigfoot.

"There he goes," said Maureen as the bear walked across the street and into the shrubs. Steve and Devin saw him leave and came in through the back door.

Becka ran to the dining room to meet them. "Devin, did you see that? Were you crapping your pants?"

"I saw him even before Dad did. It was a little scary. But Dad had his gun, so I wasn't freaking out. But I have to say, that was the most beautiful animal I've ever seen!"

"Devin, I'd have to agree with you," said Maureen.

"Yeah right! Dad would never shoot a bear! Would you, Dad?"

"What do you think I do for a living, Beck? I've shot humans. Of course I'd shoot a bear if I had to."

"But Dad," she cried, "It's an animal. You love animals!"

"Yeah, I do. But I love you guys more."

Her father's response reminded her of what he'd do to the little Bigfoot upon finding her, and Becka wanted to move the animal far away from the Farm to protect it. "I got some good pictures of it. Can we go into town now?" This was just another excuse to see Loudbear.

After everyone showered and got dressed, Steve and Devin walked Rip back to Uncle Tony's house. Tony was still on his front lawn, but napping, shotgun in his lap.

"Dad, I think you should hire him as head of security."

Steve laughed. "The bear could have stolen his cigarettes."

"Is that why he has the shotgun, 'cause of the bear?"

"I'm sure."

"Hey, Uncle Tony! Wake up! The bear's coming for you!" Devin clapped his hands loudly behind Tony's head.

Tony opened his eyes and reached up, grabbing Devin's arm.

"Guess what! We just saw the bear a little while ago. Me and Dad were outside. Not more than thirty feet from it!"

"Oh yeah?" Tony perked up. "What was he doing?"

"Just sniffing around."

"I wouldn't worry. A bear ain't looking to hurt nobody."

"Then why do you have that gun?" asked Devin.

"We brought your dog back," Steve interjected, not wanting Devin to know about Tony's ridiculous Bigfoot tale.

"Sit down, Devin, let me tell you a story. A story I told your father when he was about your age."

"You know, we really ought to go," said Steve. Maureen and Becka are waiting for us. Becka got some good shots of the bear and she's eager to get them developed." He put his arm around his son and led him away from the property, and away from the truth regarding Ben Schaefer. "We'll stop by later."

When they were out of Uncle Tony's earshot Devin said, "Dad, you were a little rude. I wanted to hear his story."

"That's exactly what it was-a story."

When they reached the house Maureen was already waiting for them on the porch. She told the kids to get their money and whatever else they wanted to bring into town with them because they planned on being out all day. Devin knew exactly where his wallet was and grabbed it and ran back downstairs.

"Let's go Beck," snapped Maureen. Devin was standing on the porch counting his money while waiting for his sister.

"You guys go to the car. I'll be there in a minute," yelled Becka.

"Where the hell is Becka," asked Steve as Maureen and Devin crawled into the Pathfinder.

"You know Beck, she forgot something or had to pee. She'll only be a minute."

"Maureen! How can you let her walk out here by herself knowing there is a huge predator in the woods across the street!"

"Chill out Steve! The bear is gone, and Becka will be fine."

Becka moved the couch out of the way and went downstairs to see the baby Bigfoot. "Here little guy. I brought you some milk." She cradled the animal in her arms and fed it milk from a water canteen. "I'll buy you some bottles today when I get into town." She smelt urine and felt her hand getting sticky on the beast's bottom. "Diapers too." *Beep beep!* "I got to go baby. I'll be back later." She kissed the animal's cheek and left the canteen with her, wondering if she could hold it herself. As she was shutting the trap door, she saw a sudden ray of light shine on what looked like the wooden bunk beds, meaning only one thing: somebody had opened the root cellar. She shoved the couch back in place and ran out of the house to the car, already scheming up a convincing story to give to her parents in defense of the little monster. Hopping in next to Devin, she saw both her parents in the front seats. Dad was driving, Mom was to his right.

Steve was obviously angry. "What the hell were you doing in there?"

Her heart raced. "Where?"

"In the house! I told you guys to walk out together!"

The car started to roll out of the driveway and onto the black, paved road. She kept her eyes glued to the side of the house as they drove by. It was at this moment that she realized her father couldn't have gone into the cellar and settled back into the car in such a short amount of time, not with his seatbelt already buckled. She turned to Devin who was looking at her with scrunched eyebrows. He was buckled in, too. On the ride to town, she found herself wondering how much time had elapsed since she was in the cellar. Was it possible she was bit by another spider and had another allergic reaction? Could she possibly have passed out again?

She looked again at Devin, who she could tell was pissed off. They had made an agreement that they would not tend to Bigfoot before speaking with Loudbear. It was obvious Becka had broken her promise. She tried to mouth an apology to Devin, but he turned his back to her.

Chapter 32

Special Agent John Galvin arrived at Margo Gargan's house with fresh pastries and knocked on the door. The morning chill was just leaving and the sun was heating up the Adirondacks. Agent John Galvin was still not used to the four different temperature settings throughout the day and arrived in jeans, a T-shirt and a windbreaker.

Margo answered the door wearing dark blue fleece pants with a matching top. "Come in. I just put up some coffee."

John entered the house and sat at the kitchen table. "I'm sorry about what happened to Mr. Whittaker. I'm also sorry to report that we found some major inconsistencies in your story."

"I told you everything I saw, as bizarre as it was."

"Why did you and Mr. Whittaker go back to his motel?"

Margo was getting frustrated at this point. "Like I told you last night, he took a walk behind the motel before picking me up. He threw a rock into the woods, and somebody threw it back at him, hitting him in the head. He got freaked out, and didn't want to sleep there, so I offered him my son's room. We went back to the motel to gather his things and check out."

"Did he have any personal problems with anybody?"

"Yes. Officers Kankro and Demitres. He had some run-in with them on the bridge the night of my son's accident."

"And how did Kankro and Demitres know where Jack was staying?"

"I don't know."

"Why were you going on a date with Mr. Whittaker?"

"It wasn't a date. I was taking him out to dinner for saving my son's life."

"Right. And your son also saw Bigfoot?"

Margo started to laugh. "I know this sounds ridiculous. What doesn't make sense about my story?"

"Well, you said you shot this 'creature' a few times. But, the only blood we found came from Whittaker."

"Did you find his body in the woods?"

"Pieces of it, yeah. The blood matched."

"Did you discuss this with Demitres and Kankro? Maybe it is a cult? Maybe it was someone with a costume with a bulletproof vest underneath," suggested Margo.

"This isn't their jurisdiction. It happened in Diamond Point. But I will go over it with them." Galvin finished his donut. "If there's anything else I need from you, I'll give you a call." And with that, Galvin let himself out.

Margo walked out after Galvin. "Since it's plural, do we call them 'Bigfeet'?"

Galvin was about to get into his car. "Huh?"

Margo chuckled. "Since there were two Bigfoots, should we call them Bigfeet?"

Galvin slammed his car door shut, remaining outside of it. "What the hell are you talking about?"

"Were you listening to my story at all last night? I told you I shot one of them, and then a much larger one came out of nowhere and grabbed Jack. I guess the smaller one recovered, or was carried. I don't know, 'cause I got the hell out of there. I told you this last night."

"No, Margo, that's not what you said. You said you shot Bigfoot, and you thought it was dead, but it must not have been 'cause it got up and attacked Jack. So what are you saying?"

Margo shook her head. "No, I don't think I said that. I mean, yeah, I was pretty shook up, but I know what happened. No, there were definitely two of them. I know, 'cause I was there."

"Were you drinking last night?"

"Well, yeah, I had a little wine, but you were twisting my words around instead of listening. You heard what you wanted to hear. If you had shut-up and listened, you would have understood last night that there were two Bigfoots. Bigfeet."

Galvin stared at Margo, analyzing her body language for an indication that she was lying. He couldn't find one. She was telling the truth, or at least what she thought to be the truth. Was she telling the truth last night as well? Or was he just not listening. She could have been traumatized, buzzed, or a little of both. He decided to go with today's story, although none of it made any sense. He had to get back to the crime scene.

Chapter 33

While Jesse showed Marc the ins and outs of running the lumbar yard, all Marc could think of was how happy he was that his mother and coach kept him on the right path to go to college. Being a running back for the West Virginia Mountaineers had to lead to more success than rotting away at a local lumberyard—even if it was his father's. He hadn't chosen any real career path at this point, but he was becoming more and more interested in anthropology, with a keen interest in cryptozoology. What if he were to discover Bigfoot? Money and success would be at his fingertips. And the women! All the woman he could handle would be lining up to get a taste of his celebrity. Who knew, maybe there would even be a way to parlay the discovery into some kind of reality T.V. show: *Into the Unknown with Professor Blake*. Marc was daydreaming about all the unknown ass he could get his hands on when Jesse noticed the boy was completely unfocused on his work. "Why are you working here this summer?" Jesse asked, "Your old man put you up to it?"

"Yeah. I hate this stuff. I don't know how you do it. Don't you get bored?"

"I design houses for contractors. It's a skill."

"I know, but you're smart. Why didn't you ever go to college?"

"Never had the money. And besides, I'm a real man, I work with my hands." Jesse laid the stack of 2 by 4's down on the cutting table. This guy had a build on him like the starting quarterback on Marc's football team. He wondered who could pick up more chicks if he and Jesse walked into a bar together. It also occurred to him the damage Jesse could inflict on him if he ever hurt his daughter.

"Where's my Dad?"

258

"He's at the Gargan's. He says you guys have been getting along lately."

"Yeah, we have. I know it sounds strange, but it's like Bigfoot opened up something inside my Dad. It's like now we have something to talk about. But I don't think my Dad believes it was Bigfoot anymore. The cops and my mom got him convinced it's Lucifer's Seeds."

"Your Dad's just confused. I think we all are."

"Yeah, but I guess me and my Dad will go back to grunting at each other for the time being."

Jesse rolled up the sleeve of his flannel cut-off shirt, wiping the sweat from his forehead on the shirt pocket. He made a muscle for Marc. "And I never once picked up a set of weights."

"Impressive," Marc responded, as if Jesse knew all the things Marc was thinking about doing to his daughter.

Jesse pulled a long bench out from under a counter and straddled it, with his hands on his knees. Marc got the hint that Jesse wanted to talk, so he carefully put down the Fat Max tape measurer and prepped himself for "the speech." He sat on the bench and waited for Jesse's opening line. To his surprise, Jesse reached into his blue jeans and pulled out a joint, lit it, took a hit, and handed it over to Marc.

Marc thought he was being tested, so he declined the offer.

"Yeah, alright then, suit yourself," said Jesse as he took another hit. "I wanted to talk to you about…"

Marc was waiting for this speech — my daughter's a virgin and if you touch her I'll break your fucking legs. Marc was prepared to talk about Danielle, and had already gone over his responses with Spencer over the phone that morning. To his surprise, however, Jesse continued his sentence on a completely different note.

"…Bigfoot. You saw it. You told me and your Dad that you saw it. You know that this thing is real."

Marc felt relieved and took up Jesse's offer on the joint. "Maybe I'll just take a hit or two. But I'm only smoking because I'm off for the summer. Once football training kicks in, I'll be on my best behavior." Marc inhaled the weed like a pro.

"A little weed never hurt anybody. I myself have never seen Bigfoot. But I know it's here. He's here. I know it, you know it, Uncle Tony knows it, and Bob Murphy knew it. I'm going to catch it, and your old man tells me you have a shitload of notes on this beast that could really help me out."

"Yeah. I took a course in Anthropology, and we focused on Bigfoot for half the semester. My teacher, Professor Ramsey, he wrote a few books on the subject. I wish I had a photo! Do you know how much money we could get if we could catch this thing in action?"

"I do," said Jesse. "But that's not why I want this thing. He killed my dog Norma." Jesse paused a moment and then repeated his words, more slowly this time. "He killed my Norma, and revenge is a mother-fucker." Jesse took the last hit of the joint, then tossed the roach into the dirt.

*   *   *

Even though the FBI was taking over the case, Tom found himself in Margo's living room listening to her side of the story, as if he were the detective in charge. Although she had seen Bigfoot, she believed it was a costume of some sorts. She was adamant about Demitres being behind it somehow.

"That man has been harassing me to go out with him for three years now! Did you know that he tried to blackmail Spencer with a DWI if he wouldn't go home and convince me to go out with him!"

"What did you do?"

"I called him over to my house and politely said I wasn't at all interested. The persistent prick that he is said he wouldn't take no for an answer and I'd sooner or later change my mind!"

Tom thought about that for a moment, again replaying in his mind the last time he was with Bob in the woods. Like a broken record, he couldn't get it out of his mind. "You know, when I first told Bob I had seen Bigfoot, his first reaction was that it was Kankro and Demitres. At the time, I thought it was the stupidest thing I had ever heard."

"And now?" asked Margo.

"What is your take on this Agent Galvin? Do you think you can trust him? Thanks to Jack, we have enough evidence to put these two shmucks behind bars."

"Galvin is not from here. He was assigned to the area to help out with the Lucifer's Seeds case, as Demitres calls it. I get the feeling that he doesn't like them."

"Yeah, he obviously doesn't think it's the Seeds, renaming the case 'The Bigfoot Butcher.' I'm going over to Jim Healy's house and will most likely bring our evidence against the cops to Galvin directly, but I want to feel him out first. Marc mentioned Spencer is coming home today. Is that true?"

"Yeah. I was supposed to pick him up hours ago, but I got hung-up with this crap. That reminds me, I have to go get him."

"This crap? Margo, your date was killed in front of you last night! I think a little more sympathy is required! Jack Whittaker was a good man. Did you know he was personally threatened by Demitres? He got it on tape, and Jim Healy has that tape."

"Yes, I know. I already told that to Galvin. What else do you want from me? My thoughts are elsewhere since Spencer's accident. He's all I have left, you know. I never re-married since Spencer's father walked out on us.

Yeah, I've had dates, but never anything serious. I guess I've learned to emotionally detach myself from the men I date. But about Agent Galvin," said Margo, changing the subject, "I will tell him of my history with Demitres. I think we can trust him."

"I didn't think Jack Whittaker was your type."

Margo turned to Tom. "Why are you so concerned with me going on a date with Jack? It was only a date! You know, dinner and nice conversation."

Tom thought about Margo's reply for a moment, then got the courage to speak the truth. "I know it sounds silly, but you going on a date with Jack knocks you out of fantasy status, you know that right?"

"No, I don't know. Please explain."

"I mean, you're real pretty, and at one time or another every man in this town has fantasized about you. But you lowering your standings for an unattractive man, well that makes it look like maybe the average guy has a shot with you. By going out with Jack, you just might have encouraged half of Warrensburg to ask you out."

"I'm flattered that you think I'm pretty, but I hardly date at all anymore. I went out with Jack because I knew it wouldn't lead to anything, and I felt he was harmless. Turns out, he just wanted to get in my pants like the rest of them. You're a good man, Tom. Sherry's a lucky lady to have a guy like you." Tom was about to mention that he really didn't have much of a marriage left but a knock on the door made him keep his comments to himself. Margo answered the door to find the devil himself standing there: Demitres.

"What do you want?" asked Margo, stepping out onto the porch so he wouldn't come inside.

"Where do you get off telling Agent Peckerhead that I wanted Jack Whittaker dead?"

"That is not what I said!"

"And what were you doing going out with a train wreck like Whittaker anyway?"

Tom heard the ruckus and came to the screen door.

"You move fast, hotpants! Can I be next in line?"

Tom stepped out onto the porch. "You got no business being here, Demitres."

"You stay out of this Tom! This little bitch is trying to set me up! Telling the FBI that I'm dressing up as Bigfoot and killing people!"

"I didn't say that. But come to think of it, the size and smell of the beast wasn't all that much different from you. And you do have a bulletproof vest, and you do live rather close to Diamond Point, and where were you last night?"

"Fuck you!" Demitres jumped off Margo's porch and kicked her deer statue, knocking its head off. He got into his car and sped off the property, spinning his tires.

"I'm sorry about him, Margo. He'll cool off."

Margo smiled. "I ain't scared of him. Listen, I have to go. We'll talk later, O.K.?"

Margo and Tom left at the same time. Tom sat in his car and allowed Margo to back out of the driveway first. As she drove away, Tom thought of Jack's last night on earth and how he spent it with a babe like Margo. That was probably the hottest woman that man had ever gotten with in his entire life. Poor son of a bitch. Tom gripped his steering wheel and pulled away from the Gargan's place. Being in Bob's neighborhood gave him the creeps.

Chapter 34

The Bettis' arrived at the Grand Union parking lot located in the center of town. Steve dropped Becka and Maureen off near the one-hour photo store and told them he was going to Madeline Totten's house to research the flowers. He told his wife about the storm, but cautiously left out the part about losing the kids temporarily. He and Devin promised to meet the girls by Loudbear's space at the church in an hour.

Madeline Totten's house was not far from the shopping center, and Steve had no problem finding it. He remembered making a left at the fork, taking note that he had never gone to the right before, curious as to where it led. Upon arriving at the old woman's house, Steve and Devin noticed a wooden statue of an Indian chief on her porch. The figure looked old, yet still in good condition.

Devin couldn't believe his eyes upon seeing the statue. "Dad! That's him! That's the ghost at the Farm! That's him! I know him! I've talked to him!"

Madeline came to the door, elated at the sight of Steve standing on her porch. "Steve Bettis. To what do I owe this visit?"

"Hi Madeline," he said as he leaned over and kissed her on the cheek and introduced her to Devin. "That's an interesting statue. Are you of Native American ancestry?"

"I've done some research on my family. I may be part of the Mohican Tribe, but there's no concrete evidence. Anyway, everything you see in and around my house has a story or two behind it." She gestured towards the Indian. "Loudbear made it. I bought it years ago from him. That is the closest replica you're going to get of Chief Ta Ta. Now that man knows his history! I told you he was harmless. Would you like to come in and have a cup of tea?"

"Would you mind if I stay on the porch?" asked Devin. "I'm amazed by the statue."

Madeline smiled. "Go ahead. Let yourself in when you're ready."

"I'd like that, thank you," Steve smiled, taking Madeline up on her offer of a cup of tea.

Madeline led Steve into her house. As Steve followed her, he felt the statue's eyes following him, and had to admire Loudbear's artistic ability. Her living room contained trinkets of all kinds ranging from old antique collectible dolls to an entire Smurf village on the far side of the room. "I like your décor. My daughter would get a kick out of this."

"That's nothing. Follow me. I'll give you the tour." Madeline pointed to the dining room, which consisted of a large table underneath an entire gingerbread village.

"Are they edible?"

"They were at one time. They're all old and preserved now. That shininess you see is a coat of spray-glue to keep the bugs from wanting to eat it." Hanging in all four corners of the rooms were life-size wooden string puppets of Goofy, Donald, Pluto, and Mickey.

Steve felt like a kid who blinked his eyes and ended up in Disney World. "Wow! Where did you get this stuff?"

"My husband was in the Navy. He traveled everywhere and came back with all these goodies. My son contributed a lot, too. You like Warner Brothers?"

"Who doesn't?"

An entrance way out of the dining room lead to a kitchen where, if you didn't know any better, you would have thought Porky Pig himself lived. There were Porky cookie jars, Porky clocks, Porky washcloths and Porky statues. "I like pigs," she told Steve. In the kitchen was a back door that opened to a small deck. "Don't be shy, go on ahead."

Steve stepped out onto the deck and couldn't believe what he was looking at. An entire fleet of antique Ford cars flooded the back yard. "The greatest vehicle is in the garage. I'll get the tea ready and call you when it's done."

Steve strolled along the property, carefully inspecting and admiring each car. He found himself wishing his father were still alive to see this, then remembered why he had come to Madeline's in the first place. It was easy to loose focus in a place like this. He followed the cement path to the garage and peeked in. To his surprise, he saw a life size sled that could have belonged to Santa Claus himself. It looked like one of those sleighs on a carousel, with real, black, leather backed seats. The body of the sled was wood, painted red with gold trimmed décor.

Madeline yelled out the back door. "Now go behind the garage!"

Steve couldn't imagine what could top Santa's sleigh, but made his way behind the garage to find a real caboose from a very old, yet classy looking train that seemed as if it was from another century. He pictured beautiful woman with long, fancy dresses and hair in rolls of curls with bonnets on their heads and carrying umbrellas as they walked on and off the train. Visions of gentlemen wearing top hats to greet them came to mind. It took him a few moments to pull himself out of la-la land to go have tea with this fascinating woman.

"I'm just amazed. I don't even know what to say."

"Thank you. If your daughter is into dolls, I have every Barbie ever made in their original boxes in my Barbie room upstairs. She's more than welcome to take a look."

"My daughter was never into dolls, but my wife would love it! If you don't mind me asking, are you well-to-do?"

"I come from a family of collector's. Most of this stuff I inherited. And when I pass, my son will get everything you see here."

"This stuff has got to be worth millions! You do know that, don't you?"

"Of course. But like I said, everything you see here tells a story of its own. And that is priceless. My son jokes around that when I go, he's going to turn this place into a museum."

"Does your son live around here?"

"My son will never have roots. His mail comes here, but he is an archeologist in Africa right now. Who knows where he'll be off to next?"

"That reminds me," Steve pulled the blue flowers from his shirt pocket. "Can you tell me anything about these flowers?"

"At least somebody listens when I talk. I feel honored that you remember me telling you I was a botanist." Madeline took the flowers in her hand. Off the living room was a smaller room, which appeared to be an office of some sorts with ancient flowers in glass cases, hundreds of books on shelves, and a small desk in the middle of the room. Unlike the other rooms in the house, this one did not have any puppets or figurines, just posters of plants and flowers. Madeline sat down at her desk, put on her reading glasses, and turned on an overhead lamp to carefully inspect the blue beauties. Steve stood across the room from her, giving her some space.

She got up and rummaged through some books on the shelves, finally deciding on the one that could be of the most assistance. Skimming through the index, she turned to page sixty-seven, and placed the book open on the desk, comparing the blue flowers to the ones pictured in the book.

Steve glanced over her shoulder as she sat down again with a magnifying glass. "That's it! We have a match!" He almost shouted.

Madeline pulled the glasses down over the bridge of her nose. "We have a match alright. But I'm afraid these are not flowers. If you recall the statue of Chief Ta Ta on my porch, you might have noticed a pouch over his shoulder. In his pouch he carried these 'flowers,' called vipor's bugloss. It's actually a rare weed only found in Michigan. I've looked it up years earlier, when I purchased the statue from Loudbear."

"What did the Indian Chief do with them?"

"That's where the story gets a little tricky. According to Loudbear, Chief Ta Ta's pregnant wife scurried into the woods with a few other women in the midst of an ambush from the white men. When Ta Ta's men found her, she was cut open and the fetus had been ripped from her stomach. She held on for as long as she could, but died within a few days of the attack. The Mohicans searched for the baby, but it was never found." Madeline paused and looked out the window. "After the passing of his wife, Chief Ta Ta went on a mission with his two strongest men. He told his people that the white men would pay for what they had done. He returned the next winter with the pouch of vipor's bugloss. The two men who accompanied the chief on this journey said that they had met up with a medicine man from another tribe. This medicine man, or spiritual leader, was filled with rage when he heard of the latest attack by the white man. He cursed these flowers, and told Ta Ta and his men to spread them around the villages of these evil white men."

Steve was not one to believe in superstitions, until he heard this story. "You mean they're bad luck?"

"Worse. The flowers were cursed and given the power to raise the beast. Stronger and more powerful than any white man or his weapons. This creature was created not only to kill the devils who had slaughtered the Mohicans, but to seek out and destroy the white man for many generations to come. They called this beast 'Sasquatch'."

*   *   *

After a sharing a calzone and half a pizza pie at Marco Polo's, Maureen and Becka walked across the street to pick up the film. Becka was surprised at how much a roll of thirty-six prints cost in such a small upstate town, then cursed silently again for forgetting her digital camera at home. Luckily for her, Devin promised to pitch in on the cost or Becka would have had no money left for the remainder of the trip. She tore open the envelope of photos while sitting on a bench outside the Grand Union, patiently waiting for Steve and Devin. Maureen looked at her watch, then sat on the bench with her daughter.

"Let me see these wolves," said Maureen.

"O.K., O.K. Let me get to them first. I think this is Loudbear's stuff. It's pictures of his jewelry." Becka ruffled through the photos to get to the dogs, secretly placing one picture under her thigh. "Here. This is Hammerhead."

"Wow, and you said they're friendly? This dog is huge!"

"I guess I have to give the camera back now. When are we going home?"

Maureen brushed Becka's hair behind her ear with her fingertip. "I'm not sure, Beck. Did you want to go soon?"

"No way! C'mon, I'll introduce you to Loudbear. He is so cool!"

They walked over to the church and up the hill to the area that once housed the big oak tree where Loudbear sold his crafts.

Loudbear was sitting on a bench sipping a canteen of water when Becka called out for him. "Look! Look! We saw a bear on our property! Here are the pictures!" Becka handed the entire envelope over to Loudbear. He stopped at the picture of Hammerhead and smiled.

"I'm Maureen," she said as she held out her hand to Loudbear.

"Hello." He looked down at Becka. "You look just like your mother."

"My kids can't stop talking about you."

"And where is Devin?"

"He and his father are at Madeline Totten's house, researching blue flowers. Do you know her?" asked Maureen.

"I do. This is the bear, I suppose," he said as he held up the photo of the bear clawing at the crawlspace."

"That's him!"

"Do you keep food in the root cellar?" asked Loudbear.

Maureen was impressed with herself that she knew what he was talking about. "No. No. We haven't opened that thing in years."

Loudbear noticed Becka wearing her necklace. He looked at her and forced a smile, immediately thinking she must have had another bad incident. Maureen caught the glance and felt awkward. "What is this," he asked her holding up one of the prints.

Becka was so proud of her painting that she had taken a picture of it. "That's the Farm. And that is our back yard. And those are blue flowers that I found. I also painted a picture of them."

Maureen intercepted. "I think they're native to the land. My mother-in-law says they are her anniversary flowers."

Loudbear handed the prints back to Becka. "I'm familiar with them." He looked down at Becka, whose eyes told him she was keeping something from him. No doubt it was her mother's presence causing the silence.

An interested customer asked Loudbear for the price of a bracelet, and Becka led Maureen away to another vendor. Becka looked back at Loudbear, whose eyes were fixated on her. Becka was hiding something, and Loudbear needed to be alone with her. The customer paid for the bracelet, and Loudbear bent down to retrieve tissue paper from under his table. The back of a photograph was resting on his box of feathers. Loudbear wrapped the bracelet, sending his customer off. He picked up the picture and turned it around. To his astonishment, he saw a picture of Devin holding a miniature Bigfoot. Loudbear knew he needed to get Becka away from her mother, and his eyes scanned the yard sale in search of her.

*   *   *

Devin and Steve thanked Madeline for her time, and Devin apologized for not coming in, but said he felt nauseous and needed to be outside. He looked as pale as a ghost. Steve asked his son numerous times if he needed him to pull over, but Devin insisted he'd be alright.

After seeing the statue of Chief Ta Ta, Devin already knew about the blue flowers, but thought he'd test his father to see if Steve would tell him the truth. "What did she say about the flowers?"

"You were right. They're weeds."

"Did she say anything else about them?"

"They originated from Michigan."

"What are they doing here?"

271

"I don't know, but you should have come in. She has a Santa Claus sled in her backyard! And a caboose!"

There goes Dad, changing the subject again. "I just want to go to the yard sale, and see Loudbear."

"What is it with you and Loudbear?"

"He's honest. I like honesty in a person. Wouldn't you agree?"

"Yeah, but you hardly know him. How can you know he's honest?"

"He saved my life in a lightening storm. He pulled me out of the way when a huge oak tree was about to land on me. He risked his life for me. City Fireman do that for money. He did it for nothing. I'll take it one step further and say that he did it for someone whose ancestor's wiped out his ancestors. Is that good enough for you?"

"O.K. That's enough."

Steve parked in the Grand Union shopping center and the two of them walked over to the church yard sale. Devin saw that his mother and sister were not with Loudbear, and told his father to look around for them and meet him at Loudbear's stand in a few minutes. Steve didn't feel like being around Loudbear, so he agreed.

"Loudbear! Did you see Becka?"

Loudbear was relieved to see Devin. "I did. She left me this photo. Is this what I think it is?"

"Yes. It lives in our root cellar. What should we do about it?"

"If you parents weren't so, well, white, we could compromise. But unfortunately, they can't be reasoned with."

"I know all about the blue flowers. My vision told me everything. There are going to be more killings, Loudbear. I saw Chief Ta Ta's statue at Madeline's house and had another vision. This one was bad...real bad. There are more Bigfoots. A lot more. And not here. North. We're talking, Canada, or Alaska. Somewhere with great amounts of snow. They will wipe out everyone there."

"Devin, you must understand that your Farm is on Chief Ta Ta's land."

"I think I know that now. Should we move the baby?"

"Do not go near the baby unless I tell you otherwise. I'm sorry. I know the way you feel about animals. I feel the same way. But these Sasquatches are not animals in the sense that we know animals. They are killing machines. If trained properly, this baby may have a chance. But it's too late for the parents. I must destroy them. Sit tight. I'll come by your Farm with a plan. I promise. And be careful."

Chapter 35

Agent Galvin sat in his temporary office at the Warrensburg precinct and mapped out his findings on a dry-erase board. Peering through the shade on the door which separated his office from the lobby area, he spotted the chubby little police secretary and held up his mug for a refill of the station-house coffee, which actually wasn't half bad.

Mrs. Schneider caught the look and fetched the coffee, bringing Galvin a new mug that bore a picture of her newest granddaughter. She knocked before opening the door, as the shade was shut again. The FBI agent opened the door for her and offered her a seat adjacent to his.

"Please. Come in."

Mrs. Schneider handed John Galvin the mug. "That's my latest granddaughter, Christie Joyce."

Galvin studied the mug carefully. "She's beautiful. She has your eyes."

Mrs. Schneider sat nervously across the table with her hands crossed on her lap, trying to conceal her anxiety. "You know, it's not everyday that a fellow from the FBI comes to this neck of the woods. 'Specially not one as young and good-looking as yourself," she blushed.

Galvin took a small sip of coffee then placed his mug on top of the table. "I was expecting Sheriff Farley an hour ago. Have you heard from him?"

The old secretary shook her head.

"O.K. Then I'll start my next step. Let me begin by explaining to you that I am going to interview everyone in this precinct. I expect that everyone will be brutally honest with me. I also expect that everything we speak about in this room, stays in this room. If you discuss anything that we speak about here today to anyone at the water cooler, you could lose your job. Do you understand?"

"Yes Sir, although I'm afraid I'm not sure what we're talking about."

Even better, thought Galvin. He started with the simple questions first: where do you live, how long have you worked here, etc. As the interrogation progressed, so did Schneider's trust in Galvin. If he hadn't kept her on track, she'd be telling him stories of her grandkids right now. "You're doing great," he assured her. "I have just a few more routine questions concerning your co-workers." Schneider took a deep breath, then nodded for the agent to continue. "Officer Demitres. How would you describe your relationship with him?"

"Oh, he don't bother with me much," she answered as she waved her hand in the air. "In fact, I really don't see much of him at all. He's not a sit at your desk kind of cop."

"Would you say that he is a hard worker?"

"That's not for me to judge."

"Whahooo! Let's give gratitude where it is earned! Demitres and Kankro have more arrests than any other pair of officers in this station combined! They stay late and sometimes come in early. Doesn't that sound like somebody who busts their ass day in and day out on the job?"

"I guess so, if you put it that way."

"Ma'am, what other way is there to put it? Now let me ask you, if Demitres was to apply for a job with the FBI, would you recommend him for the position?"

Frustration fluttered across Schneider's face. "That's not for me to decide."

"But if it was, what would you say?"

Mrs. Schneider got up and made her way to the door, slightly lifting the shade to see who was in the lobby. Satisfied with her findings, or lack of, she walked back to the agent but chose not to sit. "Mr. Galvin, he is a very bad man. Kankro too."

"If they are so bad, then how is it that they are entrusted by the people in the town of Warrensburg to protect them?"

The old lady caught the sarcasm in the agent's voice and felt reassured that this would have no bearing on her job. "Sheriff Farley, he personally recruited Kankro and Demitres."

"You have my ear. Why?"

Schneider loved to gossip. When she worked at Town Hall, she didn't miss a beat. Since she'd been at the police station, where she was the only female, the only juicy information she'd hear about was what Sam the voluptuous check-out girl at the meat store was wearing. "Word has it that Kankro and Demitres were small time bookies for the mob a few years back. Farley had a bad gambling problem and was indebted to them for a lot of money."

Galvin interrupted. "How much?"

Schneider shook her head. "I don't know. Thousands. Anyway, he couldn't pay so he offered them both jobs here in Warrensburg. They're from Brooklyn, you know. I think they may still be involved with the Mafia. But nobody ever talks about it."

"Their records show that they both live in Bolton Landing now. Is that correct?"

"I believe so. If you ask me, I'd say they started their own mafia up here."

"Not for long. I'm going to single handedly take them down and give you your town back. How does that sound?"

Schneider headed towards the door that led to the rest of the precinct. She paused before opening the door and glanced over at Galvin. "I think you need a partner. Somebody from the inside maybe." Winking at the captivating young agent, she left the room.

Galvin rested his coffee mug by his side and opened up the "Lucifer's Seeds" report written and signed by Officer Alan Kankro:

June 27, 2004 – Tara Conner, 17, recent high school graduate reported missing. Detective Desmiro from Carmel gave the case top priority. He had her computer analyzed and found a year-long history of e-mails and instant messages traced back to cult affiliates of Lucifer's Seeds, a group which originated in Putnam Lake, New York. All the recipients are not known at this time.

June 29, 2004 – Mr. Matt Moran reported that two horses and a cow had been killed on his property. The insides were missing from all animals. There were no witnesses, but Moran claims he last saw his animals alive around 8:00 P.M.

July 3, 2004 – Mr. Bob Murphy called in a complaint. He claims he saw some teenagers, all dressed in black, stealing sodas from the delivery truck that he parks on his property. He ran outside and chased them away. My partner and I responded to the call, where we found the locks had been pried open. When canvassing the area, we found a class ring we traced back to Carmel, New York. The ring belonged to Miss Tara Conner, 17, of Carmel New York.

July 5, 2004 – Tara Conner's vehicle was found in the back of the McDonald's parking lot in Warrensburg, New York. The doors were unlocked and nothing appeared to be missing. The K-9 unit was called in and traced the scent to the Schroon River. Divers went searching and found the remains of Tara Conner. Medical Examiner reported her organs were missing. We investigated satanic rituals and believe Miss Conner to be the victim, willingly or not, of the Lucifer's Seeds.

July 7, 2004 – Dale Botte reported missing by his wife, Pat Botte. Last seen fishing on Schroon River.

July 8, 2004 – Tom Blake's barn animals had been brutally butchered. Not reported until three days later. No leads. Also, Blake claims his employee's dog had been murdered too.

July 10, 2004-- Between the hours of 9 and 10 PM, Mr. Bob Murphy was at his residence alone. He was last seen at the east end of the bridge heading westbound by Marc Blake, Danielle Luongo, and Spencer Gargan. Statements from Blake and Gargan claim the victim was being chased by a large, ape-like creature. Luongo claims no recollection as she was drunk at the time of the incident. Medical Examiner states organs are missing, removed in a manner identical to Conner's. Let it be known: Murphy's body was found within a half mile radius of Conner's body. Ruled as a homicide, remains are to be put to rest.

July 11, 2004 – Johnny Walker left his house in the late evening with his dog to scare off some deer on his property. Mr. Walker claims he was gone no more than 15 minutes, but when he returned he found his girlfriend, Dina Puglesi, naked and dead on his kitchen floor. Cocaine was found on the premises and in Puglesi's bloodstream. The organs were missing, but no weapons were found. Manner of death is ruled to be a homicide.

John had read enough bullshit for the day. He closed the file and dialed the direct number to the medical examiner, Dr. Theodore Jones. "This is Special Agent John Galvin of the FBI. I need to speak to the doctor immediately." The secretary assured the agent it would only be a minute. Not ten seconds later, the medical examiner was on the other line.

"Dr. Jones speaking."

"Dr. Jones, this is Agent Galvin of the FBI. I need your final report regarding the recent killings with organs missing."

"Yes, well I'm afraid I don't have much for you. My findings are that the organs were not cut out of the victims. The victims were very much alive when these horrific incidents occurred. Worse than that, there seems to be no instrument I am aware of that could do something like this. I'd have to say that we're dealing with a very sick serial killer. A man with the strength and adrenaline, most likely doped up on speed, to rip his victims apart with his bare hands. I wish I had a definite murder weapon in order to give you something to go on. I'm sorry. I've never seen anything like this before."

"I see. In your professional opinion, would you say that it's likely there is a pair of serial killers out there, possibly working together?"

"Anything's possible at this point. But I don't see any bruising that would indicate that the victims were held down by a second party. It appears that in all cases the victims were attacked from behind. In the case of Dina Puglesi, there was an impression of a large handprint on her back. I imagine that's not very helpful to you. Do you have any leads?"

"I believe I do. I'm going to need that report on Whittaker ASAP." Galvin hung up with the medical examiner and found Mrs. Schneider at his desk again, this time holding a sealed yellow envelope. "What is that?"

Mrs. Schneider handed Galvin the envelope. "It's an official police report made by Dina Puglesi accusing Officer Kankro of molesting her."

"I went through Kankro's docket. I didn't see this."

"That's because I shredded it, on Farley's orders. But I managed to make a copy before destroying the original."

"Why wouldn't Farley want this on record?"

"I told you why. Sheriff Farley is just as crooked as his deputies. But that's not all. While you were on the phone with the medical examiner, Tom Blake stopped by, and said it was urgent that you get this tape as soon as possible."

"Who is Tom Blake? That name sounds so familiar."

"His barn animals were killed, and his son witnessed Bob Murphy's murder. He owns the lumber yard on Schroon River Road. Nice guy."

"Right, I just read that." He took the tape from Schneider and played it, revealing Demitres and Kankro threatening Jack Whittaker days before he was killed. "Where did Blake get this tape?"

"Tom Blake is in the reception area, waiting to talk to you. I'll bring him in."

Chapter 36

Danielle's stepfather agreed to give her the Jeep back, as long as she didn't rub it in her father's face. She drove to Marc's house after renting a few movies. Spencer and Marie were both home from the hospital, and Spencer insisted on spending the night watching horror films with his friends. A little weird, Danielle thought, especially after what he had just gone through. Weirder than that, Marc called to invite Danielle to watch movies with them! Still furious about Sherry's mix-up involving a girl named Allison, Danielle was ready to confront Marc.

She wore a pair of tight Levi's jeans with an even tighter white tank top. Justine suggested the outfit, saying men can't refuse a woman in a snug fitting pair of jeans. She drove to Marc's house and walked up to the porch, bending down to pet the small pig tied to a rope leash. The pig squealed with excitement, alerting Tom of her presence even before Danielle had the chance to knock.

"C'mon in Danielle." He held the screen door open for her, and looked around for anyone else. "Marc's in his room, go ahead."

Danielle hurried past Tom, feeling slightly awkward for being there, and wondering if Sherry had told her husband about how Danielle had spent the night there.

Marc was lounging in his jeans, also wearing a white tank top.

"You better go home and change, I was wearing this outfit first," he joked.

"Well, it looks better on me, so you change."

Marc got up from his bed and kissed her on the cheek. "Did you get the movies?"

"Yeah, *Friday the 13th*, parts one and two. Before we go, there's something I want to ask you."

Marc sat back down on his bed. "Shoot."

281

"Who's Allison?"

"Allison who?"

"That's what I'm trying to find out. Your mother called me Allison. Why would she slip up like that?"

Marc hadn't seen the connection at first. "Are you asking *me* to tell you what my mother is thinking?"

Danielle thought about that one for a second. "Yeah, I guess I am. It just so happens that she called me Allison while she was discussing how she doesn't want us having sex together!"

"Well, there you have it. My mother is a slick one, be careful of her."

"Seriously, do you have a girlfriend maybe at school that you don't want me to know about?"

Marc ran his hands through his thick brown hair. "Do you have any idea how different college is than high school? Or how it is to even be out of Warrensburg?"

Danielle folded her arms across her chest. "Please explain."

"I wish I could explain it. For starters, you're in a strange place and you don't know anyone. And you know that other people know each other, but you're not part of the plan. In high school here in Warrensburg, I thought I was this amazing running back. In West Virginia, I barely made the team! I can't tell my parents that I ride the bench most of the time, and only get playing time when someone better gets an injury. Before W.V., I really thought I was on my way to the NFL."

He could sense that she just wasn't grasping it. "O.K. For example, you are really hot, I mean you must know that you are the hottest girl in Warrensburg, right?"

Danielle blushed. "If you say so."

"Well, let's say that you go away to school. Forget about Warrensburg. You walk onto campus, thinking you're the shit, right? You hair looks awesome, you're finally a C-cup, or whatever."

282

"O.K. I see, go on."

"O.K., well imagine you just stepped onto campus, and you're surrounded by Pamela Anderson and Cindy Crawford look-alikes! You see your reflection on the wall, and you realize that you're not what you thought you were. Can you grasp what I'm saying?"

Danielle thought about the nightmare of not being the hottest girl in the room. "Yeah, I get it. That's awful. But it doesn't explain why you're not dating someone else?"

"Because I don't know who the fuck I am anymore! That's why! I'm with you because I finally feel comfortable again. The guys on the team, they don't respect me. Classes are tough, and I haven't adjusted yet. The last thing in the world I need at college is a girlfriend!"

Danielle eased her way to the bed, making herself comfortable on his lap. "What about us?"

"I don't know. I think we're O.K., for now. Let's not rock the boat, all right? I have enough on my plate. And as for my mother, let's just say that I barely know who she is anymore. For instance, I've been waiting for Professor Ramsey to call, you know, about all this Bigfoot shit going on. Well, I checked the caller I.D., and he's called like seven times! I asked my mother if he called, and she tells me no. Do I confront her? I mean, she knows this means something to me and my Dad. We finally have something in common, even if it turns out to be nothing. It's bringing us closer together."

Danielle kissed his forehead, recalling her strange morning with Marc's mother a few days ago. There was definitely something odd about her. "Well, there you have it. Your mother is jealous of your relationship with your father. Trust me. My parents do this shit all the time. I wouldn't' worry about it, O.K.? Let's go pick up Marie."

"I assure you, there is no other girl. Do you believe me?"

Danielle looked deep into Marc's eyes. "I do. But I don't want to get hurt. So please be honest with me, O.K.? I'm starting college in the fall, and I'm going to be in the same mental state as you. I can't predict what will or won't happen, but we have this summer together. And I like spending time with you. So don't fuck it up!"

Marc leaned in and kissed Danielle with a passion that surprised even himself. "I know it's weird, but I feel like we're in this thing together. You know? The killings, I mean. It could be any one of us. It could have been Spencer on the bridge!"

"I know." Danielle wrapped her arms around Marc and held him for a few moments before releasing her grip.

"Oh shit! I know who Allison is! Before I was born I had a sister, Allison, who died. My mom never got over it. It's a sore subject for her. I'm sorry I didn't make the connection right away."

"Oh my God! I'm so sorry Marc! I feel like an idiot!"

"It's alright. It's not your fault. C'mon. Let's get out of this crazy house."

On their way out they heard Tom and Sherry arguing on the porch. Sherry was screaming at Tom for stepping on the pig, telling him he kills everything he touches. Marc decided to exit the house from the back door, thinking his father's rebuttal was rather strange.

"I didn't touch my own son for three months because of your superstitions! So don't give me that bullshit anymore! I'm done with your insanity. You have to move on, Sherry," his father pleaded.

"Oh, I will, Tom. Mark my words, I will. I'll move on from you!"

Chapter 37

Demitres and Kankro met at Potter's diner before their meeting with John Galvin. They both ordered a plate of silver dollar pancakes and sipped coffee while waiting for their breakfast.

"I don't like this," barked Demitres. "Since when does the FBI get involved with armpit towns? I don't like the way that peckerhead was looking at me. I think he has something up his sleeve."

Kankro leaned in across the table so none of the other patrons in the diner could listen in. "Are you sure you covered all your tracks? I mean, really sure?"

"What the fuck kind of question is that? Of course I'm sure. What about you?"

Kankro insisted he also had no trails that could possibly lead back to him.

Demitres slammed his coffee mug on the table. "Where the fuck is Sheriff Farley? He's supposed to have our backs if anything goes wrong. We sure give him enough of our extra earnings!"

"That spineless fuck! You know what he's doing, don't you? He's letting us take the fall!" Kankro waved his hands up in the air.

"Hold on now. We don't know that the FBI is onto anything. This is their M.O. They're going to try to turn us against each other. Did we leave any loose strings? I want to be prepared for whatever this fuckhead throws at us."

The two men sat in silence as the waitress delivered the food to the table and refilled their coffees. Demitres stared blankly at Kankro, while he dug into his pancakes.

Kankro felt the stare and looked up at Demitres. "What?"

"Tuesday night. Where were you?"

Kankro barely finished chewing his food. "Home, why?"

"I went to your house. You weren't home."

"Yeah, why did you come to my house?"

"It doesn't matter now," scowled Demitres. "Point is, Margo Gargan was insinuating that I had something to do with Jack's murder. She told the FBI that I had a problem with Whittaker."

"So what? She's obviously wrong, isn't she?"

"Right. I had nothing to do with that. But I don't have an alibi for that night, either. I went to your house, but you weren't there, so I just drove around."

Kankro continued to cut up his pancakes. "Drove around my ass. I hope you don't plan on selling that story to the Feds. That's why we have to go over all loose ends."

"Fuck!" Demitres piled a stack of food into his mouth.

"Relax," said Kankro. "We'll just say we were together at my house drinking a few beers."

Demitres thought about it for a second. "Sounds good. But really, where were you? Your car was in the driveway, but you weren't home. You left your back door unlocked and I went in."

"Why the fuck are you sneaking around my house? Is there something you want to tell me?"

"It's nothing. Not important now, anyway. So, we were together, right?"

Kankro looked up at Demitres. "That depends. Did anyone see you Tuesday night that could say we weren't together?"

"Definitely not."

Kankro nonchalantly looked around the room, making sure no one was watching them. "There is one thing I think I should tell you."

Demitres knew his partner was hiding something, and thought this might be it. "Tell me." He smeared his

286

hash browns in the ketchup, then spooned them into his mouth.

"Dina Puglesi. The girl who was attacked in Walker's cabin."

Demitres looked up, "Yeah, what about her?"

"Well, not so long ago, I had my way with her when I pulled her over. She was a fine piece of ass!"

Kankro's perpetual habit of threatening and then molesting women was not a secret to Demitres. "So, who's she gonna tell? She's dead."

Kankro tilted his head down towards the table, making minimal eye contact, "She filed a report on me."

"Farley would never put it through." The look on Kankro's face told him otherwise. "What? You think he did?"

"I know he did," exclaimed Kankro. "I saw the file on Old Lady Schneider's desk. When I asked Farley about it, he said that Puglesi's sister came in with her to report the crime and, for the record, insisted that Schneider be there as a witness!"

"You're saying that Schneider knows?"

"Yeah, she knows Dina's side of the story. But I explained everything to the old bat and she believes me. I persuaded her not to file the report."

"What did she do with the actual report?"

"She shredded it. I watched her do it."

Demitres did not trust the old lady, and he pressed Kankro for any more info the secretary might have. "Here's what we do. We get a hold of Sheriff Farley, and avoid Galvin until we speak to him."

Kankro agreed. The two cops finished their breakfast with a growing feeling of uncertainty and, for the first time in their lives, mutual distrust. Demitres wondered what Kankro was up to Tuesday night, while Kankro thought about Demitres thumbing through his house.

When the check came, Kankro paid it while Demitres stepped outside to make a phone call.

"Warrensburg police. How may I help you?"

"Mrs. Schneider, this is Officer Demitres. Is Sheriff Farley in?

Kankro met his partner in the parking lot, watching Demitres' expression while on the phone. Demitres disconnected the call and walked fast to the police cruiser, getting behind the wheel. Kankro jumped in the passenger seat, not liking the look on his partner's face. "Did you get in touch with Farley?" asked Kankro.

"Not exactly. Let's try him at his house." Demitres pulled out of the parking lot and drove down Main Street, passing the police station and Town Hall. "Fucking Farley! I don't like it when people don't pick up their phones. He blew off a meeting with Galvin yesterday, and now he's not at the office. I didn't see his car at Town Hall either."

"You don't think he's turning us in, do you?"

"What the fuck else am I supposed to think?"

They pulled into Farley's driveway alongside the Sheriff's personal car. The ranch styled house was deceivingly larger inside than it appeared from the exterior. Demitres knocked on the front door while Kankro went to the back.

Kankro walked around the side of the property, the light winds casting off soft, harmonious melodies as they swept past Farley's collection of wind chimes hanging neatly in rows off the soffit on the side of the house. He unlocked the back gate and followed the slate path to the mahogany deck. Walking up the three steps of the deck, he reached the glass sliding doors and he peered through them, looking to see if Farley was in there. The television was off, and he didn't hear any sounds, so he knocked on the glass door. He was about to knock again when Demitres opened the door.

"How the fuck did you get in there?"

"He left a window open. He ain't here. So where the fuck is he?" Demitres stepped onto the back deck with Kankro, pushing past him.

Kankro paced around the perimeter of the deck. "Did you check the whole house?"

"What do you think I was doing in there, jerking off? Of course I did?"

Kankro looked out at the large property, neatly landscaped with decorative shrubs and walking paths to several sitting areas. He tilted his head and squinted his eyes when the hammock on the north-east side of the estate caught his attention. He nudged Demitres elbow. "Check out that hammock back there. Does it look like someone is laying in it?"

Demitres cupped his hands, shielding the sun from his eyes. "I can't tell. Let's go take a look. If I find out that Farley is handing us over I'm going to fucking kill him right here, like we should've done years ago."

"Take it easy. He's probably just hung-over."

"Bullshit," sneered Demitres. "He's been laying low for two days now. Fuck him!"

Farley was lying in the hammock, wearing a cowboy hat, blue jeans, boots, and a flannel shirt. A bottle of wine was tipped over under the hammock, and his right arm was dangling over the side, as well as his left leg.

"Hey Farley," yelled Kankro as they approached him from behind.

Farley didn't answer.

Demitres stood over the sheriff and stared in disbelief as he saw an almost perfect circle in the middle of Farley's chest, leading right through to the canvas hammock. He bent down and looked under the hammock, and where the blood had been dripping, which was dry by now. Right where the wine had spilled. Had the hat been placed over his chest, you'd never even know he was dead. "Check this out, Kankro. This killer is a fucking artist!"

"Yeah, well, sorry I don't see it. What I do see is that we are going to take the fall for this if it's true that you think Galvin already suspects us!"

Demitres snapped back into paranoia. "Alright! We'll say it's the Seeds. We'll say we got here, and we have evidence that the Seeds did it."

Kankro walked across the lawn, putting a safe distance between himself and Demitres. "We have nothing! This isn't about a bunch of kids stealing sodas from Bob Murphy's Pepsi truck. It's on a much larger scale. And we have nothing to go on! Nothing! That's why the fucking FBI is here! 'Cause we have nothing! So forget about the satanic cult! Let's start all over, and catch this mother-fucker before we lose our jobs! I don't know about you, but I like it up here. The last thing I want to do is go back to Brooklyn to break the kneecaps of deadbeats who can't pay up! Our jobs are on the line here, and with Farley dead we're on our own. This isn't good, pal. This isn't good."

Demitres knew his partner was right. Another murder, especially the murder of Sheriff Farley, would have them taken off the job indefinitely. It didn't take long for Demitres' devious mind to spring into action. "I've got an idea." Let's hide the body, then put all our efforts into finding the killer. If we find the killer before he strikes again, we kill him on the spot and Galvin will think Farley was the killer."

Kankro's eyes lit up. "You're a fucking genius! We can dump the body in the lake tonight, and it'll look like Farley left town."

"Exactly. I'm gonna gather a few of his things, like his wallet and some clothes, make it look like he was planning a getaway. You start by cleaning up the blood from the hammock."

Chapter 38

John Galvin stopped in the diner before starting another day of investigation in Warrensburg. He received many looks and a couple of nods from the patrons who were also starting their days, taking long droughts from their coffee cups, preparing for a day that was more than likely to be filled with physical labor. The friendly waitress smiled, showing off all five of her teeth. John forced a smile in return, sat at the counter and ordered a cup of coffee and a blueberry muffin. Before joining the FBI, John studied pre-law at Cornell University, graduated in the top three percent of his class, and then gladly accepted a full scholarship to Fordham University where he earned his degree in law. Passing the bar exam was considerably easy for Galvin, and his athleticism, developed from years of playing shortstop, had him more than prepared for the physical aspects of the FBI's training camp. Sitting at the diner brought back fond memories of Cornell, which was only a few hours west of Warrensburg. He remembered the uneducated looks of the locals off campus, those lacking the brains and money to make a descent living for themselves. The waitress fit this stereotype, and John pitied her, hoping to soon resolve this case and return to civilization.

The homely looking waitress placed John's coffee and muffin on the counter in front of him. "You just missed your comrades," she said.

The waitress' choice of words made John smile genuinely, acknowledging this woman's vocabulary went further than the fifth grade.

"Are you referring to Sheriff Farley?"

"No. Haven't seen him in a few days. Kankro and Demitres. You're helping them on this murder case, right?"

"That's right. I guess I'll meet up with them at the station after I finish my delicious muffin."

"I don't think they were going to the station. I overheard them saying something about going to Sheriff Farley's house. I got the impression that they had some kind of beef with him."

John lifted his mug to his lips, trying to act as if this information was not pertinent. Sometimes that makes people not want to talk, if they feel they hold the key to valuable information. That was one of the tricks he learned in his psychological training at the bureau. The waitress was easy to read, and John knew just how to get her to talk.

"Yeah, they were arguing over something on the phone yesterday," he lied. "Do you know what the 'beef' is?"

"I'm not sure, but I heard Kankro saying something about Farley reporting him. Demitres was pissed off when Kankro told him that, then they hurried up out of here. They were talking real low, so people couldn't hear them. But that made me think it was something juicy, you know, so I tuned in. I thought I would hear something about all these murders. My daughter won't even leave the house, you know. Fifteen years old, and she's locked herself inside until this maniac is caught. My mother was deaf, so she talked funny when I was growing up. My ears became very acute to all sounds, so I hear everything around here. Well just last week I heard Joe Thompson telling his wife that he's going to see a doctor about getting some of that Viagra."

John laughed. "You ought to think about a career as a spy. It was nice chatting with you." He left her a very generous tip and exited the diner.

The waitress picked up the fifty dollar bill and made change for the young agent, but he was already gone. She ran out after him. "Sir, you forgot your change!"

"No, ma'am. You deserve it. Buy something nice for your daughter, and tell her this town will be safe again real soon."

Galvin got into his vehicle and dialed Mrs. Schneider. "Could you please give me the address of Sheriff Farley?"

Chapter 39

Loudbear set his map on a tree stump that had been carved into an outdoor end table, then filled his peace pipe with marijuana and shuffled the rocks in the fire pit with his feet. Even though it was summer, the mornings in the Adirondacks were still quite chilly until the sun had time to travel a significant distance along its daily arc across the sky. His dogs gathered around him as if he was the leader of the pack: they all enjoyed the second hand smoke. They each sat with their noses in the air as Loudbear exhaled the sweet substance.

As Loudbear exhaled, he let his body relax and stared deeply into the smoke patterns of the small fire as they intertwined with the smoke trails from his mouth. The marijuana smoke looked feminine next to the fire, enticing the more masculine smoke to engage in a romantic, choreographed dance. After a few more puffs, Loudbear's body and mind were now tranquil, allowing him to concentrate without the interruption of subconscious nuisances. Mako stood up and rested his paws on the end table next to the hand-made Adirondack chair that Loudbear had carved himself out of wood from trees on his property. The sound of the map crinkling caught Loudbear's attention and he snapped at Mako to get down. He took the map off the table then patted Mako on the head. "Thanks Mako. I was just about to get to that."

He traced his finger over the map, following what was now called Schroon River Road. Seven miles from Main Street he found the land that once belonged to Chief Ta Ta. He thought about the pictures Becka had showed him of the blue flowers, and of the well. There was something vaguely familiar about that well, but he just couldn't pinpoint it.

Okeano was running around Megaladon, getting her all wound up. The dogs gave Megaladon her daily exercise by chasing her around the horse pen while Loudbear was at the church, selling his crafts to survive in the white man's world. That still bothered him: how the white men came in and destroyed everything they touched. He looked around his property and smiled. It showed no signs of the devils, except for his car. He used to ride Megaladon into town to sell his instruments, but when he expanded to furniture, he needed the car to get the pieces to the church. Meg didn't mind, though, she had the dogs to keep her busy. Loudbear calculated that it was about fourteen miles to Chief Ta Ta's land on the map, and decided to take the whole crew with him. All except for Squid, who was expecting a litter quite soon.

In the winter, Loudbear enjoyed mushing his NAIDs through the snowy hills of Warrensburg, attaching his sled to their reigns. Every summer he could feel his dogs longing for the snowfall, desperately trying to sniff out the air for the first hint of cold weather. He looked over at Mako, who was now sitting in the Adirondack chair next to him. Mako shifted his ears as if they were speaking telepathically. Loudbear stood up and Mako jumped to his feet, wagging his tail. Beluga saw the commotion and knew what was about to happen. Both dogs ran to the stable before Loudbear could tuck his peace pipe into his medicine bag. "Okeano," he called, and pointed to the stables. Okeano corralled Megalodon into the stables and the remaining dogs followed. Loudbear saddled the horse up first, then harnessed the dogs one at a time and connected them via a gang line to Meg's saddle. With the dogs in front, Loudbear could keep a better eye on them on the roads and also steer them in the right direction.

Chapter 40

The directions to Sheriff Farley's house from the diner were fairly easy. Just head west, bear right at the fork, then make a right at the country store. Two miles up the road on the right hand side was Farley's house, a ranch styled home with white fencing surrounding the perimeter of the property. "Can't miss it," explained Mrs. Schneider. The traffic was light on the way to Farley's, no more than three pick-up trucks to be exact. John had been stationed in the congested suburbs of Washington D.C. for the last two years, and the occasional open field between long outcroppings of woods made him uncomfortable enough to want to solve this case as quickly as possible. He wouldn't be spending any extra days on site after this investigation was wrapped up. He was plagued by a feeling that if he didn't high tail it back to civilization soon he might not make it back at all.

Upon seeing Demitres' police cruiser parked in Farley's driveway, Galvin pulled right in behind it. With his gun drawn, he walked up the steps and tried to open the front door, but found it to be locked. The curtains were blowing through an open window, so Galvin unknowingly followed Demitres' route. The house was strangely quiet; the only sounds he could hear came from an out of tune set of wind chimes. Galvin walked to the back of the house, where he ended up in the kitchen. It was there that the eerie sensations became a chill that slithered down his spine. He had a clear view of the deputies lifting Sheriff Farley's dead body out of the hammock and into a hefty garbage bag.

Chapter 41

Devin, Becka, and Austin were playing badminton in the back yard, or 'the field,' as they often referred to it. The sun was beating down hard on the coarse, dry grass that blanketed the property. Brown crickets were leaping from one spot to another, to avoid getting stepped on by the activities on their homeland. Maureen was mixing martinis in the kitchen while Steve sat with Uncle Tony on the back porch. The Bettis' planned on keeping today low-key, for later in the evening they hoped to venture into Lake George to ride go-carts. Although they saved a lot of money on food and lodging thanks to the Farm, Steve had already spent over five hundred dollars since they left Long Island a week ago, and he found himself getting anxious about it. He secretly wished Maureen would get a job, especially since the kids were getting older. Growing kids meant more money. The taxes on Long Island were increasing by 5% every year, and inflation was at its highest in years.

Uncle Tony looked through the screen at the kids playing badminton and began to chuckle. "You know Steve, that boy Devin of yours, what a great kid! But damn is he clumsy! In the twenty minutes since I've been here, I think he fell twenty times!"

Steve smiled. "I think that's his strategy in soccer. He falls down and the other team trips over him."

"He's nothing like you when you were a kid," recalled Tony. Maureen had joined them, handing a fresh martini to each of them.

"Thanks doll," finished Tony. "As I was saying, your husband," he looked at Maureen, "when he was a kid, all he wanted to do was go deep into the woods and follow the stream." He turned back to Steve, "Boy, you were so amazed when you discovered it went under the street and led you to the river! You were so exited your father and I thought you'd found gold!"

"I remember that. Of course I was brave because I had Jesse by my side. Jesse knew that stream flowed into the river. But he did a good job at pretending I discovered it. Jesse's a good friend. It's a shame we live so far away from each other."

"Different worlds, you and Jesse. You grew up." Tony took another sip of his drink. "I love my nephew, but he'll never change. And I wouldn't want him to! I've always treated him as if he were my own son. Smartest son of a bitch I ever met! And I'm not just saying that 'cause he's my nephew. Ahh," Tony waved his hand in the air. "Who am I kidding? He's just like me!"

Click cloc, click cloc, click cloc.

Maureen's eyes went wide. "Do you hear that? It sounds like a horse!" She opened the back screen door and walked around to the front of the house, with Steve trailing behind her. Loudbear and his entourage came into view.

"Hello Steve and Maureen." Loudbear trotted his horse onto the Bettis' property, then slid off his saddle. He tied Meg's rope to a nearby apple tree and started to unleash the dogs.

"Nice of you to drop by," said Steve, wondering how Loudbear knew where the Farm was. "Where is your car?"

"I only use that when I have to."

Maureen went to the field and called the kids who then came rushing over to see their friend and his animals. Hammerhead jumped up onto Becka as she was running, knocking her over. Once she was down, the other dogs covered her with kisses. Maureen retrieved the disposable camera that she had bought at Grand Union from the porch and started snapping pictures.

Uncle Tony had come over to see all the commotion. Steve introduced him to Loudbear.

Tony looked Loudbear up and down. "You look familiar. Have we met?"

"Maybe. I'm often at the church yard sale." Loudbear was trying to get Becka's attention, but she ran off with two of the dogs.

"Your dogs, I like them. Do they hunt?" Rip had joined the dogs along with Spike and engaged in some rough housing.

"Yeah, they hunt. But don't worry, they are well trained and very friendly. They won't hurt your hound."

Tony looked over at Rip, who was rough-housing with the much larger dogs. "I don't worry about Rip, he can hold his own." Okeano ran to the other side of the house and all the dogs followed.

Steve interjected. "I'm sorry Loudbear, can I offer you a brewski or a martini? Maureen makes the best martinis."

"I haven't had one of those in a long time. I would love to try one of your martinis."

Maureen walked to the kitchen to make a drink for Loudbear and heard commotion on the side of the house. She looked out the window and saw the dogs scratching and barking at the root cellar doors. She tapped on the window. "Knock it off!"

She went back outside and handed the drink to Loudbear. "How did you know where our house was?"

Loudbear sipped the cold drink. "I wish I had good news."

"I think I know what this is about. Follow me." Steve led Tony and Loudbear to the site of the blue flowers. He had motioned for Maureen to stay behind.

"I've already spoken to Madeline Totten about these. And Tony here has had his own experience with them."

Loudbear bent down to pick a flower. "So you know of Chief Ta Ta. What do you think?"

"I'm not sure I believe it. I don't know what to think."

Tony blurted out, "What am I missing?"

Loudbear filled Tony in on the story of the great Indian Chief, and Tony told Loudbear of Ben Schaefer.

"He lived in this house. Parents sold it to the Bettis' after Ben's death. I saw that beast. As young as I was, I could never get that image out of my mind. It's as clear to me as if it happened yesterday. They say it was a bear. Bear my ass!"

Jesse and Justine were making their way across the yard when Loudbear's dogs, along with Spike and Rip, came over to greet them. "There's my nephew," yelled Uncle Tony. "He wants to catch this beast more than anyone. It killed his dog."

"Bettis! You better not be getting my Uncle drunk and making him spill all his dirty secrets about me!" Justine politely said "Hello" to the men, then headed off to meet Maureen on the porch with a newly baked batch of vanilla cupcakes.

"Great dogs," said Jesse. "We were just talking about getting a new dog. Where can I get one of these," Jesse asked as he was petting Beluga's head, which came up to Jesse's waist.

"I'm Loudbear. I breed them. If you can wait a few more weeks, I got a pregnant one at home. I usually sell them for about a thousand dollars. You really interested?"

Jesse recognized Loudbear right away. "I know you. There was an article about you in the paper a few months ago. Said you healed a cancer patient. Is that true?"

Loudbear smiled. "Hey, I'm no doctor. But my father was a medicine man. I gave Becka a healing

300

necklace, more for protection since her incident in the woods."

As Steve listened to the conversation between Jesse and Loudbear, he felt less anxious about the Indian. Maybe he was all right after all. He had Jesse's approval, and Jesse never misjudged anyone.

Loudbear turned to Steve. "I am crazy about your kids. They are smart, intuitive, strong, and challenging."

"You got the last part right. They challenge me everyday," laughed Steve. "And I've got to say, they're nuts about you. And I never thanked you for helping Devin. He told me you pulled him out of the way of the oak tree!"

"It happened so fast. He didn't even see it coming. He says you don't get storms like that on Long Island."

"No, no we don't."

"Yeah, yeah, yeah. Let's get back to Bigfoot," said Tony.

Jesse looked to Steve who shrugged his shoulders.

Loudbear looked at the men. "Let's take a walk."

They walked off into the woods and Jesse showed Loudbear the site where Becka was almost attacked. He choked back tears when he showed him where Norma's body had been found. "I believe it was Bigfoot."

"Sasquatch," Loudbear corrected.

Jesse pulled a joint out of his pocket. "Sorry Steve."

"Go ahead." It had been a long time, but Steve wished he could take just one hit. It was too bad his job did random drug testing. He watched as Jesse passed the joint to Loudbear, then to Uncle Tony. "Now I know what a fat chick on diet feels like," he thought.

Loudbear took a drag from the illegal cigarette, letting the smoke out in small circles. "What you guys don't know," he looked at Steve, "is that your property belonged to Chief Ta Ta and his tribe."

Steve felt a sinking feeling in his stomach. "What does that mean?"

"It means that Sasquatch returns to your land to seek revenge on the white man. I believe he lives here."

Steve froze, silent, his mind racing a mile a minute. Visions of Spike scratching at the trap door, the bear trying to get into the root cellar, Loudbear's dogs barking at the cellar door all ran through Steve's mind. Uncle Tony's prior conversation with Loudbear. Do they hunt? Steve clutched his gun, which was always on his right hip.

Loudbear reached into his pocket and pulled out the map. "Here."

Steve looked at the map, which showed an array of marked spots which Loudbear explained were Tee-pees. In the midst of it all was the well. "I had no idea the well was that old. It still works," he remarked. "So that's how you knew where the Farm was?"

Tony and Jesse each looked at the map, amazed that the map itself still existed.

"When was the last time you were in your cellar?" Tony asked Steve.

"I don't know. We never use it. Listen, before we get ahead of ourselves, let's think of this situation from a realistic stand-point. Madeline Totten knows of the legend of Chief Ta Ta. She told me about it. What's to say that the story itself did not land upon the ears of a sadistic mind? The killer then bases his killings following the pattern of The Legend of Chief Ta Ta. In fact, most killers get the ideas in their heads from stories or urban legends. We don't use this house year round. Any local can see that. In fact, a guy from up the road stopped and mentioned to me that he knows I don't live here."

Jesse interrupted. "Hold up a minute, Steve. I do a good job of looking after the Farm when you're not here, and if someone was taking occupancy in this house, I would know it."

Uncle Tony and Loudbear listened as Steve and Jesse bickered about the upkeep of the Farm.

"Enough! You know what we have to do, right? We cannot wait any longer. You must get your family out of the house tonight. We must kill the creature before it kills anyone else," insisted Loudbear. "I've read the papers. I know that it's Sasquatch on the loose. I don't believe for a minute that it's cult. If it was a cult, someone would have seen something by now. And all anybody ever saw was Bigfoot."

Steve held his hands up in the air. "Now hold on a minute. I'm not saying that something isn't going on here, but did the thought occur to any of you that Bigfoot doesn't exist? I mean really, did anyone ever find a Bigfoot? A dead Bigfoot, even?"

"I found a Bigfoot!" yelled Uncle Tony.

Jesse was always fast on his feet and ignored Steve's suggestion. "Here's the plan. By seven tonight, make sure your family is on their way to Lake George. I'll have Justine make plans with them. We meet at my house tonight at seven. Agreed?" He pointed to his house so Loudbear would know where to meet them. "My friend's son thinks he has a way to lure this thing out."

Loudbear knew the baby Bigfoot was in the root cellar, and knew this was the right time to move it. "Steve, would you mind giving me a tour of the house? Becka's been telling me all about her mother's decorating. I'm into that stuff."

The men shook their head in agreement, and welcomed the change of conversation.

"I'm sure Maureen would love to show you around. Although I have to warn you, the doorways and ceilings are small. How tall are you?"

"Six foot, four inches."

"Devin was laughing, saying that the house was built for a family of shrimps."

303

"Devin makes me smile."

They all walked back towards the Farm when Jesse took orders for hamburgers and hotdogs. Smoking a joint made it lunchtime.

Loudbear spotted Devin on the tire swing and walked over to him. "Tonight's the night. Me and Jesse and those guys are meeting here tonight to catch the parents. While in the back field I spotted a tree house off in the distance. Is that your property?"

"No."

"Well, put the baby there for now. She will be safe there."

"You're parents are taking you to Lake George tonight. But you're father will be here, so I don't know how you're going to do this."

"Jesse's daughter Danielle drives. I'll ask her," suggested Devin.

"Can you trust her?"

"Of course."

"Alright then. It looks like I'm invited for lunch. You have a nice family."

"Loudbear," called Maureen, "Let me show you the Farm!"

Devin looked on as Loudbear and his mother walked into the house together. He got a glimpse of Justine sitting at the picnic table with Becka when his heart sank and he fell backwards off the tire swing.

Out of the corner of her eye, Becka saw her brother fall but didn't think anything of it since this was a more than daily occurrence. When a few moments went by with no movement from him, she got Justine's attention and they ran over to the swing.

"Devin? Devin?"

Devin lifted his eyes and tried to focus on Justine's porcelain face and blue eyes.

"Devin baby, are you O.K.?" she asked him.

304

He could see that her eyes were running out of life, that she would be the next victim, but did not know what to do. "Where is Loudbear?" he muttered.

"He's inside," answered Becka.

"I need you to get him for me Beck, now!"

Becka got up and ran for Loudbear.

Devin took Justine's hand. "I love you. You're a good person, Justine."

"Why, thank you Devin. You're a good kid, too." She ruffled up his hair before heading back to the picnic table. "I know we didn't eat lunch yet, but do you want a cupcake?"

Loudbear came outside and kneeled beside Devin. "What is it?"

"Justine is going to die soon. Bigfoot will get her."

"Not if we get Bigfoot first."

"It's too late, Loudbear."

"We will kill it tonight, I promise"

"It'll still be too late."

"Lunch is ready!" yelled Jesse.

Chapter 42

Marc scanned his notes on the computer and printed out enough copies for all the parties involved. He peeked into his parent's bedroom and saw his father trying to explain the situation to his mother. "Sherry, we're going to end this nightmare once and for all. Please have faith in me. All I need for you to do is stay home tonight, lock the doors and put on the television. Keep yourself busy."

"So you're telling me you're going on a Bigfoot crusade, just like you and your 'Nam buddies were going to do?"

"This is different! Bigfoot's out there! I saw this thing! Marc saw it, so did Spencer and Tony!"

"Don't you think I've been through enough?"

"Baby, you need to move on. It's been years since Allison's death. You gave up on everything since we lost her. You gave up on God, you even gave up on us! And you have no relationship with Marc whatsoever. It's almost like you resent the fact that he lived and Allison died."

"What I resent is not getting the fuck out of Warrensburg years ago!"

"After this we'll go on a vacation, I promise."

"Maybe I'll go on a permanent vacation, without you!"

"That's nice, Sherry, real nice." Tom shut the bedroom door and opened up Marc's. "Come on Marc, we have a big night ahead of us." Tom took the notes from Marc's hand. "I don't know how to thank you."

"You can thank me when this thing is dead."

The two of them moved up and down the driveway, loading the truck with all sorts of bait and weaponry. Then Tom disappeared into the garage for a few moments.

"Dad, c'mon. I told Spencer we'd pick him up." Marc saw the large shadow of his father painted like a portrait on the pavement and looked up to see Tom standing amongst the piles of junk with two full shot glasses in his hand. Marc smiled as his father handed him over a shot of firewater.

"I figure the Indian would approve." They both lifted their shot glasses, "To Bigfoot."

When the coast was clear, Sherry emptied the dryer of the new clothes she bought to start her new life with Professor Ramsey. Tom was right; she didn't have a relationship with Marc, or anyone for that matter. But things would be different with Ramsey. She sent him a text message to let him know that things were going accordingly, and that Danielle would be there soon with the real Bigfoot.

When Devin told Danielle about the secret in his root cellar, she recalled Marc's conversation with her about Sherry's denial of Professor Ramsey's phone calls, and took it upon herself to confront Sherry. Sherry took Danielle to meet with Ramsey, who offered a large sum of money for the little beast, and the assurance that the creature would be well cared for, and a deal was struck.

Once Sherry was alone in her bedroom, she packed the rest of her belongings for her new life, including the night vision goggles she stole from her husband, and at the last minute decided to throw a photo of Tom and Marc in her suitcase.

*   *   *

When Tom arrived at Jesse's house the rest of the gang was already there. "I hope I didn't keep you guys waiting."

"Not at all. Everybody just got here." Jesse led his militia into the living room. Once everyone was seated,

Tom handed out the notes from Marc's anthropology class. "I'll give you guys a few minutes to look over some facts that my son learned in West Virginia." He patted his son on the back as Marc helped Spencer into the recliner.

Jesse introduced everyone and served finger foods prepared by Justine. "Guys, this here is Spencer. He had the unpleasant privilege of seeing this beast up close and personal."

"That makes two of us," replied Tony with an eerie smile.

Tom took his bottle of firewater from his knapsack. "Drink anyone?"

Loudbear nodded in appreciation as they passed the bottle around the coffee table. To Jesse's surprise, even Steve took a gulp.

Steve took a stand in front of the group. "For the record, I just want to say that I believe it is a serial killer we're dealing with. As for this Bigfoot talk, I think the sick bastard may dress up as Bigfoot in an effort to throw people off course. Actually, it's a pretty clever plan. And most serial killers have high I.Q.'s. Most are white heterosexuals who are sexually dysfunctional, usually in their twenties or thirties and with low self-esteem. Many keep trophy-like body parts, such as organs, as mementos of their work. They are sadistic in nature, with a history of cruelty to animals. Some like to return to the crime scenes to fantasize about their deeds. It is not common, but it has been known that serial killers sometimes work in pairs. Now, as for the local cops around here and their "cult" theory, I'd have to throw that one out the window. For starters, cults kill in groups. Groups kill groups of people, they don't single out one person. In the case of the woman, Dina Puglesi, both her and her boyfriend would be dead if it were a cult, and the dog too. Tom, I hate to say this, but your son and his friend would be dead too if it were a cult."

"I get it Steve," said Marc. "You've narrowed it down to a serial killer dressed in a Bigfoot costume, or Bigfoot himself?"

"In other words, yeah, I guess that's what I'm saying."

"So either way you put it," said Jesse, "we're looking for Bigfoot?"

The team nodded in agreement. Spencer understood that because of his condition he was to stay inside Jesse's house and keep Spike and Rip company while Loudbear's dogs joined in on the hunt for Sasquatch.

The men marched over to the Farm, a motley group of soldiers with shotguns, rifles and even pistols dangling from homemade holsters on their bodies. Loudbear came equipped with a wicked, hand-made cross bow. Steve led the warriors straight to the root cellar, which was the agreed upon target on this mission, and waited for everyone to get in position. Tony glanced over at Loudbear and felt like he was finally going to avenge Ben Schaefer's death. He got the go ahead from Steve, and quickly pulled on the old handle of the root cellar door, exposing the insides of the alleged home of Bigfoot. Loudbear knew the baby had been moved, but did not know where the parents were hiding out.

Steve quickly went down the stairs with his gun drawn as if he was Bruce Willis in an action flick, while Loudbear took his time like a skilled hunter waiting for the prize buck. Jesse had dropped flares down from the other entrance for some extra light, but there was no movement to be seen.

Steve made his way through to the second room while Jesse and Loudbear trailed behind him. "Clear," he called as he scanned the additional room under the kitchen with a flashlight. Jesse and Loudbear met Bettis in the second room and helped collect evidence. Tony yelled to Marc and Tom that the rooms were empty and they came

309

out of hiding. The three men climbed up the stairwell holding blankets, food wrappers, bottles, Lilly pads, pillows, and fresh containers of milk. They placed their belongings on the picnic table in Bettis' yard and each just looked them over, both stunned and dumbfounded.

Tom walked over to the table. He picked up a Lilly pad. "They like to sleep on these things. I believe they use them for bedding. Bob and I found a patch of these things plucked from the pond across from the lumber yard." He lifted a lily pad up to his nose, "I'd recognize that smell anywhere. It's him."

"That doesn't explain this!" Steve handed the carton of milk to Tom. The expiration date was still a week away. "This came from my refrigerator! This guy has been in my house, taking my food!"

"Or," explained Loudbear, "your kids could've been feeding a wild animal down here. Maybe they're afraid to tell you about it, because you'd tell them to stay away from it."

Steve looked at Loudbear and knew he was right. He grew intensely angry that this man, this stranger, knew and understood his kids better than he did. Worse than that, he *knew* about what had been going on. They chose to tell *him*. "They told *him* and not *me*," Steve thought angrily.

"What's down there, Chief?" Steve got within a foot of Loudbear's chest, violating his personal space. "Little wolf pup? Harmless baby bear cub? It won't hurt you kids, you can pet it. Look at my big wolves."

Jesse jumped up in between them. "Hold on, guys. What is this all about?"

"I'll tell you what this is all about. This guy knows all about what's in my basement, don't you?" Steve stared intensely at Loudbear, waiting for an answer.

Okeano sensed the tension and whipped around the side of the house, keeping a close eye on the situation.

Mako also appeared out of nowhere, but ran down into the root cellar barking.

Steve looked at Okeano and clenched his gun.

"Don't bother," said Loudbear. "He'd be on you faster than you could draw your gun. But it's not going to get to that."

Tony followed Mako into the root cellar. "This dog found something," he called out.

Jesse averted his eyes from Steve and Loudbear for a moment and honed in on Mako. He then looked back and forth at the two men. "Loudbear, if there's something you know, what is it?"

"It's what we said in your house. Bigfoot lives down there. Nothing's changed. Except that Steve now knows we're right."

"Sorry, Jesse. I just don't buy that 'Bigfoot' has been coming in and out of my house. And now that we're on the subject, I've been reading the papers. It's more than obvious that what we're dealing with is a serial killer, not an ape. I mean really, let's be realistic. I understand that you don't see much action around here, and it would be a great tale to tell if Warrensburg was the home to Bigfoot, but it's time to get serious. People are dead. You and your cronies want to run around like a bunch of cowboys and Indians on a crusade, but you have no idea what you're dealing with. I do," he pointed to his chest. "I've dealt with serial killers before, and it's nothing you want to get yourself involved in. I've decided to pack up my family tomorrow morning and let the police take it from here, as backwards as they are. I'm going to allow myself to back down and let them do their jobs without getting in their way. It's the same courtesy that I'd want and expect. You know they called in some big wig from the FBI?"

"So, because you can read a biased newspaper, and are from the city, you think that you have it all figured out?"

Steve was clearly annoyed. "You forgot to mention the fact that I don't believe in a large ape-like creature that bears no evidence of existing! Oh yeah, and something else called common sense. Yeah, I got that too." Steve started to walk back to the picnic table by the house.

"That's O.K., Steve. Plan one failed but that doesn't mean I don't have a back-up plan." He caught up to Steve on the lawn.

"Humor me." They reached the others and Jesse stood on top of the large tree stump that Steve had been trying desperately to remove earlier in the week. Steve felt Jesse was rubbing things in by choosing to stand on it.

"Listen up, guys," announced Jesse as he pulled the notes from his back pocket. "I have another plan. Looking through the notes, which are great by the way Marc, way to pull through, I see here that the Sasquatch," he winked at Loudbear, "is attracted to music. I keep all my instruments in my barn, and I think it's time we jam!"

Steve could not have heard a more ridiculous idea. "I hear serial killers prefer opera!" He waved his hand and started to retreat into his house. "Guys, it's been a pleasure and an honor to have met all of you, but I'm pulling out. I'm sorry. My family will be back in a few hours, and I'd appreciate it if you'd all stay away from my property, especially with guns and crossbows and whatever else you guys have. I'm sorry, but this is just too asinine."

Uncle Tony got up to follow but Jesse told him not to. "Guys, meet me in my barn. I've got to talk to my friend for a minute." Jesse followed Steve into the house.

Steve was already downing a beer by his refrigerator when Jesse found him. "Steve, I know how you feel. But just listen to me for a minute. I know you've been taught to think in terms of black of white, and I'm sure it works most of the time, but this isn't the city. Hell, I'm not asking you to see the gray, I'm asking you to see the red!

Yeah, I said it! We're a bunch of fuckin' rednecks up here. Shit, we're only one step ahead of the moffits up the road! I know that's what you think of us! And you know what, I don't care what you think! I'm Becka's Godfather and I'll be damned if I'm going to sit back and let two jerk offs and a suit from the FBI sit around eating donuts while my goddaughter nearly gets killed! Around here, you need to take action into your own hands!"

Steve slammed the old refrigerator door shut but it popped back open. Kicking it shut again, he decided it was time to put Jesse in his place. "First of all, she's *my* daughter! And I happen to have enough trust in the American justice system to let the law handle this! And it doesn't make you any more of a man than I am to go out there and pretend you're above the law!"

The sound of the screen door slamming caught both men's attention and they turned to see Tom bursting in. "You got a T.V. in here?"

"Yeah, a small black and white in the living room."

Tom rushed to the television and turned the ancient knob to the local news on channel two, the only channel that came in on the set. The news reporter was just finishing a report on Kankro and Demitres. Their mug shots appeared before them and Jesse and Tom jumped up and down cheering. "Way to go Jim! This was all Healy! And I delivered the tapes to the FBI in charge! I was a part of this," yelled Tom as he pointed to the small screen. The reporter when on about how the cops may be the serial killers terrorizing Warrensburg.

This caught Steve's attention. "You mean it was you who helped put these two cops behind bars?"

"Not alone. That guy who was killed, Jack Whittaker, he recorded them threatening his life on the bridge. I just delivered the tapes. I also have them blackmailing me for my lumber. But you know what, they buried themselves! That woman, Dina Puglesi, she reported Kankro molesting her when he pulled her over a while ago. Now she's dead!"

"So who did it?"

"What?" asked Jesse.

"Who killed these people? If you think it's the cops, why are you guys searching my house for a gorilla?"

Tom rubbed his hands through his hair. "I'll be outside."

"Are you guys fucking kidding me? You framed these cops?" demanded Steve.

"Not exactly. These guys should have been behind bars years ago. They put themselves there. It's just a coincidence that they had damaging relationships with the deceased," explained Jesse.

"Do these guys have alibis for when the killings took place?"

"That's not my problem. Hey, you're the one who thinks it's a serial killer, so what are you worried about? I thought you had faith in the American justice system? They would *never* put the wrong guy behind bars!"

"You set them up!"

"I didn't set them up! I have no idea where these guys go when they're not tormenting me and my friends."

"But you know they aren't responsible for this," screamed Steve.

"That's not for me to decide. I have to have faith in the law," mocked Jesse, as he left Steve standing in his living room alone with that thought.

Chapter 43

Special Agent John Galvin walked Officer Pat Demitres into the holding cell at the State Troopers' barracks, and Officer Alan Kankro was seated next to him, cuffed to the bench. Although innocent of the crimes they were being charged, both knew other charges would arise if their houses were searched. Illegal drugs, weapons linked to other crimes, etc. Both detainees lawyered up upon being questioned, and an Italian mob attorney from Brooklyn was on his way to defend his old clients.

Technicians from the forensics labs were sent into the cell to photograph the officers' hands for defense wounds from the latest victim, Sheriff Farley. The officers were temporarily uncuffed for the occasion. "Hey tech,"asked Demitres, "Are you familiar with my case?"

The technician nodded.

"They think I'm Bigfoot," laughed Demitres.

The forensics technician smiled at him, then looked over at Kankro. "Who's he, the Abominable Snowman?"

*   *   *

Two hours had passed since Steve first heard the horrific sound of Jesse's barnyard band, or 'plan two' as Jesse called it. He couldn't take the anxiety or the music anymore, so he locked Spike in the house, got into his Pathfinder and drove into Lake George Village to meet his family. He found them at the Capri Pizza Parlor, just where they said they'd be.

"Hi honey! I ordered you a pepperoni calzone," said Maureen as she kissed her husband gently on the cheek. "You done playing with your friends?"

Steve looked up at Justine, not wanting to say anything negative about Jesse in front of her. He smiled at

315

the two women sitting across from him. "Mind if I have a slice of pizza?"

"Go ahead," answered Justine, who had just gulped down four slices herself.

"Where are the kids?"

"Next door at the arcade," answered Maureen, taking a sip of diet soda.

Maureen knew what was coming next from her ultra-paranoid spouse. "Before you freak out, Danielle is with them."

Steve breathed a sigh of relief. "Thank you. By the way, I just heard on the news that those two cops, Demitres and Kankro, were arrested today. The people believe them to be the culprits of these bizarre killings." He paused for a reaction from Justine, who was too consumed in piling mozzarella sticks in her pudgy little mouth to notice if a rocket landed in the middle of the lake. He stared in disbelief as she scoffed down some garlic knots. Maureen nodded in the direction of the pie and held four fingers up behind her head. The thought of this woman downing this much food in front of him made Steve not want to bother with the calzone. He brought it up to the counter and asked the cashier to wrap it up for him. Maureen told Justine they were going to check up on the kids and she and Steve walked out of Capri.

"There's something wrong with her," explained Maureen who was always good on stating the obvious.

"You don't say?"

"Steve, I think she's bulimic. That's a very serious eating disorder. Women binge on all sorts of food then go to the toilet and make themselves vomit. It's like they're going back in time and making all the right decisions about what foods they shouldn't eat."

"Yes dear, I believe I've heard of that. Men do it too you know."

"What's wrong with you? Why are you being so nasty tonight?"

"I think I'm just getting a little home sick, that's all. You have to admit, it's been a crazy week."

"Yes it has." They looked through the large glass windows and spotted the kids at the shooting gallery. Steve tapped on the glass and Devin looked his way. "We're going for a walk. Stay with Danielle."

Devin waited ten minutes then got Becka at the Pac-man machine. "The 'rents are going for a walk, without Justine."

Becka kept her eyes on the arcade. "When did Dad get here?"

"Don't know, but I think Justine might still be next door."

Danielle stuck her head out of the dinosaur arcade. "The exchange went as planned. Baby Bigfoot is already on her way to Canada with Sherry Blake and Professor Ramsey."

Chapter 44

Steve and Maureen held hands as they strolled around the lake. The moon was full and lit up the entire lake with reflections of the lights from the restaurants and late night cruise ships. The weather was just a little bit chilly by the water. Otherwise, it was a perfectly romantic atmosphere.

"Maureen, there's something we have to talk about."

By the tone of his voice, Maureen knew he was serious.

"What's the matter?"

"Remember I told you Jesse has issues with those two cops, the ones who got arrested?"

"No! I didn't realize it was those cops! I guess Jesse was right about them!"

"No! He wasn't right about them! He was wrong! In every sense of the word, he was wrong! Mo, he set them up. Yes, there is a serial killer in these woods, and I hate to say it, but most likely it's the guy who came after Becka in the field. But it's not these guys, Mo. The killer is still out there!"

"Are you sure?"

"Jesse and Tom admitted it to me tonight! They set them up! They know the cops are in jail and they're celebrating in Jesse's barn as we speak!"

"Steve, there is an incriminating pile of evidence linking those two officers to the crimes. The news was playing on the T.V. in Capri. I saw it. I've been a cop's wife long enough to recognize dirtbags, Steve. And those two guys are guilty."

"I'm not saying they're not guilty. But they're not killers. Do you like it here?" He asked out of nowhere.

Maureen released his hand and put a fair distance between the two of them. "What are you saying, Steve?"

318

"I'm saying I can make a difference in this town. There is a serial killer out there. A man went after our daughter. The sheriff is dead. Two cops have been falsely arrested. I have the credentials. You love the Farm. The kids love the Farm. Long Island is turning to shit. There is a job opening here in Warrensburg for me. I want this job! I want to say yes! We belong here, Maureen. I want to go into that police station right now, and tell them I want to be the first man considered for the job. I want this, Mo. We can get over four hundred thousand for our house in Long Island. You and the kids can live like royalty up here! Please say yes! A killer is still out there, and I can catch him! You know I can!"

Maureen's eyes filled up with tears. "Are you serious? Just like that? You'd pick up and move, just like that?" She snapped her fingers.

"Just like that. What do you say?"

Maureen looked at beautiful Lake George. She watched as the late night party boats were leaving the docks blowing their horns, the happy passengers waving to the people on the piers. She threw her arms around Steve. "Yes! Yes!" He twirled her around the docks and they danced to the live band playing at Shepard Park.

She kissed him passionately, then pushed him away. "Go, before someone else gets the same idea you have. Go tell them why you should get the job over everyone else. Me and the kids will catch a ride home with Justine."

"O.K. I love you, Mo." Steve scampered up the dock pier steps and galloped through the park to his Pathfinder, leaving Maureen alone with her thoughts about relocating and hoping she wouldn't reconsider.

Jesse paced around outside of the barn with Loudbear, waiting anxiously for something out of the ordinary to appear.

"Relax," said Loudbear. "He'll come."

"To all the girls, I've loved before…"

"What was that," asked Loudbear.

Jesse chuckled and peeked his head through the barn. "That is my Uncle Tony on the mic."

"You have a good group of people surrounding you," affirmed Loudbear.

"You choose your friends. It's no coincidence."

"That is true. And what of your friend Steve?"

"He's a cop. He used to be cool though. Relaxed. Not so uptight all the time."

"Want to know what I think?"

"Sure."

"I think there are two Bigfoots around here. And I think at least one will strike tonight."

"We'll get him first."

"I wouldn't be so sure of that."

"You said it yourself, your dogs can hunt."

"My dogs are no match for this beast. They can alert us, but they can also be killed, just like your dog was. Are you prepared for another death?"

"This is war, Loudbear. Of course I'm prepared."

Loudbear didn't have the heart to tell him that he would lose his lover tonight, so he dropped the subject.

Loudbear and Jesse continued their walk around the barn, with five of Loudbear's dogs by their side. The harsh crunch of sun-burnt grass sounded in the distance, and both men heard it. "Let them continue playing," ordered Jesse. Loudbear followed Jesse behind the rear of the barn when the crunching sound stopped. They stood still and waited for five minutes before taking more steps into Jesse's back field, following the ATV path. In the darkness of the night visibility was next to nothing. Jesse kept his hand on his gun and Loudbear's crossbow was ready to go.

"It sounds like two sets of footsteps," reported Loudbear.

"Never know," whispered Jesse.

Loudbear laid down in the brush and aimed his crossbow into the darkness. Jesse knelt down next to him and awaited the next movement. The sounds seemed to be going away from them, into Bettis' patch of woods beyond Jesse's field. Jesse and Loudbear inched their ways towards the sounds, keeping a safe distance between them and the perpetrator. Jesse felt like he should have warned his friends in the barn, but the Indian reassured him that those guys were all prepared for whatever barged through the barn doors.

It was now twenty minutes later, and the men were deep into Bettis' back woods. Jesse thought of Norma as he passed the spot where she was killed, wishing he had been there for her and at the same time proud of the ol' gal for giving her life to protect humans, which he ultimately knew was her job. He relished in the fact that he gave her a good life and that her death was in no way meaningless. The sounds of footsteps were leading them further into the woods, beyond Steve's property, and the dogs went ahead without making a sound. The NAIDs hunted like wolves, in silence, sniffing out their prey while sneaking up on it. Loudbear listened intensely as he heard the sounds of branches breaking and being pushed aside while pine needles crunched at the same time. He tapped Jesse's midsection. "I think we need to shine our flashlights on this thing and take him down now."

"O.K.," replied Jesse. "On the count of three. One, two…"

They both listened but did not hear the sounds of the earth being walked on. "I don't hear it anymore," confessed Loudbear. Jesse didn't hear it either.

"Scratch that plan. We can't shine the light if we don't know where to focus it. The last thing we want to do it give away our location." After a few minutes, they still couldn't hear any sounds. Jesse had another idea. "You wait here. I'll go and get back-up. We're on to this thing, Chief."

Loudbear did not like the idea of being in the middle of the woods alone with his dogs so far ahead, but reluctantly agreed to Jesse's plan.

Jesse crawled slowly away from the area at first, then got up and ran when he felt it was safe. When he approached the barn, he found Tom lingering outside.

"What's going on?" asked Jesse.

Tom let Rip out of the barn, sparing them from the awful sounds of Spencer's rhythm-less drum rolls and Uncle Tony's scratchy vocal cords. "Rip started to bark, and I heard something."

Loudbear remained lying on his stomach in the woods. He heard more noises, coming from the opposite direction. It was the footsteps of one person, not two. Figuring it was Jesse, he called out to him. "Over here."

The footsteps closed in on Loudbear, then came to an abrupt halt three feet away. Loudbear could feel someone breathing on him, and his own instinct told him it was not Jesse. He aimed his crossbow, then with the flick of a switch, shined his flashlight on the target in front of him.

Bigfoot sniffed Loudbear, acknowledging that this was not the scent of the enemy. Loudbear's flashlight shined in the beast's eyes, but he did not blink. The beast had locked eyes with Loudbear, and they both stared at each other for a few moments. For Loudbear, this was the most terrifying moment of his life. He raised his crossbow, aiming it at the monster's chest, when the sound of more footsteps broke his concentration. Loudbear briefly hesitated, and although the only illumination was that of a battery powered flashlight, he unmistakably saw the beast smiling at him, then turn away and run deeper into the woods. The beast had spared Loudbear his life. The footsteps were getting louder, and Loudbear called out to Jesse again. "Is that you?"

There was no answer, but when Loudbear shined his lights again he saw that he was surrounded by his dogs. They made no attempt to attack Bigfoot, as the creature posed no threat to their master.

Jesse hollered from the field as Loudbear tried to reflect on what had just happened. "Bigfoot had killed many humans this week, why spare me?" he asked himself. He thought about how it almost killed Becka, when all along Becka had been fighting to keep its offspring alive.

"Chief!" called Jesse.

Then it hit him. "Bigfoot spared my life, because of Chief Ta Ta's curse on the white man! I'm not a white man, which makes this beast smart enough to recognize the difference. And that means it's on a very specific mission!" He suddenly felt guilty for trying to kill the beast. "But no," he thought! "This curse is out of control! What's done is done, and killing innocent white people will not make up for what happened in the past!"

As his mind vacillated on the issue, Jesse showed up at his side, patting him on the back. "Did I miss anything?"

Loudbear made a quick decision not to tell Jesse about what happened. He acknowledged that by not killing the beast, he had just killed Jesse's girlfriend. "No."

"When you shined your flashlight a few minutes ago I thought I saw something."

Loudbear tensed up. "What did you see?"

"I thought I saw a tree house in the distance. Is that what you were looking at?"

"Uh, yeah. A tree house. I heard something from above."

"Well, then what are we waiting for? Let's go!"

Loudbear thought about his encounter with Sasquatch. The beast spared his life, but would show no such mercy towards Jesse. Loudbear was now faced with a moral dilemma. Could he kill Sasquatch for Jesse? Or did the Mohican curse need to go on?

Feeling like they were out of harm's way, Jesse held up his flashlight and switched it on, showing a tree house that was clearly built with a touch of professionalism. They walked to it and took in the scenery. There were logs that formed a circular fire pit, with markings on it showing that it was used often. Beyond the logs and beneath the tree house were steps leading to a door in the floor of the fort. Jesse climbed up and tried to open the latch but found it locked. He knocked on the door. "Is anybody in there?" As he suspected, nobody answered. He climbed down the steps and looked up at this monstrosity of a clubhouse, which had a wrap-around porch, two Anderson windows and even a hand carved front door.

"Jesse, you say it was locked? There's no lock on the outside. Looks like it can only be locked from within."

"You think it's up there?"

"Maybe. And we're here, so we might as well check it out. The footsteps led me here, and I didn't hear anything else since you left. Whatever made its way here has to still be in there." Loudbear did not believe it could still be in there, as he heard and saw Sasquatch go in the other direction. But to placate Jesse, he played it up. He was still undecided on what to do, and the idea of remaining neutral seemed to be the best way to handle the situation, for now. But he was not fooling himself when he stalled Jesse by insisting that Bigfoot might be in the tree house. He just didn't want any more casualties, on either side. Besides, maybe Devin was wrong about Justine.

Chapter 45

Maureen went back to the arcade and found Devin playing skee-ball with Austin. "Where's your sister," asked Maureen.

"Bathroom."

"Well, when she gets out, I have to talk to you two."

"Where's Dad?"

"That's what I have to talk to you two about."

Danielle and Becka came walking down the aisle of the arcade and Maureen asked Danielle if she could keep an eye on Austin so she could talk to the twins alone. Naturally, they thought they were busted but tried to play it cool. "Yeah, sure," said Danielle. Maureen and the twins left the arcade and Becka gave Danielle the choke sign through the glass window.

"Who wants ice cream," asked Maureen. In Lake George village, there was no shortage of ice cream parlors, and they picked the closest one. Devin got a triple scoop of rocky road ice cream on a cone while Becka and Maureen both got vanilla soft serve with rainbow sprinkles. They walked down towards the lake, where Devin liked to talk to the ducks.

"Your father and I were thinking, well, we were tossing around the idea that maybe we would like to move up here. What do you think?"

Becka and Devin stared at each other, both thinking they were being set up. "What do you mean?" asked Beck.

"I mean, your father is applying for a job as a policeman here. And we would live at the Farm."

"What about our friends at home?" asked Devin.

"They can come up and visit whenever they want. And Becka, I know you wanted another animal. And Loudbear said one of his dogs is expecting puppies. And up here we have the land for another dog."

"What if Dad doesn't get the job?" asked Devin.

"Are you kidding? You're father is the best cop in the world. Any police department would be lucky to have him."

Becka thought about Squid, the all black NAID, and imagined how cute her puppies must be. "I'm in," said Becka.

"Me too," said Devin, thinking the same thoughts as Becka, the black puppies.

"Me three," said Maureen.

They finished their ice cream and played a round of miniature golf. On the sixteenth hole, Steve called Maureen's cell phone. "Hello? Steve? How did it go?" We're playing mini golf. I'm sorry, I can't really hear you. Meet us at the golf course."

Maureen hung up with Steve and called Justine, explaining that she was going home with him tonight, and therefore wouldn't need a ride. That was fine with Justine, who had eaten just about all she could for the night anyhow, and was ready to go home. She gathered her own kids and called it a night.

*   *   *

Justine walked up the steps and into her home, calling out to see if anyone was there. Austin and Danielle had made a b-line for the barn upon hearing the music. She had been waiting all night to come home and purge, and now she couldn't even make it to the toilet without stepping in piss from Uncle Tony's puppy. She decided to take her business to the back of the property, where she was forced to on the nights that her bathroom was occupied. She had always wanted Jesse to add on another bathroom, but he never felt the need for two of them. Grabbing what was left of the paper towels, she headed towards the back field. Finding a decent spot, she tied her

327

hair back, rolled up her sleeves, and jammed her left pointer finger down her throat, feeling instant gratification as the churned pizza slices made their way up and out of her esophagus. She felt ten pounds lighter as the mozzarella sticks, soda and pastries made their way out of her body. Using the paper towels, she wiped off her hands then kicked some dirt over her vomit in a vain attempt to hide the evidence. Jesse had already discovered her little secret months before, when the toilet kept on backing up. He had told Justine that he didn't like it, and her response was that she didn't like him cheating on her. Neither of them ever brought up the issue again.

As Justine walked back to the house she heard footsteps behind her. Feeling slightly embarrassed, and a little angry that it was Jesse's fault she was doing this, she decided to keep on walking and pretend she didn't realize her common-law husband was trailing her. What was he going to do, tell her to cut it out? That would be opening the door for her accusations of his philandering. She cracked a smile, knowing she had the upper hand in this battle.

The scent of Justine's vomit had been attracting Bigfoot for months. He had grown accustomed to the smell of rotting food and bile and he craved the taste of it. He watched as Justine walked away from him, looking very delicious herself. He now had other responsibilities, another mouth to feed, and this woman suddenly became very appealing to him, since he recently tasted the difference between males and females. He allowed her to take another step away from him, then lunged at her, grabbing her by the ankles and knocking her down instantly. She managed to let out a scream before he twisted her neck, crushing the vertebrae halfway down her spine, and dragged her into the woods.

Loudbear and Jesse were returning from their journey in the tree house when they both heard the scream. In the open fields sounds had a way of echoing that made it nearly impossible to tell which direction they came from. There was no denying that the scream came from a female, and Jesse immediately thought of Danielle, figuring she might be back by now.

Although there was live music, Tom thought he heard something. He and Marc stepped out of the barn and found Rip with his ears up and barking. Bigfoot was here. Uncle Tony felt it and sat Austin next to Spencer and Danielle on top of the haystacks. He joined the Blakes outside with his gun drawn. Rip stayed by his owner's side. Tom led his crew to the back of Steve's and Jesse's properties.

"Where's Jesse?" asked Uncle Tony.

"He and Loudbear followed something out to the woods. They haven't come back yet," responded Tom.

"Could you make out where the sound was coming from?" asked Tony.

"It came from behind Jesse's property," said Marc.

A pair of headlights turned down the block and Steve slowed down to see that the gang was still outside. Maureen rolled down the passenger side window and leaned back so Steve could speak to them. "You guys find what you're looking for?"

Tom ran up to the Pathfinder. "Danielle's in the barn, and we just heard someone scream, so we think it might be Justine. We can't find Jesse or Loudbear. I'm going to send Marc to search Jesse's house, but the sound came from Jesse's back field. We think Justine's in trouble. Do you want to help, or not?"

Steve pulled a star shaped badge out of his wallet and showed it to Tom. "Of course I'm going to help. I'm the new Sheriff in town." Steve pulled into his driveway and walked his family into the house, insisting they all lock themselves in the master bedroom until he returned.

He was about to run out of the house when Devin took hold of his father's arm.

"Justine's dead." He didn't wait for his father to respond. Devin turned and walked up the staircase, shutting the door behind him.

Steve didn't like the look on his son's face, and grabbed his gun and ran next door to help his best friend. Marc and Danielle had gone to search Jesse's house for Justine but hadn't yet returned. Steve made Tom call Marc's cell phone to tell him to get back to the barn with Danielle since they still hadn't found Justine. When Danielle got back he told her to sit again with Austin and Spencer in the barn.

"Tony, you shine the light, and Tom, you and Marc fan out. We're going to head back behind the barn in a hundred degree angle. Let's go!" Steve didn't need to ask if anybody was ready. He knew they'd been ready all night for this.

Steve was starting to jog, and Tom was to the right of him with Marc and Tony between them. Loudbear called out to them that they weren't alone, and Jesse sprinted ahead knowing every detail of the woods on his and Steve's property. He couldn't see much while running, but he saw one of the NAIDs and knew that the dog was on to something, and decided to trail him. Rip started to bark viciously at something, then disappeared into the darkness, his bark fading with each leap. Jesse temporarily lost sight of Beluga, the white NAID, but kept running straight back, further into the woods. Marc picked up his pace and caught up to Jesse, trying hard to keep up without running into trees. As Jesse ran straight ahead, Marc fumbled with his flashlight and thought he saw Rip making his way back towards them. Jesse was past the white NAID at this point, and Marc stopped running. He pointed his flashlight at a gray NAID, and saw she was dragging something through the woods. She

330

dropped what she was carrying and barked at the flashlight. Marc ran up to her and felt sick to his stomach at what he saw. It was Justine, or a shell of Justine. Her insides were missing, and she appeared hollow. The gray NAID was covered in blood and doing her best to drag Justine out of the woods by her shirt. Maybe she thought Justine was still alive. He wondered if Jesse had seen Justine like this, and kept running. He called back to his father, who yelled that he was on his way. Marc had never seen a dead body before, other than what he thought he saw of Bob Murphy, which was now becoming all the more clear in his head, and he started to get woozy. He fell to his knees as a wave of nausea compelled him to expel everything his body had consumed within the last forty-eight hours.

Steve and Tom reached Marc at the same time, both seeing Justine's remains and exchanging glances at one another. Tom knew that Steve was relieved to see it wasn't Jesse, but his look of satisfaction quickly vanished and was taken over by an almost animalistic rage of anger and revenge. Uncle Tony and Loudbear arrived at that moment, and were speechless after what they saw. Loudbear offered to take the body back, and Tony agreed to help. For some reason the gray NAID wouldn't part with the body and went with them.

The three men walked quickly into the woods, no one speaking a word about what they had just seen, and each of them wondering if Jesse had discovered Justine's body before they did. Marc spotted Jesse up ahead. He seemed to be stopping to catch his breath, with his hands on his knees. Tom called out to let him know that they were behind him. Jesse turned around with his flashlight and pointed it to the ground. Marc followed suit and shined his flashlight on the ground, revealing a large pool of fresh blood. Steve went into crime scene mode and pushed his way in front of Jesse, forcing him to step aside.

He shined his light on the trunk of the tree, which showed a spotty trail of blood leading up. Jesse looked up in time to see a large, half human- half ape, jumping out of the tree towards the direction of his head! Tom and Steve simultaneously fired their weapons and shot the beast mid air, while Marc tackled Jesse just in time to get him out of the way. Jesse fell on his side with Marc on top of him and the beast landed right next to them. Marc shined the light in its eyes, revealing a yellow-green iris with black oval-shaped pupils. Bigfoot's nose was long and wide, his jaws large and covered in blood. It was still alive. It rolled onto its back and took a deep, long breath. As it exhaled, aspirated blood spattered out and around its mouth, creating a trail of red that ran down its hairy neck. Jesse felt no pity for this animal, and did not shoot him at close range in the forehead to put it out of its misery, as he would for any other living thing. For Jesse, this was revenge. He savored the gurgling sounds the beast made as it tried desperately to bring air into its dying body. After making sure the beast was dead, he put his hand on top of Steve's shoulder. "Let's go home."

Loudbear and Uncle Tony carried Justine's body to the barn. Tony went in first to get rid of Austin. "Seeing his mama murdered like that will scar him," said Tony. "Just as I was scarred for life when I saw Ben Schaefer get carted off into the woods like a lobster that has just been chosen by the big-boned lady in a seafood market. Poor kid will never be the same, either way." Still, Tony knew it would be the right thing to do and refused to let young Austin see his mother in that condition. He nodded to Spencer to take Austin and Danielle into the house.

Loudbear held Justine's cooling body in his arms as he waited for Tony's clearance. He heard Tony walking back towards the barn and gave the go-ahead to enter with the body. Tony laid a woolen, plaid blanket on the stage in the barn for Justine. Loudbear lowered her onto the blanket, closing her eyes and wrapping her up. Tony knelt beside her body as Loudbear recited a Mohican prayer by Chief Aupumut:

When it comes time to die, be not like those whose hearts are filled with the fear of death, so when their time comes they weep and pray for a little more time to live their lives over again in a different way. Sing your death song, and die like a hero going home.

Chapter 46

Crossing the border into Montreal had been easy for Professor Ramsey: possessing property in both the United States and Canada was almost as good as dual citizenship.

"Sherry, I can't believe you found Bigfoot."

"And I can't believe we found each other. But, it wasn't me. It was my son. And his girlfriend, Danielle. And the Bettis twins."

"But why? Why on earth would somebody give up a find like this?" wondered Ramsey aloud.

"Becka was looking for someone who she could trust not to harm it. When I mentioned you, she asked me if you'd be willing to look after the baby. Anyone else would turn this cute little creature into an experiment, shoot her up with drugs, and dissect her. And for what?"

"We're doing the right thing."

"I know. But I told you, all of this is dependent on one condition: we name her Allison."

*   *   *

Steve and Jesse walked behind Marc and Tom back to the barn. Jesse did not yet know that Steve was the new Sheriff.

"Jesse, when we get back to the barn, I'm going to give you some time with your kids, before I make the phone calls."

Jesse wiped his nose with the back of his hand. "What calls?"

Tom intervened. "Steve's the new Sheriff."

"Since when?"

"Since this evening, Jess."

"So, are you going to tell them that Bigfoot ate my girlfriend?"

"Looks that way. I'm sorry I didn't believe you. And I'm real sorry about Justine." Steve threw his arm around Jesse. When they got back to the barn, Steve left Jesse with his friends and went to tell his own family what had happened, question Devin, and get Maureen's camera.

"Dad, since Bigfoot's dead, can we see Loudbear?" asked Devin.

"It's not a good idea. Justine's body is in the barn and..."

"We won't go in the barn, we promise."

"Fine. But bring flashlights, and be back in ten minutes. Devin, how did you know?"

Becka ran out ahead, leaving Devin behind with Steve.

"If I told you I'm psychic, would you believe me?"

Steve looked at his son. "After tonight? I'd believe anything."

Loudbear was relieved to see Becka alone. "Chief Ta Ta wants it to end. His spirit has been in the Farm for years now, and he has never harmed your family. I believe he wants to put an end to the curse. I was in the woods tonight, with Bigfoot, just like you were recently. Bigfoot did not go after me, just like he did not attack you. Chief Ta Ta is trying to get the message to him to stop the killings, to break the curse, but his soul is in another place, and Bigfoot can't see him. I must go back to Michigan, to the original tribe, and start from there. I'm not saying it's going to be easy, but it must be done. Chief Ta Ta needs your help, Becka. Do you agree that innocent people have died for no cause? Both white and Indian?"

Becka looked in the direction of the barn to see Danielle crying in Uncle Tony's arms. "I do."

"What did you do with the baby?"

"I gave her to Sherry Blake. But don't worry, this Bigfoot is going to be raised to be good. Sherry and a Bigfoot expert, Professor Ramsey, took Bigfoot to his cabin

335

in Canada, where there are no people for like fifty miles. And they won't let her out of their sights. They're totally devoted. They won't kill her or shoot her up with drugs to conduct experiments on her like she's some type of alien."

Devin walked up behind Becka and stood there in silence. "I'm sorry Devin. I had the opportunity to kill him, but I did not shoot my bow. If I had, Justine would still be alive. I am so sorry."

"I know. I saw."

"Your powers are getting stronger."

"I know. Which is why I know you must go to Michigan first thing in the morning. We are moving here for good. Becka and I will take care of your dogs for you, and your horse."

"C'mon. Let me walk you home. Your father has work to do."

Becka wrapped her arm around Loudbear's waist as they walked towards the Farm. Loudbear put his arm over her shoulder, then something occurred to him.

"Becka, you said you gave the baby to Sherry Blake. Is that Tom Blake's wife?"

"Yup. Shit's gonna hit the fan in the Blake household tonight. She left him a note telling him she found a new man."

"Just like that?"

"I guess."

"You white folk are crazy."

Loudbear walked the twins to the front porch of the Farm and turned around, bumping into Steve. The porch light was dim and gave off little light, but Loudbear recognized it was Steve. "I'm sorry. I wasn't expecting to run into someone at midnight."

"That's O.K.," said Steve. "Thanks for walking my kids home. I was just here to grab a camera and take pictures of the legendary beast. Want to come back there with me? To tell you the truth, I'm still a little scared."

336

"Sure, let's go." They started walking out on the road towards the barn when they ran into Tom, who decided to take the walk with them. Although all of them were still pumped with adrenaline, Steve felt a little stupid for not believing in the mythological creature. He just didn't like being proved wrong. All things considered, he made a major bust his first two hours on the job...even if there was one loss. They got to the spot of the incident and heard growling. Loudbear's dogs started to bark, and the men automatically thought the beast was still alive. They shined their flashlights on a family of three large brown bears eating the remains of Bigfoot's body when Steve raised his gun.

"No!" Shouted Loudbear. "This is wrong."

"What do you mean, 'this is wrong'," asked Tom. "This is our only proof."

"You don't need proof. The bears need this to survive. Besides, there are three of them, and three of us. But they outweigh us. We'll never make it out of here alive. It is back luck to shoot a bear in vain. We will all be cursed. Let's go." Loudbear turned his back to the bears and headed back towards the road.

Steve snapped photos, but all he got was the large behind of a large bear. The flash of the camera pissed off another one, causing it to stand on two feet and growl at him. At that moment, Steve and Tom acknowledged that even with two guns they weren't going to defeat three hungry bears and hightailed it back to the Farm.

Tom looked on as he watched his son take Danielle into his arms, trying the best he could to console her as she learned about the death of her step-mother. Being the strong, comforting male was a role Tom was all too familiar with, and a role that he was also done with, both mentally and physically. Tossing the keys to Marc, Tom opted to walk home, in no rush to see his wife, who spent most of her energy crying about the past. Bigfoot was

337

dead. So was Justine. So was Bob. So was Dale Botte. So was Jack Whittaker. So were his barn animals. So was Allison. And so was his marriage.

Upon reaching his house, he paused at the marigold filled toilet bowl on his front lawn, a decorative accent that Sherry mimicked from a *Better Homes and Gardens* magazine. It was a horrific eye sore that all his friends teased him about. A flower pot that Marc and Spencer would pee on when they stumbled home from a night of drinking, revealing the boys' age and humor. The porch light was on, but Sherry's car wasn't there. Tom opened up the garage door, and moved boxes of junk out of the way in order to pull out Marc's mountain bike, which hadn't been used since he obtained his driver's permit. Under the work bench in the garage was a dusty, ruffled up back pack. Tom brushed it off, then stuffed it with a bottle of Gin and threw it on his back. He hopped on the bike and rode it over to the flower pot/toilet bowl, where he unzipped his pants and pissed all over the flowers, making sure to soil every one of them. Feeling a sense of great satisfaction, and a sense that he was opening up a new chapter in his life, he got back onto his son's bike and pedaled past his house, past his lumberyard, and over the one-lane bridge.

He rested the bicycle on Margo's front lawn, then walked over to the decorative deer and put its head back on. "Now that's a lawn ornament!" It was midnight, and Margo's living room light was on. Tom pulled the bottle of gin out of his backpack, then tossed the bag onto a wicker chair on the porch.

Hearing a knock on the door, Margo rested her romance novel on the coffee table and tightened her satin bathrobe, a birthday gift from her son.

Margo answered the door, expecting it to be Spencer without his key yet again. To her surprise, she

338

found Tom standing there with an unopened bottle of gin and a warm smile.

She looked behind him, wondering what he was doing at her house at this hour. "Tom, what are you doing here?"

"May I come in?"

"Of course," she held the door open for him, and he made himself comfortable on the couch.

"Do you want to have a drink with me?"

Margo smiled suspiciously at Tom, who was acting out of character. "To what do I owe this honor?" She went into the kitchen and came back with two glasses full of ice and a bottle of tonic water.

Tom made two gin and tonics, handing one to Margo and raising his own glass in a toast. "Here's to a new beginning."

Margo raised her glass and they lightly clanked their drinks together. She then sat down on a chair across the coffee table. "What happened tonight?"

"Well, Kankro and Demitres have been arrested. Your F.B.I. friend believes they are responsible for the murders around here."

"I saw on the news earlier that Sheriff Farley is dead, but I had no idea it was Kankro and Demitres! I thought they were friends!"

"They are...were friends. But, I guess we'll never know what really happened." He took another sip of his drink. "Justine is dead."

Margo's hands went to her face. "Oh no!"

"I imagine it's not going to be easy for Jesse, especially with Austin. But, they're strong, they'll both go on."

"How did it happen?"

"Bigfoot."

"I'm so sorry to hear that. I didn't really know her, but I've seen her around town and knew that she was Jesse's girlfriend. She was real pretty."

"Yeah." Tom realized that when Sherry heard the news, there'd be no turning back for her, losing her best friend. He couldn't console her again, and he didn't want to.

"But something tells me that's not why you're here?"

"Margo, I admire you. Hell, I adore you. You were completely honest with me, letting me know how lonely you were. I never imagined in a million years that someone such as yourself could feel the way you do. And you made me realize something about myself. I shouldn't feel like I'm alone if I'm with somebody. But I am alone. Just like you, Margo. My wife, she left me a long time ago. Yeah, her body is still here, but her heart and mind aren't. She lives in the past, and so did I until recently."

Margo moved over to the couch and sat beside him. "How so?"

"I thought I was over Vietnam. But after tonight, I finally know that I am over it. The events that took place this week: Bigfoot, the murders, the conspiracy. It's all over. I can finally put it to rest. I can move on."

"I'm not sure I follow."

Feeling like he had nothing to lose, Tom popped the question that had been brewing for years, and in the recent weeks, boiling. He rested his drink on the coffee table. "Margo, will you have dinner with me tomorrow night?"

"What about your wife?"

"Funny thing is, when I got home tonight, she wasn't there. Well, her car wasn't there, so I'm assuming she wasn't there. I didn't go inside to check on her. I didn't care. I felt relieved."

"It's after midnight. Where do you think she could have gone?"

Tom sipped his drink. "Like I said, I don't care."

"But Tom, this town isn't safe anymore. The cops were arrested today, but still Justine was found dead tonight! Maybe something happened to your wife!"

Tom thought about that for a moment, then stood abruptly. "You're right. I'm acting rather selfish right now." He stood up, kissing Margo on the cheek. "I'll call you in the morning."

Margo smiled at her next date. "I'm here if you need me." She watched as Tom clumsily pedaled away on his son's bicycle. Then she locked the door and returned to her book.

Tom pressed his feet down on the pedals with just enough force to push the bike forward without it falling over. The summer mountain air was warm, but not sticky, and Tom was enjoying his freedom, his loose thoughts, and his buzz. He rode across his front lawn, this time picking up enough speed to kick his right leg out and strike the "Blake" family sign hanging from a wooden post on the property, which let all the townspeople know just where he lived: an old tradition in Warrensburg. The sign shook violently, causing the rusting chains that held it up to rattle as if the winds were picking up. Tom stood the bicycle up against the garage door and went in through the front, still not concerned that Sherry's car was missing.

It wasn't until he realized that the front door wasn't locked that he knew there was a problem. His right hand jerked for the light switched as he called for his wife. "Sherry! Where are you?" His eyes quickly scanned for something out of the ordinary when something red caught his attention. On the dining room table was an unopened bottle of Jameson with a large red bow wrapped around the neck, and two new rock glasses placed on coasters sitting beside it with an envelope labeled 'Tom'.

Before opening the envelope, Tom knew what was in it. He poured himself a glass of whiskey, sat down, and opened up the letter.

> *Tom,*
>
> > *I think we both found what we were looking for.*
> *Take care.*
> > *Sherry.*

Tom Blake took a large gulp of Jameson and toasted aloud, "To Sherry." He poured another glass then went into his garage to collect his box of Bigfoot evidence. Lifting the cardboard box in one hand, he tucked it under his arm and grabbed his glass of whiskey with his free hand. He casually walked into his home office, where he rested his box on top of his desk alongside an old framed photo of his Vietnam friends.

He sat comfortably in his reclining office chair and rested his feet on top of his desk, then took another slug of whiskey, finishing what was left in the glass. He smiled to himself, then tossed the empty glass over his left shoulder and sat upright in his seat, searching through his box for the plastic bag containing the Bigfoot hair. When he found what he was looking for, he pried open the glass frame holding the memory of his friends killed in the war, and neatly placed the hair inside the frame with his friends. "Yes boys, Bigfoot does indeed exist."